W9-CFV-290

Blood of the Tribe

Other books by David S. Brody

Unlawful Deeds

Blood of the Tribe

A Legal Thriller

David S. Brody

Martin and Lawrence Press
Groton, Massachusetts
2003

Blood of the Tribe
A Legal Thriller

Published by

Martin and Lawrence Press
37 Nod Rd.   P.O. Box 682
Groton, MA 01450
website addresss: www.martinandlawrencepress.com

ISBN 0-9721687-1-0

Blood of the Tribe/by David S. Brody   1st ed.
This is a work of fiction. Names, characters, places, and incidents are either the product of the author's imagination or are used ficticiously. Any resemblance to actual people or events , living or dead, business establishments, events, or locales are entirely coincidental.

Facts pertaining to the 1970s court case between the Mashpee Indian tribe and the town of Mashpee, Masachusetts are true, as are historical facts relating to the Wampanoag chief, Metacomet (King Philip).

Cover design by **what!**design, Allston, MA

July 2003

Printed in Canada

To my daughters, Allie and Renee...
The most important legacy any writer can leave.

MY THANKS TO:

My wife, Kim, for the countless hours she spent reading, editing, revising and streamlining this story. Thankless work, but invaluable.

Richard Meibers, both for believing in this project and for offering his unsurpassed editorial skills in improving it.

Karen Sheehan, for her friendship, her passion and her brilliance in marketing.

The readers of early drafts of the story, Richard Scott, Spencer Brody, Eric Stearns, Jeanne Scott, Jeff Brody, Irene Gordon, Debra Scott, Arthur Gordon and Peter Schuhknecht, for their invaluable comments, insights and suggestions. It is, I know, no fun reading late at night with a red pen in one hand and a stack of yellow Post-its in the other.

George DeFilippo, for his many insights into police investigative procedures.

Catherine Mello Alves, for serving as my tour guide through the Lowell Law Library.

And the guys on Z's Sport Shop Softball Team, who comfort me by reminding me that, weak as my bat might be, at least my pen is strong.

Author's Note

A few year ago, I was retained by a client interested in purchasing a vacation home in the town of Mashpee, on Cape Cod. I was aware of the claim the Mashpee Wampanoag Indian tribe made in the 1970s in which the tribe asserted a legal claim to all the land within the borders of the town of Mashpee. However, when I contacted a couple of title insurance companies and Cape Cod real estate attorneys to discuss this issue, I was assured that this issue had been resolved—by the U.S. Supreme Court—in favor of the town and that no further claims could be made by the tribe.

Fortunately for my client, I dug a little deeper. It was then, and is now, my legal opinion that the tribe is not barred from reasserting its land claim. In fact, I believe the tribe is likely to do so in the near future. If and when it does so, title to over $2 billion of prime Cape Cod real estate will be up for grabs.

What follows is a fictionalized account of the chaos that might result.

PROLOGUE

[August]

Normally the feeling of bark on her skin and leaves in her hair made Dominique smile. But not today. There was no joy in murder.

She folded her large frame neatly against the trunk of the oak tree, gently blew a bee off her wrist. Nothing to do now but wait. She would not be seen—the brush on the side of the winding subdivision road had grown thick over the summer, and the morning sun shrouded her in shadows. She had always had the ability to allow the natural world to simply envelope her. Even when the natural world was nothing but a strip mall-sized wooded area left to serve as a buffer between the green lawns and cedar fences and three-car garages.

The rhythm of the woods altered slightly as a car approached. She watched a police cruiser slowly snake its way over the smooth, gray-black asphalt. The road used to be a rutted, dirt way she and her friends raced down on their bikes as children. The finish line was the lake, the same lake that was offering a soft morning breeze in futile opposition to the sticky August air.

The cruiser rolled past, pulled up alongside a knot of people huddled near where the road split into a handful of long private driveways. Most of the people were residents of the cedar-shingled subdivision. Some of them were even her friends.

The policeman hiked his pants up over his gut, wiped the sweat off his forehead with the back of his sleeve as he approached the group. "I'm Officer Cleary. I received a call about a man in a ditch."

1

Between the knot of tennis shorts and windbreakers and Prada handbags, limbs branched from the man's body at unnatural angles. "Has anybody called for an ambulance?" the policeman asked. He waited for a response. Nothing but people looking at their feet.

"Well, has anyone checked to see how bad he's hurt?" Again, nothing.

The officer radioed the dispatcher and confirmed that an ambulance was on the way. He folded his arms across his chest, tried to raise himself up to look down on his mostly-taller audience, addressed the group a third time. "Hey, does anybody know what happened here?"

A woman shrugged. "I found him here when I came out for my morning walk. I screamed, and everyone came running. I think it's Rex Griffin. He lives in the old farmhouse right as you come into the subdivision."

The policeman slid on his hip down into the culvert to the man's side, touched a blood-crusted cheek. Dominique knew it would be cold. Just as she knew he wouldn't find a pulse. He turned back to the group. "He's dead."

The officer seemed to wait for the usual gasps and screams and Oh-my-Gods. Nothing. Not from this group. Not for this corpse.

The policeman shook his head and shrugged, then bent down and reached into the dead man's hip pocket. He pulled out a wallet, thumbed through it, focused on what looked like a driver's license. A glance back at the victim's face, then a quick nod.

He hoisted himself out of the ditch, studied the faces of the neighbors for a few seconds. "Please stay away from the body. I'm going to get some tape to mark the scene." He began to walk away, then stopped and turned. "And nobody leave."

They waited until the policeman was out of view, then one man tentatively offered a handshake to another. A woman squeezed her neighbor's shoulder. A few people exchanged quick embraces.

Everyone was smiling, even as their eyes rested on the cold body lying dead in the ditch.

Chapter 1

[March]

Bruce Arrujo wondered whether he had a death wish. The other boats, even the much larger ones, had returned to the shelter of the harbors hours ago, before the midday sun had been completely swallowed by the storm. But here he was, alone in a 30-foot sloop, his mainsail flapping angrily, trying to sail through the teeth of a tropical nightmare that had whipped its way up the Atlantic coastline and was now tossing his craft around like an ant in a dark gray toilet bowl.

He was a good sailor. One of the best, in fact. Not that it was much to be proud of—put any sturdy young man at sea alone in a boat for close to a decade and he was bound to become proficient at handling the vessel. Not exactly the most profitable use of his Harvard Law degree, he knew. But, then again, alone in the froth of the Atlantic, at least he did less harm than many of his fellow law school graduates did sitting behind their desks. And none of them could touch his history when it came to misuse of a law degree.

He had long since taken down his jib and reefed his mainsail, so there wasn't much to do now other than to try to keep his bow pointed at the waves. Unfortunately, such an angle forced him to sail close-hauled, with his sail pulled in tight to the boom. And that caused the boat to tip precariously, the downwind rail actually dipping down and burying itself beneath the water's surface. But he had no choice. If he got turned sideways to the waves, a wall of water would broadside him and likely flip him over.

The fact that he was indifferent to the possibility of being capsized actually alarmed him more than his predicament itself.

From under his rain slicker, he pulled out a laminated picture. He shielded the photo as best he could from the storm, stared at the face of the woman who had exiled him to a life at sea: Shelby Baskin. The woman he had loved, then betrayed. If she couldn't spark some desire in him to survive this storm, then nothing could.

He felt a slight pang in his chest near his heart. After eight years, the thought of her still moved him. But not nearly as much as it used to. Even the spark that was Shelby was beginning to fade into the darkness that had become his existence. Without her, he would have long since allowed the sea to swallow him up.

Was today the day he just let go?

Out of the howl of the wind his grandfather's voice responded to the unspoken question. Grandpa chided him, cursed him. *Live your life, damn it! Stop feeling sorry for yourself. Stop your whining.*

Bruce allowed himself a small smile. It had been years since his grandfather's spirit had bothered to speak to him, years since the old man who had been like a father to him had deigned to offer guidance from the beyond. Perhaps time had dulled even the old man's anger. Or perhaps even Grandpa could sense how close Bruce was to simply turning the boat broadside to a wave.

Bruce took a deep breath: Shelby and Grandpa. That was really all there ever had been in his life. He had betrayed her and, by doing so, had betrayed the memory of the man who had invested so much in Bruce's upbringing. Shelby had rebuffed all his efforts at reconciliation, but perhaps he should make one last attempt to reconnect with his grandfather before simply allowing his life to expire. If he failed, there would be plenty of chances later to die.

He shook the water from his eyes, turned his attention back to the storm. Somewhere, through the walls of water and sheets of spray and oceans of darkness, the shores of Cape Cod waited for the grandson of Umberto Wild Duck Arrujo to return. And on those shores lived the people of his grandfather, the Mashpee Wampanoag Indians. The name Wampanoag meant "People of the Dawn, and the tribe had been the first to greet the Pilgrims in Plymouth.

He would go to them. Perhaps they would greet him, help him

4

find his grandfather, maybe even help him issue in a new dawn for himself.

*   *   *

The boy's skates hummed as the blades carved into the ice. Only the best skaters—those with strong legs, ideal form, superb balance—could generate that hum. It was almost as if the blades were playing the ice the way the bow of an expert violinist danced across the strings. No scrapes, no clatters, nothing but the hum. A gift.

Pierre Prefontaine took a deep breath, the familiar hockey rink smell filling his nose. Zamboni exhaust and adolescent sweat and snack bar pizza all coagulating together in a cold, gray fog above the ice surface. Sort of like the way a carnival would smell if you dropped the whole thing in a giant freezer. There were probably a hundred of these airplane hanger-like rinks across Massachusetts, and they all smelled the same.

Pierre had had no trouble finding the rink. "Look," his boyhood friend, Bob, had said. "Picture Cape Cod as an arm, with a bent elbow in the middle and a fist at the end. The fist is Provincetown, the elbow is Chatham. You know how sometimes old women get that baggy flesh under their triceps, right near their underarms? Well, that's Mashpee. The baggy flesh near the underarm." Not exactly Mapquest, but it had been years since Pierre had visited the Cape, and it did the trick. It took him an hour and a half to do the drive from Boston.

He turned to Bob. Tall and thin, the perfect build for a basketball player. But he had chosen a life in hockey instead. "So, who's that number 11?" Pierre was more than a bit surprised to hear the words come out of his mouth. Just by asking the question, he was acknowledging that he had become intrigued by the job offer. It paid about one-tenth of what he made doing commercial real estate brokerage. But it was probably twenty times as much fun.

"Name's Billy Victor. Good size, good skills, loves to compete. He's only a sophomore. Just think, you'd have two full years to ruin his game."

5

Pierre laughed, knocked the hockey stick out of his friend's hands. Carla was right—Pierre liked to hang with his boyhood pals because it allowed him to act like he was still twelve. He skated across the rink to intercept the boy. "Hey, I was watching you skate. You've got some great wheels."

The boy squinted down at him cautiously, not quite sure how to respond to the stranger who his current coach said might be his future one. Pierre saw himself through the boy's eyes—round face, tousled hair, easy smile. The right look for a polite Catholic boy whose mother wanted him to be a priest. But probably not the ideal face for a hockey coach. Maybe he should blacken a couple of teeth.

"Thanks," the boy finally muttered.

"I noticed your shots are all going high. That on purpose?"

"Nah. They just seem to sail on me."

"On your follow-through, try extending your stick forward instead of up. Usually a low follow-through will give you a low shot."

"'Kay."

Pierre skated away, moved to the side as the team began a puck-handling drill. As Billy made a turn around a pylon, his puck and that of one of his teammates collided and slid away. Billy retrieved his puck, spun back to the pylon to continue the drill. His teammate was waiting for him, stuck out a thick leg and tripped him. Billy crashed headfirst into the boards.

The boy lumbered toward Billy and skidded to a stop, spraying Billy in the face with ice dust. He was about Billy's height, but much thicker. All thighs and chest. He hissed at Billy. "Fucking Indian. Go on back to your reservation."

Billy scrambled to his feet and charged at the bully. Pierre saw Bob grab Billy's teammate and use his long arms to pin him against the boards. Pierre intercepted Billy just as he threw a right-hand punch. The punch glanced off Pierre's cheek, spinning him around. By the time he regained his balance and grabbed Billy from behind, Billy had landed a couple of punches on the top of his teammate's thick head. Pierre thought about letting him throw a few more, but he could see that Bob was still trying to separate the combatants. He wrestled Billy away.

He rubbed his cheek, smiled at Billy. "Damn. You hit hard. Now what was that all about?"

"Asshole's been on my case all year. Says he hates Indians."

"Why?"

"'Cause he's a fuckin' idiot, I don't know."

A few minutes later Pierre skated alongside Bob. "You should have let them fight. Be done with it."

Bob laughed. "I can't. Billy's too tough—once they got going, he'd never stop. And the big kid's too friggin' dumb to know when he's been beat. They'd end up killing each other. And I'd probably get sued."

"Still, it would end it, once and for all."

"No, it wouldn't. These kids' parents probably used to go at it when they were in school. Maybe even their grandparents. That's the way it is here. There are some assholes in town who hate the Indians—always have, always will. And they just pass it down to their kids."

Pierre nodded. He and his family used to vacation on Cape Cod when he was a kid, so he knew that the town of Mashpee had been splintered in the 1970s when the Mashpee tribe filed a lawsuit claiming ownership to all the land in the town. The claim eventually failed, but that didn't mean everyone lived happily ever after. Short of rape, nothing sparks a little bigotry quite like someone trying to evict you from your home.

As the practice continued, Pierre made a point of studying Billy. He seemed to be a typical teenager—horsing around with his teammates when the coach wasn't looking, slapping the puck loudly against the boards when a group of girls walked by. But he worked hard, and seemed to be a quick learner. He blasted a low slap shot that found the far corner of the net, only a few inches off the ice, then turned to see if Pierre had been watching. Pierre clapped his stick on the ice and smiled. "Nice shot, Billy."

During the scrimmage at the end of the practice, Billy's co-combatant lost control of the puck in his skates. As he looked down to find it, Billy flashed into the thug's skating lane, lowered his shoulder, and caught his teammate in the chest with a perfectly executed—and completely legal—body check.

7

As the bully lay writhing on his back gasping for air, Billy picked up the puck, swooped in on the goalie, and flipped a shot into the top corner of the net.

He dropped his stick and gloves to perform a mock Indian war dance—spinning on one skate and then the other, the opposite knee moving up and down in rhythm with his chant. "Wa-wa-wa-wa," filled the arena, Billy modulating the chant by covering and uncovering his mouth with an open palm.

Then he flashed a quick smile at Pierre and skated off the ice.

Chapter 2

Shelby Baskin stopped outside a glass office tower in downtown Boston, eyed her reflection in a smoky glass window for the umpteenth time that evening. Not bad. Sexy but respectable in a black sleeveless dress, the curves still in all the right places. And even in the dim dusk light her blue-green eyes lit up the window pane.

She sighed. Like it really mattered. What we she going to do, steal a husband away from one of her classmates? Reunions. A chance for those who had a life to gloat over those who didn't.

The law school reunion was being held on an oversized party boat, currently docked behind a hotel in one of those new brick buildings designed to look like an old one. She saw the beautiful, successful people walking up the gangplank, hand-in-hand, two-by-two, joyful in the knowledge that their genetic line would continue.

Did she really want to do this? She pictured herself laughingly repeating to scores of ex-classmates feigning interest in her social life, "No, I guess I just haven't found the right guy yet." And even that wasn't totally true—she had met him, she just hadn't been able to keep him.

Nor were any of them going to be impressed that she had made partner in her law firm—they were all graduates of Harvard Law School, for Christ's sake. They were supposed to make partner.

She turned and hailed a taxi. Those few classmates whom she had wanted to stay friends with she had. As for the rest, well, *bon voyage*.

*   *   *

Pierre eased himself out of bed, fought the urge to nibble Carla's bare shoulder, and padded his way down the hall to peek in at his sleeping daughters.

One blond, one brunette, both carbon copies of Carla's childhood pictures. He tiptoed in, skirting the dolls set up in a circle around teacups and saucers in the middle of the room. He pulled the blanket over Valerie's exposed leg, kissed her gently on her warm cheek. Rachel stirred, dropped her stuffed bunny onto the carpeted floor. Pierre picked it up, tucked it gently under her arm, kissed her as she sighed and cuddled against her furry friend.

Pierre tore himself away, peeked at the thermometer. Sixty-two degrees, and the dawn sky was clear. A hint of the summer to come. Should be perfect.

He jumped into the shower, ran a bar of soap over his body. Not the rock he was as a high school hockey player, but not bad for 42, especially considering how often he had to eat on the road and how rarely he had the time to get in a good workout.

Not to mention that spending the better part of his 35th year in jail was hardly the recipe for good health.

He left the house at 7:30, but instead of heading to his office in downtown Baltimore he swung by to pick up some roses at an early-hours florist. He returned home just as Carla was returning from dropping the girls off at the bus stop.

She eyed the flowers. "Hi there. Did you forget something?"

"No, I'm here to pick up my date. I thought we should do something fun for our anniversary. But first, these are for you. Thank you for twelve wonderful years, every one of them as perfect as a rose." It was an exaggeration. One of the years had been a thorn. A sharply barbed one.

Carla grinned, the same sparkling smile that had captivated Pierre the first time he had seen it on a sidewalk in Boston. It was a smile that enveloped her whole face; her cheeks dimpled, her eyes danced, her nose crinkled, her eyebrows arched. Even at 37, her face held the youthful exuberance of a schoolgirl. She was the freckled girl next door who got older but never grew old.

She kissed Pierre with her mouth slightly open, lingered for a second or two against his face. "So, you have a surprise planned for us. What is it?"

"A secret. Grab some coffee and get in the car."

"Do I need my passport? Maybe an evening gown?"

He smiled. "Just you."

She formed a pouty smile. "Can I at least bring some opera glasses?"

"We don't own any opera glasses. Now get in."

"But where's the limo...?"

A couple of hours later they pulled into a small lakeside marina in rural West Virginia. He had rented a 19-foot day-sailer, the kind with a small cabin for a little privacy. He had proposed to her while sailing on an almost identical boat 13 years earlier.

At midday Pierre lowered the sails and dropped the anchor. "Care for a swim?"

They were in a small cove, alone on the lake with nothing but pine trees on the shoreline facing them. The wind was steady, but the sun was out and the temperature had climbed to the mid-70s. "Sure," she responded with a smile. "With or without bathing suits?"

Pierre shrugged and kicked off his suit; Carla did the same. She was in better shape than ever—her breasts firm, here waist trim, her legs lean and strong. She took his hand, and together they jumped into the cold May water. They frolicked for a few minutes, then came together silently. They swam closer to the boat and made love in the water, Pierre resting one foot on the lowest rung of the boat's ladder for support. They moved slowly, in rhythm with the boat as it bobbed in the waves, then finally tightened their embrace and re-leased themselves into each other.

Carla drew slowly away from Pierre, smiled at him, and kissed him on the tip of his nose. "I would love to do that again, but as it is I think you're going to have to get me out of here with an ice pick."

"Yeah, me too. All my extremities are numb. Except one."

Carla splashed water in his face, then shoved him off the ladder and scampered into the boat. They dried off, pulled on some sweatshirts. "I'll be right back," he said. "I have something for you."

"Hey, that's not fair. I left your present at the house."

Pierre ducked into the boat's small hold, returned with a business-sized envelope. "Happy anniversary, Carla. I love you very much." He kissed her gently on the mouth.

Carla looked up at him quizzically. "Hmm, a sealed envelope. Is twelve years the paper anniversary? I was hoping it was diamonds or emeralds or something."

He grinned. "Just open it."

Carla pulled out a single piece of paper and began reading aloud. It was a letter from Pierre addressed to the real estate brokerage firm where he worked. "Blah, blah, blah.... Please accept this letter as notice of my resignation, effective September 1." She looked up. "I don't get it. Are you switching firms or something?"

Pierre took her hand. "No, nothing like that. I just decided I want to spend more time with you and the girls. Maybe I can do some coaching or teaching...."

"Wow, Pierre. This is so out of the blue." Moisture pooled in her eyes.

"Not really. I've been thinking about it a lot lately. I don't want to be one of those guys who goes to his kids' graduation and wonders where the years went. I've done okay the past few years, but who says that I can't just say, 'Enough'?"

Carla smiled, dabbed her eyes. "Not me, that's for sure. I'd love it if you were around more."

He nodded. She had been more than understanding about his need to dive into his new career when they had moved to Baltimore. He'd been a beaten man when they'd fled Boston eight years ago—convicted felon, sucker, fool. Looking back, he understood that it wasn't so much that they, as a family, needed the money from his new job. It was rather that he, as a husband and father, felt the need to be paid.

But that was now ancient history. He had redeemed himself, succeeded in a new career, re-inflated his ego.

"And one more thing. I sort of feel like we've been in exile down here. Maybe it's time to go back home." Pierre paused and smiled as

Carla looked up at him expectantly. He could see the hope in her eyes—she had never wanted to leave Massachusetts to begin with.

"Why don't we move to Cape Cod? Maybe even get a place on the water."

Chapter 3

[August]

Pierre stared with disbelief into the eyes of his lawyer. The lawyer—a gray suit and red tie in some big firm that Pierre's company used for corporate work—kept his eyes focused on the panoramic view of the Boston skyline visible through the conference room window. Pierre couldn't remember if his name was Herman or Herbert. "What do you mean, there's nothing we can do about it?"

Herman or Herbert shifted around sideways in the plush leather chair and shrugged. Pierre was surprised the movement didn't cause his paisley suspenders to slide down his drooping shoulders. The guy was too young—probably only 30 or so—to be wearing suspenders. And to have drooping shoulders. "The contract gives the builder an automatic extension to finish the house if he needs the time. So he wants to extend the closing until October 15."

"But our whole life is packed into a moving truck. What are we supposed to do for the next two months?"

What kind of idiot lawyer would agree to such a contract? He was in a tough spot, and it wasn't like he knew any lawyers in town he could turn to for help. Except Shelby, and she was on vacation.

It was partially his own fault—he had bought a house from a builder who owned a gift shop of all things, then never bothered to fly up and check on the progress of the construction work. He had been seduced by the lakefront site, wowed by the glossy plans. And forced into making a rash decision by an overheated real estate market. He had already lost two other houses by not jumping quickly enough, so, not wanting to be burned a third time, he had quickly made the offer. Even before Carla had flown up to see the property.

Pierre rubbed his face with his hands. "Here's the deal. We can't wait until October. The kids start school in September. Heck, we can't even wait past tomorrow. I've got a week to get everything settled here, then I have to fly back to Baltimore to wind things up at work."

"Well, you can still close on the house tomorrow if you want. Then you could begin to get settled." The attorney set down his pen, as if his suggestion was the final solution to Pierre's predicament.

Stupid advice. It was like a mechanic advising a customer not to drive so much. "But there's, like, $50,000 worth of work still to be done on the house. There's no flooring, no appliances, no light fixtures...."

"I understand that. But, legally, those are your only options—wait until October 15, or close tomorrow and have the work done after you move in."

Pierre stood up. "Wait, I see what's going on. This guy Griffin called me last week, asking all sorts of questions. *Had we sold our house in Baltimore? When were we planning on moving?* So of course I told him all our plans. Meanwhile, he knew he wasn't even close to finishing the house." Pierre stopped, surprised to see that he had been pacing around the conference room. He leaned against the shiny mahogany table, anchored himself there. "He figured he'd wait until the last minute, then tell us to take it or leave it because he knew we had no choice."

Herman or Herbert was still sitting in the leather seat, motionless. "I made a couple of calls. Apparently this guy Rex Griffin has a sordid reputation down on the Cape. He developed that whole subdivision, and almost every buyer had to sue him for one reason or another."

Pierre gripped the edge of the table. "Really? I called some of the neighbors for references, and nobody said anything."

The gray suit shrugged. "Probably didn't want to get sued by him. Anyway, Griffin says he'd be happy to close tomorrow."

"Of course he would." Pierre cursed himself. He should have found a lawyer from the Cape, someone who knew the local landscape. Or called Shelby to see if she knew a good real estate guy. He might have avoided this whole mess. "And it sounds like we don't have much choice."

*   *   *

Pierre and Herman or Herbert were back in the same conference room, sitting in the same leather chairs around the same polished oak table. They were waiting for Rex Griffin to show up. The lawyer—same gray suit, same suspenders, different red tie—was thumbing through a file, taking notes. Pierre was thumbing through the sports page. The Red Sox had blown a late-inning lead, their fourth loss in a row. At least in Baltimore you knew the Orioles didn't have a chance. The Red Sox sucked you in, then broke your heart.

He put down the newspaper. Griffin had cheap-shotted him, and Pierre wasn't quite sure how to respond. He thought back to a high school hockey game. During the post-game handshake, an opposing player, embarrassed at having been crunched to the ice during the game by a clean check from the smaller Pierre, had sucker-punched him. Pierre had spit out some blood, dropped his stick and gloves, and charged at the hulking opponent with fists flying. It had been a perfectly appropriate response—in fact, really the only appropriate response—and none of the other players, on either team, had questioned it. Just as nobody had questioned Billy making road-kill out of his teammate. But things were so much more complicated in the real world. He couldn't very well jump across the table and pummel Griffin.

Actually, maybe it wasn't such a bad idea. The last time he had sat in a law office around a conference room table, eight years earlier, his lawyer had been in the process of framing Pierre for murder so he could steal Pierre's can't-miss real estate deal. Pierre had eventually escaped with only six months in jail, though the word "only" had a bitterly ironic ring to it in light of the fact that he was innocent of every crime except that of trusting his own lawyer. And Carla had eventually exposed the lawyer's scam and saved the real estate. But Pierre's reputation in the Boston real estate community had been destroyed by the taint of the murder accusation. And he still hadn't had the chance to settle that score. Revenge may be a dish best served cold, but Pierre had no intention of waiting eight years to avenge any wrong Rex Griffin might do him.

They waited in silence for a few minutes, then a young secretary with big hair stuck her head into the conference room. "Excuse me, but there's an Attorney Shelby Baskin here to see Mr. Prefontaine."

Pierre stood up. "Really?"

"Would you like me to bring her in?"

"Actually, I'll come with you and get her."

He followed the mane of hair out to the reception area. Shelby was leaning over by the window, peering out a telescope at the Boston skyline. Pierre tried to keep his eyes from drifting down to her legs, but they were tanned and shapely and the back of her skirt had pulled up as she leaned over the telescope.... And, well, he was just a guy. He quickly focused on her face as she turned.

"Shelby, what are you doing here?"

She strode toward him, offered him one of those kisses that got partly cheek and partly lips, then squeezed his shoulder. "Hey, old friend." She pulled her face away, looked at him and smiled. "I got the message you had called a few times, so I called Carla. She told me what was up, so I thought I'd come over and see if I can help. My office is right next door...." She shrugged, raised an eyebrow, smiled again.

She was as stunning as ever—blue-green eyes, smooth skin, understated features. Pierre always thought she looked like a young Jamie Lee Curtis. But her real charm was that she didn't seem to know she was attractive. Or maybe she just didn't think it mattered.

She continued before he could say anything. "Plus, I have some stuff I picked up for the girls in London." She handed him a pair of brightly wrapped, shoebox-sized packages. "They're handmade dolls. I had one when I was a kid and loved it. Hope they do too."

"Thanks, Shelby. That's really sweet. And thanks so much for coming over. I could use some help here."

They sat on a Chippendale sofa in the reception area as Pierre described the situation.

She took down a few notes on a legal pad, glanced around to make sure nobody was listening. "Sounds like you got *firmed*. That's what we call it when you're a small client with a big firm and they don't really care what happens to you."

"Well, they do a lot of work for my company, so they should care...."

Shelby interrupted him with a hand on his knee. "But you're quitting, right? So what are you going to do, get them fired on your way out the door?"

Pierre nodded. "You're right."

"Anyway, I don't know much about real estate, as you know. But I'd be happy to sit in on the meeting if you want."

Pierre smiled. "Thanks. That would be great. He should be here in a few minutes, so let's go down to the conference room."

Pierre introduced Shelby to the attorney, mumbling the first name to cover his confusion. The gray suit sat at the head of the conference room table, Pierre sat next to him with his back to the windows, and Shelby sat next to Pierre.

At 10:00 exactly, as scheduled, Griffin knocked demurely on the open door and leaned his head in. "Oh, good, I found the right room. I hope I'm not late—there was a bit of traffic coming into the city this morning." He nodded politely, bowing his head. He introduced himself to Herman or Herbert, then moved around the table to shake hands with Pierre and Shelby. Pierre briefly clasped Griffin's hand, resisted the urge to wipe his palm on his pants. Something about shaking someone's hand as they tried to screw you....

Griffin sat down across from Pierre and unpacked his briefcase. He was a slight man of average height, about 50 years old. He was wearing basically the same outfit he had worn the previous times Pierre had met him—a white oxford dress shirt with a yellow bow tie—not a clip-on—and a pair of loose-fitting khakis. Not exactly what you'd expect from a homebuilder, but probably the perfect outfit for a huckster trying to look respectable.

Pierre studied his face. Eyes set a bit close together, glasses a bit crooked, cheeks a bit round, teeth a bit small and discolored, chin a bit weak. But there really was nothing particularly remarkable to note. Carla, who drew caricature portraits as a hobby, would have been hard-pressed to choose any feature to exaggerate other than Griffin's bow tie.

Pierre's attorney spoke. He had apparently decided it was time to show his client that he wasn't totally incompetent. Or maybe he was trying to show off in front of Shelby. "Now, Mr. Griffin, as you know, my client has agreed, rather reluctantly I might add, to close today despite the fact the house is nowhere near completion."

Griffin bowed his head and addressed Pierre directly. "I'm truly sorry for that. I assure you that I had every intention of completing the house on time. But the subcontractors...." Griffin paused here and shrugged his shoulders, then bowed his head again, taking a moment to clean his round wire glasses. With his constant bowing of his head, and his bookish glasses and bow tie, and his polite manner, Griffin reminded Pierre of a simple country minister in an old Western movie. Calling on the old widow so he could steal her money.

Pierre's attorney continued. "Yes, well, be that as it may, before we actually close today and pay over the balance of the purchase price, I feel it is prudent to set forth a written schedule of when the construction will be completed by you, Mr. Griffin, and in addition to set up some sort of escrow account to ensure that the work is indeed done. My client estimates the remaining work at $50,000, so I believe a $70,000 escrow account would suffice. When you finish the construction, the $70,000 would be released to you." Herman or Herbert sat back in his chair and smiled at Shelby, then at Pierre.

Griffin's face adopted a pained expression. "Oh, dear," he muttered, as he fumbled for a document from one of his files. "I'm very sorry, Mr. Prefontaine, but I'm afraid there has been a misunderstanding. If you would be so kind as to direct your attention to paragraph 12 of the Purchase and Sale Agreement, I believe you will see that this proposal by your counsel, although eminently reasonable, goes beyond the specific provisions of our contract. You see, paragraph 12 states that, in the event you elect to choose to close on the property despite my failure to complete construction, you do so without any adjustment in price. However, I will again offer to extend the closing until October 15 to enable myself to complete the construction."

Pierre turned toward Herman or Herbert, who snatched his copy of the contract out of the file and began to read paragraph 12. The lawyer had completed the passage and was now reading it a second time. Shelby rolled her eyes and shook her head. The attorney finished, then, red-faced, addressed Griffin. "Mr. Griffin, could you give me a moment alone with my client?"

Griffin bowed his head and left the room. Pierre's attorney spoke without looking up at either Pierre or Shelby. "Unfortunately, the man is correct in the reading of the contract. This is a standard clause, but usually the buyer can simply threaten not to close and the seller will agree to a reasonable escrow arrangement. I'm afraid that if you choose to close today, you'll have to take the house in an 'as is' condition."

"What, and just eat the fifty grand?"

"I'm afraid so. I don't see that you have any other recourse."

Shelby intervened. "Not necessarily. That may be what the contract says, but you can still sue Griffin for fraud if you can prove he never had any intention of finishing the house. Maybe get your $50,000 back that way. Actually, you'd have a pretty good case."

It wasn't much, but it was something. "Thanks, Shelby. But I don't want a lawsuit. I want a house."

"I hear you, Pierre, but I think you're going to end up with both." Shelby turned and smiled at Herman or Herbert. "And I'm sure that your lawyer is going to refund his fee. I mean, no reputable firm would accept a fee for a case that was so clearly botched."

The attorney pulled on his suspenders, stammered a response. "Well, I don't see how you can blame us...."

Shelby's eyes fired at him. "I don't blame your firm, sir. I blame *you*. You negotiated this contract. If you weren't competent to do so, you should have asked for help."

He sat up. "I am perfectly competent. I am experienced with multi-million dollar loans, and complex low-income housing deals, and...."

Shelby slapped her hand down on the polished table, silencing him. "Great for you. But you obviously have no idea how to prepare a simple Purchase and Sale Agreement. I don't do real estate, but even I know you need to put in a hold-back clause if you're dealing with new construction. I hope you weren't planning on making partner this year." She turned to Pierre. "I'll represent you if you want to sue him for malpractice."

Pierre stared at Shelby. She was one of the most mild-mannered people he knew. All of a sudden she had turned into a she-wolf. He couldn't think of anything to do but nod.

Shelby continued, gave the man an order. "Now, go tell Mr. Griffin to sit tight for a few minutes."

Herman or Herbert left, and Shelby sat back and sighed. "Sorry about that, but I hate those kind of lawyers. No way should he have let you sign that contract. Idiot."

"Don't apologize. Just remind me never to get on your bad side. And how did you know he was up for partner?"

"I looked him up in the law directory before I came over. He graduated from law school nine years ago, so this is his year. 'Up or out,' is what they say. There's probably 15 or 20 of them being considered, and only half of them will make it. A malpractice complaint wouldn't exactly help his chances." She paused, looked out the window. "Not that I would ever do that to anyone." She lifted her chin, smiled. "But he doesn't know that."

She continued. "Anyway, what are you going to do now?"

Pierre contemplated his options. They couldn't stay in Baltimore because they had already sold their house. They could stay with Carla's parents for a few days, but not a month or two. They could buy the new house "as is" and sue Griffin later. Or they could delay the closing, and live ... where? Maybe they could find a place to rent. "I'm gonna make some calls and see if there's any chance of finding a rental property."

Pierre spent the next hour phoning real estate agents on the Cape. He started in the town of Mashpee, where their new house was located, so that at least the kids could start school in town. But August, and even September, were considered high season on the Cape—houses were renting for $10,000 or more per month, and even at that price there was nothing available in Mashpee and little in the surrounding area. If they were going to spend that kind of money, they might as well invest it on improvements to their own house.

Pierre took a deep breath and phoned Carla. She agreed: none of the choices was particularly attractive, but at least by closing today they could avoid the trauma of forcing the kids to change schools only weeks into the school year. They could worry about suing Griffin later. In the meantime, they would have to tap into that nest egg of theirs to actually finish building their nest. Pierre hung up and shook his head.

This new life he and his family were starting on Cape Cod—dream lifestyle, dream house, dream views—was quickly turning into a nightmare. A bow-tied nightmare.

Chapter 4

[September]

Rex Griffin fingered his bow tie, paced slowly back and forth across the wide pine floorboards of his second floor study in the old Smithson farmhouse. Extension cords snaked around him, then wriggled out the door and down the hallway into adjoining rooms, which were otherwise empty except for the beige metal file cabinets that lined the walls. The office was equipped with a full array of modern office equipment, but the electrical capabilities of the old farmhouse were such that any given outlet could only support one or two pieces of equipment.

A black plastic wastebasket sat in the corner to catch water dripping in from yesterday's rain. The leaky roof was causing the house to rot away from the inside, and he couldn't afford to do anything but patch the shingles. Even the large blue tarp he had draped over the roof hadn't kept the moisture out. He had thrown the tarp over in late June, just after he had finalized the deal with Pierre Prefontaine to buy the last house in the subdivision. The tarp had the unintended effect of making the colonial—painted white with a red door and red shutters—look like an American flag as the 4th of July holiday approached. Now, two months later, it just looked like a tattered old tarp.

Out the window sat the subdivision he had created. Smithson Farm Estates, Mashpee, Cape Cod, Massachusetts. When he had convinced his dying Aunt Sally to sell him Smithson Bogs—35 acres jutting like a peninsula into a large freshwater pond—the land looked much like it must have in the late 1700s, when the original four rooms of the now-expanded farmhouse had been built.

The farmhouse itself had played a small part in American history. Slaves making their way to Canada on the Underground Railroad had regularly hidden in a secret room located behind a library bookcase on the first floor.

In fact, it was a bundle of papers left behind in that secret room that currently dominated Griffin's thoughts. He had found the papers just last week, wrapped in an oily cloth and tucked into a small crevice in the fieldstone wall—actually, the back of the chimney that ran up the middle of the farmhouse—of the hidden room. He had studied the papers, and he was pretty sure that they were of significant historical value. But they might also be the key that opened some unfound treasure chest. The problem was that he had no idea where to search for the chest, or even what it might look like.

Still, a treasure chest was a seductive—and distracting—fantasy.

And he needed a big score, even after earning close to $100,000 on the Prefontaine transaction. He had sold the last of the subdivision lots to them, so he couldn't tap that vein again. Yet he had a big nut to crack every month in the form of a $2 million mortgage on the Smithson Farm property, which required that he write a check every month for $22,000, then painfully watch as that sum was debited from his ever-shrinking bank account.

That the $2 million mortgage itself existed was the result of an ongoing, but brilliantly simple, deception. He had obtained the mortgage loan eight and a half years earlier, before he had subdivided the property and sold off 32 of the 35 acres. Over the years, as he sold off parcels in the subdivision, he simply forged the bank's signature to documents authorizing the sales of the parcels. He then pocketed the sale proceeds, instead of sharing them with the bank as the loan agreement required. A local lender might have noticed the sales activity, but Griffin had purposely chosen an out-of-state bank. The result was that the bank was totally ignorant of the fact that most of its collateral had disappeared. But it was a blissful ignorance, since he dutifully mailed the $22,000 mortgage payment every month. And the monthly check was all the bank really cared about. At least so far.

His problem was that his little ploy was on a collision course with itself. The loan was due in 18 months, in its entirety. And since it had been written as an "interest only" commercial loan, the entire $2 million in principal remained unpaid. He knew that if he didn't pay off the entire $2 million by the due date, his loan file would leap to the top of a pile on some banker's desk. The banker would order an appraisal of the property, which would quickly reveal the fraud, and the whole mess would blow up in Griffin's face.

He figured he could handle the monthly $22,000 payment for the next year or so. But he knew he had to find a way to repay the entire $2 million before the due date, or he would likely be looking at some jail time.

And jail was the one thing he knew he could not handle. He knew himself, knew how deeply his psyche had been affected by his years as a prisoner of war. The act of being confined, of being imprisoned and controlled and subjugated, would drive him crazy. It was as simple as that.

So he had no choice but to come up with the $2 million. The solution, he hoped, might somehow involve the stack of papers he had discovered in the old farmhouse's hidden room. Exactly how, he was not sure, but the outlines of a scheme had begun to take vague shape in his mind. It was time for another look at the papers.

*   *   *

Griffin pulled himself up into his dented and rusted pickup truck, smiled and waved at a neighbor as he exited the subdivision. She glared back at him.

He followed the two-lane road through a large wooded area, passed a few small farms, and slowed as he entered the large traffic rotary in the center of town. A half dozen roads tentacled out from the rotary, all seemingly leading to a different world. Each destination was technically a part of Mashpee, but all they really had in common was that they shared a common eye at the center.

A traveler heading south would end up in the New Seabury area—golf courses and vacation homes and luxury inns tucked tastefully up against the southern coast of the Cape. Disney World for adults. The roads going east-west were tourist routes for the middle class—fast-food restaurants and mini-golf courses and liquor stores for travelers heading east to Falmouth or west to Barnstable. Travelers to the north—those that weren't shooting up Route 130 to pick up the Mid-Cape Highway and make their way off-Cape—might come across a few upscale homes, like Smithson Farm Estates, which were being built along the shores of the many freshwater ponds and lakes in the northern section of town. But generally northbound travelers were either returning to their modest homes in the sparsely populated rural sections of the town or heading to the Otis Air Force base in Sandwich.

But all travelers had to come to the rotary, to the eye. And, alongside the eastern edge of the rotary, like a giant multi-colored eyebrow, some smart entrepreneur had built a massive retail area called Mashpee Commons.

Griffin turned into the Commons, found a parking space in a lot behind a new brick building designed to look like an old mill. The fake mill sat between a red clapboard building designed to look like an old schoolhouse and a bright yellow structure that looked like a Wild West saloon. His bank was located in the saloon building.

He waited in line for service. He would be met with the same cold hostility at the local bank as he had encountered on the way out of the subdivision; he would have preferred it to be otherwise, but he couldn't have it both ways. He had long since abandoned any pretense of supporting himself through his construction business, and the gift shop he ran in the old barn of the farmhouse brought in only a few bucks during tourist season. He hadn't gone so far as to make up business cards that read, "Rex Griffin, Professional Litigant," but he might as well have.

He had sued, or been sued by, almost 50 of his fellow Mashpee residents. The cases brought against him mostly involved shoddy construction work on houses he had built, including those in the Smithson Farm Estates subdivision, as well as attempts to collect unpaid bills from him. The cases he had initiated could have been used as a law school curriculum—everything from dog bites to trespassing to libel to assault. Few, if any, of them were legitimate. He

26

couldn't very well now be surprised that he was so abhorred in the community.

Not that he cared. He had always been a loner. Maybe it was because his brother Donald suffered from autism, and kids used to tease Rex about it. Or maybe it was because his parents spent all their time and attention on Donald, leaving Rex to himself. Or maybe the shrink in the army was right—maybe Griffin felt guilty that he was normal while his brother was not. Whatever. Donald now lived in a group home with other autistic adults in suburban Boston. Griffin didn't hate him, or even resent him. But he was happy not to be burdened by him.

After all, he had his hands full with his sister. Denise had been born when Rex was already off fighting in Vietnam, after his family had moved from suburban Boston down to the Cape. She would have been better off had he never returned. He closed his eyes, replayed the nightmare for the thousandth time.

"Rex, Rex, come watch me on the monkey bars."

"Be right there, Dennie."

"Look, I can hang upside down. Look at me!"

"I said I'll be right there. Just let me finish reading this article." To this day, Griffin could visualize the headline from the *Boston Globe*: "Real Estate Prices Expected to Rise." He was going to make a killing investing in real estate.

"Rex! I'm slipping. Help!"

"Okay, okay, I'll be right there." He had started to amble over, his eyes still on his newspaper.

"Rex……!"

He looked up just in time to see his 8-year old sister's head split open on the corner of a cinder block some kid had been using as a stepstool.

Denise was now 28 years old, going on 9. She was a striking woman, just as she had been a beautiful kid—bright blue eyes, a freckled nose, dark brown curly hair, a smile that belonged in a toothpaste commercial. But, though she had grown into womanhood physically, and even physiologically, her intellectual growth had been stunted by the accident. She was an 8-year old trapped in a woman's body. All because her brother had been too busy with his newspaper.

27

Since their mother's death, she had lived with Griffin in the old farmhouse. He really didn't mind—she was cheerful and sweet, and helped out by doing many of the basic chores around the house. He didn't let her use the oven, but she could make toast and dry the dishes and do some laundry. And it didn't hurt that her inheritance money and monthly Social Security checks helped pay the bills.

The biggest problem he had was keeping the boys—or, rather, men—away. She was just mature enough to have learned how to flirt a bit, and men seemed to sense that she was a juicy piece of fruit that had grown ripe on the vine. Lolita in a Baywatch body.

Griffin's musings were interrupted by the arrival of a stern-faced bank officer. She reminded Griffin of the assistant principal of his junior high school. "Can I help you?"

Griffin, for the third time, explained that he wanted to get into his safe deposit box. He knew they were being purposefully obtuse—they no doubt preferred that he bank somewhere else. But he refused to allow his irritation to show. He smiled wanly at her, fingered his bow tie.

She sighed. "Come this way." She marched him into the vault, then left him as he locked himself in a small room and spread the contents of the box onto a table. Thirty-one sheets of yellowed paper, covered front and back, all written in longhand in the years before the Civil War. He had preserved each page in its own plastic casing, though the 150 years spent in the dampness of the old farmhouse's secret room had caused the papers to fade and mildew. Griffin removed a magnifying glass from his pocket and began to examine his discovery.

The sheets of paper were a handful of pieces to a much larger historical puzzle, like stray pages that had come free from the binding of a long novel. He hummed as he postulated and theorized and conjectured, attempting to weave together a story around the fragments of history spread in front of him.

The pages comprised a single document entitled, "Modern History of the Wampanoag Indian Tribe of Marshpee, Massachusetts." The document, true to its name, recounted the history of the Wampanoag Indians of the Mashpee area of Cape Cod, then known as "Marshpee," beginning in 1807 and ending 60 years later, in 1867.

28

The pages consisted of a series of yearly entries, each entry summarizing the highlights of the tribe's activities for the year and concluding with a listing of the newly elected tribe officials. The handwriting indicated that the same person had written all 61 entries, though the scribe's hand had clearly grown unsteady by the time it had scribbled the final few entries. Griffin touched the paper. A poet, he knew, would try to visualize the changing face of the tribe historian as he or she dutifully marked the passage of years from young adulthood to old age, would note that the passing years were reflected not just on the yearly tribal entries but on the wrinkles forming on the scribe's face like rings on a tree trunk.

When Griffin had first uncovered the documents, he assumed that they might be of value to some collector of Native American history. He had read that the Pequot Indians, owners of the Foxwoods Casino in Connecticut, had opened a museum of Native American history; perhaps they would be interested in purchasing the discovery from him. But in the past few days Griffin had become preoccupied with the sentence that was written—almost ritualistically—across the bottom of all 61 entries: "The tribe knelt at the grave of the great sachem, Metacomet, then we left the land of the smooth stones and returned to our homes."

Griffin had immediately suspected that "the land of the smooth stones" referred to an area of the Smithson Farm land that was marked by a mound of fist-sized smooth stones piled in a clearing near the farmhouse. He was not sure what the significance of the stones were, but they were located close enough to the original farmhouse so that they had not been disturbed when the subdivision roads and homes were built.

But who was Metacomet, and why was he buried at Smithson Farm? Griffin read through the documents, but could find no additional clues. So he scribbled the name "Metacomet" on a piece of paper, returned the documents to the safe deposit box, and drove to the local library.

He first searched back through the town records and learned that Smithson Farm had been owned in the mid-1800s by a man named Attaquin, who had been a leader of the Mashpee tribe and a successful merchant and farmer. That, at least, explained why the tribe's historical documents were hidden in the farmhouse's secret room.

And Attaquin's Indian heritage also helped explain the farmhouse's use as a stop on the Underground Railway. From what Griffin had read, the Mashpee tribe members had frequently interbred with freed slaves in the early 1800s. As a result, many tribe members also had African-American blood. And, presumably, sympathy for the plight of the slaves.

Griffin then turned to the name Metacomet. This was the given name of the Wampanoag chief known to the Colonists by his Christian name, Philip. The Wampanoag tribe occupied the land of what is now southeastern Massachusetts, Cape Cod, Nantucket and Martha's Vineyard. Philip, nee Metacomet, became chief following the apparent murder by poisoning of his brother by the English settlers in Plymouth, Massachusetts. Fearing that the English would eventually wipe out the entire Native American population, Metacomet organized the various southern New England tribes in the mid-1670s and led them in battle against the Colonists in what became known as King Philip's War.

The Colonists eventually prevailed in the war with the Native Americans, but not before many Colonial towns and settlements were burned. Eventually the English troops shot and killed Metacomet, effectively ending the war. After Metacomet's death, the English beheaded him and quartered his body, then displayed the head on a pole in Plymouth for 25 years as a warning to other Indians.

Could Metacomet's quartered body, and perhaps eventually his head as well, have been brought to Mashpee for burial? It was likely that the political climate in the nearby Plymouth area would have made it difficult for the remaining Wampanoags to erect any kind of shrine for Metacomet in Mashpee, where many of the Wampanoags had been forcibly resettled after the war. But could the Wampanoags have quietly transported Metacomet's body to an unmarked grave where they could mourn their fallen leader without drawing undue attention to themselves?

*   *   *

The kids were staying with Carla's parents for a few days in their condo near Boston, but Pierre and Carla—along with a constant stream of local craftsmen—were working practically round-the-clock on the house.

Yes, the house. A four-bedroom, three-bathroom center entrance Colonial with a three-car garage and finished basement. Set on three partially-wooded acres that rolled gently down to a small sandy beach on a pristine lake. Just like the other dozen or so houses that ringed the tennis racket-shaped peninsula that comprised the subdivision.

Except that the other houses were actually habitable.

Pierre was returning from what seemed like his twentieth trip to the local Home Depot. Back and forth he had gone, along with a trip to a number of other stores and shops, and he hadn't even laid eyes on the ocean yet. Mashpee, he was beginning to learn, was not the sandy beaches and gentle surf of the Cape Cod vacation guides. There were some nice beaches on the southern edge of the town, but they had become largely inaccessible to the general population as a result of the New Seabury development. This was a working class town—the locals spent their recreational time hunting in the woods or fishing on the ponds and lakes, not lying on the beach. It struck him that he could just as easily have been in upstate New York or rural Maine.

He saw the blue tarp of the farmhouse ahead, turned into the subdivision. Carla met him in the driveway, yellow rubber gloves on her hand. "What's wrong?" he asked.

Her shoulders slumped. "Just that this house is a disaster."

Pierre sighed. Carla rarely allowed things to get her down. "What's wrong now?"

"I flushed the toilet down in the basement, and it all just came right out and flooded everything. I called the plumber, and he says that there's not enough slope to the sewer line, so things just back up. He thinks we need to re-do the whole line."

"I'm not sure I want to know how much."

"Probably five grand, including the carpentry work. Damn it, Pierre, nothing in this house works." She yanked off the gloves, tossed them into the dumpster sitting in their driveway.

"I know. It's my fault. I should have known better than to fly out here in a weekend and try to pick out a house. So much for being a real estate expert. I just fell in love with the water views."

Carla forced a smile. "I guess he can't ruin those, can he?"

Pierre appreciated Carla's attempt to let him off the hook. But he knew he deserved to be boned and filleted. "I should have researched Griffin better. Just take a look at the old farmhouse he lives in—the thing probably could be really charming if he'd just take care of it. The paint's peeling, the grounds are overgrown, the chimney is falling down...."

"Not to mention the tarp on the roof. The house looks like an over-sized 4th of July float."

Pierre laughed. "You're right. And it's not like it would take much digging to get the scoop on this guy. He built all the houses in the subdivision and pretty much every neighbor I've talked to has horror stories about the shoddy work."

"They can't be as bad as this, Pierre—they're all still standing. It's like he hired the kids from Sesame Street to do the construction work."

"Actually, that's not far from the truth. Apparently he uses the high school kids from the Voc Tech as his workers. He pays 'em next to nothing, and they get to practice building houses for high school credit. On top of that, he's got brown teeth. Never trust a man who doesn't take care of his teeth."

"You're right about his teeth—they're gross." She sighed. "But we've got to do something. I don't mind cooking outside while we wait for the kitchen to be finished, and I even don't mind living with plywood floors for a while, but the bottom line is that this house is a piece of junk. We're going to have to redo almost everything—plumbing, electrical, the roof—and it's not going to be cheap."

"I know. I'll call Shelby. No sense waiting—we might as well sue Griffin right away."

*   *   *

Armed with a newly-purchased metal detector and backpack, Griffin spent the next few days exploring the 35 acres that comprised Smithson Farms in hopes of finding Metacomet's grave. It was sweaty, dusty work, especially dressed in khakis, loafers and a bowtie, but the neighbors might be watching so Griffin wanted to stay in costume.

Wampanoag burial practices of the 17th century consisted of burying the deceased in a dirt or gravel grave, with the head facing to the southwest, where the souls of the dead were believed to reside. More importantly for Griffin's needs, the deceased were buried with tools and weapons for use in the afterlife, with the more important members of society being buried with the greatest quantity of material goods. As a chief, Metacomet would likely have been buried with an arsenal of knives and tomahawks, as well as perhaps a gun or some bullets captured from the colonists. Hence the metal detector.

Already this task had become more complicated than Griffin had expected. Originally he had thought that the mound of smooth stones had been erected to mark the grave. However, his research revealed that these stone piles were instead the result of the ancient Wampanoag practice of dropping stones into a pile along a path to ensure good fortune on their journey. So the stone pile had nothing to do with the grave itself, other than to confirm the fact that Metacomet was buried along, or near, a well-traveled Indian path.

Still, Griffin was fairly confident he could find the grave. The body would likely be buried on higher ground—much of the lower lands flooded naturally every spring, which was one reason why the land had been suitable for permanent use as a cranberry bog. And he expected that the grave would be relatively close to the mound of smooth stones. Even so, that left more than five acres that still had to be meticulously searched.

Finally, after days of pacing the property, the metal detector sang out as it glided over the crest of a small clearing tucked within a grove of trees. He dried his sweating hands on his khakis, adjusted his bow tie, and moved the detector back and forth across the earth. The metal objects seemed to be arrayed in a rectangular pattern, approximately six feet long by four feet wide. Griffin nodded— according to his research, the body would have been laid out on its side, in a fetal-like position, with the burial goods ringed around it. On a southwest to northeast axis, as this was.

Griffin carefully brushed aside the blanket of freshly fallen leaves and examined the earth underneath, then pulled out a trowel and began to scrape the soil aside along the borders of the rectangle. He worked slowly, humming, the sun warming the back of his neck and the dirt cooling his fingers. He penetrated the topsoil, then used his hands to gently push the earth away. Once he determined the depth of what he hoped was a grave, he could use a shovel to move more quickly, but for now he didn't want to disturb his treasure with a careless slash into the earth.

His fingers bumped up against a hard, smooth object only 18 inches below the surface. At first he thought it might be a rock, but its edges were too straight and its width too uniform. He probed deeper, tucked a finger under the edge, tugged gently. The earth held on to its bounty, then reluctantly yielded as Griffin tugged harder. It struck him as a bit poetic—reclaiming for man that which man had buried.

The item came free, dirt falling from its darkened surface as the sun illuminated it for the first time in over 300 years. Not a knife or an ax or a tomahawk as Griffin had expected, but a horseshoe. Griffin examined it, smiled, slipped the heavy iron piece into his backpack. He would plunder nothing else from this grave, but he would keep this piece. He could use a little luck. Metacomet would just have to find his own blacksmith in the afterlife.

He moved to the southwest end of the rectangle, tried to guess where the head would lie, began digging. A foot below the surface, his trowel scraped against a fabric of some kind. He nodded again—sometimes the bodies were buried wrapped in a blanket. Working carefully, he pushed the dirt away, probed beneath the decaying blanket fragments with his fingers. Something hard, round. Probably the skull.

He pushed the blanket fragments aside, reached into the cavity, caressed a cantaloupe-sized object. He pushed more dirt away, confirmed with his eyes what his fingers had told him—a skull, adult-sized, turned on its side. He found the jaw, pushed away some more dirt, reached for the neck, the clavicle. Nothing.

He probed further, his fingers searching for the bones of the body that belonged to the skull. But instead of bones, his fingers found more fabric. Another blanket. Why would there be a second blanket? Could there be a second body buried in the grave? If so, he

34

had the wrong burial site. Metacomet, he had theorized, was buried alone—buried in secret by his loyal followers while his head was displayed on a pole in Plymouth. So why would there be two bodies?

Griffin slapped himself on the thigh. Idiot. There weren't two bodies, only two blankets. The body had been wrapped and buried first; years later, after its years on the pole, the head had been added, wrapped in a separate blanket.

Together, the head and the body made one corpse. And, wrapped separately, they proved that the corpse was that of the beheaded Metacomet.

The site was shielded by trees from the other homes in the subdivision, and nobody seemed to have observed him. However, the grave was, unfortunately, located partially on land he no longer owned. Part of the site was technically on the land he had sold to the Prefontaines. If only he had known, he could have simply re-drawn the lot lines before the closing. But at least the site was unlikely to be disturbed. The Prefontaines had their hands full just finishing the house—they were unlikely to do major landscaping, especially with the winter months approaching. Still, it never hurt to be safe. He yanked the two property stakes out of the ground and re-inserted them on the other side of the burial spot. The ploy wouldn't fool a professional surveyor, but it would probably keep the Prefontaine family away from Metacomet's grave.

He had no intention of telling anyone of his discovery. Eventually he'd be able to cash in on it, but in the meantime was content to let the beheaded Metacomet lie peacefully in his grave.

It had now been almost two weeks since Griffin had discovered the tribal history documents. In that time, he had educated himself on King Philip's War, located King Philip's, or Metacomet's, grave, and deduced that the Smithson Farm property was likely the historical gathering spot for the yearly tribal council meetings of the Mashpee Wampanoag Indians. All of this was of historical interest, but it wasn't going to make him rich.

Yet Griffin sensed that he was on to something. The town of Mashpee still had a sizable Indian population, and Griffin's discovery would likely be of tremendous interest to them. In fact, since Metacomet had created an alliance with almost all the tribes in southern New England, his burial site might be of interest to all Native American tribes in the area. In some ways, Metacomet was like the George Washington of the New England Native Americans. Would the tribes, some of whom were flush with cash from casino operations, be willing to overpay for Smithson Farm in order to preserve the burial site? Or could the local Mashpee Indians be maneuvered into pressuring the town of Mashpee into overpaying for the land for the same reason?

In order to answer this question he had to better understand the history and the dynamics of the relationship between the Mashpee Wampanoag Indians and the town of Mashpee. Griffin had moved to the town in the early 1980s, just as a court battle between the Mashpee Indians and the town of Mashpee over title to the land in town was winding down. The town had prevailed in the action, and there had been years of bad blood in town over the whole dispute, but that was really all Griffin knew about the case.

*   *   *

Griffin changed into a clean pair of khakis and a fresh oxford shirt, retied his yellow bowtie, and hopped in his truck. He crossed the Sagamore Bridge and arrived less than a half-hour later at the library in the town of Plymouth. He knew better than to expect to get much help from the librarians in Mashpee, and more importantly he didn't want any of his nosy neighbors to know what he was researching. In Plymouth, which was "off-Cape" and therefore really part of a whole different world, he could work in anonymity and also expect a bit of courteous assistance if he needed it.

Griffin had no trouble finding a long list of newspaper articles reporting on the Mashpee lawsuit filed in the late 1970s. He skimmed easily through the legalese; scores of lawsuits had long ago made him fluent in legal jargon. He hummed to himself contentedly; this was exactly the type of project that he enjoyed. Pick up a stray piece of seemingly unimportant information, then connect it to a bunch of other equally innocuous scraps of data. It was like some kind of children's connect-the-dots coloring game. Sometimes the result was nothing more than a random collection of minutiae—scribbles on a page, to continue the metaphor. But once in a while a picture emerged, invisible to all eyes but his.

The gist of the Mashpee Indians claim was that the state of Massachusetts and the Mashpee tribe had signed a treaty in the early 1800s which distributed the tribe's reservation land to the individual tribe members. The tribe now argued that the treaty unlawfully took away the tribe's ancestral land and that the land—essentially, the entire town of Mashpee—should now be returned to the tribe.

Specifically, the tribe argued that the treaty was illegal under the terms of the Nonintercourse Act passed by Congress in 1790. This law stated that only Congress could enter into treaties and agreements with Indian tribes. And since the original agreement between Massachusetts and the tribe was not approved by Congress, it was not legal. The tribe's argument was a legally strong one—the tribes of northern Maine had made a similar argument in the late 1970s in a case that was settled for $30 million, and the Oneida tribe of upstate New York was currently pushing for a return of 250,000 acres of land in a case that had the support of the U.S. Justice Department.

Unfortunately for the Mashpee members, the tribe never really got to argue its case. The judge had ruled that the case could not be heard until the Mashpee Indians first proved that they fit the definition of an "Indian tribe" under the applicable federal statute. The court heard forty days of testimony on the question, and a jury found that at some point between 1842 and 1869 the tribe had abandoned its "tribal identity" and assimilated into the mainstream of American society. Even though the tribe "re-organized" itself in the early 1900s, the judge concluded that, under the terms of the federal statute, this "abandonment of tribal identity" in the mid-1800s precluded the tribe from bringing the lawsuit today.

Griffin paid a few dollars to have a copy of the actual court decisions printed out for him. He could feel his heart beginning to race, could see the dots beginning to connect. He dried his hands on his pants, took a deep breath, adjusted his bow tie, and began to read the cases carefully, paying special attention to the appellate court's summary of the specifics of the jury's conclusions.

In essence, the jury concluded that between 1842 and 1869 the Mashpee Indians had ceased to interact as a unified tribe and had instead begun to function as individual members of American society. The Mashpees were unable to provide any evidence to the jury that during this period the tribe maintained a centralized government, kept a tribal history, participated in community decision-making, or congregated for group worship. The jury simply didn't buy the testimony of the expert witnesses who testified on behalf of the Mashpee Indians that the absence of this evidence was likely due to the fact that most Indian cultures kept oral, rather than written, records of tribal history, events and meetings. The jury wanted to see written evidence, and the tribe, despite the tens of millions of dollars that were at stake, had none to offer.

Trying to contain his excitement, Griffin searched for follow-up articles on the Mashpee case. He could find nothing further after the tribe's appeal to the Supreme Court had failed. He understood human nature—it was not unexpected that after such a high-stakes defeat that the deflated tribe would take a few years to rally again. But Griffin was surprised that in the intervening 20 years nothing more had transpired in the case. After all, the merits of the tribe's claim to the land had never been heard, and, in fact, many legal commentators at the time believed the tribe's case to be a strong one. Would the Mashpee Indians so easily have walked away from an eight- or even nine-figure windfall? Griffin doubted it.

He tried a different approach. He sat down in front of an empty computer, logged on to the Internet, and ran a search using the words "Mashpee Indians." Eureka. Buried in a Bureau of Indian Affairs summary of pending cases, deep in the bureaucratic bowels of the federal government, he found the tribe's response to its court defeat. In 1990, the Mashpee tribe had officially applied for federal recognition as an Indian tribe. The Bureau, which moved at glacial speed, was still a year or two away from a final decision, but federal recognition of the tribe would constitute a successful end-run around the earlier court decision. Griffin nodded at the ingenious subtlety of the tribe's tactic—once the federal government had recognized the tribe, the tribe could re-file its lawsuit and force the court to rule on the case on its actual merits.

If the lawsuit filed by the tribe in 1976 had been a nuclear attack against the town, the application for federal recognition was a brilliant piece of guerrilla warfare. Unlike in court where both sides have an opportunity to present their side of the case, it was unlikely that town officials were even aware of the tribe's 1990 federal recognition application. And even if any officials had been aware of the filing back in 1990, it is doubtful that those same officials would still be in office today, more than a decade later. As a result, in all likelihood the tribe's application would be ruled on without the town of Mashpee ever even having had the opportunity to offer evidence in opposition.

But a clever strategy would not be enough by itself—the tribe still had to prove its case that the Mashpee tribe had not "abandoned its tribal identity" back in the mid-1800s. The tribe had failed in its attempt to convince a jury of that fact, so it was far from certain that the Bureau would rule in its favor, especially in light of the existing court decision to the contrary. Without new evidence, it would be difficult for the Bureau to reach a conclusion that directly contradicted a federal court opinion that had been upheld by the Supreme Court.

Without new evidence. That was the key. Griffin sat back in his chair, closed his eyes, and allowed himself a tight smile.

As exciting as the discovery of King Philip's grave had been, the true value of the tribal documents he had found lay not in their revelation of Philip's burial spot but in the mundane details of the 61 yearly historical entries. Every election of tribal leaders, every mention of tribal worship customs, every recounting of petty tribal disputes, every debate over which crops to grow, every tabulation of tribal income and expenses—each of these was compelling evidence that the Wampanoag Indians of Mashpee, Massachusetts indeed existed and interacted as a tribe during the first two-thirds of the 19th century. They had not assimilated into mainstream society as the jury had concluded, but rather had maintained their tribal identity.

And Griffin now knew that there were people who would likely pay millions to be able to prove this very point: Metacomet's descendents.

And perhaps also their enemies.

*   *   *

Griffin left Plymouth and headed back to Mashpee. He had done the drive a thousand times—over the Sagamore Bridge, past the Christmas Tree Shop's thatched roof, down the Mid-Cape Highway, exit in Sandwich, past the Air Force base, into Mashpee. Never anything particularly interesting about the drive. But at least he had avoided the traffic—during the summer the half-hour drive could become an all-morning ordeal.

In eighteen months he needed to pay off his $2 million mortgage. And in the meantime he needed to write a $22,000 check every month to the bank just to stay current.

The problem was that at this point only the Mashpees would understand the value of his find. But the Mashpee tribe was a poor one. And Griffin had no interest in taking an I.O.U.

The other potential parties to the litigation—the town, the land-owners, the title insurance companies—had deep pockets. But they had no idea that the tribe was about to hit them with a sneak attack. Griffin could warn them, but the act of warning them might itself make his discovery worthless—given time, the town and landowners could mount a successful political campaign in Washington to defeat the tribe's claim for federal recognition.

A catch-22. The only people who valued his discovery were the ones who couldn't afford to pay him for it.

Worse still, if he gave the Mashpee tribe the documents now in exchange for a promise that they would pay him at a later date, the documents themselves would enable the tribe to break that very promise. Griffin connected the dots: First, the tribe would use the documents to achieve federal recognition as an Indian tribe. That would make the Mashpee tribe a sovereign nation, immune from the civil laws of both Massachusetts and the United States. And as a sovereign nation, the tribe could simply renege on any promise it might have made to pay Griffin.

From what Griffin had read, he doubted a court would even hear his case to enforce the tribe's promise to pay him—the doctrine of sovereign immunity stated that no sovereign entity could be sued without its permission. And even if he was wrong, and a court for some reason allowed the suit to go ahead, how would he ever collect on his judgment? Griffin, better than most, knew what it was like to be judgment-proof. No court would order the seizure of tribal property—such an action would be akin to a court ordering that Montreal be seized to satisfy a Canadian debt to a U.S. resident.

His dilemma reminded him of the old mantra recited by the leaders of the Soviet Union: "The capitalists will sell us the rope with which we will hang them." Griffin would be giving the tribe the very documents they would use to screw him.

So he was stuck. He needed some way to hold the tribe to its promise, some way to neutralize the trump card that their sovereign status would give them. Some way to slip the rope over the Mashpees' necks instead of his.

Chapter 5

[October]

Pierre slammed the screen door shut.

"What's wrong, Pierre?"

"I'm gonna kill that guy. I swear." He regretted the words even as he spoke them. He had spoken in hyperbole, but, even so, he didn't want the girls to hear him talk like that.

"What?"

"Come on, I'll show you."

Pierre led Carla out the side door of their new home and marched through a wooded area. There were a number of ponds that dotted the subdivision, remnants of the property's prior use as a cranberry bog. Still within their property lines, they stopped at the edge of a small pond. A freshly painted, red- and white-streaked pond.

Carla gasped. "Oh my God. That asshole. I can't believe he did that."

Pierre reached in and pulled one of the floating paint cans toward him, tossed it aside. "We gotta clean this up, Carla. It's gonna seep into the groundwater, into the lake, into the wells...."

"Us? What about Griffin?"

Pierre shook his head. "We're gonna have to clean this up first, worry about him later."

"How long do you think it's been like this?"

"Well, some of the cans still have some paint in them, so not very long."

"I bet he got the letter from our attorney yesterday and then sneaked down here last night."

Pierre nodded. "Makes sense. We told him to finish painting, so this is his response. The guy's a nut. The Builder From Hell. I'm so sorry, Carla—I should've researched this better, found a different house."

"It's not the house I'm worried about, Pierre. I'm scared. This guy's crazy. And he lives so close to us. Who knows how many other times he's slithered over here onto our property?"

A voice in the distance interrupted them. "Mr. Prefontaine? Mrs. Prefontaine? Hello, hello?"

Pierre sighed, shook his head. "Why do I have a bad feeling about this? You might as well wait here; I'll go see who it is."

He cut back through the woods, spotted a middle-aged man walking around the house. "Can I help you?"

"Oh, yeah, hi. Sorry to bother you. I'm Bill Burke, with the Cape Cod Conservation Commission. We got a call this morning, somebody reporting a hazardous spill situation."

"Let me guess—anonymous tip, right?"

Bill looked down at his clipboard, shrugged. "Doesn't say here. Could be. Know what this is all about?"

Pierre sighed again. "Yeah. Follow me."

Pierre led the man to the pond. A light breeze kicked up, mixing the white and red paints together. A slimy pink coating spread, Pepto-Bismol-like, to the far side of the pond.

Bill Burke removed his cap. "Oh. Oh, my."

Carla responded. "We're pretty sure we know who did this."

Bill shook his head. "Doesn't really matter right now. We gotta contain this before it spreads down to the lake. Mind if I use your phone? See if I can get a team out here right away."

They walked back toward the house. As they cleared the woods, Bill Burke stopped suddenly. Pierre watched his eyes focus on their half-painted home. White, with red trim.

The government official turned away from Pierre and Carla, muttered a few words while shaking his head. "Folks, you might want to call your lawyer."

*　　　*　　　*

Rex Griffin stroked his bow tie and peered through the window of the old farmhouse, watching as the team of environmental experts and clean-up specialists wormed their way through the subdivision.

He hoped the paint wouldn't contaminate the lake–he enjoyed an occasional swim. And he, like most, preferred that the lake be tinted blue, not pink. But from the looks of the size of the army of environmentalists, they would contain the spill before it spread too far. It would probably cost the Prefontaines a fortune. But he had to show them that they were out of their league here–they should call off their lawyer, take their loss and just move on. This was a fight they could not win.

Griffin looked at his watch. Time for another neighborly visit.

He scrubbed his hands clean of any paint residue, grabbed a work apron and a tool box, and cut across his front lawn to the gift shop he ran in the old barn. The shop was filled with the typical gift shop schlock–t-shirts and coffee mugs and beach towels emblazoned with neon-colored outlines of Cape Cod, cheap costume jewelry made from sea shells, a few dozen different wind chimes and wind socks and weathervanes hanging from the barn's exposed wooden beams. Plus the basic provisions a beach-going vacationer might need. He had hired one of the local blue-hairs to watch the shop for him while he attended to his construction business.

"Ethel, I'm going to be out for a while."

"Yes, Mr. Griffin. Should I check on Denise while you're gone?"

"That would be nice of you, Ethel. Thank you. See if you can get her to do something besides watch those soaps." The last thing he needed was for her hormones to start running wild.

"Do you want me to bring her over here with me?"

During the summer the shop often filled with young men on vacation looking for sunscreen or postcards or a paperback book, so he tried to keep Denise away. But it was unlikely that the singles crowd would be on Cape on a weekday in October. "All right. Thanks."

Griffin strolled cheerfully through the subdivision, then rang the doorbell of a sprawling Tudor he had recently built. As he waited, he ran his finger along the cracks that had already begun to appear in the stonework on the front of the house. He was a bit surprised the stonework wasn't in even worse shape—it had been the Voc Tech kid's first attempt at masonry.

It still amazed Griffin that people bought the houses he built. Sure, he provided palatial floor plans and elaborate designs and amenities, but anybody with even a cursory knowledge of the building trades could see that he cut every corner he could find. From experience he knew that, on a $200,000 home, the buyers would obsess over the quality of construction; but at $600,000, all they cared about was the size of the master bedroom suite and the brand names on the appliances. They were paying a Mercedes price, so they simply assumed that they were getting quality construction. It never occurred to them they were buying an oversized Pinto.

Built with weather-damaged lumber, resting on a foundation poured on loose soil, framed with two-by-fours instead of two-by-sixes, encased with mold-inducing synthetic stucco. The town building inspector had shaken his head at Griffin's work, but signed off nonetheless; he knew Griffin wouldn't hesitate to sue if provoked. And the homebuyers, like most, were far more concerned with paint colors and tile choices than in whether their house would survive the decade. Or even the winter.

Eventually, of course, they would sue him. Or, more accurately, sue the shell corporation he had formed to perform the construction work. They would spend ten or twenty thousand dollars, obtain a judgment from the court, then ... nothing. The corporation had nothing, so their judgment was worthless. And he had put the farmhouse in Denise and Donald's name, so nobody could touch that either.

Amisha Raman opened the door, straightened her skirt. She was strikingly beautiful—mocha skin, watery chocolate-colored eyes, straight white teeth framed by a pair of cherry red lips. In his younger days, when he chose to indulge in those types of delicacies, he would have found her just delicious.

Her features hardened as her eyes focused on Griffin. He nodded a hello, raised his toolbox a few inches. "I'm here to work on the repairs." He had recently received a letter from the Ramans' attorney threatening all sorts of legal actions if he didn't repair some defects.

Amisha spoke as if she had learned her English in a boarding school in London. "Very well, Mr. Griffin. You may enter."

The list of work was a long one, but Griffin had no intention of completing it. Or even starting it. He puttered around for an hour or so, then yelled down the stairs. "Mrs. Raman, don't come up the stairs for a few minutes. I've just put fresh grout around the tiles."

He spread a work cloth across the stairway landing for show, then made his way into Mr. Raman's office. Griffin had done his homework—Rajiv Raman was an executive with a biotech start-up company, one that had recently gone public. He remembered the man from the closing—a scowling, snorting man with a singsong voice and a bad case of dandruff. But he apparently had an aptitude for biotechnology, and had leveraged that single proficiency into a trophy wife and a trophy home.

Griffin sat down at the computer, logged on to the Internet. He quickly opened the e-mail program, then typed a message: *Company profits splendid this quarter. Announcement coming Friday. Stock sure to rise—fine time to buy. Do NOT confirm receipt of this e-mail or respond to this e-mail in any way! Rajiv.*

He sent the message to everyone in Rajiv's address book, then deleted the message from the 'Sent' file. The Ramans would never know the message had been sent. Until, that is, the Securities and Exchange Commission brought charges against Rajiv for insider stock trading. Or until his friends called, furious that the stock had plunged. Either way, it would be ugly.

Griffin left the computer the way he had found it, slapped a little fresh grout around the tiles to make it look like he had done some work, and said his good-byes. "I'll be back tomorrow to finish up."

Amisha offered Griffin a small smile, gracious in her victory in having pressured him to make the repairs. "Good day, Mr. Griffin."

"Yes, thank you. It has been."

Chapter 6

Pierre—or Coach Pre, as he was now called—had held three practices, and he was starting to get comfortable with the players. He noticed that Billy's Neanderthal teammate still glared at him, but for the most part the kids left Billy alone. And the bully never went so far as to directly challenge Billy again.

Pierre had made a practice of ending the sessions with a series of wind sprints. Unlike most coaches, he participated in the sprints as well—it was always better to lead by example. Plus, it kept him in shape.

But Pierre's sprints had a twist. At the end of every half-lap, the players had to drop to the ice and do twenty push-ups. Unlike soccer or basketball, a hockey shift was a series of short sprints, interrupted by a series of brief wrestling matches as players fought for control of the puck. Pierre's drill was designed to replicate those conditions.

Pierre made a point of skating next to Billy, pushing the boy and pushing himself. "Come on, Billy, I'm an old man. Can't you keep up?" Billy was actually the faster skater, but Pierre was able to complete his push-ups faster and gain a few seconds of valuable rest time while Billy was still prone on the ice.

Billy almost nipped Pierre on the final sprint, but Pierre held him off. It wouldn't be long before the boy overtook him.

They skated slowly for a few seconds, gasping. "Good practice, Billy. Way to work."

"Um, Coach, I'm not going to be able to come to practice tomorrow."

"All right. Everything okay?"

"Yeah. I just gotta work."

Pierre looked at his watch. The girls would already be asleep, and he knew that Carla planned on painting tonight—a couple of the local galleries were already displaying her watercolors, and one of the Newbury Street galleries in Boston had contacted her about showing her work. So Pierre knew he wouldn't be missed, though he was never totally comfortable leaving his family alone with Griffin living only a few hundred feet away.

He turned to Billy. "You wanna stay for a few minutes now so we can work on some stuff I was going to go over? No one's using the ice."

"I guess so."

Pierre dismissed the team, made a quick call on his cell phone to Carla to make sure everything was okay, then skated back to Billy. "This actually applies even more for you than the other guys. I noticed when you're carrying the puck down the wing, you always either shoot or pass. You never try to beat your guy wide. But with your speed, you should try to take him."

Pierre dropped a few pucks on the ice at center ice. "Here, I'll play defense. Come in at me and try to go wide."

They practiced for a half hour, Pierre showing the boy how to freeze the defenseman by faking a pass across the ice before bursting past him to the outside, and then how to tuck his shoulder into the defenseman to shield the puck and create shooting space. By the end of the session, both skaters were panting and sweaty.

"All right, Billy. That's it for me. But I expect to see at least two goals from you next game with that move."

"Okay, Coach."

"Hey, you need a lift home?"

"Sure."

They showered and dressed, then grabbed a Gatorade from a vending machine. The ride from the rink to Billy's house took only about fifteen minutes, but brought Pierre to an area of Mashpee he had never seen before. Which was a bit surprising, since it was only a couple of miles from the Smithson Farm subdivision.

This was the Mashpee as it had existed before it had been "discovered" in the late 1960s by Bostonians looking for a summer getaway. Simple ranch- and Cape-style homes, many vinyl-sided, tucked together side-by-side, the smell of burning wood filling the cool night air. Sort of the rural version of where Pierre had grown up just outside of Boston. Behind a row of houses he could see the moon reflecting off a pond.

"That where you learned to skate?"

"Yup. Johns Pond."

Pierre smiled as a childhood memory came to him. "Ever fall in?"

Billy shrugged. "Couple of times. But it's pretty shallow where we skate."

Pierre nodded. He had played a lot of pond hockey, and Billy's nonchalance about falling in reflected the attitude of the other pond players he had known. The air was cold, and the ice was rutted. You might even find yourself neck deep in an ice bath, gasping for breath and flailing toward shore. But the game beckoned and so you played.

Pierre wanted to keep the conversation going, wanted to draw the boy out. He knew Billy's father was dying of cancer, but wasn't quite sure how to go about trying to be supportive. He crossed himself, offered a silent thanks that his girls had not yet had to deal with death in their young lives. "Did you always live here?"

"Yeah. Dad grew up down the street. This is it, right here on the right."

Pierre was curious to see the inside of the house, to meet Billy's family. "Hey, mind if I use the bathroom?"

"Okay."

They entered through a side door, into a small kitchen and dining area. Pierre smiled as he noticed the mustard-colored appliances—the same ones he had grown up with. The smell of a hot, hearty dinner hung in the air, the haze diffusing the overhead light into a grayish blend of ribbons and streaks. Two girls, younger than Billy but older than Pierre's daughters, sat doing homework at a square wooden table tucked underneath the front window of the room.

They smiled shyly at Pierre, then buried their heads back into their books.

"Billy, that you?" It was a deep, commanding voice. But not unkind.

"Yeah, Mom. Coach Pre is here, needs to use the bathroom."

"Just one second." Pierre could hear a scurrying sound from the next room, pictured Billy's mother tidying up. "All right," she called. Billy led Pierre through the kitchen into a small living area. A jigsaw puzzle lay half-completed on the coffee table separating the brown couch and the television set, and a dozen or so hockey trophies sat on top of a bookshelf. But the room was empty of people. And neat.

"Bathroom's right over there."

When Pierre came out, both of Billy's parents were sitting on the couch. They stood as he smiled at them, then introduced themselves. Pierre felt a pang of guilt—it was late in the evening, and these people had probably settled in for the night. His intrusion had forced them to scramble to get dressed and receive him properly.

"I'm sorry to intrude on you folks."

Billy's father started to respond, then buried his face in a handkerchief as a coughing spell hit him. Billy's mother took over.

"Not at all. Thank you for driving Billy home. And it's nice to meet you—Billy speaks of you often."

She was a large woman, with full features and a deep voice. Pierre studied her face. She smiled at him kindly, but her deep dark eyes locked onto Pierre's and held them, probing and questioning and exploring. Dominique was her name, and aptly so—she seemed to dominate the room, both with her physical size and an imperial-like presence.

Pierre thanked them for their hospitality and said good night. He held Dominique's gaze for a few seconds. Squeezed into a small home, probably only a lost paycheck or two away from poverty, her husband only months from death, she stood proudly—almost majestically—in front of him, stared him down, and looked straight into his soul.

He was glad he had no secrets to hide.

*   *   *

50

It was warm for November, and Bruce had the day off from his job at the local marina, so he decided to spend the morning exploring the cemetery located behind the Indian Meeting House.

The meetinghouse was a typical New England Colonial-era structure—simple in style with horizontal white clapboards and 12-paned windows framed by black shutters. The grounds surrounding it were filled with tombstones and grave markers—not neatly laid out like a modern-day cemetery, but haphazard as if it never occurred to the planners that there someday might exist a scarcity of land. There weren't many trees to break up the landscape, but those that did exist were tall and thick and sturdy.

His grandfather wasn't buried here, but he thought he might find some tombstones of some of his other dead ancestors. He had already met some of his living ones.

He had arrived in Mashpee just as the summer was ending and, for the most part, they had welcomed the grandson of Umberto as the distant relative that he was—they invited Bruce in, offered him coffee, shared with him some family memories and history. But it wasn't like he felt he had found the connection to his grandfather that he was searching for. He would stay through the winter, then head back to sea if he hadn't found some peace of mind here in Mashpee. He still hadn't decided whether he would make one final attempt to reconcile with Shelby.

He ambled leisurely across the grassy lawn, tried to imagine how these people had lived in the 19th century. Actually, he knew how they had lived because he had researched the question: they farmed and fished and clammed and hunted, much as they had in the 18th and even late 17th centuries, when the Wampanoags from around the region had been rounded up and resettled in Mashpee. So the colonists could keep an eye on them.

In fact, it was not until the 1960s that the outside world began to interfere with the tribe's hunting and fishing and clamming activities. Until then, Mashpee was essentially ignored by the rest of Massachusetts. Though located near the entrance to the Cape from the mainland, Mashpee was not considered an attractive vacation destination—its shoreline was marshy, its harbors shallow, its soil full of rock.

But at a certain point the town's proximity to the mainland led to the development of the town as a vacation, retirement and second home destination. The new residents erected fences and barriers around their oceanfront and lakefront properties, blocking age-old paths and byways and preventing the local tribe members from fishing and clamming and hunting as they had for centuries.

There wasn't really anyone to blame for the conflict between the tribe members and their new neighbors—it was inevitable, given the differences in outlook and expectations between the two groups. But the end result was that the tribe elected to attempt to reclaim title to the entire town through a lawsuit in the late 1970s. Things had gotten ugly.

So ugly, in fact, that Grandpa had stopped coming down. He had plagiarized from a popular song: "'Clowns to the left of me, jokers to the right.' These people have no clue. Mashpee is one of the first towns you hit when you get onto the Cape. It's in a perfect position to make itself a real destination spot. I mean, who wants to keep driving down to Chatham when you can get out of the traffic an hour or two earlier? And there's plenty of land to make sure that the tribe can keep hunting and fishing and clamming. But this lawsuit is going to kill it for everyone. Nobody's gonna want to go down there if the Indians are protesting against Thanksgiving and the White folks are driving around with rifles in their pickup trucks. People go down there for a vacation, for Christ's sake...."

And there was still a good amount of residual hostility in town. The townspeople still harbored resentment over the tribe's attempt to evict them from their homes. And tribe members resented what they perceived to be their increasing marginalization in the town—they no longer controlled the town government, they no longer had unfettered access to the woods and waterways, and they hadn't really participated in the economic boom that had made so many of their fellow townspeople wealthy.

In fact, the only Native Americans in town who seemed truly content were the ones buried beneath his feet. Which meant he fit right in.

*　　　*　　　*

Pierre and Carla raked leaves into a broad pile, while Rachel and Valerie took turns running down the sloped lawn and vaulting into the growing mound. Carla had pulled their hair back into matching ponytails, which bounced up and down as they skipped along. Valerie was blond like her mother, and Rachel was brown-haired like Pierre, but there was no doubting that they were sisters. Luckily for them they looked like Carla—blue eyes, cute little upturned noses, happy mouths. Valerie was in the fourth grade, still a few years away from boys and bikinis and braces. Rachel was more outgoing than her big sister, the self-appointed social director of her second grade class. Pierre guessed that Carla had probably been the same way as a kid.

Every few minutes, when they thought their father wasn't looking, they snuck up on Pierre and stuffed leaves down his shirt. He would scream out in surprised agony, then chase them back to the leaf pile and toss them gently into the cushioned mound.

After one such foray, he returned, huffing, to Carla's side to continue raking. "Wow. Either they're getting faster and heavier, or I'm getting older."

"I think it's both, darling. Our little babies are growing up." She paused here, and Pierre could see a shadow cross her face. "I'm glad they have each other. There really are no other kids around here for them to play with."

Pierre nodded. "I know. Add that to the list of things I should have checked out before buying this place. But in the summer there were plenty of kids around."

"Yeah, the Cape's like that. Anybody you've ever known your whole life comes to visit. Labor Day hits, and they all go home. They send a Christmas card in December, a nice note as soon as the snow melts in the spring, then show up again the next summer. It's a Cape tradition."

"But I know there are kids down here—the schools are full of them."

"Sure, just not in this subdivision. You used to sell real estate, you know how it is—most of these new houses sell to retired people or to people who use them just as second homes. The locals can't afford $600,000 for a house."

"Maybe this was a bad idea, Carla. Maybe we should sell the house and just start over. Find a neighborhood."

A shiny black Cadillac rolled down their winding driveway. A burly, middle-aged man, completely bald, stepped out and waved. Pierre and Carla waved back, then made their way toward the visitor. As they got closer, Pierre could see the faint definition of muscle under the man's flesh—he reminded Pierre of a retired pro football lineman he had once met. Even his head looked like it had muscles.

"Sorry to bother you folks, but I'm one of your neighbors. Name's Ronnie Lemaire. Just wanted to come by and introduce myself."

He offered a beefy hand and a warm smile, and Pierre returned both. Carla, too, offered her hand, and Ronnie gently folded his gnarled fingers around hers.

"Welcome to the neighborhood. Sorry we haven't come by sooner, but...," Ronnie paused and glanced at the still unfinished house.

"Mr. Lemaire," Carla asked, "would you like to come in for a cup of coffee?"

"Thanks, but I'll have to pass on that. And please call me Ronnie. But a group of us in the neighborhood, we're getting together tomorrow night. Just to talk about some issues here in the subdivision, you know? Eight o'clock. Maybe you could join us?"

*   *   *

It was a brisk autumn evening, but Pierre suggested they walk. "It doesn't seem right to drive to visit our neighbors."

"Fine with me. Just let me grab a flashlight, it's dark out there. And stick the cell phone in your pocket—I told the babysitter to call if she needed us."

They walked along the crushed-stone driveway, holding hands, Pierre kicking rocks along the way. Their noses and ears filled with the smell of freshly fallen leaves and the sound of the woods coming alive for the night.

To the left, the main subdivision road led past Griffin's farmhouse and to the town highway; to the right, the route looped around in an oval shape, driveways branching from it toward the homes that lined the perimeter of the wooded peninsula of land that jutted into the lake. Not including the old farmhouse, there were 11 homes in the subdivision, all of which fronted directly on the lake.

A dog yelped, interrupting the serenity of the night. Carla swept the flashlight beam across the road in front of them, then stopped as the light found the dog and its master.

"Good evening, Mr. and Mrs. Prefontaine." A bow-tied Rex Griffin, a yapping terrier at his feet, smiled and waved. The dog pulled at his leash and growled, then offered a final bark of warning.

"Hello," Pierre said, before his eyes had focused on the man in front of them. He and Carla hurried by. A few steps further on, Pierre spoke. "I wish we had driven. I could have run him over."

"Pierre, stop it." Carla punched him playfully on the shoulder. "That's horrible."

"What? I wouldn't have hit the dog, I promise."

They laughed and Pierre slipped his arm around Carla. The last couple of months had been pretty unbearable, but she never complained, never blamed him for choosing the House from Hell, never once suggested that life had been a lot easier when he *wasn't* around to help. "I'm just thankful you haven't made me go sleep with the terrier."

"I've considered it. But why should you get to sleep in a warm, cozy doghouse while the girls and I have to deal with cold drafts and leaky windows?"

"Plus, I'd miss you all terribly."

Carla smiled teasingly. "And the girls would miss you, too, Pierre, the girls would miss you."

Pierre returned her smile, kissed her gently on the cheek. It said a lot that they could now joke about him being separated from the family. Valerie had been only two when he had served his jail time, and he had almost missed Rachel's birth. For a long time afterwards he refused even to take overnight business trips. "I love you, you know."

She leaned into him as they continued walking. "I love you, too, sweetheart. But next time I get to pick out the house."

Ronnie Lemaire's house was a grand, center-entrance colonial, with wings on either side and a four-stall garage connected by a breezeway. Biggest house in the subdivision. Professionally land-scaped lawn, immaculately maintained, with a softly lit pond built into a small rock formation in the front yard.

"Look, Carla, that's a koi pond—you know, those big Japanese fish. I read that people go around stealing them; they're worth a couple hundred bucks each."

"The whole place is gorgeous. I wonder where he got his money?"

Pierre smiled. "Believe it or not, he pumps septic systems."

"You're kidding!"

"No, I saw his truck the other day—big red letters on the side: 'Lemaire Septic and Pumping.'"

"You know what then? He deserves everything he's got. I wouldn't want that job."

Ronnie Lemaire greeted them at the door. In the bright light of the foyer, Pierre could see the razor stubble on Ronnie's shaved head; as Pierre had guessed, the shaved head was by design, not circumstance. Ronnie escorted them to a large, sunken room in the rear of the house with picture windows looking out over what now was a blackened expanse of water. The views during the daylight must have been spectacular. Like the exterior of the house, the home's interior was well kept and neat—though a bit too modern for Pierre and Carla's taste—with the smell of freshly-cut flowers and pine trees wafting through the open floor plan.

Ronnie introduced them to his wife, Loretta. She was probably 20 years his junior—petite, big hair, a bit heavy on the make-up. But she was gracious and friendly, and she guided them around the room to meet the other 15 or so neighbors. Ronnie watched her finish the introductions, then cleared his throat to begin the meeting.

"You all just met Carla and Pierre Prefontaine. They bought the house over on lot 10, the new one that Griffin just built. Seems they've had a few problems with Griffin themselves. So I invited them tonight. Might as well jump right into it. Let's go around the room—Justin, you can start."

Justin McBride was all eyebrows—gray, wild tufts of hair that drooped down and obscured his eyes. He had a small button nose and thin mouth, so that's really all there was to his face: eyebrows, with some pinkish skin in the background.

Pierre guessed Justin's age at about 70, though he sensed a vibrancy about him that made it hard to think of the man as old. Justin leaned forward in his chair and sighed softly. "Well, I'm a bit embarrassed to say that the court has ruled that our friend Mr. Griffin may proceed with his case against me. This is not to say that he will win, but he has put forth enough of a case so that it will go to a jury."

Ronnie cut in, addressing his comments to Pierre and Carla. "Justin is a lawyer. Griffin is suing him.... Actually, Justin, you tell the story."

Justin smiled kindly. "Mr. Griffin is suing me for legal malpractice. It's a rather—how should I put this?—unique claim, in that I was never his lawyer."

Carla asked the obvious question. "Then how can he sue you for malpractice?"

Justin nodded. "That's the beauty of his suit. It's very difficult to prove a negative in court. Let me give you an example: Can you, Mr. Prefontaine, prove to me that you did not promise Mr. Griffin that you would mow his lawn this weekend? He claims you did tell him so, and produces a picture of an un-mowed lawn as his evidence. Pretty flimsy case, right? Well, what evidence can you produce to refute him?"

"I guess it would just come down to his word against mine."

Justin reached over and lightly banged his open hand on the coffee table. "Exactly. And when it comes down to that, who can say what a jury will do?"

Carla asked, "So is that what's happening in your case, Mr. McBride?"

"Essentially, yes, though it is a bit more complex than that. He claims that he hired me to represent him in the purchase of some land he was interested in buying, that I ignored the case, and that my failure to represent him adequately caused him to lose out on a profit of upwards of half a million dollars. Well, to begin with, the thought of representing this man is totally repugnant to me—over a year ago I filed a lawsuit against him for his failure to build the tennis courts he promised and to pave the roads and finish the landscaping in the subdivision. So not only do I have no interest in associating with the man, I also would be barred from acting as his attorney by the code of legal ethics.

"But here is what Mr. Griffin has produced as evidence to support his case. First, a copy of a letter he alleges he mailed to me in which he encloses the real estate transaction papers and thanks me for agreeing to represent him. My response to that, of course, is that he never sent the letter. Second, his phone bill, which shows three long distance telephone calls from his house to my office in Boston during the weeks in which he claims I was acting as his attorney. This is a bit harder to explain, but I believe that he simply phoned my office, asked the receptionist to put him on hold for a few minutes while he took another call, then simply waited seven or eight minutes before hanging up."

Justin paused here to take a sip of water, then continued. "And for his final piece of evidence, and here is where I really have to tip my hat to the man, he produced a copy of a canceled check for $500 made payable to my law firm with the notation 'Retainer for Attorney McBride" written on it. Apparently what he did was send a check to the Accounts Receivable department of my firm. The bookkeeper innocently deposited the check, and, well, you can imagine my surprise when the check was entered as Exhibit A in Mr. Griffin's lawsuit. And as I said before, I have no evidence to support my claim that I am not his lawyer. In fact, I can no more readily prove that point than I can prove that I am not Mr. Griffin's doctor. Or his lover, for that matter."

The group, as one, chuckled. Pierre jumped in. "Or that I did not promise to mow his lawn." He was enjoying listening to the older man, enjoyed his upbeat demeanor even as he recounted the details of Griffin's villainy.

Justin smiled and nodded, satisfied that his young student had absorbed the lesson. "So, now, my simple lawsuit attempting to get Mr. Griffin to complete the subdivision work has mushroomed into quite a little nightmare for me. There is, of course, the small matter of a half-million dollar lawsuit against me for malpractice. But, in addition to that, my malpractice insurance company immediately doubled my premium. And Mr. Griffin reported me to the Board of

Bar Overseers and asked that my license to practice law be revoked. All of this, of course, is intended by Mr. Griffin to get me to drop my suit against him."

With that, Justin sat back in his chair, smiled at Pierre and Carla, and nodded to Ronnie that he had concluded his tale.

Ronnie sighed. "So there's one example of what you can expect from this guy." He shook his head. The man climbed in and out of cesspools all day, yet it seemed that Rex Griffin was the thing that truly revolted him. "Amisha, what about you?"

Amisha stood. Carla leaned over and whispered into Pierre's ear. "My God. She looks like she belongs in a make-up commercial."

"Or in a James Bond movie."

Amisha's words came easily from her mouth in a gentle, English-accented voice, though Pierre could see the anger in the fire of her dark eyes and the flare of her nostrils. "As you know, this Mr. Griffin has created quite a tempest for my husband and me, quite a tempest indeed." She recounted how Griffin had sent the damaging e-mail from their home computer. "My husband, of course, knew nothing of this message. Until a few weeks later when he received quite a disturbing letter from the Securities and Exchange Commission. He may well yet be facing criminal charges for insider stock trading."

Carla interjected. "I'm sorry, but why would Griffin do this? What did he hope to gain?"

Amisha laughed scornfully. "Well, for one thing, you can be sure that we have no intention of ever allowing that scoundrel into our home again! And, knowing this, of course he has returned on a number of occasions with the stated purpose of attending to the repair items. And since I have refused him entrance to the house, he now has taken the position that he is relieved of the responsibility of completing the repair items. Game, set and match to Mr. Griffin, as they say."

Justin McBride spoke up. "Well, if it will help, I'd be happy to talk to the SEC investigator on your case. My bet is that he's pretty skeptical about your story. But I can at least confirm that Griffin is fully capable of doing as you claim."

Other neighbors also voiced their willingness to help out. Pierre sensed that, though the neighbors had spent a few evenings together, they had not yet reached a comfort level as a group. Justin's offer was a step in that direction.

Amisha bowed her head. "Thank you all. We have had quite a time with this man Mr. Griffin, quite a time. The man is a perfectly dreadful creature. He has put my husband and me through our paces, that is for sure. And it won't do to let him get away with it, it simply won't do!"

"See, there's a simple pattern here." Ronnie Lemaire was now addressing Pierre and Carla. "If you sue Griffin, or even threaten to sue him, he responds with an atom bomb. Everyone in this room here has a similar story. He sued D.J. over there—says he slipped on the ice in front of D.J.'s house. All because D.J. tried to get him to fix his leaky roof. And he sued me for ... what was it Justin? That contract thing?"

"Intentional interference with contractual relations."

"Yeah, whatever the hell that is. Says he lost a buyer because the buyer called me for a reference, and I told him Griffin was a crook. So he sued me."

Pierre nodded. That explained why none of the references he called had warned him away from the subdivision. Nobody wanted to get sued by Griffin. Pierre couldn't really blame them.

Ronnie continued. "Anyway, we can't seem to think of a way to get back at him. We can't prove anything, and he doesn't seem to be afraid of us. He puts on his bow tie and walks that little terrier of his every night after dinner, right through the subdivision, waving and nodding to us like he's our best buddy. And nobody goes near him."

Pierre noticed that Ronnie's face—which had been tanned and leathery—was now red, and Pierre saw him clench, then unclench, his massive fists. Ronnie spoke quietly. "What he's really doing is rubbing our face in it. And we can't seem to do anything about it." Pierre gave the man credit for his self-control. Ronnie seemed like a man of action—this type of sitting around and talking, instead of actually doing something, must drive him crazy. Pierre remembered how he had been tempted to jump across the closing table and stuff Griffin's bow tie down his throat.

Carla's voice interrupted Pierre's thoughts. "You've probably all heard about Griffin dumping paint into our pond. I think we'd all like to meet Rex Griffin in a dark alley some day." As Carla spoke, she leaned over and picked up a nutcracker from the coffee table in front of her. "I know what I'd do to the little weasel." She casually lifted a walnut, slipped it into the nutcracker, and snapped it open with a single twist of her wrist. She caught the walnut with her free hand before it fell to the floor, popped it into her mouth, and crunched down with her teeth. Then smiled.

Amisha clapped. "Here, here, Carla. Bravo. Save some of that nut for me."

"You got it, Amisha." Carla paused to let the laughter fade, then continued. "But seriously, I think one of the things we should think about is hiring one attorney to represent all of us. It seems to me that part of the problem is that none of us can prove anything against Griffin because we have no hard evidence. But together, as a group, we have some pretty good circumstantial evidence that something fishy is going on around here. It's like Justin said when he offered to talk to the SEC investigator for Amisha—we can all sort of support each other's stories. I mean, if we all go in front of the same judge, and all tell a similar story about what we think Griffin is doing, it will be a lot more convincing than if the judge just hears it from one of us."

Justin McBride nodded in agreement as Carla spoke, then responded. "Exactly. I was going to suggest a similar plan myself."

Ronnie Lemaire turned to Justin. "Justin, why don't you take the case?"

"Sorry, but I don't think I could, given my personal involvement. But I'd be happy to assist whomever you choose."

The room was silent for a moment, then Carla spoke again. "Pierre and I are friendly with a lawyer who used to work for the District Attorney's office in Boston. And I know for a fact that she's had plenty of experience with sleazeballs like Griffin. Now she's a partner at a law firm in Boston. Her name's Shelby Baskin. Maybe she'd be a good choice. I'll see if she can come down and meet everyone, if you want."

The group accepted Carla's recommendation, and the meeting broke up. A couple of neighbors came over to chat, and Carla soon had planned a small dinner party.

Carla smiled at the small group around her. "At least around you guys I won't have to feel embarrassed about all the cracked tiles and leaky faucets! But I can't promise we won't talk about Griffin. I can't get him out of my head because he's living right here with us. Every time I leave the subdivision or look out the window, I see his house. I mean, a home is supposed to be your refuge, but he's right here with us."

Amisha concurred. "I know what you mean. We can view his house from a few of our windows, so I leave those curtains closed throughout the day."

Carla laughed lightly, though Pierre could sense there was no joy in her voice. "Here we are, beautiful homes, right on the water. People think we've got it made. If they only knew."

*   *   *

A bunch of neighbors had accepted Carla's invitation and come for a cook-out. "So," Carla asked, "did you have fun? The stunt kite was a big hit."

Pierre was sitting on the floor at Carla's feet, one of her legs draped lazily over his shoulder. The neighbors had left, the girls were in bed, the dishes were done. They were taking turns sipping from the same glass of wine. "You know, it's funny. You bust your butt— work crazy hours, ignore your health, short-change your family. All so you can afford to buy a big house on the water and go fly a kite. That's what success is these days—being able to afford to take time off and go fly a kite any time you damn well feel like it, just like when you were a kid." Pierre paused for a moment. "We had no idea how rich we were when we were twelve."

Carla took his chin, turned his face to look at hers. "Well, besides that, Mrs. Lincoln, how did you like the play?" She smacked him gently on the forehead with an open hand.

He smiled, sighed. "Sorry about that."

"Well, *I* had fun. What did you think of the neighbors?"

"Hard to tell. Everyone was pretty cautious."

"Yeah, I think Griffin has everyone a bit uptight."

"Speaking of Griffin, did you hear back from Shelby?"

"Yeah, she called this morning. She's coming down next week to meet with us. I invited her to stay here and spend the weekend."

"Great. It'll be fun to hang with her for a while. How's she doing?"

"She seems okay. But I don't think she's over Bruce. At least not totally."

Pierre could feel himself tense up at the mention of the young lawyer who had first befriended him, then cheated him, then framed him. Carla gently massaged his shoulders as he spoke. "I'd like to lock Bruce in a room with Griffin and see who comes out with a stake through his heart. Dracula versus Frankenstein, two out of three falls. Maybe put it on pay-per-view."

Carla smiled, and Pierre continued. "But you really think she hasn't gotten over him? It's been seven years. And the guy is pure scum." Actually, Pierre knew that wasn't a totally complete description of his enemy. Bruce also happened to be brilliant and charming and dynamic. "I mean, I could see how Shelby fell for him. I just don't understand how come she hasn't gotten over him yet."

Carla spoke softly. "At first I thought it was because she was gun-shy, but seven years is a long time to have your guard up. I've offered a few times to fix her up with guys we know, but she didn't really seem interested. And it's not like there aren't plenty of guys who would love to go out with her."

"I'm not so sure about that. She's almost too much for most guys—too beautiful, too smart, too sophisticated, too successful. I think guys like to be around women who don't challenge them so much."

"Except you, of course."

"Of course." Pierre turned his head and smiled up at Carla. "You, Carla, are truly a challenge."

She removed her leg from his shoulder. "Yeah. You'll see what kind of challenge I am when we get into bed tonight."

"Ouch." He took a sip of the wine. "Did Shelby have any thoughts about Griffin?"

"Just that it sounds like his strategy is just to make us spend so much money on lawyers that we stop fighting him."

"Which we're doing."

"But at some point this has got to end. The whole neighborhood is being dragged through the mud. I'm worried that somebody's going to snap and do something stupid."

"You know what? Maybe that's exactly what Griffin is hoping for. Somebody to do something stupid."

*   *   *

The two men sat across from each other in a corner booth of a Burger King, away from the bustle of a five-year old's birthday party. The lunch rush was over and the restaurant was otherwise almost empty. Justin McBride was tempted to reach across the table and squeeze Rex Griffin's bow-tied neck until his eyes popped out of his head and splattered against the inside of his wire-rimmed eyeglasses.

Instead, he took a sip of coffee.

Griffin looked out the window for a few seconds, processing the information he had just been given from the bushy-eyed lawyer. "So you've formed a little support group. Do you sit in a circle and hold hands?"

"No, we stick pins in a little Rex doll. It's a furry little rodent with glasses."

"Easy, Justin. You and I have a simple business relationship; there's no reason it has to turn personal."

"Where I come from, blackmail is personal. And if you mess with me on this, if I hear so much as one whisper about what my son did in Vietnam, so help me Griffin I'll stuff that smiling face of yours into a meat grinder."

Justin had forced his son to fight in Vietnam—a father's pride outweighing a parent's love. The boy had snapped under the pressure, had totally lost it. Fired his machine gun on a group of unarmed kids hiding in the tall grass. A young combat photographer was standing around with nothing better to do than snap pictures of the whole bloody mess. Didn't even try to stop it.

Justin wasn't sure whether the fact that the photographer was sitting across from him now, 30 years later, was a coincidence, or whether Griffin had been following the boy's political career all these years and had somehow orchestrated the intersection of their lives, blackmail at the ready.

Griffin laughed softly at Justin's threatening words. "Calm down, Justin. I can't afford to have you straining that heart of yours. I invested too much in our relationship."

"What do you mean by that?"

"Well, you don't think that we became neighbors by accident, do you? I had to give you a $30,000 discount to get you to buy that property, but it was worth every penny."

Justin looked back at Griffin, tried to hide the surprise from his face. So, Griffin had indeed orchestrated the intersection of their lives.

Griffin continued in a mocking voice. "What, did you think your superior negotiating skills won you that discount? Or did you think I was just dying to have a lawyer as a neighbor? Please, Justin. As soon as I saw your name, I figured you must be young Justin's father. I'd been holding those pictures for 25 years, waiting for the chance to use them. Then you came along. I wasn't going to just let you walk away."

"You're a sick bastard, you know that?"

"Yes, well, that seems a bit odd coming from the father of a mass murderer." He held up his hand, stopped Justin from responding. "But don't worry, Justin. As long as you keep your end of the bargain, Junior's dark little secret will remain just that. After all, what's a half-dozen dead kids between friends? And he can continue to serve the good people of Massachusetts up at the State House. Doing all sorts of good, no doubt."

The Styrofoam coffee cup burst in Justin's hand, hot coffee splashing into his lap and over the table. He had no idea he had been squeezing so hard.

Griffin grinned, showing small brown teeth. "Awfully tense, aren't we Justin? You can trust me on this one—there's no benefit to me in ruining Junior's political career. As for the coffee, well if it were me I'd feel compelled to sue Burger King. That must have been a defective cup, and I'm sure hot coffee in the lap could cause permanent damage. Even for someone your age."

Justin took a deep breath. If this had been a boxing match,

Griffin would be one or two punches away from knocking Justin out. He had to calm down and think clearly. He knew he was an excellent attorney, and had always prided himself on his ability to keep his emotions in check during high-stakes negotiations. But this was not about some client, this was personal. What was that old cliché? *A lawyer who represents himself has a fool for a client.*

He ignored the dig at his age. Time to focus. "All right, Griffin, what do you want me to do?" The children were now singing Happy Birthday to the lucky five-year old.

"Just more of the same. I want to know what your little group is planning. From what you say, you've found some attorney who's going to put together a unified defense against my suits. Do you think that will work?" Griffin paused here and smiled, then lowered his voice in a conspiratorial tone. "You are, after all, my attorney."

Another dig designed to get a reaction from Justin. Griffin was good, Justin had to admit. He knew which buttons to push and when to push them. Justin had heard that Griffin had been subjected to psychological, as well as physical, torture in Vietnam. He apparently had learned a few things about the human psyche.

Justin again fought to keep his emotions in check. "She's going to have a tough time with it. The cases are spread around in different courts and with different judges. On purpose, no doubt...."

Griffin showed his teeth again and bowed his head.

Justin paused as a mother hustled a squirming party-goer into the bathroom. "So it's going to be hard to get a single judge to focus on the whole group of cases. Judges are very careful not to step on each other's toes. Plus, they're all so busy that they're not exactly looking to increase their caseload. But, if she can put together a nice, tight package, with some compelling evidence, she might get a judge to look at it."

"How soon are we talking?"

"It'll take her a while to walk this through. So probably a few months."

"All right, what else can you tell me about your little group?"

"Well, people are angry. But they're also frightened. It may be that some of them get cold feet and bow out of the group. Or maybe some of them decide to take justice into their own hands." Justin watched for a reaction—it was his first attempt to knock Griffin off-balance.

But Griffin merely nodded. "Which ones?"

"You mean besides me?"

"Please, Justin, don't insult me. You're a lawyer. What are you going to do, over-bill me?"

Justin felt his face turning red. "I'd say Ronnie Lemaire would love to get his hands on you. And that new guy, Pierre Prefontaine, would probably be right behind him."

"Who else?"

Griffin was trying to be casual, but Justin could sense that the information was important to him. "Hard to tell. It's not like we know each other that well."

Griffin studied him. "How much influence do you have with them?"

"I'm not sure what you mean."

"Let's say that the group was presented with an offer to settle all the lawsuits. Could you convince them to accept it?"

"It all depends on the terms."

"Obviously, Justin." Griffin snorted. "But if they were fair, could you convince them?"

Justin glanced over at the kids eating the birthday cake. "I think everyone would like to get you out of their lives. So if it was a reasonable offer, I think I could convince them to take it."

*   *   *

Carla pulled her SUV into the dirt lot in front of Griffin's gift shop, Treasures From The Barn. She wouldn't have stopped if she had seen Griffin's truck parked out front or in the farmhouse driveway, but it wouldn't hurt to look around a bit as long as Griffin wasn't around. Maybe get a better feel for the guy.

An older woman worked the cash register. A younger, pretty woman was helping her bag a few knickknacks. That must be Denise.

Carla grabbed a sweatshirt off a rack, went straight to Denise. "Hi, can you help me? My sister is about your size and I was wondering if you could try this on for me."

Denise glanced at the older woman for approval, then smiled and nodded. She came out from behind the counter, skipped behind Carla as Carla purposely led her away from the register area.

They tried on a few different sweatshirts as Carla hemmed and hawed over her decision. "Of course, my sister isn't as pretty as you, so I'm sure it won't look so good on her."

Denise blushed a bit, looked down at her feet, offered a quiet, "Thank you."

Valerie had reacted in almost the identical fashion to a compliment a few days ago. Denise's earrings were stick-on hearts, straight from some third-graders dress-up party. This beautiful woman standing in front of her was really just a girl. A little girl living with a monster.

Carla wanted to reach out and give her a hug, take her home and let her play dolls and tea party and tag with Valerie and Rachel. She sighed, felt her eyes well up.

*　　*　　*

Griffin stood in a short but slow-moving line at the Registry of Deeds in Barnstable, the county seat.

He had learned two crucial things in his meeting with Justin McBride. First, that the natives were not only getting restless, they were so frustrated that they were ready to resort to violence. Griffin knew he would always win that type of battle—he had no fear of pain.

The second thing he had learned was that McBride believed he could sell the group on a reasonable settlement. And Griffin was prepared to make such an offer. Whether he abided by its terms was another matter entirely.

McBride had asked him once whether he felt any remorse for those whom he victimized. It was a ridiculous question. He deprived them of nothing more than their money. They would simply go out and earn more, and if they did not, then they would just have to do without some of their toys. No new SUV this year. No Caribbean vacation. Maybe they'd even have to move to a smaller house away from the water. But he did no evil—he orphaned no children, na-palmed no villages, tortured no innocents.

He himself knew evil, knew what it was like to be tortured until he passed out, to live in a rat-infested pit, to eat ants and cockroaches and drink urine to survive. His victims thought they were suffering when he took their money, but they were no different than a three-year old crying over a lost toy. It may seem like the most important thing in the world to the child, but he was the adult who knew better, the adult in a world of children crying over lost toys.

Which is not to say that he did not want the toys for himself. He would like to have them, but he could live in a shack in the woods if he had to, and still think it a life of luxury compared to what he had once known.

Finally, he handed the recording clerk a document entitled "Discharge of Mortgage." This document, true to its name, discharged the mortgage on the farmhouse land. It was signed by a vice president of the bank, whose signature was duly notarized. Griffin normally preferred not to be so blatant in his forgeries, but it could not be helped this time. He had recorded similar forgeries every time he sold off a parcel of the subdivision, so this was merely the last in a long line of fake documents purporting to unencumber his land. Again, as long as he paid the bank their $22,000 every month, he was betting they would never notice the fact that they no longer had any collateral to secure their $2 million loan.

Now that the farmhouse property was unencumbered, he could offer it up to his neighbors in settlement for the claims they had against him. When the time was right, of course. The property was probably only worth a few hundred thousand dollars, but Griffin was counting on the fact that McBride could convince them that it was the best they could hope for, especially since Griffin had no other traceable assets.

And more than the money, Griffin knew his neighbors would put a high value on the possibility of him forfeiting the farmhouse and having to move from the neighborhood. Not that any of them would be around to enjoy it.

*   *   *

Shelby stood as Ronnie Lemaire entered the room. She had spent the day in Pierre and Carla's study, meeting with each of the subdivision neighbors. She had hoped to spend a half hour with each, just to get a quick overview of everyone's case against Griffin. Instead, most of the meetings stretched beyond an hour—it was now early evening and she was exhausted. But at least this was the last one.

She extended her hand, smiled at the burly, bald-headed man. She sat on one side of a blue- and white-striped couch that she was pretty sure—based on the throbbing in her lower back—converted into an equally uncomfortable sleeper unit. "So," she said. "Who won?"

He raised an eyebrow as he sat down on the same sofa. Shelby never liked to meet with a client while sitting behind a desk. It generally made people uncomfortable, like they had been sent to the principal's office or something. "Who won what?" he asked.

"The football game. It's a Saturday in November, you're nose and head are sunburned, and you wanted to meet late in the day. I figured there must be a big high school game today."

He grinned. "Sharp girl. How do you know I didn't just come from the golf course?"

She looked at him for a few seconds. He was one of those guys who could call you a girl without it being offensive. Perhaps because he was of an older generation, or perhaps because she knew he was a blue-collar guy, or perhaps just because she knew he meant no disrespect. "Nah. You golf early in the morning, not late in the afternoon."

She knew she had hit the mark. "And how do you know that?" He was eyeing her intently, intrigued by her powers of perception.

"Because of the way you walked in, like your legs were a little bit tight from exercise. But it takes a few hours for muscles to tighten, so you must've finished before lunch."

Now he was bug-eyed. "Wow, that's amazing. Pierre said you were sharp, but...."

Shelby laughed. "Well, not that sharp. I called your house this morning and your wife said you were out golfing...."

Ronnie laughed, then shared his history with Rex Griffin. An hour later Shelby walked Ronnie to the front door of her friends' house and said goodbye.

Ronnie yelled over her shoulder to Carla. "Hey, good choice. She's sharp as a tack." He turned back to Shelby. "And like I said, I got this son who's single...."

She smiled, gently pushed him out the door. "Thanks, but no thanks. I've got my hands full with the father right now."

She sighed, turned to her friend. "Carla, I'm just gonna change into some jeans. But I'd love a glass of that wine you're drinking when I get back."

"You got it."

Shelby navigated her way back to the guest room. Actually, guest suite was a more accurate description, though Carla had warned her that there were still a number of items that needed to be "de-Griffinized." The room itself was easily as big as the living room in her condo downtown, plus it had its own outside deck. She smiled to herself at the irony—when she had first became friendly with Carla, Pierre was on his way to jail and they were only a whisker away from bankruptcy. Not that they had deserved either fate.

On her way back to the living room, Pierre met her at the bottom of the staircase, one girl slung over each shoulder in a fireman's carry.

"Say goodnight to Shelby, girls."

They offered her a cheerful goodnight, which quickly degenerated into giggles and shrieks as Pierre tickled their feet and toes. They responded by pulling his ears, and the three of them ascended the stairs in a swarm of writhing and squealing. Shelby watched them disappear up the stairs, turned to see Carla eyeing her from a soft couch in the living room.

"They love the dolls you gave them. They sleep with them every night. I hope you bought a couple of extra in case you ever need them."

Shelby laughed as she walked through the open room toward her friend. "Am I that transparent?"

"Well, you're not wearing a sign that says, 'Impregnate Me,' but..."

"Ouch!"

Shelby flopped into a beige oversized easy chair facing the lake, closed her eyes for a moment. "Carla, I keep meaning to ask, how's the painting going?"

Carla's legs were curled underneath her. She sipped a glass of wine. "Actually, really well. I did a series of scenes from the Cape—you know, people at an ice cream stand, a group of bicyclists riding at sunset, a family at the beach. Just everyday stuff. But a couple of galleries down here are selling them, and I got written up in *Boston* magazine. I've sold almost a dozen of them in the past few months."

Shelby looked at her friend. "That's great, Carla. I don't know the first thing about painting, but it always struck me that you've got a great eye. You always seem to be able to paint a picture in a way that makes me feel like I'm inside the scene...."

Pierre returned. "Hope I'm not interrupting anything."

"No. I was just telling your wife how talented she is."

Pierre sat down with Carla on the couch, cuddled up next to her in front of the fireplace. Shelby studied them for a minute. What was it about them that made them so, so ... content?

Carla and Pierre seemed truly satisfied with their lives. Aside from the whole Griffin thing, of course. Shelby thought about that for a moment—she didn't know anybody else whom she could say that about. Including herself.

Her hosts were well off, but Shelby knew for a fact that they had given away far more money than they had kept. 'Blood money' was what they had called the funds they had received from suing Bruce's law firm. The firm had paid generously to keep private the news of one of its lawyers trying to frame a client for murder. They had held out for top dollar, then paid off some debts and donated most of the rest of it to charity. So it wasn't just about money.

And they had a nice house, but they used it to entertain friends and family rather than to impress them. An open door, a warm hearth, a full refrigerator, a shed full of beach toys. A place to come and have fun. A place where joy settled in and stayed.

They had had some misfortune, then caught a lucky break and made the most of it. Now they defined happiness for themselves, in a way that brought them satisfaction. If life was a journey, then they were definitely driving the car. Shelby could feel her eyes begin to well up. Why did she so often feel like she was merely a passenger?

It wasn't supposed to be this way. She had gone to law school with the expectation that she could be an advocate for truth, for goodness, for justice. But, in fact, only rarely did a client walk into her office wearing a white hat. Mostly she dealt with grays. Sometimes, when she was lucky, it was light gray. And she still had enough integrity that she ushered the dark gray clients out the door. This case, at least, offered her the promise of going to sleep at night secure in the knowledge that she was fighting the good fight.

But practicing law was hardly scintillating work. Her friends seemed to all be creating things—hatching companies, writing screenplays, cultivating cancer-fighting drugs. And, yes, making babies. But all she created was paper. Letters. Motions. Briefs. She killed trees for a living.

She stared at the fire. It was always hard being around Carla and Pierre. It was bad enough that their contentment stood in such stark contrast to the life she was leading. Even worse, being around them always unleashed a rush of Bruce memories that flooded her senses—anger, betrayal, bitterness, longing. It was exhausting. If she didn't like them so much, she would have given up the friendship years ago.

Pierre interrupted her introspection. "Something about the first fire of the year. People always talk about the smells of spring, but I love the smell of a fire on a cold fall night."

Shelby took a sip from the glass of wine Carla had poured her. "I know what you mean. We didn't have a fireplace when I was a kid, but we took a ski trip every year up to Vermont. That smell makes me think of skiing."

Carla spoke. "Sorry to bring up work stuff, but how did your meetings go today?"

Shelby smiled. "Well, you guys sure do attract 'em. First Bruce Arrujo, now Rex Griffin. Remind me never to let you fix me up with anybody."

"Yeah, like you need help getting dates."

"No, Carla, dates I have plenty of. Second dates, now that's a different story."

Pierre jumped in, teasing her. "Hey, Justin McBride's a widower. And he's a lawyer, just like you...."

Shelby swatted Pierre with a sofa pillow. "Thanks, Pierre, but I'll pass. I know it sounds shallow, but those eyebrows of his make me think of one of those kids' toys where you use a magnet to drag little metal shards around on a face. It's like some kid used all the pieces for the eyebrows, and there's none left for a nose or mouth."

Carla laughed. "That's exactly it."

"But I do feel sorry for him. He's supposed to be semi-retired, and he's gotta deal with this malpractice crap. But to answer your question, Carla, your intuition was right. There's enough going on here so that we should be able to get a judge's attention. I mean, where there's that much smoke, there has to be fire." Shelby smiled. "I dedicate that cliché to you, Pierre, in honor of your first fire of the year."

"Thank you," he said as he raised his class to her.

Carla continued. "Shelby, what's the time frame on getting this in front of a judge?"

"I can have something drafted in a couple of weeks, then send it out for you guys to review. My bet is that everyone's gonna want to run it by their own lawyer, and you can imagine what it's like trying to get a half-dozen lawyers even to agree on what time it is. Plus the holidays are coming up. We can probably get something to the court just after the first of the year. Then they'll schedule a hearing for thirty days later. So middle of February, though Griffin could delay it for another month or so if he tries."

"Do you think he'll fight it?"

"I have no idea, Carla. I haven't even had the pleasure of meeting the creep. But it's weird—from talking to everyone today, it seems like Griffin hasn't really done anything on any of these cases for a couple of months. He's doing what he needs to do to keep them going, but it's almost like he's not really focused on them."

Shelby sipped at her wine and stared into the fire. Something was gnawing at her, but she was having trouble articulating it. "Actually, maybe it's not so weird. Griffin must know he can't win any of these cases. It's almost like he's just harassing you all for no reason. But that doesn't make sense either. It just doesn't all add up to me. I feel like there's more going on here than we know about, but I have no idea what it is. All I know is, if I were you guys, I'd be careful."

Chapter 7

[December]

It was a sunny, warm morning in December, the weekend after the four-day Thanksgiving break. The entire neighborhood seemed to be out raking leaves or simply enjoying what was likely to be the last jacket-free day of the year. Many had just returned from church.

At a convenience store in the center of town, Griffin dropped a quarter into a pay phone, completed his call, and drove back to the farmhouse. And waited. Fifteen months until the $2 million loan was due.

A half-hour later, a pair of sedans—one a police cruiser—turned into the subdivision and pulled into Griffin's rutted driveway. Two men stepped out of the unmarked car and walked toward his door, their hands resting on their gun holsters. Another two uniformed officers stood crouched on either side of the squad car, their bodies shielded by the open doors. Griffin straightened his bow tie, went outside to greet them.

A clean-cut man in his mid-thirties addressed him. "I'm Detective Foster and this is Detective Cataldo. Mashpee Police Department. Are you Mr. Griffin?"

"Yes, Officer. What can I do for you?"

"Mr. Griffin, we've received a complaint that there are bomb-making materials being stored in your garage. Mind if we take a look?" Griffin noticed that Detective Foster was speaking in a loud voice, probably so that the uniformed officers—tensed and alert—could hear the exchange. Meanwhile, the other detective had edged over to the garage. It was really nothing more than a glorified shack—Griffin doubted whether it would last the winter, which was why he hadn't bother to paint it or repair any of the broken windows. Even so, the detective was peering in through the window with a flashlight, one eye still on Griffin.

Griffin also noticed that a few of the neighbors had gathered near the end of the driveway. They were no more than four or five car lengths away—it was likely they could also hear what was being said.

"I'm sorry. If you want to search the property, you'll have to get a search warrant."

"Very well, Mr. Griffin." Detective Foster turned toward his partner. "See anything?"

"Sure do. We got a dozen sticks of Solidox and a couple of bags of sugar, along with a scale and a mortar and pestle. All the stuff you'd need to make yourself a nice little bomb."

"What's Solidox?" The detective eyed Griffin as he spoke to his partner.

"Plumbers use it for welding pipes. It's really just solid oxygen—you can get it at any plumbing supply store. But when you mix it with an energy source, like sugar, you can get a pretty big explosion. Perfect for a pipe bomb."

Detective Foster continued to keep his eyes trained on Griffin. "All right. That'll be enough for a warrant. Cataldo, you go back to the station and swear out an affidavit." He raised his voice, addressing one of the uniformed officers. "Brandon, radio the station and tell them to get the judge on the line. Tell him we got bomb-making materials in plain view, and we're coming in with an affidavit and we want a search warrant. Also, call the Fire Department and get them to send an engine over. And call the state bomb squad and have them send a team. And secure the area—nobody any closer than they are right now." He turned back to Griffin. "Mr. Griffin, I'm afraid I'm going to have to ask you to stay right where you are."

Griffin sat on his front step and waited. Most of the neighborhood had now gathered behind the police lines at the end of his driveway. All eyes were on him.

A few minutes later, a State Police van pulled into the driveway and two men wearing jumpsuits and work boots stepped out. They conferred with the Mashpee detectives for a few minutes, then marched over to the garage and peered in through the windows.

Griffin looked at his watch. Almost one o'clock. He had resigned himself to being arrested. But if things got delayed until late afternoon, they might have trouble finding a judge to hold a bail hearing before the next morning. Griffin shivered at the thought of jail, even for a single night. Maybe he just should have let them search the garage without the warrant. If they weren't back within the hour, he'd just let them in. Any later than that and there was no guarantee he would make it home tonight.

Five minutes later Detective Foster again approached Griffin. "We've obtained a search warrant." He flashed it in front of Griffin, who nodded. "Would you please open the garage for us?"

"Okay, Detective." Griffin tried to hide his relief—at least he wouldn't be spending the night in jail.

"And also the house."

Griffin hadn't expected that. "You also have a warrant for the house?"

"Yes, sir."

Griffin sighed and opened the door. He didn't like the idea of a bunch of cops going through his papers. Not that they were smart enough to understand most of them. And he could sue them later if anything had been disturbed; actually, he could sue them even if nothing had been disturbed.

Ten minutes later one of the bomb squad officers came out of the garage and conferred with Detective Foster. The detective then approached Griffin. "Mr. Griffin, you are under arrest for possession of bomb-making materials." He handcuffed Griffin, then read him his rights.

A uniformed officer escorted Rex to the waiting cruiser. The neighbors stared, disbelieving. Could Griffin really be that evil? Would he really go that far? Griffin could see the fear in their eyes, imagined their outrage when he posted bail later that day and returned to the subdivision to haunt them. There was a monster in their midst, and there was nothing they could do to vanquish him.

*   *   *

Griffin looked at the small tree Denise was busy decorating in the corner of their living room. The ceilings were only seven feet high in the 18th-century home, so that meant they had to get a short tree. And, of course, Denise was much taller than the average American child. Which meant she was probably the only person in America who both still believed in Santa Claus and could also put the star on the top of the Christmas tree without any help.

Christmas. And that meant Griffin had to drive to Boston, pick up Donald, and bring him back to Mashpee for the holiday. "Try to finish up, Dennie. We have to go pick up Donald."

She clapped her hands together. "Goodie." For some reason she liked it when Donald came to visit. Maybe because, other than Rex, she had no other living relatives. They hopped in Griffin's pickup, easily made their way across the Sagamore Bridge and onto the mainland. Denise fiddled with the radio as Griffin concentrated on the road—a light snow had begun to fall, and the roads were getting slick.

"Do you have your seatbelt on, Denise?"

"Of course." She gave him one of those furrowed brow looks that kids sometimes give when adults ask stupid questions. He smiled—along with the soap operas, she loved to watch public television, where they no doubt emphasized the importance of seatbelts.

They had been driving an hour now and had just reached the Boston suburbs. As the city loomed in the distance, Griffin began to feel the anxiety rising in him, the tension creeping through his body. He loosened his grip on the steering wheel, slipped a piece of gum into his mouth to prevent his molars from grinding. It had been two months since he had last visited Donald, sixty-two days since he had had to try to cope with the unpredictable life form that was his brother.

His mother had been convinced that Donald's autism could be traced back to a visit to the doctor when Rex and Donald had been young children—Donald, with no signs of autism at that point, was given a series of vaccination shots, while Rex, who was running a fever that day, received his shots a few months later. A bad batch, his mother had always said about Donald's shots, though it wasn't until decades later that researchers began to search for a link between autism and vaccinations. Recently, Griffin had read that it might have more to do with the use of a mercury-based preservative than the vaccine itself.

As a child, Griffin's life had been governed by Donald's needs. Their routine was unalterable—breakfast at 7:20, lunch at 12:05, dinner at 5:30, bed at 7:45. A few minutes either way, and Donald would dive to the ground and smash his head against the floor, sometimes until he lost consciousness. Trips outside the home were impossible, Donald screaming until he was returned to his familiar environs. He couldn't walk from one room to another without first stopping in the doorway and rubbing the doorframe on his way through. Even the simple act of opening the window or changing the television station risked sending Donald into a spiral of rage and self-abuse. He simply was unable to cope with the world around him, especially when that world changed in even a normally imperceptible way.

Yet Donald was not retarded, was not without intelligence. By the time he was three, he had learned to read, had memorized the license plate numbers of every car in the neighborhood, could recite the 50 states in alphabetical order. Backwards. But he could not begin to comprehend what was meant by a favorite color, even as he insisted on drinking only from the blue cup. And he couldn't tell you what made him sad, even as he banged his head on the wall every time his mother left the room.

By the time Griffin had returned from Vietnam, his mother had finally relented and placed Donald in a group home for autistic adults. She had devoted her adult life to nurturing the needier of her two sons, acutely sensitive to the widely held belief in the medical community that autism was caused by "refrigerator parenting"—cold, unloving parents whose indifference pushed the child to withdraw into himself rather than to develop normally.

Finally, her devotion and years of sacrifice to Donald were re-warded with an unexpected mid-life pregnancy. And the birth of a beautiful, healthy daughter, Denise. And then Rex had ruined even that for her.

Denise interrupted his thoughts. "Is it true that you and Donald are twins?"

"No. Why do you say that?"

"Mom said you were."

"She must have said we were 'Irish twins.' That's what they call kids who were born the same year but aren't really twins."

"No, Mom said you were twins."

Griffin could see the veins on the back of his hand as he gripped the steering wheel. Nothing like trying to argue with an eight-year-old. "We're nothing alike. How could we be twins?"

"I don't know. But Mom said so." She turned her attention to the radio dial.

"Okay, Denise, look straight ahead. See those big buildings?" They could see the Boston skyline rising in the distance.

"Whoa. Are they taller than trees?"

"Sure are."

"Do you build buildings like that, Rex?"

He laughed. "No, not that big. I build houses, not big buildings."

They passed through the city, found the Medford exit, followed the familiar route to Donald's home. Rex tried to visit every month or two. Partly because he felt he should, and partly because he needed Donald's social security checks.

It was mid-afternoon when they arrived, and a few inches of fresh snow coated the neighborhood. The home was a large yellow Victorian on a tree-lined street near Tufts University. The neighborhood seemed like a typical middle class one—kids out building snowmen, minivans in the driveways, Christmas lights and wreaths decorating most of the homes.

Inside, they waited in the foyer for someone to come greet them, then gave up and followed the noise of a television set to a large, brightly lit living area in the back of the house. Something about fluorescent lights in Victorian homes always struck Griffin as disconcerting.

Donald was sitting in a hard-backed chair, rocking gently back and forth just as he had when they were children, watching a game show with two or three other residents. He looked up, greeted his siblings in a loud voice. "Hello, Rex. Hello Denise." Then he returned his gaze to the game show. Or more accurately, one eye focused on his show. His right eye focused on some spot a few feet to the right of the television. In addition to the other cards in the winning hand Donald had been dealt, he suffered from strabismus, commonly known as a wandering eye.

Denise hopped over, gave her brother a quick hug. She squeezed his crew-cutted head against her breast, his heavy plastic glasses twisting against his face and his mouth resting against her nipple. Rex shook his head—neither of them had the slightest idea. He had read a vampire novel once in which a young girl was turned into a vampire and given immortality. She had matured into a woman, lived to be hundreds of years old, but the fact that she no longer aged meant that physically she was forever stuck in the body of a 6-year old. That was Denise, except in reverse—her child brain had no clue how to manage the adult body that had sprouted out around her.

Donald continued to stare at the television, so Denise released him from her bosom and bounced back to Rex's side. Rex spoke. "Hello, Donald. You're looking well." It was a silly thing to say to someone with no concept of beauty or aesthetics, but he was just trying to fill the space with words.

"Rex, can I have your keys?" Donald had always been obsessed with keys, had always wanted to hold and count and memorize them.

"Here you go." Griffin handed him his set, watched Donald's left eye study them.

"Fourteen keys instead of thirteen. This one is new, Rex. What is it?" Even the question was asked in the same loud monotone that Donald had used since he was a child.

Griffin smiled to himself. On their last meeting, Donald had asked what each key was for. He apparently still remembered, two months later. "You're right, that one is new. It's for a safe deposit box."

"A safe deposit box. Okay. Can I hold your keys, Rex?"

"Sure. But we have to go now. Do you remember you're coming back to Mashpee with us for Christmas?"

"Yes." Donald rocked. "Today is Christmas Eve."

"That's right, Donald. And families should be together on Christmas. So get your bag and come with us." Griffin watched as his

81

brother nodded, then lifted himself out of his chair and walked stiffly up the stairs to his bedroom.

He put his arm gently on Denise's shoulder. Yes, families should be together on Christmas. Even dysfunctional ones like his.

Chapter 8

[January]

Griffin sat in the back corner of the gift shop, shielded from the public by a curtain hanging from a wire strung along the beam above him. The desk surface was clear, other than a file he had just extracted from a metal file cabinet. He thumbed through the papers in front of him, found Billy's employment application. He had reviewed it almost daily over the past week, but the sight of the words on the paper still brought him pleasure.

Full Name: William Blackfoot Victor
Age: 16

Griffin's eyes jumped down the page, to his favorite, although admittedly illegal, part of the application.

Ethnicity: Native American (Mashpee Wampanoag)

A Mashpee Wampanoag Indian. Finally. Eleven boys filled out the stupid form before he had found Billy. It sure would make things easier if the Indians would just wear their headdresses around town so you could tell who they were. Griffin slipped the file back into the drawer and looked at his watch. It was only mid-afternoon, but he was anxious to get on with the evening.

Billy was folding and shelving some sweatshirts. Denise was nearby, attaching price stickers to some coffee mugs.

Griffin watch as Billy's eyes peer down Denise's open-necked shirt as she bent over her task. She understood that boys liked girls, and even understood that they liked to hold hands and kiss, but it had never occurred to her that her breasts were of particular interest to the opposite sex, so she made no effort to hide them.

Griffin allowed the boy to leer for a few more minutes, then stood to leave. "Billy, please watch the shop while I'm gone. I'll be back in an hour. Come on, Denise."

He drove her into the town center to a small beauty salon. "This is my sister, Denise," he explained to an older woman with frosted hair and too much make-up.

She winked at Griffin. "We'll take care of her." She reached out, took Denise's hand. "Come on, honey."

Griffin returned an hour later. Denise was sitting in a chair, waiting with a stylish haircut, some make-up on and her nails done. Best looking woman in the place. No contest.

"You look pretty, Denise."

She smiled broadly. "Thanks."

That smile. It was her mouth that caused the most problems. Lips, teeth, tongue—these were the things that men fantasized about. They may think they like tits or legs or asses, but just watch what happens to them when a pretty girl parts her lips and runs her tongue along her teeth. And Denise had perfect wet, white teeth framed by a pair of eager red lips.

"Let's go. I'm going to bring you home, then I'll be back later on with Billy. I'll order a pizza. He's going to have dinner with us, maybe hang out for a while afterwards. So put on a nice dress and some perfume, and don't mess up your hair."

She flashed him another big smile. "Okay, Rex."

He glanced over at her. "Why are you smiling so much? Do you like Billy?"

Denise looked away, her face a bit pink now. "No.... Well, he's all right I guess."

"Yeah, he's a good kid, that Billy."

Back at the gift shop, he found Billy sweeping the day's debris off the wide pine floorboards. Griffin nodded at the boy, locked the door to the gift shop and turned off the front lights.

"We're going to close the shop early today. I want you to come with me to Rhode Island, down to Providence. I have to pick up some more of that costume jewelry, and it's a bit of a rough neighborhood."

"All right."

They were in Providence in an hour, finished loading the truck by 4:00. Now it was time for their real mission.

"Hey, you ever been to the Foxy Lady? It's right around the corner."

Billy shook his head. "No."

"Ever heard of it?"

"Yeah, some of the guys talk about it."

"Come on, let's go check it out."

"I don't know...."

"What's wrong, you gay?" Griffin almost laughed out loud as he said the words. But he knew the natural adolescent impulse would be to recoil from the accusation.

"No."

"All right then. I'll even pay for you."

Griffin didn't wait for an answer. He pulled into the parking lot, escorted Billy to the front door of a windowless, nondescript building in an industrial neighborhood. It was a Tuesday afternoon in January, so there was little likelihood they would be turned away because of Billy's age, but Griffin slipped the doorman a fifty-dollar bill just to be sure. There were, after all, millions of dollars at stake. Which is why he had driven all the way to Providence when there was a perfectly seedy strip club right in Mashpee—Griffin didn't want to be seen by any of the locals at Zachary's. Especially with the boy in tow.

They entered a smoke-filled room, their feet sticking to the beer-soaked floor. Griffin made a face. "Upstairs is for the low-lifes." He led Billy down a wide staircase. A tall blond in a short skirt and halter-top greeted them at the bottom. They sat at a table, ordered a couple of soft drinks. Within minutes, a couple of dancers approached, wearing nothing but a thin G-string. They swung their breasts and thrust their pelvises in Griffin's direction.

He smiled, nodded toward Billy. "This is his first time here." He handed each of the girls a hundred dollar bill. "Make sure he remembers it."

One sat on each of Billy's thighs, began to run their fingers through his hair and their breasts against his cheeks. Billy turned toward Griffin with a look of panic, but Griffin just shrugged and headed for the men's room to pee.

A half hour later they were back in Griffin's truck. Billy's face was flushed, his breathing labored. Sweat stained his armpits and moistened his hair. The dancers had earned every penny of their fee, bathing him in a sea of jiggling flesh and silky hair and gyrating pelvises.

Billy stared out the window, silent. But Griffin knew that the images that were being projected into his mind were not the same ones his eyes saw on the side of the road.

*   *   *

Griffin squinted through a crack in the door, the room illuminated only by the television set and whatever light the full moon provided. His sister Denise lay on one of their mother's old oriental rugs, splay-legged, her eyes tightly shut as Billy drove himself into her. A beer bottle, half-empty, rested uneasily on the edge of a coffee table, teetering slightly in concert with Billy's teen-aged thrusts and Denise's soft moans. Or maybe they were whimpers. The porn tape ended and the fully clothed characters of The Love Boat, Denise's favorite show, popped onto the screen and danced silently on the television in the background.

The spectacle lasted only a few more minutes, then Billy rolled away, his head resting on an empty potato chip bag. He pulled up his pants and turned to look at the half-naked body curled up next to him. Griffin watched intently, unconsciously adjusting his bow tie. This was a key moment—if the boy was totally repulsed, Griffin had little chance of luring him back again. And though he could cajole or bully Denise into almost anything, getting her to agree to a repeat coupling might be stretching it if Billy didn't so much as say goodbye.

Yet Billy was a decent kid—probably better than most hormone-raged boys his age. But he was no match for the combination of alcohol and smut that Griffin had bathed him in that night. Not to mention the Ecstasy pill Griffin had ground up and sprinkled under the cheese of his pizza, just to make sure the boy had lost all inhibitions. Now Griffin needed the "hug drug" to continue to do its work on Billy—hopefully a feeling of pity or compassion or even kindness would fight its way through the fogginess and lust and alcohol and manifest itself in a word of comfort or a squeeze on the shoulder. Just something positive for Denise to take away from the ordeal.

Billy sat still on the floor, dazed and disoriented. He reached his hand out slowly toward Denise, hesitant to touch the woman he had just ravaged. He brushed her hair away from her eyes, then leaned closer to speak. "I hope I didn't hurt you." He waited for a moment for a response, and, when he realized he wasn't going to get one, covered her with the sweatshirt he had been wearing and pulled himself to his feet. He found his jacket, caught himself before he fell, and staggered toward the door.

Griffin retreated ahead of him and returned to his study. He fingered his bow tie and peered out the window as Billy, head bowed, stumbled down the driveway. Five beers, no water. The kid was clearly dehydrated, perhaps dangerously so. Dehydration was a dangerous side effect of the Ecstasy drug, which was why users weren't supposed to mix it with alcohol. But Billy was a strong kid, an athlete, and Griffin knew that most of the Ecstasy fatalities involved teenage girls, not boys. Besides, there was plenty of snow on the ground if Billy got thirsty on his walk home.

Griffin went back to the den. Denise was still lying on the floor, shivering. He entered, draped a blanket over her, turned up the heat a few degrees, left without saying a word. He thought about reminding her to clean up the mess before she went to bed, but figured he could let it go until morning. Maybe he'd even clean it up himself.

*   *   *

Bruce Arrujo sat in a hard-backed chair in the public library, a yellow legal pad and a ballpoint pen flat on the oversized mahogany table in front of him.

He read what he had written so far: "Dear Shelby:"

Or maybe he should leave out the "Dear"?

He went for a quick walk, splashed some water on his face in the men's room. He tried again, this time just letting the pen form whatever words it may:

Dear Shelby:

I was a pretty good guy until my grandfather died when I was 19. For the next 7 years I did a lot of rotten things, many of which you know about. For the last 7 years I've been paying for my mistakes. I guess what I want to ask you is this: If you don't think I've paid a high enough price yet, after 7 years, then you'll never think I have.

I'm in Mashpee, on the Cape, trying to reconnect with my grandfather. There is some of him that flows through me, and he was a great— and good—man. I'm trying to find that part of me.

Will you see me?

Bruce

It wasn't poetic, and it wasn't dramatic, and it wasn't romantic. But it said what it needed to say.

*   *   *

"Rex, is it Friday again?" Denise was standing in front of an old off-white ceramic sink, one of the many things in the kitchen that Griffin had meant to modernize but had never quite gotten around to.

Griffin looked up from his newspaper and took a bite of croissant before answering. "Yes, it is. And Billy's coming over to visit again tonight right after we're done work, so make sure you take a shower and comb your hair, just like last week. And don't forget the perfume—boys like that."

Denise pulled out a drying rag, rubbed at a plate until it squeaked. "I don't want him to come visit me anymore," she murmured.

Griffin looked up again, softened his voice. "I don't understand, Dennie. He's just like the boys in those soap operas you watch all day. You said you wanted to meet some boys, right?"

"Yes...."

"So you got what you wanted." Griffin paused for a minute, then continued. "And you know what he told me at the shop yesterday? He told me that he really loved you. He said he thinks about you all day long, just like in those TV shows you watch. What do you think about that?"

Denise's eyes had filled with tears. "Well, I don't think I like it very much. When he loves me, it smells funny. And ... and it hurts."

Griffin nodded—she sometimes had some surprisingly accurate insights into life. "You know what? Bad smells and a little bit of pain—that's all part of love. But there's lots of good things about it, too. Didn't it make you feel special when he was holding your hand and kissing you?"

"Well, yes."

"You'll get used to the other stuff like the funny smells, and I bet it won't hurt so much next time either." He stood up, put his hand on her shoulder in one of his few displays of physical affection toward his sister. *That*, at least, was one thing nobody could ever accuse him off. "Listen. You're 28 years old already, and you know Mother wanted you to find yourself a husband. So do as I say, and make sure you make yourself pretty and clean before Billy and I get home tonight."

"Yes, Rex."

"Good. Now I have to go open the store. Do your chores, and I'll see you tonight."

＊　　　＊　　　＊

Griffin watched as Billy helped a customer choose a sweatshirt. The kid had a nice way about him. He looked like a typical teen-ager—black t-shirt, single earring, pants that dragged on the floor. But he was courteous and helpful to the customers, and they seemed to quickly take to him. The woman he was assisting ended up buying two sweatshirts.

"All right, Billy, closing time. And it's Friday night—I expect you're joining us for pizza again." Griffin had decided not to say anything about Billy's "date" with Denise the previous week. As far as Billy knew, Griffin thought Billy and Denise had just watched music videos. Not surprisingly, Billy hadn't brought up the subject either.

"Um, I'm not sure I can come over tonight." Billy, focusing intently on refolding the sweatshirts, avoided Griffin's gaze.

Griffin slowly approached the boy. He had anticipated Billy's hesitancy, rehearsed this moment. "Wasn't that your father I saw dropping you off here yesterday?"

"Yup."

"He's not looking well. Is he gonna make it through the winter?"

Billy brought his hand to a pimple on his cheek, shifted his weight. "Doctor says he hasn't got long. Less than a year."

"That leaves only you to support your mother and sisters, right?"

"Mom works. She's the school nurse."

"Still, you'll be the man of the family."

"Yup."

"So it seems to me like you really need this job." Griffin had made a point of continuing to give Billy a full 20 hours per week after school and on weekends, even though the small gift shop had been basically deserted since Christmas. He had even accommodated the boy's ice hockey schedule.

Billy looked up at him, a flash of anger in his dark eyes. "Yeah. I do." He was a few inches taller than his boss, and more solidly built. Though that wasn't saying much.

Griffin removed his wire-rimmed glasses and cleaned them with a soft cloth he kept in his pocket. He didn't really need glasses, but he wore them because he felt that the round rims softened his face, gave him a less beady-eyed look. Made him appear more trustworthy. Just like the bow tie. "And I like having you here, son, I really do. You're a hard worker, you're honest, you're good with the customers. In fact, I was thinking that it's about time I gave you a raise." He paused. "But I also have to think about my sister a bit. She's all excited that you're planning on coming over tonight. Now, I told you she's a bit retarded, but she's a sweet girl and she's just a bit lonely. But she's not all that bad to look at, right?"

Billy shrugged.

"And I'll tell you what. I'll pay you just as if you were still working here at the shop. So what could be better than that? You get to eat pizza and watch TV, listen to some music if you want, and I pay you for it. So do we have ourselves a deal? Every Friday night?"

Griffin smiled broadly and shoved his hand out to the boy to seal the deal. The boy, or course, had no way of knowing Griffin would be drugging him again. Billy looked down, took Griffin's hand quickly in his own, gave it a quick squeeze, then released it.

For the first time, Griffin noticed how massive the boy's hands were. He looked down—huge feet as well. He felt a quick pang of sympathy for his sister, then ushered the boy out into the cold winter night.

Chapter 9

[February]

Griffin sat in the folding chair in his office, extension cords snaking around him. He lifted the oversized envelope off the metal desk, weighed it in his hands. He knew what it contained—about three pounds worth of legal motions and briefs. His spy, Justin, had warned him that Shelby Baskin would be filing her papers the first week of February.

Griffin also weighed his own options. Normally he would dive in, anxious to begin the chess match, ready to sift through the boxes of paperwork in search of those key documents that would allow him to delay, to obfuscate, to blur, to sidetrack. A lawsuit was like wet clay, and he was the expert sculptor, shaping it to his needs. Rarely did he win a case, but rarely did he have to. Most of his adversaries settled the case simply to be rid of him—rid of his petty procedural disputes and his overreaching discovery requests. Of course, these stratagems—or, more accurately, harassment tactics—cost him nothing, since he represented himself. But they cost his adversaries thousands of dollars in legal fees, without in any way moving the case along. This was, he knew, the key to all civil litigation: force the other side to spend so much money on legal fees that they would come begging for a settlement.

It was a tried and true strategy. He had been involved in more than 100 lawsuits in the past decade, and only lost a handful.

Better still, not a single one of those triumphant adversaries had ever collected a cent from him. Yes, they had their court judgment, but he had made himself essentially judgment proof. No bank accounts to freeze, no stock portfolios to attach, no wages to garnish. Nothing but a few knickknacks and postcards in the gift shop. When he won a case—or, more accurately, extracted a sum of money in settlement—he quickly converted the proceeds into cash or precious metals and stashed them in a safe deposit box. And when he lost, he smiled at his opponent and invited him to go ahead and try to find any assets to satisfy the judgment.

But even he was beginning to become distracted by the lawsuits with his neighbors. There was no real upside to them; none of them would go far toward helping him pay off the $2 million mortgage, due in only 13 months. They had succeeded in buying him some time, but that's about the best he could hope for from them.

And his mind was now on other matters.

Billy had coupled with Denise twice in early January, though he had refused to return for any future "pizza dates." He probably realized after the second time that Griffin had been drugging him. Griffin was hopeful that the two couplings would suffice—he had scheduled them to coincide with Denise's peak fertility period, and had added to her fertility by purchasing a supply of fertility drugs from an Internet dealer. And now Denise was over a week late for her period. Nine glorious days, to be exact. It wasn't something he was particularly proud of, but it was as much for Denise's good as his own.

The potential payoff from these couplings far exceeded anything at stake in his neighborhood skirmishes. It was time to focus on the bigger prize, time to put his neighbors on the sidelines. At least temporarily.

Griffin tried to analyze the conflict from the neighbors' point of view. In some ways, he was surprised they had had the balls to continue to fight him. He knew they were terrified he would slip a bomb into their garage, and he had witnessed a steady stream of home alarm company vans entering the subdivision over the past two months. Perhaps now would be a perfect time to capitulate—they would pat each other on the back for standing up to him, and credit their brilliant legal strategy for forcing him to his knees. Hell, they would probably have a neighborhood potluck dinner to celebrate. Little did they know.

He opened the envelope and began scanning the legal pleadings. Basically, Attorney Baskin had submitted a series of motions on the various cases requesting that all of the suits involving the neighbors and Griffin be transferred to a single judge. It was a sound strategy, and she made compelling arguments why both justice and judicial economy would be served by the action.

He pulled out a legal pad and a pen and began jotting down some notes. The best deals he had ever made were the ones where he sold something that actually already belonged to the buyer. It was like kidnapping, but with property rather than people—steal something valuable, then sell it back to its rightful owner. In this case, he had taken both money and peace of mind from his neighbors. He would simply offer them back to the neighbors in exchange for something of value.

After a few minutes of scribbling, he picked up the phone and dialed Shelby Baskin's number. Her secretary put her on the line.

"This is Shelby Baskin."

"Ms. Baskin, this is Rex Griffin. I was calling about the motions that were sent to me today by your office."

"Mr. Griffin, I'm going to have to ask you to hold for a moment." Griffin waited for almost a minute, then she returned. "Mr. Griffin, I have begun to tape record this conversation. You may, of course, choose not to continue to speak with me. But if you wish to stay on the line, you must understand that this conversation, and every subsequent conversation you and I have, will be recorded. Is that acceptable to you?"

Griffin smiled, made a mental note. Technically, she had begun to record the conversation *before* gaining his consent, which was illegal. In any event, a nervous lawyer meant nervous clients. "That's fine, Ms. Baskin. Record away."

"Good. Now what can I do for you?"

"As we've been discussing for the past half-hour...."

Shelby cut him off, as he knew she would. "For the record, Mr. Griffin, we have just begun our conversation. The time now is 4:37 in the afternoon, and the date is February 5th. I'm sure the telephone records will show that this call began no earlier than 4:35."

Griffin nodded to himself. This Shelby Baskin would not be a pushover, just as he had sensed when he had met her briefly last summer in Pierre's lawyer's office. "Whatever. I was calling to see if your clients would be interested in some type of global settlement."

"What did you have in mind?"

"I'm not ready to go into specifics right now, but what I envision is a situation where I put a sum of money into a pot to settle all claims against me. Your clients can then divide the pot as they see fit. There is, however, one caveat: I'm not in a position to pay the money at this time, but I would agree to offer my home in Mashpee as collateral. If the money is not paid in 18 months, your clients could take the property and liquidate it."

"How much money are you talking? And is the house currently encumbered?"

"Again, I'm not willing to offer a specific figure at this time. But the property is currently unencumbered, other than some overdue property taxes."

"And I assume you would also release all claims you have against my clients?"

"That's the idea."

"Give me your number. I'll make some calls, then get back to you if my clients are interested."

*   *   *

"Well, here's a surprise for you." Carla put down the phone and sat down at the table next to Pierre. "That was Shelby. She just got a call from Griffin, asking if we'd all be willing to settle the litigation."

"On what terms?"

"Shelby didn't have many details, but she wants to come down tomorrow night to meet with us as a group and explain what's going on."

"You know, any kind of settlement's going to be tough. All the cases are so different, and everybody has a different agenda." And everyone was scared. Especially since the bomb incident. Griffin had convinced the judge that he was an amateur chemist merely conducting an experiment, and that he had no evil intent. The police had been unable to find any evidence that Griffin was targeting anybody with the bomb—in fact, there was no bomb, only materials to make one. So the judge had dismissed the charges and released him.

That would have been the end of it, except a few days later Griffin showed up at the police station threatening a false arrest lawsuit against the town. He eventually agreed to drop the suit, but only after the police gave him a written apology and returned the mug shots and fingerprints they had taken at the time of his arrest. The only good news was that the mayor hadn't been pressured into actually presenting Griffin with the keys to the town.

Pierre shook his head—the price of living in a free society was that dangerous criminals often were allowed to walk the streets. Or live next door.

"Well, we all agree on one thing...," Carla noted.

Pierre smiled. "Yeah, but since it's illegal to tar and feather him, we're going to have to somehow figure out some other way to get everybody on the same page. I don't envy Shelby."

*　　　*　　　*

Shelby took a deep breath, stood up, and prepared to address the group of neighbors scattered around Carla and Pierre's living room. Some sat in chairs, some on bar stools, others on the oak floor. A few stood, leaning against the walls. Five or six had their own lawyers in tow.

She really didn't want to be here—not only was getting all the neighbors to reach a consensus going to prove to be an almost impossible assignment, but she was missing a night at the theater with the Big Sister chapter she oversaw. She expected that the dozen volunteers and their Little Sisters would enjoy the show without her. She had no such expectations for her own evening.

She took a second deep breath, looked out the window, paused again. She imagined Griffin, only a few hundred yards away. Watching the house with a pair of binoculars. Observing the comings and goings of his enemies. Plotting his next move.

Shelby had heard about the bomb-making incident—if Griffin were really so inclined, now would be the ideal time to use the bomb. Sure, Griffin had promised the judge he wouldn't build any more bombs. But that hardly gave her, or the neighbors, a high level of comfort.

She trembled for a moment, involuntarily scanning the room for an out-of-place duffel bag or unattended briefcase. She began to understand the toll the threat of Griffin's terrorism must be taking on the neighborhood residents.

"All right, everyone. I have a feeling this is going to be a long meeting, so we might as well get started. I'm Shelby Baskin—I think I've met most of you. As you know, I filed a series of motions last week in the various cases you all have involving Griffin. Well, he called me yesterday and wanted to know if we were interested in some type of global settlement. Basically, he's offering a pot of money for you all to divide as we see fit, which would settle all current claims. The catch is that he claims he doesn't have any money now, so he wants to delay payment for 18 months."

Ronnie Lemaire interrupted. "You're kidding, right? He expects us to settle this based on his promise that he'll pay us later? Come on." He spoke in a deep, laughing voice. Not condescending, but street-smart and commanding. So much for having charmed him at their first meeting.

"Please, Mr. Lemaire, let me finish." She actually liked Ronnie, but she needed to control this meeting. "Griffin's offering to put the farmhouse up as collateral. So if he doesn't pay like he's supposed to, you can take the property."

Justin McBride spoke up. "Of course, we'd need to do a title search to make sure the property is unencumbered."

"He says it is, but of course we'd double check. And he doesn't even actually own the house—it's in a trust for his siblings. But since he's the trustee, he can pledge it."

"Excuse me, but how much money is Mr. Griffin willing to put into this pot of his?" Shelby smiled at Amisha's singsong cadence, and at her literal interpretation of Griffin's proposal.

"He wouldn't give me a figure, but it must be more than a few bucks if he's offering his house as collateral."

Ronnie Lemaire shook his head, raised his beefy hands above his shoulders. "I don't think we should trust this guy. I wouldn't even bother sitting down with him, you know?"

A few people nodded, then Justin surprised Shelby by jumping in and countering Ronnie. She had been told by Carla that the kindly lawyer and the gruff sewer man were close friends. "Let's not rush to judgment, Ronnie. I don't think it hurts to hear what the man is offering. I don't trust him either, but at some point this all has to end."

"Come on, Justin. Do you really think Griffin has any reason to settle with us?" He shook his head, laughing knowingly. "Nothing against Attorney Baskin here, but it's not like we have him on the run or anything."

Carla responded. "Maybe we do. Maybe Griffin's afraid that all this is going to end up in front of one judge."

Ronnie shrugged and smiled. "Look, I'm not a lawyer or nothing, you know? But I know this Griffin, and I've been thinking about this whole idea. So what if the judge throws the book at him? You're never gonna collect a penny from the guy. The farmhouse ain't in his name, so you can't touch it. And he's got no money. So waddya think you're gonna win?"

More than a few people nodded. The meeting was getting away from her, and she hadn't even had a chance to finish describing the settlement offer.

Justin McBride spoke again. "In some ways, Ronnie, your point cuts against you. You're right—Griffin is judgment proof. All we can really hope to gain from Ms. Baskin's strategy is to get his cases against us thrown out. But that's why his offer is attractive. He's actually willing to put some assets on the table, into the pot as it were." He smiled at Amisha, bowed his bushy eyebrows at her. "Look, he may just be playing games with us. But it doesn't really hurt us to play it out and call his bluff."

Ronnie shook his head, shrugged his broad shoulders. "All right Justin, you're the lawyer. But I think you're all wasting your time. The guy's not gonna settle until he has to. And right now we got nothing on him. I don't know what he's up to, but I wouldn't be spending that money he's promising us just yet." He sat back in his chair, still shaking his head.

Shelby took the opportunity to move the meeting along. She felt strongly that it wouldn't hurt to play out the negotiations. "All right then. The thing we need to decide tonight is how much we'll take to settle, and then how do we divide it up. I think the best way to do that is for everyone to write down on a piece of paper the amount they feel that Griffin owes them."

Amisha raised her hand and interrupted. "That is a rather difficult calculation. The repairs that Mr. Griffin failed to perform on our home really don't amount to much. But the damage to my husband's career is quite sizable, I can assure you."

"Good point. I think we need to limit ourselves to specific, out-of-pocket expenses and economic damages. In your case, Amisha, I would think that would include both the cost of repairing your home, and also whatever attorney fees you've had in defending the SEC investigation, plus any fines your husband had to pay."

One of the other attorneys cleared his voice. Shelby was surprised it had taken the other lawyers so long to jump in. "Are you suggesting that everyone should include their attorney fees?"

It was a fair question. Everyone had spent money on attorneys in their battles with Griffin. But these fees were normally not recoverable in a civil trial. And what about other litigation costs? Shelby listened to the debate swirl around her for a few minutes, then sighed in frustration. The group was splintering apart rather than jelling together. And they hadn't even begun the discussion—at this point more likely to be an argument—about how to divide up whatever pot of money Griffin offered. She began to wonder whether this had been Griffin's plan from the beginning—undermine the group's unity by throwing out the idea of a settlement. The applicable clichés ran through her head: Divide and conquer. The devil is in the details. A room with five lawyers will have six opinions.

Justin McBride, again, came to the rescue. He stood. "Everybody, please. This is not productive, I don't think. We are getting bogged down in process when there are substantive issues that need to be decided. Why don't we defer the issue of attorneys fees until a later time? I think what's important now is for everyone to spend a minute in honest reflection, contemplating the following question: *What would it take to make you whole, to put you in the same position financially as if Griffin never came along?* Put aside attorneys fees for now—we've all incurred them. And put aside mental anguish and all that—we've all been traumatized to varying degrees. And please be honest, both with yourselves and with your neighbors. We will all be living together here, hopefully in peace and harmony, for a number of years. So let's try to be fair. Keep in mind not only the economics of the situation, but also the psychological and emotional benefits of putting this matter behind us. When we're all done, we can add up all the figures and see where we are."

Shelby waited a few minutes, then went around the room asking for numbers. She decided to start with an easy one, a couple whose house Griffin never completed.

"We're out about $65,000. That's what it cost us to finish the house, and to fix Griffin's screw-ups."

"Good. Carla and Pierre, how about you?"

Carla responded. "Cost us $70,000 to finish the house, not including our labor. And the best estimate we've got is $120,000 to clean Pepto-Bismol Pond and the wetlands around it. That includes draining it, then removing the silt at the bottom and getting rid of it all. Plus $20,000 for the consultants. And then there's 18 bucks for a bottle of vodka, 'cause we really needed it."

Shelby chuckled along with the others in the room, thankful for Carla's attempt to lighten the mood. "Thanks. Any chance of your insurance company paying?"

"Not much. They're having trouble believing our story that our neighbor came over one day and threw cans of paint into our pond."

Shelby nodded. "All right. Justin, how about you?"

"Well, my original claim against Griffin was that he didn't finish the subdivision tennis court and landscaping. We're probably talking $40,000 here, and that's for the subdivision, not for me. My other damages relate to the increase in my malpractice insurance premium. But I also recognize I have the most to gain from settling with Griffin—his malpractice case against me, bogus though it is, goes away. So I'm willing to absorb the increased insurance cost myself."

Shelby was surprised that Justin didn't push for more. He was under-selling himself. But that was his choice. "So that's it, just the $40,000 for the subdivision improvements?"

Justin nodded, his gray eyebrows flopping up and down. Shelby half-expected to feel a fanned breeze.

"Okay, thank you. Amisha?"

"We have only perhaps $20,000 worth of claims for work on our house. But the SEC investigation is continuing still. There may be fines and other penalties. They are very serious about this insider trading, we have learned."

"What if, as part of the settlement, Griffin admitted to sending the e-mail from your husband's computer?"

Amisha smiled at Shelby, then turned to consult with her attorney. Shelby couldn't help but noticing how classically beautiful Amisha was—Cleopatra in modern garb. And with a naughty twinkle in her eye and a song in her voice. She wondered what her husband was like—was he dark and dashing as well, or had this been some type of arranged marriage? She would have to ask Carla later.

Amisha turned back to address Shelby. "Our counselor believes that such an admission would go quite a long way toward exonerating my husband."

"All right." They were making some good progress, and Shelby was becoming more hopeful that the group would be able to work toward a consensus on a strategy for responding to Griffin.

She turned toward Ronnie Lemaire, who had taken a seat in the back of the room, and took a deep breath. "Mr. Lemaire, I know that you aren't in full agreement with the way we're going about this...."

He interrupted her. "No, it's all right. I'll go along with you guys for a while on this. I doubt it will come to anything, but I guess it can't hurt to talk to the guy. What do I know, anyways?"

Shelby smiled. Maybe she had won some points with him at their first meeting. "Good. Now what do you have for damages?"

"I don't really care about the money. I just want the guy out of my sight, before I kill him or something stupid like that. My big thing with the guy is that he ran down my dog. See, I caught him stealing my electricity—what he did was tap into my electrical main and run a cable to his house. So I was paying for all of his electricity, genius that I am. I don't know, maybe five grand worth. So I finally figured it out, and I go to his house and lift the little bastard up in the air and shake him around a bit. I wasn't planning on hurting him, you know? I just wanted to scare him a bit, let him know not to mess with me."

Ronnie looked around, as if seeking affirmation that his actions were not unreasonable. Satisfied with the nods he received, he continued. "Anyway, a couple hours later, the cops show up at my house. The guy's pressed charges against me, plus he's got a restraining order. Cops tell me I gotta stay a hundred feet away from the guy. That's no big deal, but it means I can't drive in and out of the subdivision 'cause it means driving by his house, you know? So my wife and I go stay in a hotel that night, just to stay away from the guy. I figure I'll get my lawyer to straighten the whole thing out in the morning. Next day, I come home and my dog's lying dead in the street. I didn't see the guy run him over, but I'm not stupid, you know?"

Shelby could see the anguish, and the anger, in the man's face. After a slight pause, he continued. "That was quite a dog, raised him from a puppy." Shelby noticed his fists clench. "So I told the guy that I'd wring his neck next chance I got. And he's stayed far away from me ever since."

Shelby watched as Justin reached over and squeezed his friend's shoulder. It was a kind gesture, almost parental.

"Why don't we take a quick break?" Shelby suggested.

*   *   *

They finished an hour later. Eleven neighbors with claims against Griffin. Shelby did some quick math: $760,000, not including attorneys fees.

"So we've got over $700,000 in claims, plus probably another couple hundred in attorneys fees."

Ronnie stated the obvious. "No way he's paying us close to a million bucks."

"I agree. But the question is, how much would we take? My suggestion is that, whatever number he offers, the pot should be divided up proportionately. So if he offers, say, $380,000, everyone would get half of their claim. Does that sound fair?"

One of the neighbors responded. "I don't really think it is. It's great for people who have no legal fees to pay, but some of us are out some big money for attorneys and we're not getting anything back."

Shelby could see Amisha nodding, along with a few others who had contributed generously to their attorneys' kids' college funds. It was a fair point.

But so was one of the neighbors' response. "But you'll never get that money back, even if you win your cases against him. I think I'm right, but courts almost never award attorneys fees, even to the winner." He looked to Shelby and Justin McBride for affirmation.

Shelby was happy to let Justin respond. "As a rule, that's correct. Courts rarely award attorneys fees to the winning side. But I've also seen many cases settle where one side contributes to the other's attorneys fees, especially where the case is a strong one. And to be fair, most of the cases against Griffin are strong ones, so it's not totally unreasonable to conclude that some recovery for attorneys fees would be appropriate here. May I make a suggestion?"

It was a rhetorical question, an approach Shelby recognized from her litigation days. Justin wanted to make sure he had everyone's full attention, and silence was often the best way to get an audience to refocus on the speaker.

He continued. "My suggestion is to divide the pot into two. Put, say, eighty percent of the settlement funds into a pot for damage claims, and put the remaining twenty percent into a pot to pay legal bills. Each would be distributed proportionately, as Shelby had recommended."

The group debated this proposal for a few minutes, then eventually settled on an 85/15 split of the settlement proceeds.

They were in the home stretch. Shelby looked at her watch—eleven o'clock. "All right, it's late and we've done a lot tonight. I think the last thing we need to do is to decide how much we would take for a total settlement, then I can go back to Griffin and try to get a firm offer from him."

Justin interjected. "May I make one more suggestion?" Shelby nodded. "Why don't we all write down a figure we feel would be acceptable, then we can take the average as sort of a place to start.

Nobody will be bound by this, but it will at least give us an idea of where consensus might lie."

The group murmured its approval. For the second time that night everyone scribbled a number on a piece of paper, and for the second time Shelby polled the group.

The numbers rolled in: $300,000; $345,000; $200,000; $550,000.

Then it came to Ronnie Lemaire. "I say $10 million." He stood, laughing. "I'm sorry, but here's the way I see it. Whatever number he offers, I hope he can't pay it. 'Cause then we can take his house and sell it and be rid of the guy, right?" Justin nodded. "See, I don't care about the money, I just want the guy gone. So if it's a choice of him paying us some money on the one hand, and on the other hand the choice is us foreclosing on his house and getting rid of the guy, and we get our money that way, well then why not take the best of both worlds?"

Shelby smiled to herself. His logic was impeccable, though it sure made her job more difficult. "So you'd rather me cut a deal for some number that we know he can't pay?"

He crossed his arms in front of his chest. "Exactly."

"Does everyone agree with that?"

Mostly nods around the room. A few shrugs.

"You realize that's a tough assignment, don't you?"

Ronnie laughed. "Sure. But Carla and Pierre say you're pretty good...."

Shelby turned to her friends and smiled. "Thanks a lot." She should end the meeting on this light note. There was no consensus on what number the group would take from Griffin, but otherwise there was general agreement that she should go back to Griffin and solicit a firm offer from him. That was enough for tonight. She wanted a good night's sleep before she called Griffin in the morning.

*   *   *

Griffin watched from the woods as the neighbors came out of the Prefontaines' house and made their way to their cars. He was counting on the full moon to illuminate his handiwork.

Ronnie Lemaire reacted first. "Hey, does anybody else smell something funny? Like sulfur?"

A voice Griffin didn't recognize. "Yeah, I smell that. And there's a bunch of wire scraps over here on the ground near my car."

Ronnie's voice boomed through the night air. "Get away from your cars! Everybody stay away from the cars!"

"Why?"

"Because I think that mother-fucker booby-trapped them!"

The neighbors scampered away from the road, huddled together in the shelter of the Prefontaines' porch. Griffin smiled to himself. He could make out their shivering forms. None of them wanted to run cowering into the house, yet they danced around each other in a kind of theatrical pantomime, each trying to shield his body with that of his neighbor.

Another voice, this time Amisha's. "Shouldn't somebody call the constable?"

"Good idea." Griffin watched a half-dozen bodies push toward the front door. One fought its way through to make the call; the others edged further away from the street.

Griffin smiled again, trudged through the snowy woods back to the farmhouse. You couldn't build a bomb with just sulfur and wires. But none of them knew that. All they knew was what they had seen on the nightly news—buses and cars and buildings ripped apart in Jerusalem and Belfast and Caracas.

He stopped after a few steps, turned back toward his neighbors. He filled his lungs, exhaled with all his strength. "Boom!" The taunt was not part of his plan, did not really advance his cause in any way. But sometimes you just had to let loose and have a little fun.

The police would arrive, would investigate, would find his footprints. But they wouldn't find any bombs, so what did it matter? The neighbors might insist they arrest him for assault or disturbing the peace or making threats, but the reality was the only thing he was guilty of was littering.

Littering. Griffin shook his head. A country that had carpet-bombed entire villages in Vietnam actually had laws against littering. And sometimes even enforced them.

He prepared for bed. He would sleep well tonight, though he

knew his neighbors would spend the night listening to the sounds of the dark.

*   *   *

Griffin returned from breakfast with Justin McBride and checked the caller ID on his telephone. Two calls from Shelby Baskin's law office. No message, but she was obviously eager to talk to him. Just as Justin had reported. This Shelby Baskin was sharp, but she didn't know that one of her clients was a mole.

He sat back and waited for Shelby's call. She would be wary of him, expecting deceit and duplicity. If she didn't find it, she might become suspicious. So he needed to plant some type of booby-trap in the deal he proposed, some subtle provision designed to blow up in the face of the neighbors. But not so subtle that Shelby couldn't ferret it out, disarm it and report back to her clients that she had saved them from impending disaster.

But she would never then expect a second booby trap. It was basic human nature. He would exploit that weakness now, just as the Viet Cong had taught him.

He left his office and found Denise in front of the television set in the den, watching a soap opera. "I want you to answer the phone next time it rings."

She looked up at him in surprise, them flashed a big smile. She was under strict orders never to answer the phone. "Really? Okay, Rex."

"By the way, you feeling okay?" He had spent the morning reading up on pregnancy issues—it was almost time for her to be feeling some morning sickness.

"I'm good, Rex."

"All right. So answer the phone, find out who it is and then come get me."

"Okay."

A half hour later the phone rang. Denise answered it as instructed, called to him that Shelby Baskin was on the line.

Shelby was expecting an asshole, especially after last night, so he decided to give her one. If he was too nice, she might smell a rat. He held the phone away from his mouth, closed the door and yelled as if to his sister. "Didn't I tell you never to answer this phone, you imbecile! Next time you touch this phone I'll send you to live with the other retards!" He waited a few seconds, then spoke again, this time into the phone. "I see you called twice before this morning. Why didn't you leave a message?"

She recovered nicely. "I wasn't sure who else might hear what I said. I figured I'd err on the side of caution."

"Nobody here but me and my retard sister. Did you talk to your clients?"

There was a long pause. "I did. They'd rather have the money up front. They don't want to wait for it."

Nice try. She was going to let him win this point, then expect him to give in on the next one. "Don't waste my time, and don't insult me. They get their money in 18 months. How much do they want?"

"They're waiting for your offer."

"I thought we agreed you were going to call me back with a number." That was not at all what they had agreed, but Griffin wasn't trying to impress Shelby with his honesty. He just wanted to manipulate her.

She remained unruffled. "No. You asked me to find out if they were interested in a settlement. We spent four hours together last night, and the end result of the meeting is that they're willing to entertain an offer from you. We don't have a number yet."

"Fine. Here's the deal. All claims released, going both ways. In two years I'll pay them $150,000. I'll put the farmhouse up as collateral."

"It was supposed to be 18 months, not two years. And $150,000 isn't going to do it."

"How do you know $150,000 isn't enough? I thought you didn't have a number."

"I don't know what they'll accept, but I know what they won't accept." Again, she didn't miss a beat. "And you can put the $150,000 into the 'Not a chance in Hell' column."

"All right, then make me a counter offer." He wanted her to commit to some number, no matter what it was. By doing so she would become intellectually allied with the concept of a settlement.

107

At that point, in her mind, the negotiations would be reduced to a question not of if, but only of how much. And, according to Justin, Griffin was going to need her to be an advocate for the deal in order to sway Ronnie Lemaire and Pierre Prefontaine.

"I can't do that."

"Look, this is silly. I gave you a number. You don't like it. Fine. So make me a counter. But don't sit there and expect me to negotiate against myself."

"I really can't give you an exact number. But I think, at a minimum, you'll have to double your number."

"That's crazy. Let me ask you. You've reviewed the cases—what do you think is fair?" Justin had said she was as honest as they come. So she might try to dodge the question, but she wouldn't lie. Too bad for her.

"I'm not that familiar with the cases, so I'm not comfortable giving you a number."

"Come on, don't insult me. You wrote a 22-page brief—you've read the cases."

"Well, given that you seem to be judgment proof, and given that my clients are spending boatloads of money on legal fees, I think it makes sense for them to settle with you. That's why I called you back. But it's their call, and they're not going to take $150,000."

"All right then. I'll go to $200,000. But remember, it's gotta be all the neighbors. If even one holds out, then it's no deal."

Shelby set down the phone and took a deep breath. She knew some lawyers who actually enjoyed negotiations that were more like full-contact chess. But she was not one of them.

Nor had she been prepared for Griffin to be so adversarial. Everything she had heard about the man had led her to believe that he would be polite and demure, like a pit bull that showed no sign of aggression before tearing into the neck of its victim. But he had been overtly hostile, snarling and drooling. And his treatment of his sister had been even worse.

Shelby focused on Denise for a minute. What was her life like? Living with a heartless brother, imprisoned in his home day after lonely day. Did she have any friends? Was there anyone to hug her when she was sad? Nobody in the subdivision had ever seen her leave the farmhouse, other than to retrieve the mail or go help out in the gift shop. What were her dreams? Did she even have any?

She sat for a moment to collect her thoughts, then spun her chair toward her computer. She had learned long ago that saving the world was not part of her job description. If she had wanted it to be, she wouldn't have gone to law school. But maybe she had made the wrong career choice. Harvard Law School looked good on a resume, but it didn't offer much in the way of comfort for the Denise Griffins of the world.

She typed out an e-mail to the subdivision neighbors, reporting Griffin's $200,000 offer. She could accept it, reject it, or offer a counter, whatever they decided. But they needed to give her some clear direction, especially in light of last night's latest scare. She had no idea how Griffin's terrorism would affect the group.

In the meantime, she would order a title examination of Griffin's property—he said the farmhouse land was unencumbered, but he wasn't the type of guy you took at his word. Other than that, she would do nothing until she heard back from the neighbors.

Five minutes later, she received an e-mail response from Carla: "I'll try to get everyone to agree on a number. Hopefully I'll get back to you before the end of the week. Wish me luck!"

*   *   *

Shelby hung up the phone. She hoped it would be for the last time today—they never told you in law school that being a lawyer really meant arguing with a person on the other end of a phone line all day. At least when you argued in person you could see their facial expressions.

Last call or not, it was late, she was tired, and the day had not gone well.

Her clients had authorized her to go back to Griffin with a counter-offer of $285,000. He had responded by increasing his offer to $220,000, and Carla had been able to convince the neighbors to come down to $250,000. But there it sat. Eleven separate phone calls, and the sides were still $30,000 apart.

The phone rang again. Shelby looked at her watch, started to pick up her jacket, then reached for the phone. It was Carla. "New development. We'll take the $220,000."

"Really? What happened?"

"Well, Justin McBride offered to throw in the extra $30,000. He said he felt strongly that this was a good deal for us, that it would be more than worth it to get Griffin out of our lives."

"Wow. That's very generous of him."

"Yeah. Made us all feel pretty cheap. So we told him to forget the $30,000—it's not his responsibility to make up the difference. So we'll just take the $220,000."

Shelby laughed. "Sounds like he shamed you into it."

"Yeah. I bet the old owl knew all along we wouldn't take his money. It was just his way of pushing us to do the deal."

"You're probably right. So I'll call Griffin tomorrow and tell him, then draft a settlement agreement for everyone to review."

"Great. Thanks for all your help, Shelby. It'll be nice to have this whole thing behind us. You know, I make the girls wait in the house now when I start the car...."

"I hear you, Carla. I know you'd like to have this behind you. But it's not a done deal yet. It's going to take a few weeks to get the agreement documented, and these settlement agreements can get a bit dicey. And we're not exactly dealing with a man of his word here."

*   *   *

[Early March]

Bruce stood in the late winter shadows, peering through the binoculars into Rex Griffin's study. Boring work, especially because Griffin never seemed to do anything worth noting. But tedium was a relative state—four hours in the slushy woods was no worse than four months in the cold Atlantic.

And it wasn't like he had anything better to do. There was no work at the marina, and he had visited with everyone who might have any connection to his grandfather. And Shelby still hadn't answered his letter.

So when he got a call from Dominique Victor asking if he had

110

any free time and wanted to earn a few bucks, he figured, why not? He had met her when he had arrived in Mashpee because she was on the tribal council, and now she wanted him to learn what he could about this Rex Griffin character.

"I think he may be using Billy for some sick porn stuff," she had said. "He took Billy down to some strip club, then drugged him and left him to have sex with his sister."

Salacious stuff. But from what Bruce had seen so far, Griffin seemed far more interested in law books than in sex. Which, in and of itself, was strong evidence that this guy was either really sick, or really dangerous.

*   *   *

Griffin pored through the settlement documents that Shelby had drafted. He didn't really care what they said, just as he didn't really care whether the settlement figure was $220,000 or $220 million—the neighbors were never going to see a penny of his money, no matter how many pages of legalese she produced.

But he did want to continue the illusion that he was agreeing to the settlement only because he had somehow booby-trapped the arrangement. It would then be up to Shelby to defuse the trap at the last minute. After all, the neighbors were expecting some type of shenanigans from him. They would never let their guard down until their fears had been realized.

Griffin scribbled notes on a legal pad for the better part of the afternoon, then picked up the phone and called Shelby.

"I have a number of problems with the terms of the settlement agreement." He listed close to a dozen provisions he wanted revised, none of which mattered a bit to him. Shelby listened politely, and asked a few questions of clarification, but did not respond substantively to any of his comments other than to say she'd have to review them with her clients.

"The last problem I have with the agreement is this language in the Mutual Release. It says I release them from all claims I have against them. That's not the deal—the deal is that we're settling all the lawsuits, nothing else. No way am I giving these people a free pass. What if they're trying to screw me on stuff I haven't even figured out yet, or don't know about yet?"

"It's standard release language, Mr. Griffin."

"I don't care if it's standard or not. The deal is that we're settling all the claims that are *pending*, nothing else. This is not negotiable."

"Very well. I'll speak to my clients and get back to you."

*   *   *

Shelby looked over the notes she had made. None of Griffin's requested changes to the agreement were of particular consequence except the last one.

Why would anyone want to limit the release language? In most settlement agreements, both sides were looking to employ broad language that made it clear that there were to be no further claims by either party against the other. It was like a divorce—the parties wanted to move on with their lives, wanted nothing further to do with each other. Ever.

But Griffin was not like most litigants. Perhaps this was his ploy, his angle—end the litigation, but leave the door open to more suits against his neighbors in the future. He could simply settle these lawsuits and then fabricate a whole series of new ones. Shelby would advise them to avoid Griffin at any cost, but she couldn't change the fact that they had had numerous interactions with him in the past that would be fodder for new lawsuits. Bottom line: by the time the neighbors got around to trying to collect the $220,000, he would have asserted a stack of offsetting claims of his own, which would probably be enough to block the foreclosure of the farm house.

Ronnie Lemaire had been right. Griffin had no intention of really ending the litigation—he was merely trying to buy some time. Call for a temporary truce, then use the ensuing calm to re-arm for another series of battles.

Shelby sat back in her chair, contemplated her options. One option was to advise her clients to accept the limited release language—but that would be like sending Griffin an inscribed invitation to sue. A second option would be to push Griffin to accept Shelby's release language. But Griffin—not surprisingly, given what Shelby believed to be his strategy—had made it clear that the point was non-negotiable. A third option was to simply abandon the settlement.

But was there a fourth option, some way they could use the discovery of Griffin's strategy against him?

Shelby knew she was out of her league here. She had spent a lot of time in the courtroom, but didn't have much experience in drafting and negotiating complex civil settlements. After a moment of hesitation, she grabbed the folder and walked down the hall to the office of one of her law partners.

She had never liked this particular partner, and not just because he constantly leered at her. He was in his mid-forties, twice divorced, and the poster child for the conniving attorney. He lied to other attorneys, lied to judges, lied to clients. And he probably lied to his partners. But he knew every sleazy trick in the book. She made sure the top button of her blouse was buttoned, took a deep breath and knocked on his door. Sometimes the ends justified the means. Or so she hoped.

She explained the case to him. He nodded knowingly. "Sure. I've seen it before. This guy Griffin wants to have the wife at home and still keep his girlfriend."

Shelby looked at him blankly.

"You know, he wants to have his cake and eat it too. He wants the settlement because it'll buy him some time, but wants to come back later and sue your guys again."

"So what would you do?" Shelby was almost afraid to ask.

"Who's his attorney?"

"He doesn't have one."

He smiled a toothy, yellow smile. "There you go then. You gotta slip something in to the agreement that goes over his head."

"He's pretty sharp, sharper than a lot of attorneys I know."

"Doesn't matter. Try putting some stuff in the 'Defined Terms' section—nobody ever reads them anyway. Hell, you could write a definition that says that every time the word 'guilty' is used it really means 'innocent' and I don't think half the attorneys would catch it. That's what I would do."

Shelby nodded and made her escape. "Thanks for your help."

She returned to her office and pulled the Mutual Release document from the folder. It was a simple two-page document, with a reference that all capitalized terms were to have the meanings as defined in the Settlement Agreement document. Her law partner was right—she had barely skimmed the six pages of definitions recited in the Settlement Agreement.

She focused on the language Griffin wanted changed. The clause stated that the parties released each other from all pending claims, whether asserted in the lawsuits or not. Griffin was demanding a simple revision—he wanted the release limited to only those claims actually asserted.

Shelby turned back to the Defined Terms section of the Settlement Agreement. The term "Claims" was defined, but not the term "Pending Claims." She pulled up the document on her computer and inserted a simple definition: *The term 'Pending Claims' shall mean all Claims, known or unknown, that have been asserted or could have been asserted in any pending Lawsuit.*

There. Done. The term "Pending Claims" had been re-defined in an *Alice in Wonderland*-like manner to include claims that weren't even known yet, much less asserted and pending. If Griffin wasn't sharp enough to notice, well, that was his problem.

Shelby sighed. It was her problem, too.

Deceiving a party who was not represented by an attorney in this way was a clear violation of her ethical standards. She could justify it in her mind as an acceptable violation—rarely had she been involved in a case where the white hats and black hats fit so neatly. But it was a rationalization nonetheless.

This was what her law professors always referred to as the first step down the slippery slope. Was it possible to be just a little bit unethical, they asked? Shelby had struggled with the question for many years, and had reached the conclusion that the concept of the slippery slope was actually a bit insulting—her professors would have her believe that her decision to sneak a definitional change into a settlement agreement with a snake-like adversary was the first step down the path toward a life of crime.

But she knew it was not, no more than a glass of wine inevitably led to a life of alcoholism. And if she lost a bit of sleep because she felt guilty for the ethical violation..., well, that was better than her clients lying awake at night in fear of a bomb-wielding terrorist.

*   *   *

Shelby actually slept fine that night. At noon she arranged a conference call with the neighbors to update them on the case. It would be up to her clients to decide what to do.

Shelby began the conversation. "First of all, I want to tip my hat to Ronnie Lemaire. Ronnie, you were right, Griffin was just trying to buy some time. He had no intention of ever paying. But now that we've figured out what he's trying to do, I think I've found out a way to turn it against him." She described both Griffin's attempt to booby-trap the settlement agreement and her proposal for disarming the device.

"So, it's up to you guys. What we're doing is a bit..., let's use the word 'aggressive,' but I'll draft the documents if you tell me you're okay with it."

Shelby was not surprised that the group unanimously approved her plan. People were funny—they loved to criticize lawyers for using "dirty tricks." But, in the end, lawyers only did what clients asked them to. The Mashpee neighbors were good, decent people, yet they didn't think twice about the morality of attempting to deceive Griffin.

It reminded her of the way people criticized politicians. The solution was simple: vote for someone else. The same was true with lawyers: don't hire the sleazy ones.

She sighed. "All right, then. I'll make the changes to the documents and see if he bites."

She revised the documents that afternoon and faxed them to Griffin. He had agreed that, if they reached an agreement, he would sign first to prove to the neighbors he was sincere. Then she would collect signatures from her clients.

The next morning the settlement agreement arrived back at her office in a Federal Express envelope, the signature of Rex Griffin scrawled across the bottom. It had been almost too easy.

Chapter 10

[Middle of March]

Billy was unpacking some brass wind chimes from a cardboard box, untangling them and hanging them from some hooks on the barn's beams. He replayed last night's hockey game in his mind, smiled as he relived his breakaway goal.

His boss' words cut through the daydream. "We just came from the doctor, Billy. Denise is pregnant. She says you're the father."

Billy tried to focus on Griffin's scowled face, then felt himself sink to the ground. His first inclination was to run, but he couldn't even convince his legs to stay between his trunk and the floor. He sank slowly, stared at a spot on the far wall, tried to slow his breathing.

Griffin stood over him, arms crossed, nostrils flared. Billy waited. *What had he done?*

Finally Griffin spoke. "Well, are you?"

Billy forced his jaw to unclench. "I, I don't know. Maybe."

"Get out of my store. Right now."

Billy rolled away from Griffin and pulled himself to his feet. He steadied himself against a display rack and tottered toward the door.

He never should have touched Denise, especially after the first time. He knew it was wrong, knew it was a mistake. But something— and he knew now that it was the drugs—had made him feel so ... affectionate toward her. She was like a cuddly kitten, all soft and warm. Plus she was gorgeous, with a killer body. He had examined and explored and stroked her body more out of a sense of discovery and wonder than any uncontrollable passion. Of course, once her clothes came off and her breathing quickened and he began to remember the strippers at the Foxy Lady....

Still, what kind of idiot gets involved with a retarded girl to begin with? And what kind of jerk takes advantage of her and gets her pregnant?

He began to run. He ran as fast as he could, his long straight hair bouncing off the back of his neck, his eyes watering as the cold wind of life slapped him in the face.

* * *

Griffin wasn't sure what Billy would do after staggering out of the store that morning, but he wasn't surprised when the phone rang that afternoon and a man with a raspy voice identified himself as Billy's father.

The man was dying from lung cancer. The news that his son had impregnated a retarded woman would hardly be likely to brighten his final days. Oh well. Eleven months until the $2 million loan was due.

"Yes, Mr. Victor. What can I do for you?"

"Mr. Griffin, I believe that it would be best if we met in person...."

They met an hour later at a Dunkin Donuts, sat around a wobbly table in the corner as a steady stream of mid-morning customers grabbed coffee and pastries to go. Billy wasn't there, but Billy's mother was. In Vietnam, Griffin had been beaten and tortured, drugged and starved. So he was fairly immune to the stare of a steely-eyed adversary. But even he was a bit disquieted by the way Billy's mother focused her large eyes on a spot a few inches beyond his forehead.

He suppressed a shiver, tried to return the woman's stare and study her as she was studying him. He had read about the history of the Wampanoag tribe, knew that the death of most of the male tribe members during the Colonial period had resulted in the intermarriage of many of the tribe's women with freed black slaves. He could see that history in the face of the large-boned woman sitting across from him—full lips and a wide nose from her African heritage; high

117

cheekbones and straight dark hair from her Native American one. Not a particularly attractive face, but resolute and august. Almost imperial. And, Griffin had learned, she was the tribe's Medicine Woman, whatever that meant. Not that he really believed in that sort of voodoo stuff. Even so, he sensed he would need to be careful around Dominique Victor.

Billy's father—Vernon was his name—was tall and lanky, much like his son, with the same large hands. Griffin guessed the body seated across from him was at one time a powerful one, but today it was slumped deep in its chair and its leathered skin was pallid and ashen around yellowed eyes. The sounds and smell of spring may have filled the air outside, but Billy's father reeked of the death of winter.

Griffin tugged on his bow tie, waited for Billy's parents to set the tone. They had called for the meeting, so they must have an agenda. Griffin was curious to hear what it was.

Finally Vernon spoke. "I am not here to offer any apologies to you or your sister. From what Billy tells me, he is not the only one responsible for this situation."

Billy's father stopped here, waiting for Griffin to respond. They probably knew Griffin had been getting the boy drunk, and perhaps even knew Griffin had been drugging him. Griffin refused the bait. "Please continue." Two ears, one mouth; use them proportionately.

"Be that as it may, we have a situation that needs to be addressed." A thick, gravely cough interrupted the man's response for a few seconds, then he continued. "Is your sister planning on having this baby?"

"Yes. Abortion is not an option."

The man nodded slightly, turned to look at his wife. Griffin got the sense they were actually relieved that Griffin had closed this door so tightly. "Is she planning on keeping the baby, or is adoption a possibility?"

"Adoption is not an option either. My sister wants to raise this baby."

Billy's mother spoke for the first time. Her voice was deep and low. "And what do you want, Mr. Griffin?"

"What I want is that this never happened!" He regretted the

comment as soon as he said it; he had overplayed his hand, and Billy's mother wasn't buying his righteous indignation act. She drummed her fingers on the table, waited for a meaningful response. Griffin surprised himself by trying again. "Putting that aside, to be honest, I'd prefer that Denise put the baby up for adoption. But she is insisting on keeping the child, so I'll do my best to support her. But I'll need some help from the father and his family."

"When you say 'help,' do you mean financial assistance, or just general support?"

The woman sure did cut right to the chase. "Frankly, Mrs. Victor, I'm not sure Billy's in a position to offer either. He's hardly ready to be a father figure, and my understanding of your family's financial situation is that I shouldn't expect much help there either."

Billy's father began to protest this point, but Mrs. Victor silenced him with a gentle squeeze of the arm. "So what kind of help are you referring to?"

"I'd like support from the Mashpee tribe. I'd like the child to be recognized—legally—as a member of the tribe. By that I mean a full share in all tribal benefits and programs and rights."

"I don't see that as a problem. The child will by blood be half Mashpee."

Griffin bowed his head. "There's more. I will be the child's legal guardian. And Billy and your family must agree to have nothing to do with the child. Billy will be the father by blood only—he will have no visitation rights of any kind, and no contact with the child. The child will be a child of the Mashpee tribe, but not a child of the Victor family. And all this will be agreed to in writing."

Billy's father made an attempt to straighten himself in his chair. "Why would you demand this?"

"I'm not going to debate with you about Billy's fitness to be a father, or about your family's fitness to help raise the child. Those are my terms. If Billy doesn't accept them, then he can start supporting the child financially right now, beginning with Denise's medical care. But he can't have it both ways."

"I see." Vernon pulled himself to his feet and dropped a couple of dollars on the table to pay for their coffee. "My wife and I will speak to our son, and to the tribal council, and let you know our decision."

Griffin sat back and replayed the conversation in his mind. Not bad, other than the fact that the mother might turn out to be a more formidable adversary than he had expected. In truth, he didn't care whether or not Billy or his family took any interest in the child, and didn't really even care whether Billy sent over a few bucks every month for childcare expenses. But he knew the most effective way to negotiate was to insist on something you didn't really want, and then to concede the point later. He had insulted Billy's family, and they would likely come back and insist on having a role in the child's upbringing. Fine. Griffin would eventually accede to the demand, and the family could take the baby and put him to sleep in their wigwam for as many weekends as they could stand his crying.

All of which would only reinforce the one thing Griffin really cared about—that the child's legal status be beyond question. The child would be a member of the tribe.

Chapter 11

[Late March]

"Come on, Billy, get your head in the game." Pierre knocked the teenager's hockey stick from his hands. "The tournament's next week and you look like you'd rather be home in front of the TV."

Billy bent over slowly and lifted his stick from the ice. "Sorry, Coach." He began to skate away.

Pierre followed. Was this typical teenager malaise, or something more? He softened his tone. "Something bothering you?"

Billy continued skating, his eyes focused on the ice in front of him. "Just some stuff going on."

"Want to talk about it after practice?"

Billy shrugged. Pierre smiled to himself—a shrug was often teenager-speak for yes. "Good. We'll go grab a burger and catch the Bruins game."

An hour later they were seated in front of a big-screen TV at Bobby Byrne's Pub, eating popcorn and waiting for their burgers. Pierre and Carla had eaten there a few weeks earlier, passing the time reading the love poems and philosophy inscribed on the wall in the dining room. He figured Billy would prefer the hockey game on TV to Yeats on the wall. "So. What's bothering you?"

Billy played with his straw, let out a sigh. His voice was little more than a whisper. His long hair, still wet from the shower, shrouded his face. "I got this girl pregnant."

Pierre wasn't sure how to respond. "Ouch. Is she going to keep the baby?"

"Yeah."

"She your girlfriend?"

"No, nothing like that."

"Feel like telling me about it?"

Billy shrugged again. "I was working in this store. My boss invited me to come over after work on Friday nights to hang out with his sister. Actually, he was paying me to come over."

"Paying you?"

"Yeah, she's, she's ..., I can't think of the right word, but she's not normal. She looks normal and everything, but she's, you know, retarded. He said she was lonely." He paused, took a sip of his Coke. "So I went over there the first time, and it was really weird. I didn't want to go again, but he sort of pressured me into it. Then, after the second time, I knew he was drugging me or something. My parents took me to the hospital the next morning and they did a blood test. They found drugs in my body—Ecstasy."

"I don't understand. Why would he drug you?"

"I don't know."

"Come on, Billy. Give me a guess."

Billy shrugged a third time. "Maybe he did it so that I'd think I was having a good time with his sister. He knew I didn't really want to go over there any more. Ecstasy is supposed to make you feel all happy and stuff."

"Yeah, they call it the 'hug drug.' Do you think he wanted you to have sex with her?"

Billy pondered the question for a minute. "I don't know. He always left us alone, and he gave us lots of beer. And both times I was there he left us music videos to watch, but when the music ended porn came on."

"So he leaves you in a room alone with his sister, gives you beer, drugs you with an Ecstasy pill, and puts porn on the VCR. Sounds pretty strange to me."

"He's a strange dude."

"Not just strange, I'd say sick. Maybe he was watching you guys, or making a video. So what's going to happen?"

"Well, she wants to keep the baby. The brother, my boss, he met

122

with my mom and dad and told them he wants to be the baby's guardian. And he wants us to stay away from the baby."

Pierre felt a pang, remembered what it had been like when he had been kept away from Valerie for six months. Other inmates complained about the food or the violence or the monotony of jail life. For him, the worst part was not being able to hold his baby. On more than one occasion he had actually cried himself to sleep. What kind of asshole would deny a father the right to see his child? "Why does he want to keep you away from the baby?" Pierre remembered Billy's mother, tried to picture her agreeing to such a condition. "I can't see your parents going for that."

"No. They're going to insist that we get to have the baby on weekends. If he won't agree, then we're going to the police and tell them about the drugs."

Pierre nodded. "But you're going to let him be the guardian?"

"We talked to a lawyer. We don't have much choice. The mother usually gets to keep the baby, and since he's Denise's guardian, it makes sense he'd be the baby's guardian also. And it's not like I can keep the baby myself."

"I see what you mean." Pierre paused for a moment. "The whole thing just sounds bizarre. Who is this guy?"

"His name is Rex Griffin."

Pierre dropped his burger onto the table, missing his plate. He should have seen this one coming—gift shop, retarded sister. Of course it had to be Griffin. "Whoa. Hold on here. Let me think for a second." This had suddenly gone from a tough-luck story to a full-fledged horror show.

Pierre closed his eyes, tried to connect the dots. There was no way that Denise getting pregnant had been an accident; nothing happened in Griffin's world except by design. But why would Griffin want to impregnate his own sister? And then insist on being the baby's guardian? Pierre couldn't come up with an answer, but he sensed the same kind of complex scheming and puppeteering that Bruce Arrujo had employed to send him to jail. "Listen, Billy, I have no idea what Griffin's up to. But I know this guy; I'm sure he's planning something pretty ugly."

"Like what?"

"You got me. Our whole neighborhood is fighting him, and none of us can figure him out either. If you don't mind, I want to talk to my wife and our lawyer about this. They might have some ideas what he's up to."

"Yeah. Sure."

"In the meantime, try to stall him a bit. And don't tell him that you know me—that's the one thing we have on him now."

*   *   *

Carla was still awake, painting in her studio above the garage, easels scattered around the room with partially-completed paintings and drop clothes crumpled together in balls atop the cheap linoleum floor. The moonlight shone in through the skylights, and also through the windows as it glistened off the lake. She was just about done for the night when Pierre called and said he was on his way home. "Please wait up for me. I just found out some more stuff about Griffin."

She sighed, rinsed out her brushes, opened a bottle of wine. This had become their nightly routine—put the kids to bed, open up a bottle of wine, talk about Rex Griffin. She was beginning to wonder whether Griffin's terrorism was more psychological than physical. He had done no actual harm to anyone, bomb scare or not, but he had succeeded in tormenting them, infecting their lives with fear and anger and despair. She shrugged—that's why they call it terrorism.

She had responded to the Griffin battle by refusing to allow it to change her life. She had put it into perspective—this was a fight over money, nothing more. It would all end soon, and their lives would return to normal.

But Pierre was beginning to drown in it, in his obsession of all things Griffin. In many ways, she knew, Pierre saw this as a rematch of his battle with Bruce Arrujo, a second direct challenge to his manhood, another test of his ability to protect his family. And, even more fundamentally, he saw it as a battle between good and evil, between that which was right and just and noble and that which was base and vile and sinister. He had ridden his white horse into battle

124

once before, the champion of all that was good, and had lost. He could not allow it to happen a second time.

Unfortunately, the battle was taking its toll on Pierre, on their marriage. They had fought over Pierre's insistence on buying a gun, argued over his refusal to let the girls play in the yard without supervision, bickered over his obsessive need to peer through the telescope he had purchased to spy on Griffin.

She heard his car pull into the garage. She met him at the door, kissed him, noticed again the dark circles under his eyes. They moved to the sofa, sipped wine from a single glass.

He recounted Billy's saga.

"What a horrible thing for a kid to have to go through," she said.

With a shaking hand he touched the glass to his lips, then stood and paced. "Look, Carla, you're better at this stuff than I am. I always see things as black and white. You're better at the grays. But to me this Griffin is just plain evil, like the devil."

"There's no gray, Pierre. It's all black this time."

He nodded. "That's the easy part. But the gray part comes in when I try to figure out what to do about it. Should we really be making a deal with him? Isn't that really what he wants?"

"Not necessarily. It's a good deal for us, too."

"Only because we're so damn afraid of him. He's like the neighborhood bully—he steals our lunch money, then gives us a nickel back if we promise not to tell on him. Well, that's bull. It's our money, he shouldn't get to keep any of it."

"And you think this settlement lets him keep the money."

"Don't you? I mean, all of these lawsuits are totally one-sided. So why are we giving him anything? Why are we settling?" Carla was silent; the question was rhetorical. He continued. "Because we're afraid of the guy. We're afraid of the bully."

He slumped into a chair, looked up at the ceiling, then continued. "I'm starting to think Ronnie Lemaire is right—we should keep fighting the guy."

"I see your point. But remember, he's got no assets, so we probably wouldn't get anything from the litigation. So in that sense it's a pretty good settlement." *Plus, we can get on with our lives.*

"Maybe so, Carla. But I just don't think it's smart to back down to bullies. All it does is make him think he can get away with it the next time. The guy terrorizes us, then starts building bombs, and we go running to make nice. Well, screw him."

"You know it's not that simple, Pierre."

"Yes it is, Carla. People always make things more complicated than they have to be." She closed her eyes. *He honestly sees this as a battle between good and evil. And maybe he's right.*

He continued. "All I know is that every time I compromise on stuff like this, I end up regretting it later."

Carla nodded. He was referring to his decision to accept jail time for a crime he did not commit. It had been a strategically sound option—six months in jail, as opposed to the possibility of a murder conviction. But it had never sat well with him. He'd been framed, been set up. He should have fought for the truth, for justice.

She swirled the wine in the glass for a few seconds. He would hate himself, and probably her, if he walked away from this fight. And it wasn't like she didn't know about his idealism when she married him—she couldn't ask him to just switch it off and on, when it suited her needs. She looked up at him, saw the tired, anguished man itching for a fight. "Sweetheart, I can't very well argue that you should go against your conscience. It's one of the things I love best about you. If you feel that it's wrong to settle with Griffin, then I'm with you. We'll keep fighting him."

*   *   *

Pierre brushed his hand against his wife's cheek, slipped out of bed. They had made love, and Carla was sleeping peacefully next to him. That should have been enough, used to be enough, to lull him to sleep. But not anymore.

Even their lovemaking had changed, had been affected by the Griffin nightmare. What used to be a celebration, two people sharing their passion for life, had become merely an opportunity to escape, like getting drunk or taking a nap or going to the movies. Get naked, forget about Griffin for a while.

And here he was, choosing to prolong the nightmare that Griffin had made their lives. He could make it all end by just agreeing to settle the lawsuits. Even Carla wanted to just put this behind them. All he had to do was cave-in, fold his tent. It was tempting.

But it was the wrong thing to do. He knew he might lose Carla if this battle continued much longer. But he also knew he would lose her for sure if he betrayed his conscience and surrendered to Griffin.

He had no delusions—he knew many of Carla's friends and family thought she could have "done better" when she married Pierre. He was just another guy. But what he did have was a code of ethics and a sense of morality that, from the beginning, she had been drawn to. In that sense he was the antithesis of her father, a bank executive who lived in a lily-white Connecticut suburb with his blue-blooded country club friends, cheating on his taxes and lamenting the fact that the Jews and the Catholics and the Blacks and the Asians had infiltrated so much of American society. She had been enchanted by Pierre's work in a soup kitchen, flabbergasted by his refusal to allow a family friend to get him out of a speeding ticket, spellbound by the solemnity with which he said his prayers every night. He was the vehicle by which she moved from a world of entitlement and privilege to one in which morality and benevolence dictated behavior.

So how could he now agree to a settlement with Griffin that made a mockery of every tenet and value and characteristic for which Carla had married him? He could be untrue to himself—for Carla, for his girls, he would do that. But he could not be untrue to that which Carla had fallen in love with. Not and expect his marriage to survive.

*   *   *

Shelby was at her office by nine o'clock, which was early for her. She had settled into a routine of working late, then taking the time for a workout the following morning. It was one of the few nice things about not having a family—she could set her own schedule. The phone rang a few minutes after she arrived.

"Hi Shelby, this is Pierre."

"Good morning. What's up?"

"Have those settlement documents with Griffin been signed yet?"

"Actually, I just got them back from Amisha's lawyer yesterday.

Griffin's already signed, so you and Carla are the only signatures I still need. Why do you ask?"

"Sorry to throw this at you at the last minute, but I don't think Carla and I should sign them. Griffin's got something going on here that's bigger than just a bunch of lawsuits against the neighbors." Pierre described to Shelby his conversation with Billy. "So, bottom line, I don't want to sign anything until we figure out what's going on."

Shelby was silent for a moment. "As sick as the whole thing with this boy sounds, I don't see how it could have anything to do with the settlement agreement. It's your call, but I think you should still sign it. It's a good deal, especially with the language we put in."

"I just don't trust this guy."

"I understand, I don't trust him either. But I still don't see how the thing with Billy should change your feeling about the settlement agreement. One has nothing to do with the other."

"Except the timing is the same—the guy litigates for years, then all of a sudden he wants to settle. Before he has to." Pierre paused, then continued. "Have you bought a car recently?"

Shelby laughed. "Yeah, last year. Why?"

"Did they try to pressure you to lease instead of buy?"

"Yeah, big time. Told me what a great deal leasing was."

"Same thing happened to me. I wasn't sure how the numbers all worked out in the end, but I figured if they were pushing me so hard to lease, it must be a great deal for them and a bad one for me. So I did the opposite—I bought."

"Okay...."

"Well, it's the same thing with Griffin. I don't know exactly why he wants us to sign the settlement agreement, but if it's good for him, it must be bad for us."

Shelby started to respond, then stopped. The lawyer in her was prepared to point out to Pierre that his logic was flawed—his distrust of Griffin actually was a good reason to sign the settlement because it boxed Griffin in, gave him less room to maneuver. But her instincts told her to listen to the meaning behind the words, the message Pierre had failed to deliver. "Is that the only reason, Pierre? Just that you don't trust him?"

Silence, then a kind laugh. "No, you're right, Shelby. I didn't want to bore you with all the morality stuff, but it's more than that. It's not just about the deal. It's about me. It's about not giving in to this guy."

"I guess I can understand that." In fact, she agreed with it. But it was not her job to take moral positions on behalf of her clients. Her job was to point out the legal ramifications of their decisions, to play the devil's advocate if necessary. Which she did. "But it's not like he's going away. Settle or not, he's still going to be your neighbor, still going to be tormenting you."

"That's exactly it. To me, a settlement means we all shake hands and walk away. Clean slate. But I don't want to shake his hand, and I don't trust him to just walk away. He's still up to something. Griffin is evil, and I can't help but think that we're wrong to agree to anything with him. It's like doing a deal with the devil. And I won't do that. I can't."

*   *   *

Griffin put the phone down, stared out his window at the home of Pierre and Carla Prefontaine. He had to give them some credit—it had taken them six months, but they had finished the landscaping and painting and exterior trim and deck. The house looked pretty good, at least from the outside.

Justin had been right about Pierre. He had turned out to be the hard-liner in the group, refusing to enter into this little truce of convenience. As Justin described it, *refused to do a deal with the devil.* Even after Justin had sat down with Pierre and tried to resell him on the merits of the settlement.

The problem, Griffin knew, was that Pierre had publicly staked out a position based on principle. He was a man of high morals, he had proclaimed to his neighbors, and as such could not make peace with the evil Griffin. Unfortunately, he couldn't very well reverse his position down the road without branding himself a hypocrite. No amount of logic or reason or even coercion would likely succeed in convincing the zealot to get off his high horse. Later on he could be knocked off, but for now Griffin would have to adapt to the fact that Pierre would not be signing off on any neighborhood peace pact.

It would make things more difficult for Griffin. But not impossible. He had hoped to only have to fight a war on one front. Now, he would have to continue to do battle with the neighbors while at the same time he engaged the Mashpees.

As for Pierre, it seemed he had let his emotions—or, more accurately, his morals—get in the way of what should have been a simple business decision. Best to let him have his little victory for now. He would pay for it later.

Chapter 12

[April]

Valerie bounded into the kitchen, her blond ponytail bouncing, a big smile on her face and in her blue eyes. She kissed Pierre on the cheek, her little nose squishing into him, and plopped down onto his thigh. He closed his eyes for a moment. In a few years, he knew, his little girl would be focusing on boys, not on Dad.

"How was school, Val?"

"Good, Dad. We had a sub in gym class—he said he knows you."

"Me?" It wasn't really that surprising. Pierre knew lots of people in town from the hockey program.

"Yeah, he asked if you were my father."

"What was his name?"

"Mr. Griffin."

Pierre's heart pounded. He spun Valerie around to face him. "Sweetheart, tell me everything that happened in gym class."

She shrugged. "We did gymnastic stuff—tumbles, vaults, stuff like that. Oh, and he sent home a letter for you." Valerie dug through her backpack, handed Pierre an envelope.

He opened it, unfolded a piece of notebook paper, turned it so Valerie couldn't read along:

Dear Mr. and Mrs. Prefontaine:

I thoroughly enjoyed having young Valerie in Gym class today. What a precious young lady—I had no idea such an angel lived right down the street from me! I served as her spotter on a number of gymnas-

tic exercises and found her to have exquisite muscle tone, body shape and flexibility. I couldn't believe she is only 9 years old; to my eye and touch she seemed instead to be quite the young woman! I look forward to having further opportunities to instruct her in gymnastics—and perhaps in other proficiencies necessary to a young woman's education as well—in the near future.

Your neighbor,
Rex Griffin

Pierre let the paper drop to the floor, hugged his daughter. It was one thing to threaten Carla and him....

*   *   *

Shelby put the note down on the conference room table, shook her head. Pierre and Carla had driven up to Boston from the Cape to meet with her, to get her reaction to Griffin's missive. She had ordered sandwiches for lunch, but they sat, uneaten, on a plastic serving dish in the middle of the table along with a tray of office supplies and pitcher of water.

Carla spoke. "Well, do you think we're just being paranoid?"

"No, you're right. The letter is just ambiguous enough so he could deny any evil intent, but the message is clear. My first question is how did he get to be a substitute teacher?"

Carla responded. "We called the school, but as far as they're concerned he's totally qualified. College degree, no criminal record, no complaints from parents. They need people, so they hired him. And by substituting for the gym teacher, he knew he'd get Valerie as one of his students at some point during the week."

"The guy leaves nothing to chance," Pierre added. "My guess is that he poisoned the regular gym teacher."

Pierre was not one to be easily intimidated, but Shelby could see the fear in his face. His demeanor made her decision an easy one. "Listen, there's something I've been wrestling with for a couple of weeks. I wasn't going to mention it to you, but now I think I should."

Carla raised her eyebrows. "What is it?"

"It's about Bruce Arrujo. I got a letter from him a month or two ago. He's on the Cape, in Mashpee."

Pierre sat up. "In Mashpee?"

"Afraid so."

"What's he doing there?"

"I'm not sure—he mentioned something about having relatives in town, about trying to reconnect with his grandfather."

Carla reached and took the pitcher, poured a glass of water for both Pierre and herself. "I didn't even know you kept in touch with him," she commented.

"An occasional letter, that's all. I think he sees me as his only link to the real world. He's been living in his boat for seven years now, just sailing up and down the coast. This is the first time he's actually stayed on land for a while. It's almost like he's asking me for permission to end his exile."

Carla looked intently at her friend. "Wow. How do you feel about that?"

Shelby saw a mixture of sadness and compassion in her friend's eyes. Carla was a romantic at heart—she really believed that, somehow, true love would win out and Bruce would return to regain the heart of the fair Shelby. Shelby held no such delusions.

And she really didn't feel like talking about Bruce at all. But he had become relevant. "Listen, I know you guys came up here to talk about Griffin, but believe it or not Bruce coming back might play into to all of this. So, to answer your question, part of me still hates him, never wants to see him again. But part of me says, hey, seven years is a long time to hold a grudge."

Shelby paused, swallowed, then continued. "He used to like to think of himself as some kind of clipper ship, a combination of the turbulence of the ocean and the stability of the land. Sort of the best of both worlds—creative and passionate and wild on the one hand, grounded and cold and intellectual on the other." She looked out the window at the gray-blue waters of Boston harbor in the distance. A couple of passenger boats, but no clippers. "Before he left I told him I thought he had a point, that he really was a combination of the ocean and the land. I told him it was called mud."

Pierre nodded, chuckled. "Good one. What did he say to that?"

"Actually, nothing. He sort of agreed. I think he really did feel bad he had betrayed us."

"Well," Pierre said, "I'm having trouble feeling sorry for the guy. He was in a sailboat. I was in jail."

"Look, Pierre, I don't feel sorry for him either. I told him he was unfit to live in a civilized society, told him to go sail away and not come back until he was ready to be a human being. But I really never thought he'd be out there that long. I figured he'd wait a few months, then dock his boat and go scam somebody else. But it's been seven years...."

"And you think he's really changed?" Pierre asked.

"I really don't know. And I'm not sure I even care. But Rex Griffin changes everything."

Carla said, "What's Griffin got to do with it?"

Shelby turned, faced her friends. "I'm really worried about Griffin. Worried about you guys."

Pierre looked at the note from Griffin sitting on the table in front of him, nodded at Shelby to continue.

"I'm not just talking about the paint in the pond or the bomb threats or even the notes to Valerie. That stuff scares the heck out of me, but the really scary thing is that everything he does seems to be part of some bigger plan. And none of us has any idea what it is. Who knows what he might do next? The guy's a psychopath. All we're doing right now is reacting to him—he does something, then we respond. For all I know, we're doing exactly what he wants us to do." She paused, took a deep breath. "I really think we need someone to try to figure out what he's up to. Someone to match wits with him. Someone whose mind works in the same conniving and obsessive way his does."

"You mean Bruce, right?" Carla asked. Pierre turned away.

Shelby said, "Yes, Carla. I know you both want nothing to do with the guy, but I really think he might be able to help us."

Carla and Pierre exchanged glances, then Carla spoke. "What could he do?"

"Follow Griffin, study him, look at all the legal papers, try to get inside his head. Might take a few weeks, might take a few months. But if anybody can figure it all out, Bruce can. In many ways, they're the same person—Griffin is a crook who likes to play lawyer, and Bruce is a lawyer who's really a crook."

"I don't know," Carla said. Shelby knew she would defer to Pierre on this.

"Look, obviously it's your call. At least think about it. But I think we need someone to play chess with Griffin, someone who has both a legal background and a criminal mind. Maybe Bruce is the wrong person, but I can't think of anyone else...."

"All right. We'll think about it. Probably talk about it the whole drive home."

Shelby walked her friends to the door, then returned to her office and kicked off her shoes. She looked at her law school diploma framed on the wall—that's what she was, a lawyer. Was she allowing her personal feelings to cloud her professional judgment? Unfortunately, she wasn't even sure what her true feelings were, so she couldn't even begin to answer that. On the one hand, the few months she had spent with Bruce were the happiest of her adult life. He had invigorated her, challenged her, vitalized her. She had never felt so alive before. Or since.

Then he had betrayed her. Faced with choosing between her on the one hand and a couple of million dollars on the other, he chose the money. Actually, that's not entirely accurate—his choice was to try to have both her *and* the money. In the end he got neither.

At his core there was a decent human being lurking inside of Bruce. The question was whether he had been able to peel away the layers of greed and rot and slime to get to it. In the end, the only way to answer that question was to let him back into her life and judge him for herself. That would mean taking a huge chance, opening herself up to him again, leaving herself vulnerable, trusting him. It would mean actually allowing herself to feel again. But she had played it safe for the past seven years, and it had gotten her nowhere. She had the same boring career, the same boring life now as she did the day Bruce sailed away.

Maybe it was time to roll the dice, time to get back into the game, time to play the cards she was dealt. There were a hundred clichés that applied. And they all conveyed the same message: She couldn't win if she didn't play.

*   *   *

Carla reached across, squeezed Pierre's knee as he navigated his way out of Boston. This used to be their city—they used to walk its streets, eat in its restaurants, picnic in its parks. But that was before Bruce Arrujo had taken it away from them.

"Hey, want to grab a quick bite in Chinatown? If we hurry we can make it back in time for the school bus. We didn't have any lunch yet...."

He sighed. "I'm sorry, I'm just not in the mood. And I'd rather not risk it. What if we get stuck in traffic?"

She nodded, took a deep breath. No sense in trying to distract him. "Well, what do you think of Shelby's idea?"

He offered her a half smile. "I'm not too crazy about it, obviously. It's bad enough that he's living in Mashpee right now. I didn't really expect to invite him back into our lives again."

"No. Me neither. But I hadn't planned on Rex Griffin, either. My feeling is that we don't have to like Bruce. We don't even have to trust him. We'd just be using him to track Griffin."

Pierre sighed again. "I'm really torn on this. I don't *want* him in our lives, but I also recognize we may *need* him. Like Shelby said, Griffin's a psychopath. I can't let my feelings about Bruce jeopardize our family. But still...."

"Look, Pierre, you're one of the few people I know who actually *lives* a so-called Christian life. Most people I know just pay it lip service. But you give to the poor, you pray from your heart, you treat people the way you'd like to be treated. And you forgive people when they wrong you."

Pierre glanced at his wife, offered a wry smile. "So I should forgive Bruce...."

"No, I didn't say that...."

"Yes you did. So I'll answer your question: Bruce hasn't apologized. And if he did, I wouldn't believe him."

"But what if he did apologize, and what if he really was sincere about it?"

Carla watched as Pierre wrestled with the question. "Those are some big assumptions you're making. But, if he really was sincere about it ... I mean, he would have to really prove it to me, then I suppose I'd forgive him. But that's a big 'if.' And even then, I wouldn't want anything to do with him."

Carla reached over, rubbed his cheek. "You know, darling, I knew what your answer would be. If you had said you couldn't forgive him, then he really would have won, he really would have changed you. He hurt you, I know, but he couldn't kill the essence of who you are."

Pierre blushed. "And what made you so sure?"

She smiled. "That's easy. If he had changed you like that, I wouldn't still love you so much."

*   *   *

Bruce was the last to arrive, which was only fitting since he had traveled the furthest to get there. He had journeyed beyond himself, then painstakingly charted a return voyage.

He knew tales of sailors who had left family and friends to explore distant ports and lands and adventures. Sailors who dreamed of returning some day to the unchanged, idyllic life they had left behind. Bruce's hopes were different. He hoped to return to find himself totally unrecognizable.

Today should be a good test. The people seated across the table from him would be studying him, examining him, searching for the monster that used to be him. He approached the room, scanned it quickly before entering. Typical law office conference room, much like the one he used to host Pierre in while trying to scam him. The requisite wall of windows with a view of the city, this time of the Charles River winding its way past Fenway Park to the west. A long, polished conference table, this one of golden oak. A portrait on the wall of some old geezer who founded the firm, this particular geezer in a World War I uniform. And, as was often the case in law firm conference rooms, a group of angry people waiting for a fight.

He watched three sets of eyes focus on him. Their reaction to him did not surprise him—he had recoiled a bit himself when he looked into a mirror a few months ago for the first time in years. No longer the tall, dark young lawyer with the boyish grin and the piercing eyes and the rugged good looks. Instead, he was gaunt, even a bit jaundiced through the leathered skin. Worse than that was the look of despair in his eyes. His eyes used to shine with intensity and purpose and confidence. But seven years at sea, essentially alone, will suck the swagger from a man.

They were at the far end of the room, seated around the far end of the table. As far from him as possible. None of them stood or greeted him in any way. Just eyes. Angry eyes.

He straightened himself and met each of their stares with a small smile. First Shelby. A million times he had seen her face—in the swirl of bubbles cascading out from under the bow of his boat, in the streaks of sunlight breaking through the morning mist, in the shadows the fluttering sails made against the foaming sea. She looked back at him impassively, only the fire in her blue-green eyes revealing her inner turbulence. She nodded slightly, then swallowed. "Hello, Bruce."

He tried to speak, realized he couldn't force any words out, offered another small smile, and turned to Pierre, seated in the far corner of the far end of the room. This time Bruce found his voice. He spoke quietly, his hands clasped behind his back, and looked directly into Pierre's eyes. "I was hoping I would see you again someday, Pierre. I just want you to know that I never meant for you to go to jail. That was never my intention. The other part I won't even try to apologize for—you trusted me and I screwed you. But the jail part I never meant to happen."

Pierre's forehead reddened and his teeth clenched as Bruce addressed him. Pierre didn't respond for a few seconds, then stood up and moved around the table to face Bruce. Pierre wasn't as tall as Bruce, but he was solid and fit.

Pierre stared into his face for a few seconds. Bruce resisted the urge to move his hands in front of his body to protect himself. Bruce could see him trying to control his breathing, trying to keep his fists from flying out in hatred. He was like coiled metal, forced into an unnatural shape, straining to free itself from its restraints. Finally he spoke. "Go to Hell, Bruce. It's going to take more than your little bullshit speech for me to forgive you." He gritted his teeth, forced himself to turn away and go back to his chair.

Carla broke the awkward silence. In the end, she was the one who had bested Bruce, had denied him the millions he had schemed and scammed for. "Look, Bruce, it's safe to say that nobody in this room likes you. But Shelby says you've changed, says you'd like to make amends for what you did to us. So we agreed to at least hear what you have to say."

"Fair enough. But, as Pierre said, my words aren't really worth that much. Especially in this room. But Shelby said you guys have a problem that maybe I can help with. I'd welcome the chance to try to redeem myself a bit in your eyes."

Shelby looked at her friends seated to her left, who nodded at her to continue. "As you said, Bruce, we have a problem. And the irony is that we need you, or someone like you, to solve it."

"What kind of problem?" Bruce was still standing near the entryway to the room. Nobody had offered him a seat, but he didn't mind standing in front of the three of them in some kind of position of supplication.

Shelby responded. As she did, she raised her left hand above the table for the first time. Bruce's heart jumped as he saw there was no wedding ring on her finger. "We'll go into the details later, but the bottom line is that Carla and Pierre, along with a bunch of their neighbors down in Mashpee, are involved in some nasty litigation with the developer of their subdivision. I'm representing them in the lawsuits."

"Well, it sounds like you guys are in good hands."

"That's part of the problem," Carla answered. "We are in 'good' hands, but I think we need to be in some hands that aren't so good. Some hands that know how to get dirty and know how to scratch and claw. We're pretty sure he's trying to screw us, but we can't figure out his angle. A few weeks ago we found out that he got his mentally retarded sister pregnant by drugging some high school kid who worked for him...."

Bruce interrupted. "Rex Griffin."

Pierre had been turned sideways to Bruce, facing the window but occasionally glancing over his shoulder to follow the conversation. He spun now to face his old enemy. "You know him?"

Bruce nodded. "I've become friendly with Dominique Victor. She asked me to follow him, see what I could learn."

Pierre continued in a low, even voice. "Which is what?"

"Not much. He spends a lot of time working on legal pleadings. I think he's one of those self-trained lawyers. But it's not like he's making porn tapes or anything like that. And he's been spending time at the library researching the history of the Mashpee Indian tribe...."

Pierre cut him off. "He's been *what*?"

Bruce looked at him quizzically. "Doing research on the Mashpee tribe. Why?"

Shelby looked at Pierre and Carla, then addressed Bruce. "We didn't know he was interested in the tribe. But it makes sense. Our feeling is that everything is somehow related, but we can't figure out what the sleazeball is up to."

Pierre interjected. "So we figured we needed a sleazeball of our own to help us."

"That's not helping, Pierre." Carla's voice was quiet, but firm.

Bruce spoke softly. "That's okay, Carla. I'm a big boy."

Shelby continued. "We need someone who can think like this guy Griffin, play chess with him. Someone who might be able to figure out what his plan is."

"So this meeting is sort of like Batman and the other Superheroes asking the Penguin to help catch the Riddler."

The three of them stared back at him impassively. Tough to keep the sense of humor honed when you're at sea. Carla responded. "We're not actually trying to catch him, just figure out his next move."

"As I said, I'd be happy to help out, and in fact I already am. But you know I've been disbarred, right?"

Shelby nodded. "We're not asking for your legal services, though your legal skills and training will come in handy. What we need is for someone to help us connect the dots. We've got plenty of lawyers, too many even. But we don't have anyone who's looking at the big picture and trying to see how all the pieces fit together. Like I said, we need someone to play chess with Griffin."

Bruce lowered his voice, focused on Shelby. "Do you really think I'm the right person for this?"

Shelby looked down at her hands. "I'll be honest, Bruce. I don't know. There's so much bad blood between you and the three of us. Plus you've been basically living the life of a hermit for the past seven years, so I have my doubts about how quickly you'll be able to jump back into the fray. It may be that we're all just wasting our time. But you've got a unique set of skills, and they happen to be exactly what we need."

Bruce smiled. "Sort of like the 'devil that you know' argument, huh?"

Shelby responded. "That's a good way to look at it. I spent a lot of time going over the details of how you tried to scam Pierre. Your attention to detail was almost scary. It made me realize that you weren't just cold and calculating, but obsessive too. And, as much as I hate to admit it, your plan was brilliant. And that's just what we need, an obsessive genius. Someone who has no other distractions, no family or kids or job or hobbies."

"Someone with no life." He had spent the better part of the past decade doing nothing but sailing, drinking rum and engaging in imaginary one-way conversations with his dead grandfather. Once in a while he'd crew on a charter boat to pick up spending money, but for the most part his contact with other human beings—live ones, that is—had been limited to sending a monthly postcard to Shelby. The postcards were a thin, tenuous connection to his old life, and Shelby seemed to be able to sense when the connection was fraying and would respond occasionally with a restrained, but not uncaring, card of her own. Her last card had surprised Bruce by requesting this meeting, though she had made it clear that the encounter would not be a social one.

Shelby raised her chin and looked Bruce in the eyes for the first time since he had entered the room. Bruce thought he saw a hint of concern in her eyes. "Look, Bruce, you've been out there trying to find yourself for seven years now. It's time to get on with your life, time to do something productive. Maybe this job we're offering you isn't the right thing for you, but you've got to get off your boat and rejoin the real world."

Bruce looked out over the Charles River below. A handful of

small sailboats zigzagged their way down river. One of his first dates with Shelby had been spent doing just that.

Bruce wanted to tell her how much he just wanted one more chance to do the right thing, how much he wanted the chance to win her back. But it was not the right time, or the right place. And he was not at all sure that he was truly capable of doing the right thing. All he could do was look back at her. "Before I decide, there's one thing you should know."

"What's that?"

"I have some Mashpee blood in me. That's actually why I'm in Mashpee right now. My grandfather was one-quarter Mashpee Indian. He used to go down to the Cape every summer to visit some cousins and go to the tribe's reunion. That's how I met the Victors."

"I thought your grandfather was Portuguese," Shelby said.

"He was, but not totally."

"Well, even better then. Having cousins in Mashpee may give you some connections you need to track Griffin. And from what you've said about your grandfather, they should welcome you with open arms."

Shelby was right—Grandpa had been a great man. Too bad he had died before Bruce had finished growing up. Bruce knew Grandpa never would have allowed him to turn into such an asshole. Bruce nodded. "You're right. They might be able to help."

Shelby looked at Carla and Pierre, waited for them to nod their assent. "All right. Let's give it a try." Shelby tossed a manila folder in Bruce's direction. "This is some background info on Griffin, and on the cases. It'll give you a feel for how sleazy he is."

"Even worse than me, huh?" Bruce regretted saying it right away. It was a transparent attempt to elicit a kind word from Shelby.

Shelby, as Bruce guessed she would, ignored the invitation to stroke him. "As for money," she said, "we'll pay your expenses, but otherwise you'll be doing this simply because you want to help out."

"Sort of like my penance for past crimes."

"You can look at it that way. But a healthier outlook might be to believe you're doing it because it's the right thing to do. We need your help, you need to get back into the land of the living, and this guy Griffin needs to be stopped. Seems like a win-win situation."

*   *   *

Griffin sensed as much as heard the man's presence in the wooded area just off the drive. It was a skill he had learned in Vietnam—an ability to discern a break in the rhythm of the night, to perceive a shift in nature's haphazard pattern of sound and movement.

Barrister sensed it too, growled softly toward the darkened night. Griffin lifted the small dog. "Shhh, honey, it's okay. Quiet."

The presence of an unseen adversary didn't surprise Griffin. Regarding the attack, it had always been more a matter of when than if. And his regular evening walk with Barrister was the obvious time to strike—eight o'clock every night, regardless of the weather. He looked around. He was out of sight of any houses, and the cool April night had kept his neighbors in their homes. Not that any of them would likely have stepped up to help him.

The man attacked quickly, leaping through the brush and charging at Griffin. Griffin turned his back to the onslaught, but a baseball bat to his shoulder sent him sprawling to the pavement. He covered his head and face with his arms, curled himself into a ball, and prepared to absorb what he knew would be a torrent of kicks and blows.

He willed his mind to escape his body, to distance itself from the moment. His flesh was nothing but a vessel in which he carried himself—it was not alive, it could not feel, it was not him. Let it be punctured and split and breached. His bones were merely the framework for his hulk—they were not alive, they could not feel, they were not him. Let them be fractured and splintered and shattered. None if it mattered. None of the blows could reach the Rex that existed within, the Rex that was steeled away so deep that no amount of torture or defilement could begin to touch him.

The beating continued. Griffin was aware of the blows, heard the hollow thud of the kicks as they echoed through his body, sensed the crack of his bones as they buckled beneath the force of the bat. But he did not feel anything, even as the assault knocked the air from his lungs and the light from his eyes.

And then it was over. Griffin heard the man run back to the woods, felt the soft whimper of Barrister as he gently licked his bloodied face. Griffin tried to pull himself off of the cold pavement, but could not. Barrister nuzzled against him, then barked as if in a plea for help. It was early still—somebody was sure to pass by before the neighborhood slept, and Barrister would draw their attention to the beaten man splayed on the road.

Griffin closed his eyes and waited, the warmth of Barrister's breath on his face and the thought of better days to come the only gifts of this cold, dark night.

*   *   *

Bruce squatted behind some brush in the small wooded area, watched as the black-clad figure crouched behind a tree near the side of the road. It was just past dusk, and the subdivision road was empty except for Griffin walking his dog. The masked figure was—quite obviously—stalking Griffin. Bruce saw the baseball bat, felt its heft from fifty feet away.

It would likely be ugly. So be it.

The thug gave Griffin one final kick, then plodded his way back to the woods. Bruce broke into a run, angling to intercept the masked assailant. He hadn't stopped the attack when he had the chance, and he wouldn't go to Griffin's aid now. His job was to figure things out, to win the chess match. Not to play the Good Samaritan.

He sprinted through the lightly-wooded landscape, bulling his way through the brush and branches, closing on his unsuspecting prey. The assailant stumbled along, panting, apparently spent from his assault on Griffin. He was a big man, but thick and soft. He wouldn't likely put up much of a fight once Bruce knocked him to the ground and took away the bat.

Bruce leapt, buried his shoulder into the man's kidney, wrapped his arms around him as they tumbled together through the under-brush. The man blustered a curse. "What the fuck...?"

Bruce pinned the brute to the ground, cut the words short with a short, quick punch to the man's jaw. "Shut up."

The man fought to free himself. "Listen, mother-fucker...."

Bruce hit him with a second shot, this one a quick jab to the

Adam's Apple. The man gagged, flooding Bruce's nostrils with the stench of stale garlic. "I said shut up."

Now Bruce could see the fear in the man's eyes. He gasped a reply. "Okay."

"Who sent you?"

Griffin's attacker shook his head. "I don't know what you mean."

Bruce pulled off the thug's ski mask, raised his fist, smashed it into the man's nose. Blood gushed out, flooding the man's face and streaming into his panting mouth. "Answer me."

The thug coughed and spit, finally found some oxygen. He snorted a response. "All right. My boss sent me. Dickie Viola."

"He doing someone a favor?"

The man held up a hand in fear. "I don't know. Honest! He didn't tell me nothin'."

Bruce saw the panic in the man's eyes, knew he was telling the truth. "All right, where you from?"

"Brockton." Bruce nodded. Just as he expected—an out-of-towner, a professional job. The buffoon had no idea why he had beaten a man nearly to death. Or even who had hired him. The guy knew nothing. Which was, still, just what Bruce knew—nothing.

* * *

On his fifth day in the hospital, the drugs finally cleared a bit and Griffin reached for his own medical chart to take stock of his injuries: concussion, punctured ear drum, fractured ribs, broken wrist, dozens of deep bruises. It hurt to breathe, it hurt to think, it hurt to move.

A policeman came to interview him the next day. It was, he noticed, the same detective who had arrested him on the bomb-making charge. Foster was his name. Clean-cut, mid-thirties, straight back, probably ex-military. If he remembered the bomb incident, and Griffin was sure he did, he didn't let it show.

"Mr. Griffin, this was a pretty serious battery. If some of your neighbors hadn't heard your dog barking, you might have bled to death."

Griffin didn't think things had been quite that dire—it took a lot more than a few blows with a baseball bat to kill him. But he nodded nonetheless.

Detective Foster continued. "Were you robbed as well, sir?"

"No."

"Any idea who the assailant was?"

"He was wearing a ski mask, so I didn't see his face. He came right out of the woods, almost like he was waiting for me. Attacked me with a baseball bat."

"Can you provide a physical description?"

"I don't know. It was dark. And he hit me from behind. But pretty big, I think. All I really saw was the bat."

"Do you have a regular routine that he might have anticipated?"

"Yes. I walk that same road every night with my dog, Barrister." The detective rested one foot on the cross-brace of a chair, wrote down Griffin's answers in a small notepad.

"Same time every night?"

"Yes, at eight o'clock. Usually for a half hour."

"Do you have any enemies who might want to see you hurt?"

Griffin nodded, sadly. "As I believe you're aware, Detective, I haven't been getting along with a few of my neighbors. Plus, I've had some unpleasant dealings with a local family whose son got my sister pregnant."

The policeman nodded. "Can you provide me with some names?"

"If I had to guess, I would say you probably want to talk to Pierre Prefontaine, Ronnie Lemaire, Justin McBride, Amisha Raman and her husband—those are the neighbors I've been feuding with. And Billy Victor is the boy who got my sister pregnant. Any one of them could have been behind this."

He spelled the names and provided addresses for the policeman, then continued. "Please let me know what you find out, Detective. I'm going home tomorrow. But I'd hate to think they might come back and try to finish the job."

Chapter 13

[May]

Griffin walked into the den, the same room that Billy had screwed Denise in. She had only recently started watching television in here again—for months she had watched on the small set in the kitchen.

Denise was sitting on the old red leather sofa that had been in the family forever, watching some silly sitcom. He smiled kindly at his sister's bulging midsection. Nine months until his $2 million loan was due. But only five months until Denise was.

He was set to meet that night with the tribal council, the meeting having been postponed for two weeks while he recovered from his injuries. He still had occasional headaches, and still sported a cast on his wrist, but otherwise he was close to fully recovering from the attack a month earlier.

In the council members' minds, this was a meeting to discuss the future of the baby—issues like custody and visitation rights still had not been resolved, and he expected the council to be prepared to battle over those issues tonight.

But Griffin had no intention of waging battle this evening. His agenda was totally different. This would be his first opportunity to make contact with the individuals he would need to partner with in his attempt to revive the lawsuit against the town. Griffin would gladly sacrifice points relating to the child's upbringing if by doing so he could gain the confidence of the tribal council members.

"Denise, are you ready?"

"Yes, Rex."

"Good. Let's go."

"Will Billy be there?"

The question caught Griffin a bit off-guard. Griffin looked at his sister, saw the moisture forming in her bright blue eyes. It had never occurred to him that she had developed any feelings for the boy. Or maybe the tears were tears of pain or anger. Or even hormones. Whatever the cause, a few well-timed tears would make her appear even more sympathetic to the council. He would have to remember to mention Billy to her again right before the meeting began. "I don't think he'll be there. But his parents will be."

They climbed into Griffin's pickup truck for the drive to the meeting. "Don't forget to buckle your seat belt."

"Okay."

Griffin had read that when the town of Mashpee had been first incorporated, the tribal council also served as the town government. Even over the years, as the town slowly gained non-Indian residents, the tribe was able to maintain control over all town functions. But in the 1960s, a rush of development forced the Indians to share governmental functions with non-tribe members. So a tribal council was re-formed to deal with exclusively tribal matters. Like Denise's pregnancy.

The meeting was meant to be an informal one, so they met at The Flume, a dimly-lit restaurant owned by an ex-chief of the tribe. The restaurant, a dark-wooded structure set in some pine trees by the shore of a small pond, specialized in traditional Wampanoag cuisine. It was still pre-season on the Cape, so the group spread out around a long table in the corner of the main room and ordered some coffee.

Griffin eyed the group around him. Billy's parents he had met, and he made a point of seating himself so that he wouldn't have to face the icy glare of Billy's mother for the entire evening. Otherwise the group was fairly nondescript. A mix of a half-dozen men and women, mostly middle-aged.

Griffin remembered that, ironically, the Indians' nondescript appearance had been part of the tribe's problem in its previous lawsuit against the town. The tribe members were trying to prove to a Boston jury that they were part of an active Indian tribe, but the jurors had trouble believing that the individuals seated around them in the courtroom were anything but everyday Americans. No headdresses. No moccasins. No war paint. They may have Native American blood in them, the jurors concluded, but how could they claim to be members of an active Indian tribe? It hadn't been a particularly enlightened conclusion, but coming from a bunch of jurors whose only exposure to Native Americans was from watching Westerns on television, it wasn't totally unexpected.

Griffin jumped right in before his agenda could be redefined. "I want to thank the council for agreeing to meet with us tonight. And I also want to begin the evening by apologizing to Mr. and Mrs. Victor." He paused for a moment here and bowed his head toward Billy's parents. "As you may have already heard, I previously took a rather extreme position regarding the Victor family's rights to participate in the upbringing of the baby, which we now know will be a boy. That was wrong of me. I was acting out of anger and frustration at the unfortunate situation we find ourselves in."

Griffin paused again, glanced kindly at his sister, his eyes resting directly for a moment on the unfortunate situation in question. "But upon further reflection, I understand the importance of the baby's father and his family taking an active role in the baby's life. And I have also learned that the Victors are fine, upstanding people and will surely be an asset to the child. So I welcome their assistance in raising the child, and also welcome the tribe's involvement in the child's life."

The speech had the effect Griffin expected. The council members had no doubt seen Griffin's attitude toward the Victors as arrogant and perhaps even racist. They had arrived tonight ready for a fight—a fight for justice and respect and honor. But Griffin had handed them their victory before the battle had even been engaged, and now they weren't sure what to do with it. Other than to stare back at him blankly.

He continued. "I must continue to insist, however, that I will be the baby's legal guardian, just as I am Denise's legal guardian. After all, the baby will be living in my house and I will be responsible for its health and welfare." He turned and looked again at Billy's mother. "But at some point in the future, when Billy becomes an adult, I would be more than willing to revisit the guardianship question."

Again, blank looks. It was time for an escape. "Well, then. Thank you all for your time, and I again apologize to Mr. and Mrs. Victor for my previous behavior. Good night to you all."

*　　　*　　　*

Griffin arrived at the library just as the doors were opening for the day. The building was one of those impressive, heavy stone structures with lots of turrets and a mansard roof.

He had with him a list of the tribal council members he had met with the night before, along with a bag full of quarters to make copies. He flicked on a microfiche machine and began scrolling through the local newspapers from the late 1970s. He wasn't looking for headlines, but rather for letters to the editor.

The tribe, as an entity, had elected to sue the town of Mashpee. But within any entity, some individuals are combative while others are conciliatory. Griffin guessed that the same was true of the Mashpee tribe. There must have been a few individuals who were at the forefront of the tribe's decision to take an aggressive stance against the town, and they often identified themselves by writing letters to the editor. Maybe at least one of these letter-writers was still a member of the tribal council.

He didn't have to look hard before he found what he was looking for. Clayton "Ace" Awry, now a member of the tribal council, had written a series of letters during the mid-1970s, each of which argued passionately in support of the rights of the Native Americans, first in response to the armed clash between federal agents and Native American demonstrators at Wounded Knee in 1973, and later in support of the Mashpee Indians' claims to town land. The letters weren't particularly well-written or well-reasoned, but the guy definitely had a chip on his shoulder.

Hopefully it was still there.

Griffin turned off the microfiche machine and moved to a computer terminal. He logged-on to the Internet and pulled up the on-line version of the local newspaper. A quick search for Ace Awry showed a recent article commemorating the twenty-fifth anniversary of Ace's Donut Shop.

Griffin suddenly had a craving for a cruller.

*　　　*　　　*

For the next week, Griffin began his day with a donut and a cup of coffee at Ace's Donut Shop. It was really more like a diner—an 'L'-shaped room with ten or twelve stools at a Formica lunch counter as you entered, and a dozen round tables off to the right in the leg of the 'L'. The locals sat at the counter, and the tourists sat at the tables, and the flies sat wherever they could find a tasty morsel. Which was as likely to be on the floor as on a plate. A few tired ceiling fans pushed the stovetop fumes and the cigarette smoke and the coffee steam around the room.

Ace was there every morning, an apron around his bulging mid-section, his long hair pulled back into a gray ponytail, gabbing with the customers and barking at the help. Griffin sat at a stool, his bow tie contrasting sharply with the work clothes and dungarees of his fellow customers. But they left him alone as he sipped his coffee, purchased lottery tickets, and listened to the conversations around him.

In some ways, Griffin found it a therapeutic way to spend his mornings. He had assumed that everyone in Mashpee knew—and despised—him. But the Mashpee that Griffin lived in was a different world from the Mashpee of Ace's Donut Shop. Griffin's Mashpee was the Mashpee of second homes and summer vacations and miniature golf. The people who shared breakfast with him at Ace's reflected the grittier side of the Cape. They were the laborers and craftsman and fishermen, the people who viewed the Cape as a home rather than a theme park. Most of them had never heard of Griffin. Or his lawsuits.

One morning Ace lumbered over to re-fill his cup. "Didn't I meet you a couple of weeks ago over at the Flume restaurant?"

Griffin smiled. "You do look familiar, but I couldn't place your face. Yes, that was me. I'm Rex Griffin." Griffin held out his hand to Ace, who gave it a firm shake. Griffin offered a self-deprecating smile. "I'm the one who insulted Mr. and Mrs. Victor, then had to stand up and apologize for it."

Ace nodded, smiled. "Well, you took us by surprise that night. We were set for a battle."

"Yeah, well, it took me a while to get over my anger. It's sort of a bad situation...."

"I hear you. But the Victors are good people. I've known 'em all my life."

The men exchanged small talk for a few more minutes, then Griffin paid his bill and left. He returned every morning for the next couple of weeks, sometimes chatting with Ace and sometimes not.

Throughout his life, he was always amazed at how easy it was to win people over—all he had to do was be courteous, laugh at their jokes and assume a demure demeanor. Almost without fail, people trusted their ability to judge character. Many people would admit to being of only average intelligence, or to being bad with money, or to being unathletic. But he never knew anybody who admitted to being a bad judge of character.

Griffin, of course, knew how often they were wrong. In fact, he made a living from it. The only true way to judge someone was to see how they behaved in times of extreme pressure or stress. Did they cower in fear when faced with enemy fire? Did they share their rations when food was scarce? Did they spare an enemy soldier when he lay wounded and defenseless in the mud?

But if Ace wanted to warm to him because he was a loyal customer, laughed at Ace's jokes, and left a generous tip every morning, well, that was Ace's problem.

On a particularly slow morning at the donut shop, Griffin decided it was time to show one of his cards.

"Can I ask you a question?"

"Sure."

"Do you know who Metacomet is?"

"You bet. He was one of the Wampanoag chiefs back in the 1600s. You probably read about him in high school—his English name was King Philip. Why do you ask?"

"Well, I found some stuff buried in a hidden room of my house a few months ago. Some papers. And they keep referring to Metacomet's grave."

"Really? Nobody is sure where he's buried. Some of the old-timers say the tribe members used to go visit his grave every year, but nobody knows where it is anymore."

"That makes sense. These papers were from back in the 1800s. They look like some kind of Mashpee tribal records."

"Really? What kind of stuff?"

"It looked like minutes from the yearly meetings; what do you call them, powwows?"

"Yeah, believe it or not, that's actually a Wampanoag word. Pow-wow."

"The minutes talked about tribe elections, business decisions, ceremonies, that kind of stuff." Griffin could see Ace's eyes widen, knew that Ace understood that this might be exactly the evidence the tribe needed to pursue its lawsuit against the town.

But Ace played it cool, ran his hand along his ponytail. "Huh."

"If you want, the tribe can have the papers. Put 'em in a museum or something."

"Yeah, thanks. I'll talk to the other council members. Maybe we could use them. Bring 'em down next time you come, I'll take a look at them."

Chapter 14

[June]

Griffin didn't want to bring the papers into the donut shop—some slob was likely to spill coffee on them. And he preferred that the neighbors not see him meeting with Ace in his home. So he suggested that Ace come by the gift shop one afternoon to look at the tribal papers.

Meeting at the gift shop reminded Griffin of his practice as a child of not bringing playmates to his house because he was embarrassed to have them meet Donald. Things had definitely changed—he used to hide Donald from his friends because he feared being teased. Now he paraded Denise around with him because it made him seem kind. It was a sign of his evolution as a manipulator; if he was going to be burdened with Donald and Denise as siblings, he might as well try to make the best of the situation.

That morning, he had taken the documents out of the safe deposit box and removed them from their plastic coverings. The last thing he wanted was for Ace to know that Griffin thought them valuable. But he knew they would be in safe hands—Ace would treat them gingerly once he realized their significance.

Griffin escorted Ace into a small storage room in the back of the shop, where he had set up a card table and a couple of chairs. He pulled the documents out of a brown paper bag and dropped them on the table in front of his anxious guest. Only eight months until his loan was due.

"See, each page is a summary for a different year. There's 61 entries, beginning in 1807 and going to 1867." Griffin wanted to make it clear to Ace that he knew exactly how many pages were in the collection and would quickly notice if any disappeared. "Take your time, read through them. Kind of interesting stuff."

He sat back and watched Ace thumb, ever more gently, through the documents. Ace could not hide his excitement. "I have to tell you, these documents would be of great value to the tribe. Historical value, I mean. We'd love to have them."

"Actually, what I was thinking was that I would give them to the baby. After all, he's going to be half Mashpee Indian. It might be a nice keepsake for him as he gets older and wants to explore his Native American heritage." Sometimes Griffin even amazed himself.

Ace blustered a response. "Hey, that would be a nice gesture. But would you mind taking extra care of them? Maybe put them in a safe deposit box or something? I'd hate to see them damaged."

"Of course. And one more thing I wanted to show you. I was wondering why these papers were hidden in my house, you know? And they kept talking about Metacomet's grave as being at the land of the smooth stones. Well, I remembered a mound of round stones on my land, out back behind the farmhouse. So I started looking around nearby, and I think I found Metacomet's grave. Want to see it?"

*   *   *

Ace dialed the number in Washington. He tried to do so as infrequently as possible—it seemed like these guys charged $500 just for saying hello. But he had learned that if you wanted to fight the White Man's government, you had to first hire the White Man's lobbyists.

He was connected to a hearty voice with a Texas accent. "Ace, old friend, how are you?"

Ace skipped the small talk—at $500 per hour, every six minutes of conversation with this guy cost the tribe 50 bucks. He had tried in the past to talk to some underling, but then he noticed he was being billed first for the original conversation with the underling, and then again for the time it took the underling to write a memo to the lobbyist, and then yet again for the time it took the lobbyist to read the memo. So it was cheaper just to rush through a conversation with the top guy.

"Actually, pretty good. I found some documents that I think could seal the case for us—historical papers that summarize tribe meetings for 61 years in the 1800s. They show the tribe making group decisions, having elections, that kind of stuff. They're exactly what you said we need to prove our case to the Bureau of Indian Affairs."

"Great. Send them on down. But remember, I can't guarantee how they'll rule. Those days ended when Clinton left office and that idiot over at BIA overruled his staff on a bunch of decisions on his last day in office."

"I understand...."

"But I can guarantee that they'll look at your application right away, put it on the top of the pile. That's how it works down here, that's what you pay me for. I can't change the decision, except maybe a little bit on the margins." He chuckled. "But without me, your application could sit down there for another decade without anybody so much as spilling coffee on it."

*   *   *

Bruce had been at the job for more than a month. He had expected that it would take him no more than two weeks to figure out what Griffin's plan was. Either he was rusty from inactivity, or this Griffin guy was a real master.

Bruce was seated around the kitchen table at Billy Victor's house with Billy and his parents. They were waiting for Shelby, Pierre and Carla. It would be cramped, but Billy's father wasn't up to traveling. Plus Bruce sensed that Pierre and Carla didn't really want him in their home.

Which was fine. For the last couple of weeks Bruce had been living in a small cottage behind the Victors' house. It was little more than a shack, but he had been living on a sailboat for the past seven years, so it wasn't exactly a hardship for him. Slowly he was getting used to being around people again; he even had eaten a few meals with Billy and his parents. The food was thick and hearty, but best of

156

all, Dominique Victor, Billy's mother, had some old pictures of summer powwows that included his grandfather.

She had laughed when Bruce first pointed him out. "That's your grandpa?" she had chuckled. "I was only a little girl at the time, but I remember how he used to take us all out sailing on the lake and then tip the boat over and make us swim to shore."

Bruce had laughed in turn. "He used to do the same thing to me when I was a kid. He loved to sail." He had felt the need to tell Dominique more about Grandpa. She had listened intently. "He used to say that the world was divided into two groups of people—ocean people, who were wild and creative and spontaneous, and continent people, who were solid and stable and hearty. But there were a few people who were the sailboats—creative and free-spirited like the ocean, but also stable and steady like the landmass. He always wanted me to be a sailboat."

Dominique had nodded, asked the obvious question. "And, are you?"

"No. I thought I was once, but I was just kidding myself."

She had reached over, patted his knee. "Or maybe you just ran aground...."

Whatever the truth, it had felt good—finally, after months here in Mashpee—to reconnect with his grandfather's past, to see the pictures, to hear the stories about him that Dominique remembered from her youth. Grandpa was really the only person Bruce had ever loved. Other than Shelby.

Shelby. Almost on cue the doorbell rang; Bruce could see her silhouette through the sheer curtain over the glass pane in the door, then her full face as Dominique opened the door and she glided in. Still as captivating as ever, her blue-green eyes firing out from behind dark lashes, her intensity chiseled into her high cheekbones and pursed lips and angular nose. But those features could quickly melt in a lighter moment, washed away by a wet smile and a pair of dancing eyes, her face radiating energy and warmth and life. Parisian runway model meets Princess Diana. He stood.

Shelby greeted Dominique warmly, nodded at Vernon and Billy. Then she lowered her eyes, spoke his name. "Bruce. Hello." She took a seat at one of the corners of the square table. Far from Bruce.

"Hi, Shelby," he said. He would have to win her back slowly, if at all. Hopefully today would be the first step.

Bruce began the meeting. It didn't surprise him that Pierre and Carla hadn't invited the other neighbors; as far as he knew, they didn't even know about him. Keeping them out of the loop was probably the right call—Bruce knew he was still a wildcard, still not completely trustworthy. In espionage parlance, he was a rogue agent. The fewer people that knew about him the better. And that was fine with him—it lessened the likelihood of someone blowing his cover.

He didn't need notes—his brain had been empty for years and easily accommodated and retained the information he had learned about Griffin. But first he wanted to make sure his 'clients' were being straight with him. "Before I tell you what I've learned, I need to know if any one of you had anything to do with beating up Griffin."

He studied Pierre and Carla, Billy and his parents, even Shelby. He saw no duplicity in any of their faces as they looked back at him blankly. He waited a few more seconds, then continued. "Well, the guy who beat him up was a professional. So somebody hired him."

Not surprisingly, Pierre challenged him. Bruce could tell Pierre the water was wet and Pierre would be skeptical. "How do you know?"

"I was there, watching."

Bruce waited for the next question, the obvious one. Carla asked it. "Did you try to help?"

"No. That would have blown my cover. But I chased the guy through the woods, tackled him. A professional, muscle for some leg-breaker up in Brockton. But he doesn't know who hired him. My guess is it's someone with a Mashpee address."

The statement hung in the air for a few seconds, then Pierre spoke. "When you say it would have blown your cover, do you mean you've been following him around?" Bruce noticed Pierre's question changed the subject.

"Sort of. What I'm really trying to do is learn Griffin's routine, so I don't have to follow him. It's a lot better to be waiting for him when he gets there, if you know what I mean. That's why I was in the woods that night—he always walks his dog at the same time. And apparently I wasn't the only one who noticed."

Shelby spoke. "All right. So what else have you learned?"

Dominique stood and pulled some soft drinks and a pitcher of lemonade out of the refrigerator. She poured while Bruce answered. "Well, let me start by saying I still haven't figured out what Griffin is up to. I just don't have enough pieces of the puzzle yet, partly because he's been in the hospital or in bed most of the last few weeks. But I do know one thing: He definitely is working off of some intricate blueprint."

"Why do you say that?" Dominique looked at him intently, her eyes trying to read him. She had been studying him in that manner for the past month. Bruce's sense was that she was used to being able to judge people's character, but still hadn't figured out Bruce's. Which made sense, since he was in the process of totally redefining himself. There was nothing to judge yet.

"A couple of reasons. First of all, this guy leaves nothing to chance; he doesn't have an impulsive bone in his body. I spent all of last week reading through the court cases he's been involved in over the past five years—do you know there's over 50 of them?"

Carla responded. "I'm not surprised."

"Anyway, if you read through the cases, you can see that Griffin was planning the lawsuits from the very beginning. Most lawsuits are the result of something going wrong—you slip on the ice and fall, a car rear-ends you, a contractor has cash-flow problems and can't finish the job, stuff like that. But with Griffin, everything was calculated. He'd look for the icy spot to slip on, look for the banana peel in the supermarket."

Pierre interjected. "Or, in our case, he looked for an out-of-town buyer who wouldn't be around to keep an eye on the construction."

Bruce nodded. "Right. My bet is that he never planned on finishing your house. From the beginning, he knew you'd take it 'as is' because you had no choice. So, with a guy like this, I have trouble believing that anything he does is just by chance. Nothing is impromptu. There's no way he'd invite Billy over for pizza on a Friday night just because his sister was lonely. It just wouldn't happen. He had something planned from the beginning, and based on the strip club and the beer and the Ecstasy and the porn tapes, it's pretty obvious his plan was for something to happen between Billy and Denise. I don't know if he just wanted to blackmail Billy somehow, or he was taking videos of them, or if he really wanted her to get pregnant. But it wasn't an accident."

Dominique nodded, affirming Bruce's conclusion. A bit of vindication for her boy. Bruce saw her reach down and squeeze her son's knee under the kitchen table, then she spoke. "You said you had a couple of reasons for concluding he had some plan. What's the other one?"

"Right. The whole settlement with Carla and Pierre and all their neighbors doesn't make sense. He had no reason to do that, at least not yet. Shelby was working on some stuff that may have gotten the cases consolidated, and maybe at that point he would have been willing to settle, but his whole m.o. is to make people spend as much money on legal bills as he can before he settles. So why not force Shelby to spend another ten or twenty grand in legal time? Why settle when he did? Again, I don't know why, but whatever the reason, it's part of a bigger plan that I haven't figured out yet."

Shelby spoke for the first time. "So what information are you missing, what pieces of the puzzle are you still looking for?"

He had hoped she would keep talking. That way he would have an excuse to continue staring at her. But she was done, and it was his turn to speak. He wondered if Dominique noticed the way he looked at Shelby. He smiled to himself—of course she noticed. She noticed everything. He was beginning to learn that a Medicine Woman was as much an expert in matters of the mind and spirit as in those of the body. Or maybe they were just all connected.

Bruce answered Shelby's question. "What I don't have yet is some kind of link between what's happening with Billy and his sister on the one hand, and all the lawsuits with the neighbors on the other. My gut tells me there is one, but I don't know what it is."

Billy's mother and father exchanged a long glance. Vernon nodded, and Dominique turned to address the group. "I think we may know what that link is. But I need you all to promise the information will not leave this room." Dominique paused, watched as Shelby, Carla and Pierre all nodded. She turned to Bruce, who nodded as

160

well. She eyed him for a minute, gauging his sincerity, then, seemingly satisfied, continued.

Dominique stood, paced slowly around the small kitchen as she spoke. "Thank you. We had a tribal council meeting a couple of nights ago and Ace Awry—he's one of the council members—was all excited about finding some documents that he thinks will help the Mashpee tribe take the land back from the town."

Carla interjected. "I thought that case was already over."

Dominique nodded. "Most people think that. We went all the way to the Supreme Court, and lost. But the case itself was never heard; we got thrown out of court before we ever got to present our case. You see, what happened was that before our case could be heard we had to prove we were still an Indian tribe, and had been since the early 1800s. The town was arguing that we..., the term they used was that we had 'abandoned our tribal identity.' So we had to prove that we hadn't disbanded the tribe. Well, it's a lot like answering the question, 'When did you stop loving your children?' The answer is never, of course. But how do you prove something like that?

"It really was ridiculous—every one of us grew up with the burden of being a minority in this country. We all heard the war cries when we were kids. We all had to listen to the comments about smoking peace pipes and scalping people and doing rain dances. We all were called 'Half-breed' and 'Indian Giver' and 'Honest Injun.' But, hey, it was okay because we had our heritage, we were proud to be Native Americans. But then to have some lawyer stand up in court and tell the jury that we weren't really Indians.... Well, then, what are we? We have to be something, don't we? It just defied common sense."

Shelby nodded. "I remember reading about this case in law school. Wasn't part of the problem that the tribe didn't have any written records?"

"That was a big part of it. We didn't have the same kind of formalized government that Western societies use; we governed ourselves more informally, through consensus and general agreement. So we didn't have a lot of the governmental records that would prove to the court we were governing ourselves like a tribe."

"But wouldn't that be true of most tribes? How did all the others prove their legitimacy?"

Dominique nodded. "Good question. The problem really only comes up with the tribes on the east coast. The eastern tribes were all recognized by the *state* governments before the Revolutionary War, and that's who we signed treaties with. Congress never bothered to officially recognize us because nobody thought it was necessary— they had taken all our lands already, so what more needed to be agreed to? But, after the Revolution, as the country spread west, the new tribes that the settlers encountered were officially recognized by Congress. They had to be so that treaties could be signed."

Shelby spoke. "So it really is just a question of timing. It has nothing to do with which tribe is legitimate or not."

"Exactly." Dominique paused here, shook her head. "But, anyway, we did have some stuff, some church records and other records the state made us keep. And that's when the lawyers took over. When we produced those records, the town's lawyers held them up as evidence that we had assimilated into mainstream society and abandoned our tribal practices. 'Look,' they said, 'the tribe had adopted Christianity and Western forms of government. They had rejected their Indian ways.' The whole thing was absurd—we were forced to assimilate by the state and the missionaries, and then it was used against us, as evidence that we had abandoned our tribal identity."

Shelby nodded again. "So what you really needed was some records kept by the tribe, but not stuff that the town could argue showed you had assimilated."

"Right. And that's what Ace claims he's found. He says he's got minutes from 61 years of tribal powwows from the 1800s. Stuff that shows tribal elections and ceremonies and historical events."

Shelby interrupted. "I'm a little confused. If the case has already been decided, what good would these records be?"

Dominique again paused, as if considering whether to answer this question. "I'll let you all figure out the legalities. But Ace thinks these records will help us re-open the case."

The room was silent for a few seconds. This was an interesting piece of information, but Bruce still didn't see the connection to Rex Griffin. "So how does Griffin fit into all this?"

Dominique turned to face him. She lowered her voice. "Who do you think gave Ace Awry the records?"

More silence, then nods. Dominique continued. "And it gets better. Ace also says Griffin showed him a gravesite. Says that Metacomet is buried there—you all might know him as King Philip. He was the Wampanoag chief who led the Indian fight against the Colonists back in the 1600s. If it really is his grave, it would be an extraordinary find."

Carla spoke. "Where is the gravesite?"

Dominique focused her large dark eyes on Carla. "Go home and look out your back window."

*   *   *

Dominique walked her guests to the front door, then stood and listened to the sounds of the summer night. Her husband was dying of cancer. Her son had been drugged and then bred to a mentally impaired woman. And now her tribe and her town were on the verge of a battle that would likely tear apart the community.

And yet the sounds of the night continued, blissfully ignorant of the turmoil in the world of the humans.

She listened for a few more minutes, then sighed and re-entered her home.

Vernon had fallen asleep on the couch, exhausted from the night's exertion. She draped him with a blanket, kissed his cheek. It wouldn't be long now—this kind, decent horse of a man she had married had outlived the doctors' predictions, but the battle had left him weak and spent.

It was now Billy's time.

As if sensing his mother's thoughts, Billy walked silently into the kitchen and sat down at the table.

Dominique sat opposite him, looked deep into the dark eyes of her only son. He held her gaze, steady and serene. A boy with a man's problems. And responsibilities.

"My boy, my son, I need your advice."

Billy nodded, still silent.

"We are at a time of change, a time of confusion. Your father will soon die, perhaps before your baby is born."

Billy nodded again.

"But there's more. The tribe, I'm afraid, will soon be at war with itself. And at war with the townspeople."

"Because of the documents that Ace Awry found?"

"Yes, because of that, and greed. You weren't even born when we went through this the first time. But it was a nasty fight. The way the townspeople saw it, we were trying to take their land, their homes. In our minds, we were just trying to take back what was ours. There's still some bad blood, almost 20 years later."

"I know. I hear it sometimes from guys on the hockey team."

Dominique nodded. She was a school nurse; she heard what the kids said, knew how cruel they could be. "But what you don't hear about is the divisions that almost tore apart the tribe. Many of us were not in favor of the action the tribe took."

"Why not?"

She spent a moment organizing her thoughts. "Well, there were really three reasons. The first had to do with fairness. It's a bit ironic, actually. For centuries the government took our land, but they always made sure to do it 'legally,' by buying it from us or signing a treaty with us. Then, later on, when we argued that the land was taken from us unfairly, they waved the documents in our face. 'A deal's a deal,' they would say. As if that somehow made it moral and just and fair and decent.

"But in Mashpee, for once, the government really was trying to do the right thing. Back in the 1800s, the state appointed overseers to govern our affairs. Of course, they were stealing from us left and right. So the tribe members pushed to have the tribal lands deeded to the people, so the land wouldn't be held in a reservation anymore. Why, they argued, should we not be given the same rights to own land as other Massachusetts residents? And the state actually agreed. They let us incorporate as a town, let us govern ourselves, let us own the land as individuals. With dignity."

"So how could we sue?"

"Well, as it turns out, back in 1790-something, Congress passed a law that said only Congress can make land deals with the tribes. States can't. So our lawyers were arguing that the original decision by the state of Massachusetts to break up the reservation and give the land to the tribe members was illegal. And since it was illegal, all the land should go back to the tribe and be considered reservation land again." She smiled. "That was the irony of the situation—what we were asking for may not have been fair, but it was the law."

"How much land was it?"

"All of Mashpee, every acre. At one point, the tribe members owned everything in town. Over the years, of course, people sold stuff off, and that's why there's been so much development."

"So the tribe was trying to get back everything?"

"That's right. Homes, stores, restaurants, beaches, everything. It was all originally part of the reservation. But, as I said, to some of us the whole thing didn't seem right. Sure, it was nice to use the law against the government for once. But that didn't make it right. Remember, it was the tribe that originally asked the state to let us divide the land among our members. It's almost like we were admitting that we weren't sophisticated enough to handle the land ourselves, that the state shouldn't have trusted us with it to begin with. To me, it seemed like the whole case rested on the argument that the state should have been protecting us from ourselves. I had trouble with that argument. Still do."

"But the tribe still sued."

Dominique nodded, rested her hands on the table. "Yeah, we did. Things sort of got away from us. Originally we just wanted to negotiate something with the town, maybe get some land for some parks and a few bucks from the title insurance companies. But things got pretty heated, pretty fast. Next thing you know, we were in court." Dominique smiled at her son. "The whole town. Cowboys on one side, Indians on the other."

"Sounds like some B-movie."

Dominique shook her head. "Actually, it was a miserable time. A few of the town residents supported us, but mostly people thought we were trying to steal their homes. Can't say that I blame them—in some ways, we were. There was a lot of anger, a lot of hatred. Which was the second reason some of us didn't want to sue. We knew it would tear the town apart. And it did. Friendships ended, neighbors stopped talking, people switched churches. They boycotted our businesses, so a lot of our people went bankrupt. It was ugly. Even a few marriages broke up."

"Over a lawsuit?"

"This was more than just a lawsuit. People really thought they were going to lose their homes, their businesses. We never would have pushed it that far, but they didn't know that." She paused for a second. "At least, I don't think we would have pushed it that far. I don't think we would have been that stupid."

"What do you mean?"

"See, what nobody understood was that we only filed the suit to get a settlement from the title insurance companies. We never wanted to have all the land put back into a reservation."

"Why not?"

"Because that kind of decision from the court would apply to everyone, including us. This house we're living in right now would have become tribal property. Same with Ace Awry's donut shop, though I'm not sure he's thought that far ahead. Basically, everything in Mashpee would become part of the reservation. Including anything owned by tribe members. Nobody wanted that. So that was another reason why some of us didn't want to file the lawsuit."

"But, Mom, it might have been worth it. For the tribe, I mean. If we won."

Dominique looked hard at her son. "Why do you say that?"

"Well, there are a lot of poor people in our tribe. The money would come in handy."

Dominique stood up, walked over to a door and pulled out an accordion file. Inside she pulled out a stack of newspaper articles, thumbed through them until she found the one she was looking for. She handed it across to Billy. "Read this later. It's an article about a tribe in California that suddenly got very rich from opening a casino. I'm talking huge amounts of money—maybe a couple hundred thousand per year for every tribe family. Well, next thing you know, they're fighting over it. One guy runs for chief, runs against his first cousin. When he wins, he re-writes the tribe's constitution so that his cousin no longer qualifies to be part of the tribe. Same amount of Native American blood, but now the cousin has been kicked out, excommunicated. So the cousin sues, says he's as much Native American as everyone else. Know what the court says?"

"What?"

"Says the tribe is a sovereign nation, so the court has no jurisdiction over it. Says it's totally up to the tribe to decide who its members are."

"So what happened to the cousin?"

"He gets nothing. The tribe's got millions, but he's on welfare. And half the tribe's not talking to the other half."

"You think that could happen in Mashpee?"

Dominique nodded. "No doubt. We file that suit again, it'll be Cowboys and Indians all over again. And if the Cowboys don't kill us, we'll likely kill ourselves."

*   *   *

Ace Awry had been awestruck when Griffin brought him to Metacomet's grave. Griffin wasn't much for sentiment, but he remembered being impressed when, as a boy, he had visited George Washington's home on a school field trip. For a Wampanoag Indian, whose recent history was marked by three continuous centuries of being defeated and subjugated by the European settlers, Metacomet was war hero and father of his country rolled into one. Even if he did eventually lose the war.

Ace's awed reaction to the grave was a crucial part of Griffin's plan. It was essential that Ace, and, later, the other Mashpee Indians, become emotionally attached to the gravesite. Griffin had researched the matter—unfortunately, the Mashpee band of the Wampanoag tribe had not fought alongside the other regional Indian tribes and had instead maintained neutrality during King Philip's War. So, technically, the Mashpees' ancestors had never even followed Metacomet into battle. But would these details matter over 300 years later, even if they were known? Probably not. Griffin expected that the tribe would take pride in their Wampanoag forefather's spirited attempt to defend the Native American tribes from the invading Colonists.

In fact, his plan depended on it. The 19th century tribal documents were merely the bait he had dangled in front of the tribe, an attempt to appeal to their economic interests by providing them the means to re-open their land claims case. But, as his plan had evolved, the real payoff for Griffin hinged on the tribe's interest in re-claiming and preserving Metacomet's gravesite and surrounding area. If their interests were merely economic, and not spiritual, they would be indifferent to the gravesite and Griffin would fail. But, at least based on the way Ace had stood reverentially at the edge of Metacomet's grave, Griffin was hopeful he had snagged a hook in the Mashpee tribe's heart as well as its wallet.

Too bad for the subdivision neighbors that their houses happened to be in the way. In Vietnam, they had a term for harm caused to innocent bystanders: collateral damage. The euphemism was typical of the military, but the term aptly described the loss the neighbors would suffer when they lost their homes. Though, in some cases, they weren't so innocent. But that would all flesh itself out later.

For now, Griffin pulled out a couple of old law books he had found in the library and sat down to work at his computer. He had never drafted a trust document before, but, other than a few key terms and provisions that needed to be tailored to the particular situation at hand, the language of the standard trust document had changed little over the centuries.

He entitled the document, "The Griffin Family Trust," and named himself as the sole trustee. As trustee, Griffin would control the trust, but he would not be entitled to any of the assets or income earned from the trust, which was technically owned by the trust's beneficiaries. It was like a corporation—Griffin was the President and Chairman of the Board, and he therefore made all the decisions, but the shareholders were entitled to all the dividends.

Griffin first named his brother Donald as the beneficiary holding 49% of the trust. For the remaining 51% beneficiary, he wrote, "The oldest of any living child, born or unborn, of Denise Griffin, if any; otherwise Denise Griffin." He couldn't name the unborn baby as a beneficiary yet, but he wanted to make it clear that, once born, the baby would have a 51% interest in The Griffin Family Trust. He had toyed with making the baby the 100% beneficiary, but there was always the risk that Billy and his family would try at a later date to gain custody of the baby. And his assets. If they were to succeed, it would be better to lose half the loaf than the whole thing.

Not that it really mattered who the beneficiaries were—Griffin treated anything that accrued to his brother or his sister as his own. It would be the same with the baby, so long as Billy's family kept out of the way. But, in the eyes of the law, the written document was paramount. It was one of the few good things about having such a nut job family: he could place assets in his brother's and sister's names and away from his creditors, yet never lose control of the assets themselves.

Next he prepared a short gift letter. He, Rex Griffin, was gifting to the trust the Mashpee historical documents he had found. The result of all this was that, once the baby was born, the child would own a 51% interest in the trust and, by extension, the tribe's historical documents. All thanks to dear Uncle Rex.

Chapter 15

[July]

The neighbors met, again at Ronnie Lemaire's house. The mood at the original meeting had been one of unified rage—they had all been wronged by the demon, Griffin.

Tonight their feelings were more complex. One of them, presumably, had hired someone to beat the demon practically to death.

Ronnie had ringed the large living room with seats, perhaps 35 in all. In addition to the stark white living room furniture, he had brought in an assortment of cherry dining room chairs and yellow metal kitchen chairs and green plastic deck chairs and chrome bar stools, most of which clashed with the thick black and white carpet. There were actually far more seats than bodies, which allowed people to keep their distance from their neighbors. Not that anyone felt much sympathy toward Griffin, but the fact that one of the people in the room may have caused such a beating was disquieting.

And, perhaps more worrisome, many feared that the beating might provoke Griffin into further escalating the violence. It was July in one of America's premier vacation spots, yet most of the neighbors rarely ventured from their dead-bolted homes.

Pierre looked around the room. Nobody met his glance—in addition to their edginess, almost everyone was angry with him for scuttling the settlement. It had been, at least on its face, a good deal. Now it was a good dead deal.

He had tried to explain himself to each of the neighbors—they were, for the most part, polite. Then they asked if he'd reconsider. By the time he had spoken to the sixth or seventh neighbor, he'd almost agreed to bend to the will of the majority. But then he looked into Carla's eyes, realized what he'd be risking by bowing to the neighbors' pressure. They were his neighbors, but she was his wife. Maybe they'd even thank him someday.

But they definitely weren't thanking him tonight. To make matters worse, over the past week each subdivision resident had been served with a new lawsuit from Griffin. In it, he alleged that the neighbors had conspired to hire someone to assault him. The suit recounted Griffin's various injuries, related the history of bad blood between him and the neighbors, detailed how the residents had joined together to oppose him, and requested damages of tens of millions of dollars. To make sure he could eventually collect his damages, he had requested that the court immediately grant him attachments on the neighbors' properties and freeze their bank accounts. Shelby had said that they could probably defeat Griffin's request to freeze the bank accounts and attach the property, and likely would eventually be able to get the case dismissed. Unless, of course, Griffin could prove that one of them really did mastermind the attack. In any event, it would keep a boatload of law firms busy for a few years. At $250 per hour.

So here they all sat, back at square one, looking at the floor and fiddling with their pens. But they were here nonetheless, joined in their battle against Griffin. *The enemy of my enemy is my friend,* Pierre thought. *But that doesn't mean I should trust him.*

Ronnie Lemaire stood, sighed. "All right. Here we are again. Carla, I know you had some stuff you wanted to tell us. But before that, anybody else got any news?"

A thin, middle-aged woman in a sundress cleared her throat. She was a dentist from New York, only here in the summer and an occasional holiday weekend. "Well, this Griffin fellow has succeeded in ruining our credit. We went to refinance our mortgage, and, what with all these lawsuits he filed against us, we got turned down cold."

Another hand went up. The preppy guy who was doing okay on the professional golf tour. "Same thing happened to us. Got turned down for a car loan."

Justin responded to the comments. "I think we can all expect that our credit has been affected by all the litigation. Banks don't like to lend money to people who might end up bankrupt."

Amisha shook her head, sighed. "This is all just too much. Maybe we should all just sell our homes and move away from here."

Justin turned, smiled kindly at her. "I'm sorry, my dear, but you can't even do that. Griffin may not be able to put attachments on our properties right now, but as soon as you put the 'For Sale' sign up on your house, he'll run to court and convince the judge to give him the attachment. And you can't sell with an attachment. Even without the attachments, it sounds like none of us would be able to get a mortgage to buy another home anyway. It seems to me that we're all stuck here until things are settled with Griffin."

Pierre turned to Carla, winced. Attachments on their homes, ruined credit—more reasons to be angry at Pierre for scuttling the settlement.

Justin's comments hung in the air for a few seconds, then Ronnie looked across the room at Carla. "Carla, you have something...."

Pierre and Carla had agreed that she would be the better choice to address the group. She remained on her bar stool, legs crossed, her long denim skirt hanging almost to the floor. "Thanks, Ronnie. First of all, I know that many of you don't agree with our decision to reject the settlement."

Amisha jumped in, challenging. Even in a green plastic chair she seemed exotic and glamorous. "It was a bit odd, Carla. You were the one who was championing its cause for the longest time." Pierre knew that Amisha's husband, Rajiv, was still battling with the SEC on the insider trading charges. Plus, Amisha and Rajiv had come out of pocket to cover the losses their friends and family had suffered by following Griffin's e-mailed stock tip. Close to $100,000. And Rajiv's company, like most others, was taking a beating in the stock market. So it was not surprising that she was a bit edgy.

Carla nodded. "I know. But I don't want to rehash that tonight. We've got some other information we thought you all should know. It might even make some of you come around to our way of thinking."

Amisha nodded a cautious consent. Carla continued. "One of the reasons we weren't comfortable with settling with Griffin is that it never made sense that he would want to settle in the first place. That's what Ronnie was saying all along."

Ronnie responded. "Look, I may not have fancy degrees like a lot of you have, but I happen to be a World War II nut. And what Griffin is trying to do reminds me of Hitler signing that treaty with Stalin. He knew he would turn around later and whack Russia, but first he needed to buy some time so he could attack to his west. So he made that deal with Stalin."

Carla nodded. "That's what we were thinking with Griffin. The only reason he would want to settle is so that he could buy some time while he focused on something else. Well, we think we've figured out what that something else is...."

Justin McBride leaned forward in his chair. "We're listening."

Carla sighed. "This is complicated, and I want to present it clearly." She looked down at some notes she had prepared. "Okay, this all starts back in the seventies when the Mashpee Indian tribe filed a lawsuit against the town. They were trying to get back all the land in Mashpee. The entire town."

Justin nodded. "They lost that case. Took it all the way to the Supreme Court, if I recall correctly."

"You're right, Justin—the tribe did lose the case. But we think Griffin has found a way for them to file the case again."

Justin looked at Carla skeptically, arched one bushy eyebrow. "Once you lose in front of the Supreme Court, that's it, you've lost."

Carla was less than comfortable arguing legal points with Justin, especially because her promise to Dominique meant she couldn't reveal any of the details of Griffin's discovery. But she took a deep breath and plowed ahead. "We asked Shelby to look at this for us, and she says the case was never really decided. It was just thrown out on a technicality."

The old lawyer sat back, closed his eyes for a few seconds. "I wouldn't call it a technicality, but, yes, the case was thrown out before the tribe's actual claim was heard. If I remember correctly, it was an issue of standing—the tribe first had to prove that it really was an Indian tribe before the court would hear the case. And they couldn't prove it."

Carla continued. "Right. Well, with Griffin's help, Shelby thinks that they've got a good chance to re-file the case. I'm sorry, but I can't tell you any more that that." Dominique had authorized her to give only the most basic details to the group, nothing more.

Justin leaned forward in his chair. He seemed willing to accept Carla at her word. For now, at least. "Well, that would be a huge development." He lifted himself off the edge of the easy chair, moved around behind it and rested his hands on the back. "Absolutely huge. Everyone thinks that case is dead. But if the tribe can re-file, they've got a real good chance of winning. I don't remember the details of their original claim, but I remember that we all thought they had a better than 50-50 chance of winning if they could get the case heard."

Ronnie Lemaire cut in, his tanned arms folded tightly across his thick chest. "Now wait a second. I happen to be a member of the Mashpee tribe—my mother is half-Indian. And I was around during that first lawsuit. I thought it was a crock, and I wanted nothing to do with it. You don't sue your neighbors and try to take their homes, not if you have half a brain."

Justin broke in, smiling. "Or unless your name is Rex Griffin." Ronnie chuckled. "Right. But anyway, that case is over. The tribe lost. End of story."

Justin responded. "The tribe did lose, Ronnie. But I think Carla might be right. The case was never really decided—the tribe could re-file."

"All right then, so maybe the tribe re-files—and by the way, I haven't heard anything about that—and everyone fights it out in court again. I always figured the state would have to kick in some money to settle the whole thing anyway, if it ever got to that point. I mean, it was never about the land. It was always about the money. But here's my question—where does Griffin fit in with all of this? I have a little trouble believing he's just trying to help out the tribe just because he's a good guy, you know?"

Slowly everyone's head turned to Carla for an answer. "Well, here's where it gets really interesting. Turns out that one of the old Indian chiefs from the 1600s is buried right over there." Carla pointed out the window, toward Griffin's farmhouse. "Right between Griffin's house and our house."

Pierre could see Ronnie's face soften. "Really? Right back here? Which chief is it?" He may have opposed the tribe when it filed the lawsuit, but he apparently still identified with the tribe's culture and history.

Pierre figured it would be okay for him to jump in now. His refusal to sign the settlement was ancient history in light of the newest Griffin news. "Metacomet is his Native American name. We learned about him in school as King Philip."

"No way," Ronnie said. "Metacomet's buried in your backyard? You're shitting me." He grinned at Pierre, shook his head in disbelief. "Unbelievable. Metacomet...."

There were a few whispers as spouses and friends explained to each other who King Philip was. Most of them, if they recognized the name all, probably thought he was a European monarch of some kind, not a Native American. So Pierre wasn't surprised that they didn't share Ronnie's enthusiasm.

Pierre addressed Ronnie's question. "Well, if you believe the survey markers, the grave's technically on Griffin's land. But I paced it off. According to our plot plan, it looks like the grave sort of straddles our property and his. Not that I think Griffin would ever move the lot markers around or anything...."

Ronnie interrupted. "How do you know it's Metacomet?"

"The tribe had some expert up here looking at the grave. Based on the stuff they found buried with him, they're pretty sure it's him. Plus, the head and body were buried separately, which makes sense if it was Metacomet. The stuff I read says he was beheaded and his head was displayed on a pole in Plymouth after he was killed."

Ronnie nodded. "Holy shit." He sat back, stared out the window in the direction of the gravesite.

Amisha shrugged her shoulders. "I don't see the connection between this dead King Philip and our all-too-alive Rex Griffin. Though it might not be a bad idea to bury one Rex next to the other...."

Justin McBride was clearly amused by the word play, but how many others knew that 'Rex' was the Latin word for 'King'? Luckily, Pierre had been reading the girls a book about Tyrannosaurus Rex. He continued. "I'm not exactly sure of the connection either,

Amisha. But here's one more piece of information to add to the puzzle. You've all seen Griffin's sister, right?"

A few nods, but also some blank looks. Not surprising—Griffin rarely let her out of the house. "Well," Pierre explained, "Griffin has a sister named Denise who lives with him. She's mentally retarded, probably about 25 years old. I'll spare you the details, but Griffin arranged to get her pregnant by a 16-year-old kid who worked for him in his gift shop. The kid is a Mashpee Indian."

A number of voices filled the room. The one Pierre heard most clearly was Ronnie's wife, Loretta. "He pimped his sister? What a sick bastard." She turned to her husband, her dark hair flying. "You know what? You go right ahead and kick his ass if you want. I won't stop you."

As Loretta spoke, Pierre noticed Justin grope for a glass of water and swallow it greedily.

Ronnie smiled sadly at his wife, turned to Pierre. "Who's the boy?"

"Billy Victor."

Ronnie nodded. "Good kid. Nice family."

"The problem," Carla concluded, "is that we still haven't figured out how to connect all the dots. But it seems pretty obvious that Griffin is going to help the Mashpees in their lawsuit. Beyond that, who knows? Maybe he gets money, maybe he gets land...."

Ronnie stood up. Pierre could see the veins throbbing in his neck and along the side of his bald head as he spoke through clenched teeth. "Well, I'll tell you one thing. He's not getting my money. And he's not getting my land. And I'll be damned if that son-of-a-bitch thinks he's going to use Metacomet's grave to help him line his pockets."

*   *   *

Griffin woke even before the summer sun had crested on the horizon. Actually, to be accurate, he had been awake most of the night and got out of bed early. And even that was not entirely accurate—he no longer slept in a bed, but rather on a mattress he had dragged onto the flat portion of the farmhouse roof. He simply found the walls of his bedroom too confining.

But even sleeping outside on the roof, he had been plagued the past few weeks with nightmares—all with the same theme. Locked in a cage. Trapped in a cave. Stuck in an elevator. Buried alive. He knew it was his subconscious revolting against the ever-growing possibility of being confined to a jail cell.

It was time for one of his bi-monthly visits to Donald, this time without Denise. The $2 million loan was due in seven months. And, if anything, the stakes had increased for him over the past few months. He needed to pay off the loan to stay out of jail, of course. That was paramount. But he also needed to retain control of the farmhouse property in order to barter Metacomet's grave to the Indians. And if he didn't pay off the mortgage, he would lose the property.

On the one hand, jail and destitution. On the other, freedom and a small fortune. Even Donald could get this one right.

But he had some work to do to get there. According to Justin, the neighbors had begun to suspect that Griffin's plan went beyond simply terrorizing them for economic gain. They hadn't figured it out yet, and he wasn't about to share his plan with Justin, but it had finally occurred to them that they might be caught in the middle of something that went beyond a few measly lawsuits.

Unfortunately for them, Pierre Prefontaine's refusal to make a deal with the devil now meant they might all have to go through Hell.

Griffin killed a couple of hours doing paperwork, then hopped into his truck, headed toward Boston. The old pickup had no air conditioning, so he opened the windows against the July heat. Most of the traffic was coming on-Cape, so, once he fought his way through Mashpee and onto Route 6, he moved freely along. He drove almost mechanically, the sights and sounds of the highway barely registering in his consciousness as his mind worked through the details of his plan for the next hour. Like all plans, it had evolved, grown, mutated. He had originally hoped to simply broker a deal between the Indians and the neighbors—the tribe would get Metacomet's grave and a fat check from the title insurance companies, the neighbors would get out from under the mountain of lawsuits Griffin had buried them in, and he would walk away with a pile of money for putting the whole thing together. All before his mortgage came due.

It would have been a good deal. A deal everyone could have lived with–and one nobody would have had to die for.

Now, unfortunately, it looked like the deal itself was dead. There was no way Pierre would sign off on it, no way Pierre would agree to anything that involved Griffin walking away with a pile of money. And Metacomet's grave was partially on Pierre's land, so his cooperation–voluntary or coerced–was essential.

The problem was that it had become personal with Pierre, had become a matter of pride and principal. And hatred. Griffin knew– from experience–that there was often a high price to pay for making enemies, and he had made one in Pierre. Now, unfortunately, he would have to pay that price.

It was time for Plan B.

Griffin had called ahead so the staff could warn Donald of the visit and prepare him for the change in his routine. He wasn't planning on staying long, and he didn't want to waste any time waiting for Donald to adjust to him.

Griffin let himself in, followed the familiar path to the television room. Donald was sitting in his hard chair, rocking, his good eye on the television set.

"Hello, Rex. These are my friends, Rex." Donald pointed in the general direction of his housemates. "That's Christopher. And that's Clark. And that's Russell."

"I know, Donald, I've met them before." The Rainbow Coalition. One was Asian, one Black, and one White, though Griffin had no idea which was which. Apparently, disability didn't discriminate on the basis of race. "I'd like you to take me to your room now, okay?"

Donald rocked in his chair for a moment, then let out a deep sigh as if struggling to maintain self-control. His show wasn't over yet, Griffin realized. "Not yet, Rex."

"Okay, Donald, but just a few more minutes. And while we're waiting, give me your glasses so I can clean them." Donald's glasses looked like something Buddy Holly wore back in the 1950s–thick plastic frames, large rectangular lenses, a wide nose bridge. He held them up to Rex, who pulled out his shirttail and wiped months worth of fingerprints and eyelash grease and dust off the lenses.

Donald's show ended and he pushed himself from his seat, accepted the glasses back from his brother. "My room's upstairs. Number 4."

"I know, Donald." For some reason Rex was particularly impatient with his brother today. He took a deep breath, followed Donald up the stairs and into a good-sized bedroom on the second floor, stopping in the doorway as Donald rubbed the doorframe before entering.

Griffin stepped into the room. He turned toward his brother. "Please get your social security checks, and also your ledger. You've been writing down everything you spend, right?"

"Yes, Rex. I'll get them for you, Rex." Donald opened his closet, dug for a small fishing tackle box tucked in the back. His movements, Griffin noted, were as they always had been—rigid, stiff, almost robotic. He opened the box, handed the checks and ledger to Griffin.

Griffin glanced at the ledger, nodded approvingly at the few dozen items entered in child-like lettering on the pages. "Good. You've done a good job conserving your money. Mother would have been very proud of you." Then again, other than ice cream, what was there for Donald to spend it on?

Griffin stood up. "Come on. Let's go to the bank."

They climbed into Griffin's truck. Donald fumbled with the keys for a few seconds, then found the ignition key and handed it to his brother. "Thank you, Donald," Griffin sighed.

They rode for a few minutes in silence, Donald rocking against his shoulder belt. Griffin noticed his own knuckles whiten, relaxed his grip on the steering wheel. "Why don't you tell me about what you've been doing, Donald, tell me about your days."

"I wake up at seven o'clock. Then I have my breakfast. I eat Fruit Loops with milk and a banana, except on the weekends we have pancakes...." Donald continued in a near-shout for another ten minutes until they arrived at the bank.

The teller recognized them, greeted them cheerfully. Griffin cashed Donald's checks, escorted his brother to one of the benches in the bank foyer. He handed his brother a stack of 50 singles. "This is for spending money. But don't spend it all." He then handed him a roll of quarters. "And this is for doing your laundry. But don't wash your clothes more than once a week, otherwise they'll get threadbare. And we don't have the money right now to buy you new ones." The remaining couple of thousand dollars he stuck in his pocket. Where none of his creditors—or enemies—could reach it.

They climbed into the truck, headed back to the old Victorian. Donald, rocking again, began identifying the cars parked along the side of the road. "1997 Toyota Camry; 1999 Nissan Pathfinder; 1997 Ford Taurus...."

Griffin started to ask him to stop, then had a thought. "Donald, do you still know all the cars?"

"Yes, brother."

"And can you still memorize license plates?"

"Yes, brother. Yours is CI2317."

Griffin nodded, smiled. "Excellent." Maybe Donald would be of some use after all.

Griffin parked the pickup, walked with Donald back to the group house. At the front door he accepted a quick hug from his brother, then snatched his keys out of Donald's hand and returned to his truck for the trip back to Mashpee.

*   *   *

Bruce sat in his car, spooning the last of a Hoodsie ice cream cup into his mouth with a wooden stick. Griffin had been gone from the old Victorian house for about ten minutes now. He had left with another man, but Bruce had elected not to follow. Griffin wasn't stupid—he probably wouldn't be aware of being followed on a major highway, but he might notice if a car pulled out behind him on a small side street and mirrored his path.

In some ways, trailing Griffin was like spying on himself. Or at least spying on the old Bruce, the one that plotted and schemed and cheated and stole. He didn't know enough about Griffin yet to understand the man's motivations, but he recognized the focused intensity of the man's pursuit. Like Griffin, Bruce had been on a quest to secure his fortune. Was Griffin's quest as misguided as his own had been?

Bruce had assumed that the money would fulfill him, would somehow fill the void of loneliness and despair that existed within him. As a child, he had compared his own dysfunctional family with those of his friends and neighbors. The difference? Theirs had money, his did not. It was a simple conclusion for a young boy to draw, and a difficult one for a young man to reject. Eventually, Shelby had shown him that he was wrong—it was not money that had been missing from his life. Just as it was not money that was missing today.

Unfortunately, by the time he had figured it all out, Pierre was in jail for a crime he didn't commit. And Bruce was a thousand miles out at sea in a sailboat, filled with more despair than ever before, exiled there by an incensed ex-lover who had declared him unfit to remain in civilized society. All in all, hardly a successful quest.

And, actually, he hadn't really figured it all out, even after seven years on the open seas. He knew that Shelby was the only thing that could fill that void within him. And he knew he would never choose any amount of money over her. But he still wondered why he couldn't somehow have both....

Bruce left his car and approached the house. If Bruce had his way, Griffin would fail in his own quest just as catastrophically as Bruce had.

He stopped on the porch to look at the mailbox. There were six names listed. The second one down caught his eye: "Griffin, Donald." Obviously, this was the man Griffin had left with.

Bruce walked back toward his car, slowed his step when he heard a couple of kids on scooters approaching. He smiled as they passed him. "Hey, who lives in that big yellow house over there?"

"A bunch of autistic guys. You know, like in that movie, *Rain Man*."

"Thanks." Interesting.

He waited another hour, watched from a distance as Griffin finally returned with his companion and parked his truck. The two men walked together up the front steps of the Victorian. Bruce thought about following, but Griffin had never seen his face and Bruce wanted to keep it that way. It was much easier to hunt prey that was blind to you. He would wait.

He didn't have to wait long. Griffin quickly returned to his truck and drove away. Bruce ambled back up the porch stairs, knocked on the door of the Victorian. The door swung open, but nobody came to greet him. He stood in the entranceway and yelled in. "Hello, hello. I'm looking for a Mr. Donald Griffin." It was likely that the man was related to Griffin. Could he be his son? His father? His brother?

Bruce heard someone yell for Donald, then watched as a figure descended stiffly down the staircase rising in front of him. He looked away for a second, and when he looked back he was face to face with a crew-cutted middle-aged man whom he assumed was Griffin's brother. The face was a bit fleshier, and the eyes not as furtive or intelligent—in fact one eye didn't seem to work at all. But there was no doubting the familial resemblance, right down to the small, brown teeth.

Donald stood, facing Bruce, impassive. Bruce tried to think of an excuse as to why he had come to visit Donald, realized it didn't matter. Donald would accept any reason he gave. "I'm sorry, I was looking for an old friend by the name of Donald Griffin. But you're not him."

Donald's one eye continued to stare back at him through thick, heavy glasses, so Bruce simply turned and left. "Sorry to bother you. Wrong Donald Griffin. Goodbye."

Donald remained silent for a few seconds, then called out to Bruce in a loud, flat-pitched voice as Bruce reached the bottom stair.

The shouted words stunned Bruce, saddened him, somehow reconnected him to both the richness and the despair that was the human existence. "My name is Donald Griffin. I can be your friend...."

Chapter 16

[August]

Billy reclined on his bed, lights off, music on. He had just finished a four-hour lunchtime shift waiting tables; now he had a couple of hours to kill before heading back for the dinner crowd. Despite working 60-hour weeks since school had ended, he didn't feel tired. It was tough work, but at least his boss didn't try to ruin his life.

He thought back to the previous summer. Before cancer and Ecstasy and pregnancy and Rex Griffin. Too young to get a real job, he had spent the summer mowing lawns for spending money. But mostly he had hung out at the beach with his friends, practicing his moves both on the girls and on his skateboard. The skateboard, at least, he had mastered.

It seemed like a lifetime ago. His father was the father and he was the son. Soon, his father would be dead and his child would be born. He would be the father.

Would he be as good at it as his dad had been? Sure, he was young. But if he loved the baby, and if Mom helped out, why couldn't he be a good dad? He would teach his boy to ride a bike, to catch a ball, to track a deer.

But, more to the point, would he have the chance to find out how good a dad he could be, or would Rex Griffin deny him even the opportunity to be a father to his baby? Griffin said he would allow Billy to have the baby on weekends, but could he really be trusted?

Billy spun onto his stomach, buried his head in his pillow. Somewhere out there his baby was growing in a womb. His baby, his own flesh and blood and genes and DNA. And the same monster that had drugged him and bred him like a farmyard animal could now be plotting to deny him the right to be a parent to the child. His child.

Billy lifted his head, got to his knees. There was no way anybody was going to keep him from his baby.

He pounded his fists into the pillow—left, right, left, right, over and over, scores of times, until he dropped back onto the bed, exhausted.

*　　*　　*

Outside Billy's bedroom, his father leaned heavily against the doorframe and heard the sounds of his son's anguish. Being sixteen was hard enough without having to be an adult at the same time.

He sighed, slid to the floor. He felt so feeble, so powerless. His family was under attack, and the most he could do was meet the enemy for coffee. And even that had wiped him out for the day.

But the prospect of near-term death was also somewhat liberating. All through life, he had believed that actions were followed, like a dog on its leash, by their consequences: smoking begets cancer, as he could attest to; laziness begets poverty; crime begets punishment.

But, now, with death imminent, he wondered if the equation was still valid. If he ate too much, would he really get fat? If he nodded off in church, would he really be chastised by the priest? If he killed a man, would he really go to jail?

*　　*　　*

Justin sat across the table from his son, tucked into a quiet corner of a trendy new Brookline restaurant Justin, Jr. had been raving about. It was a Thursday night, and the Boston area usually emptied out in August, but The Fireplace was packed. Fortunately the owner knew Justin, Jr. and had saved them a table overlooking Beacon Street.

He listened as his son spoke, tried to morph his anguished reaction into a look of joy and pride. "That's great, my boy! Just great.

184

You'll make a fine candidate, a fine Congressman. Your mother would have been very proud of you."

He tried to purge the image from his mind's eye, but the vision of his son—machine gun by his hip, firing into a crowd of women and children—never fully left his consciousness. Justin understood on an intellectual level how the pressures and terrors of war could make otherwise decent people commit savage deeds, and he tried not to judge his son, but he could never fully accept the fact that his own boy had been the author of such an atrocity. And his son had no idea Justin even knew of the massacre.

State Senator Justin McBride, Jr. lifted his drink, tilted it slightly to his father. "Thanks, Dad. I wanted to tell you first. We're holding a press conference tomorrow; that's why I wanted you to come up to Boston. I hope you can stay for it."

Justin eagerly put his drink to his lips, held it there to cover his face. If Griffin found out—and how could he not hear the news?—the blackmail would begin all over again. So far Griffin had been content to limit Justin's use to that of a mole, a double agent. But with a seat in Congress at stake, who knew what the fiend might demand in exchange for his silence?

And this latest news of Griffin breeding his sister to the Indian boy was utterly barbaric. Who would ruin two lives—plus that of the baby—merely for financial gain? The man had to be stopped.

Justin knew that he had already given too much to Griffin, had allowed himself to be used as some pawn in a complex chess match Rex Griffin was playing. And pawns could be easily sacrificed. But pawns could also checkmate an unsuspecting king.

*   *   *

Carla dragged a green plastic lawn chair off the deck, sat in the shade a few feet from the new cedar playground set they had just bought the girls. She watched the girls climb and slide and swing and hang, then closed her eyes and tried to let their joy and laughter wash away her despair.

No luck. But she painted a smile on her face, hoped the mask would fool the girls. No reason they should be haunted by the Griffin monster.

Carla watched the girls play. In the entire neighborhood, that swing set was probably the only island of joy. Griffin had effectively sucked the life and spirit from the subdivision.

She had just spoken to the bank. She and Pierre, like their neighbors, could not get a mortgage. Griffin's lawsuit had ruined their credit rating.

So, almost unbelievingly, they were in a financial predicament. When they had sold the property she had rescued from Bruce's scam, they had been left with almost $2 million after paying taxes. They had funded their retirement account and the girls' college funds, paid cash for a house, put a few hundred thousand into the stock market, and given the rest—close to a half million dollars—away to family and charity. Their feeling was that, without a mortgage and college and retirement to worry about, they would only have to earn enough to pay the weekly household expenses.

But they hadn't planned on the stock market crashing. And they hadn't planned on moving back to Massachusetts and paying $600,000 for a house. And they definitely hadn't planned on Rex Griffin. Already he had cost them over $100,000 to clean up Pepto-Bismol Pond, plus close to that again to rebuild their house. Not to mention legal fees. They owned the house without a mortgage, but now they couldn't even tap into that equity because of Griffin's lawsuit. And though they still had fat retirement accounts, Shelby had warned them that if they accessed them and converted them to cash that the money would be fair game for Griffin to go after.

The truth of the matter was that they were asset-rich and cash-poor. And even that would have been tolerable if their lives weren't so dreary. It was bad enough that Griffin tormented them on a daily basis, but she sensed that Pierre had begun to drift away from her over the past few months, especially since his refusal to agree to the settlement. She had tried to be supportive of his decision, but she knew he could hear her unspoken words: *This all would be behind us if you had just signed the settlement agreement.*

Not that she would ever voice those words. She knew how important it was to Pierre's psyche to win this battle. It had taken Pierre

186

half a decade to rebound from playing Pinocchio to Bruce's Gepetto. She and her girlfriends used to joke about it, but the male ego really was a fragile thing. Pierre was anything but a chauvinist, but that didn't mean he didn't pride himself on being able to support and care for his family.

But he had bounced back, started over again in Baltimore, re-established himself as an Alpha Male.

And then Griffin had bested him again, humiliated him. What was the phrase they used in boxing? *Slapped him silly.* That's what Griffin was doing to Pierre, slapping him silly. They all knew it, and it was making Pierre miserable.

✳ ✳ ✳

Griffin and Justin settled in to their regular booth at the Burger King in Plymouth. A young man wiped down their table, then moved a few feet away to empty the garbage bin.

Griffin noticed a glob of ketchup that had survived the wipe-down. It was the type of thing that drove him crazy: How could you miss a quarter-sized glob of red ketchup in the middle of a white table? He turned toward the worker. "Boy, you missed a spot here."

The young man apparently didn't hear him. Or was purposely ignoring him. Griffin read the worker's nametag, snarled at him in a low, steady voice. "I said, *Bruce*, that you missed a spot here. Clean it please. Now." It was the way he had to speak to his dog sometimes. It usually worked.

And it did this time as well. The young man scurried over, wiped up the spot, rubbed until it squeaked. "I'm sorry, sir."

Griffin nodded, watched as the worker fussed over the adjoining table as well. Griffin pulled at his bow tie, turned his attention to Justin. "Well, Justin, I see that Junior has set his sights on Congress. He'll fit right in with the other criminals, I'm sure." Griffin had worded his comment that way on purpose. His second sentence—by saying "he *will* fit in" rather than "he *would* fit in"—pre-supposed that Junior would, indeed, be elected. And that pre-supposed that Griffin would not sabotage the campaign. Justin was sharp—he would understand the implications of Griffin's words, would look past the aggressive tone Griffin had used to deliver the message. Sure, it would have been easier to be more direct with Justin. But this kind of nuanced message served to distract Justin, to keep him a bit off-balance.

Justin nodded his understanding, eyebrows flopping. "I'm glad to hear that you're still willing to honor our deal."

Griffin paused here, sipped from his coffee. What he was about to ask of Justin was not particularly onerous, but he wanted to make the old lawyer squirm for a few seconds. It would make him that much more likely to agree to the relatively painless request. He played with his coffee lid for a few seconds, then purposely dropped a few french fries on the floor and watched in satisfaction as the worker scampered over to sweep them up. He turned back to Justin. "As I've always said, I have nothing to gain by ruining Junior's political career. But I will expect a favor in return. In addition, of course, to your continued spying."

Griffin waited patiently for Justin to respond to his comment. Finally, Justin sighed deeply. "I'm listening."

"It's really not so bad. In fact, you may even like the idea. I wanted to talk to you about my mortality."

Justin cut him off. "You're right. I do like the idea. I'm all in favor of it."

Griffin smiled, nodded. He enjoyed the repartee with the bushy-eyed barrister. So much of his time was spent alone in thought, plotting and scheming. Or in the company of his sister, Denise. "Well, then, you'll be happy to know that I'm feeling particularly vulnerable right now. The recent attack on me has made me wonder whether it might happen again."

"So what is this, a deathbed confession? I've only got a couple of hours."

"Good one, Justin. But I don't need you to hear my confession. I need you to help me put my affairs in order."

"What do you mean by your affairs? Do you want me to sue your doctors after you die?"

"Another good one!" Griffin banged the table in mock appreciation. "No, I mean my siblings. I am the legal guardian for Denise and my brother, Donald. He's autistic, so they're both legally incompetent. I am also to be the guardian for Denise's baby. You know, don't you, that she is pregnant?"

"Yes, I heard about it. You're quite a little matchmaker. Sick, if you ask me."

Griffin bowed his head. "Yes, well, I admit it was far from my finest moment. But necessary, I assure you. In any event, if something happens to me, I need someone to be executor of my will, take care of Denise and her baby, act as their guardian, make sure the trusts I have set up for them are managed correctly. I know I might not strike you as a doting brother, and I know it might sound a bit maudlin, but I promised my mother before she died that I would take care of Donald and Denise. And, quite frankly, I'd rather see them get my money than have it fall into the hands of my creditors. We have an old family friend up in Maine who can be Donald's guardian, but Denise and the baby will need someone close by."

"You realize that you can't be the legal guardian for the baby until the baby is born and the court appoints you, right?"

"Yes. But the baby's father and his family have already agreed to it. My understanding is that the court generally will rubber stamp something like this."

"That's right. But they agreed to you being the guardian, not me."

Griffin smiled. "Do you think they'd really mind if I was out of the picture? They'd do cartwheels or smoke their peace pipes or whatever it is they do."

Justin shook his head. "I don't know, Griffin. I'd think anybody would be thrilled to have a Neanderthal like you responsible for their child."

"Well, be that as it may, what the Victors have actually agreed to is that the baby will have the same guardian as Denise, whether it's me or somebody else."

"What if I decide the baby would be better off living with the father?"

Griffin shrugged. "Personally, I don't really care where the baby lives, Justin. But I do ask that you take Denise's feelings into consideration. Otherwise, I just want to make sure the Victors don't get their hands on any of the trust money."

"I see. So, other than the small matter of blackmailing me into it, why choose me? It's a pretty obvious conflict of interest for me."

Griffin waved away the conflict comment with his hand, then dropped his eyes and lowered his voice. "Well, quite frankly, because I don't know anybody else I could ask. I had a bit of a disagreement with the attorney who use to handle my affairs...."

"Yeah, I bet."

"Anyway, you're a lawyer, so you're qualified to handle the job. And the court would definitely approve of you. And so would the Victors. Plus, you seem, for the most part, to be a man of integrity."

"Thanks for reminding me."

"You're right, perhaps integrity is too strong a word. What I really mean is that you're too old to chase girls or buy fast cars, so I trust you won't need to steal *too* much from my heirs." Actually, he had no doubt that the duty-bound old lawyer would serve selflessly and faithfully. Unless, perhaps, somebody else had pictures of Junior. Griffin paused to offer a small smile to his adversary. "Look at it this way, Justin. If I were to die, it would be a bit of a hassle for you, dealing with my will and my sister and the baby and all that mess. But just think of the bright side. Junior would be in Congress. And I wouldn't be around to outsmart you anymore."

*   *   *

Pierre scampered to his left, lunged for the ball. It ticked off the tip of his glove, skidded into center field. Base hit. Or maybe error, shortstop. Either way, the runner was standing on first base. And Pierre was feeling every one of his 42 years.

He slammed his fist into his glove, pulled on one of the leather glove laces as an excuse to avert his eyes from his teammates. At 22, he would have skipped to his left, reached down and snapped the ball off the dirt with his glove, maybe even styled a bit to add some flare to the play. At 32, he would have moved to his left before the ball had even hit the bat, anticipating the flow and recognizing the patterns of the game, and again made the play routinely, his body rotated to make the throw to first even before the ball had settled into the leather web. But, at 42, he had lost both his quickness and his feel for the game. The quickness part he could, grudgingly, accept—he wasn't the first athlete whose reflexes had slowed. But there was no excuse for the loss of his baseball intuition—that was simply a matter of focusing, of concentrating, of engrossing himself in the task at hand. None of which he had been able to do since Rex Griffin had entered his life.

Having Griffin as a neighbor was like having water in your ear while you tried to hear the breathless words of your daughter in her first school play. Or dirt in your eye while you tried to watch your wife's reaction as she lifted the lid on that special anniversary jewelry box. But it was worse than that, because it was constant. No matter what Pierre did, he couldn't forget the fact that Griffin was out there, somewhere, plotting and scheming and terrorizing. Everything in his house reminded him of Griffin. When he looked at his girls, his first thought was to protect them from Griffin.

And when he played softball, the aluminum bat gripped tightly in his hands, he saw Griffin's face on the ball as it arced slowly toward him....

So, to be fair, it wasn't all bad. He couldn't field very well any more, and he missed the ball almost as often as he hit it. But when he hit the ball, he hit it hard. And it felt good. Real good.

* * *

Amisha dreaded the sound of her husband's car pulling into the garage. Sure, it was lonely in the house without companionship—isolated from family and friends, alone in a new country, a terrorist living only a few houses away. But it was worse when Rajiv was home.

This was supposed to have been her dream home. She had worked for months with a professional designer to find just the right balance—she didn't want opulence, she had said, she wanted dignified good taste. They had settled on lots of cherry-wooded furnishings and cabinetry to give the feel of old world elegance, but had offset if with skylights and oversized windows to soften the sobering effect of the dark wood. It had seemed like a good idea in theory, but no matter how many floral arrangements or fruit bowls or knickknacks she added, the home simply refused to feel warm. But she knew she couldn't blame the designer for that.

Tonight would be ugly. She would have to tell Rajiv about the latest in the Rex Griffin saga. He had been away on business, so he didn't know about the lawsuit and the possibility of an attachment on their house and a freeze of their bank accounts. She hoped he wouldn't beat her, as he had when she had allowed Griffin to access his computer.

But she feared the worst. He might not know yet about Griffin's latest offensive, but he did know that his company's stock price had dropped to $3 per share, down from a high of $140. And he did know they had a major problem with the IRS, a result of some arcane rules relating to the exercise of stock options. Amisha didn't exactly understand it, but the end result was that they owed the IRS close to a million dollars on "income" they had never seen, all because Rajiv had exercised some stock options back when the shares were trading in triple figures. Unfortunately, Rajiv had stubbornly refused to sell any of the shares, unwilling to acknowledge the reality of the high-tech stock crash, and had therefore missed any chance of cashing in on the stock's inflated value. So not only did they lose close to ten million dollars in share value by not selling, but they also now owed the IRS $900,000 for phantom "gains" on the very shares that were now virtually worthless.

Rajiv trudged through the door, dragging a garment bag and a small suitcase behind him. He had only been gone five days, but it seemed to Amisha as if he had somehow grown even rounder while on his trip.

"Namaste," she said, greeting him in their native language. But they did not kiss, did not embrace. He would mount her later, she knew, panting and pawing, but otherwise their marriage lacked intimacy. It did not have to be so, even for an arranged marriage. But for Rajiv, the weekly rutting was enough. That, and his work.

She switched to English, as was his preference. He wanted to be in the habit of it for when they had children. Not that they'd had any luck in their attempts so far. "Come, I have dinner waiting for you." The smell of curry filled the room. "How was your trip?"

Rajiv grunted, waddled into the kitchen, dropped into a chair.

"Not good." She gritted her teeth—he spoke in that exaggerated singsong voice that so many Indians and Pakistanis used. She knew that Westerners mocked it, and she prided herself on not being so melodic when she spoke. "The economy is so bad that nobody is willing to invest in any new technologies. I will have to leave on another trip tomorrow morning." He pinned a flight itinerary on the refrigerator with a magnet.

Good. Another trip. "I am sorry to hear that." She took a deep breath, turned toward the stew on the stove. She never should have married below her caste—Rajiv may have been a successful business-man, but he would never have the culture or refinement of one born into the Brahman class, as she had been. He was of the Kshatriya class, and always would be—money and an expensive car could never change that. But he had been captivated by her beauty and had made her father a financial offer he could not refuse. So it had been done.

And based on his behavior in this life, the Kshatriya class was as high as Rajiv's soul would ever ascend. In fact, he'd be lucky in his next life to return as anything more evolved than an insect. Amisha smiled at the thought—Rajiv, and Griffin too, both punished for their sins in this life by reincarnation in the next as mosquitoes, fated to be flattened into oblivion by the slap of a hand before they even had their first taste of blood. The Hindu religion was a bit rigid at times, yet at least it offered the promise of punishment in the next life for the wicked people of this one.

But, in this life at least, she was stuck with ill-tempered, ill-mannered, abusive Rajiv. She had thought about leaving him; indeed, she thought of little else lately. But she had no friends or family in the country, and he kept her passport locked away. Not to mention the stigma divorce still carried in the Indian culture—when she had complained about Rajiv once to her mother, her mother had re-minded her that she must think of her husband as her god, and to fast and pray for his long life. Even so, divorce was possible here in America. She had no money, but the house had been put in her name to protect it from Rajiv's creditors. If only she could access the equity in it.... But to do that she'd first have to get rid of Griffin and his lawsuit. "Rajiv, I have some more unfortunate news. Rex Griffin has filed a new lawsuit against us. It relates to the attack on him a few months ago. He has alleged that it was a neighborhood conspiracy, that we all had a hand in his assault."

Rajiv waved a hand. "More bunk. This man is a charlatan."

Amisha remained focused on the stove. "I agree. But the result is that we will not be able to get a mortgage on this house, or to sell it."

Rajiv slapped his hand on the table. "Why is that? We need that money to pay the tax authorities!" His voice squeaked as he yelled.

"It seems that a bank will not lend us money while we are involved in litigation...."

Rajiv stood, moved toward her. He was not a tall man, and was close to twenty years older than she, but he was thick-chested and powerful. She backed up against the stove, reached behind her for a knife she had been using to cut vegetables. He had regularly slapped and cuffed her during the course of their marriage, but the beating he gave her after she had allowed Griffin to access his computer had been brutal, savage. Her face had been bruised and swollen for almost two weeks, and her ribs sore for twice that long. She swore it would not happen again.

"Woman, the affairs of the house are your responsibility! You chose this house. Then you let that monster into my office, left him unattended to use my computer. What else did you do with him while he was here—perhaps suck his dick, you whore?" She could see his breathing quicken, the veins in his neck throb. "And now you tell me you can't even get a simple mortgage! You are nothing but a pretty face. You have failed to give me children and you have failed to manage our home!"

He raised his hand to strike her.

Instinctively, Amisha swung the knife around to shield her face from the blow.

The world seemed to move in slow motion—Amisha was able to see that Rajiv had closed his eyes as he swung his hand, had time to conclude that he never saw the steel point blocking the path to his wife's cheek. And then watched as his meaty, cuffed hand plowed through the air and split open on the scallion-speckled blade.

Amisha froze for a second as her husband's eyes opened in astonishment, watched as he brought his hand to his face and stared disbelievingly at the blood gushing from it.

She knew she should be afraid, or angry, or even sorry. But all she felt was power—the power of having a lethal weapon in her hand, the power of seeing the brute that was her husband drop to his knees and cry out in pain, the power of no longer being a victim.

Not sure what else she could do, and afraid of what she might do if left alone with her husband on his knees and a knife in her hand, Amisha took a deep breath and screamed as loud as she could. By the time she finished, Rajiv had fled, a dishtowel wrapped around his hand and hatred in his eyes.

*   *   *

Amisha held the knife in front of her face until she heard Rajiv's car squeal out of the driveway, then collapsed into a kitchen chair. Okay, now what?

She let the knife drop onto the butcher-block table, noticed the blood pooling between the knife and the table like a thick, reddish chocolate sauce. She stared at the blood as the pool slowly expanded over her custom-made table. She knew it would likely stain the blond wood. And she didn't care a bit.

Well then.

She was pretty sure Rajiv would go straight to the hospital for stitches—he was a child when it came to pain, and he would also be concerned about infection. He loved himself too much to forego proper treatment.

So that gave her at least an hour, maybe two, before he returned. And he would return—his ego would demand he come back and re-take his castle. She preferred not to be here when it happened.

But where could she go? And for how long? An hour or two simply wasn't enough time to re-organize an entire life. If she was going to leave Rajiv.... Even the thought made her cringe as she realized the difficulties this would cause her family back in India. It simply wasn't done, a wife leaving her husband. Her youngest sister would be forever tainted, the product of a family unsuitable for marriage. Her mother would be shunned. Her father's business would dissolve. And she, she herself would likely be ostracized from her

195

own family. At the very least they would refuse to support her in any way. Even her sister in Los Angeles would likely denounce her.

Yet she couldn't stay with Rajiv. That, at least, was clear. But it was equally clear she couldn't just walk out the door tonight—she needed to get some money, make some preparations, concoct a plan. Rajiv was going on another business trip tomorrow. She would have to avoid him until he returned, use the time while he was away to try to figure something out.

She pulled out a note pad from the kitchen drawer, began jotting down lists of things she would need. Money, personal papers, family heirlooms, medical records, clothing. Rajiv would probably cancel her credit cards....

The phone interrupted her thoughts. She checked the caller ID—Rajiv's cell phone. She took a deep breath, reached for the knife, lifted the receiver. "Yes." She was proud of the fact that she hadn't fled yet, wondered if Rajiv was surprised to find her still at home.

"Listen to me, woman. I will show you how a *man* properly handles a problem."

Amisha looked at the clock—8:15. It was later than she thought; he had been gone more than an hour already. She tried to keep her voice steady. "And what is that supposed to mean, Rajiv?"

"You will see, woman." Click.

She stared at the phone for a few seconds, then rushed upstairs into her dressing room and threw some clothes and toiletries into a leather overnight bag. Where was Rajiv? Just leaving the hospital? Halfway home? Pulling into the subdivision? She separated the velvet curtains fronting the over-sized Palladian window, scanned the street below. Nothing but a man, probably Rex Griffin, walking his dog.

She snatched her bag off the bed, sprinted down the curved staircase and rushed back to the kitchen. She grabbed the knife, slid it into the side pocket of her bag. She'd rather not flee the house if possible. But if Rajiv was returning, she could not stay. Not with him likely bent on revenge.

She found her pocketbook, rifled through the contents. Seventy dollars in cash, a few credit cards. Good enough; the Cape was full of hotels. She ripped a flight itinerary off the refrigerator—Rajiv was set to leave on a 9:00 A.M. flight out of Boston the next morning. She scribbled a quick note on a scrap of paper, set it down next to the pool of blood on the table: *I will phone you early tomorrow morning.* She would call, attempt to placate him, beg for his forgiveness. It might temper his rage a bit.

Amisha peeked out the window to make sure the coast was still clear, then strode toward the garage door. She reached up to her cheek, felt the sting of his last beating, increased her pace. She grabbed a long leather coat out of a closet—it was a humid August night, but she had been shivering ever since she had knifed her husband. She pushed the button to open one of the three garage doors, climbed into her black BMW, backed out of the driveway.

Now where? On the one hand, she could abandon her home, go straight to a hotel. But what if Rajiv did not return? Did she really want to capitulate so easily? And if he did return, she wanted to get a sense of his mood. *Know thy enemy.* But from a safe distance.

She turned left, away from the subdivision entrance. She drove a few hundred feet, turned her car around in a driveway, steered back toward her own driveway. She stopped before she got there, pulled tight onto the side of a bend in the road, left the car running. It was just now dark, and she couldn't see much of the road from where she sat because she was tucked in behind a grove of trees; likewise, the trees would hide her from Rajiv if he indeed chose to return to their home. Or, rather, their house. It would never really be a home again.

She looked at the digital clock on her dashboard. 8:42. She had stabbed Rajiv at about 7:00, and he had called at 8:15. Was he returning?

She waited a few more minutes. Six, to be exact. 8:48.

A sudden screech of tires speeding over the pavement. She couldn't see any cars for a few seconds, then a pair of headlights suddenly appeared through the trees. Rajiv's red Mercedes.

She held her breath, watched as his car shot down the subdivision drive and swerved into their driveway. He didn't bother to pull into the garage. But he didn't get out of the car, either. She watched, waited. Had he seen her?

He opened the car door, and through the trees she could see his square head illuminated in the driver's seat. It looked like he was resting his forehead on the steering wheel. She had neglected to close the garage door, so he would see that her car was gone, would deduce that she had fled. A few seconds passed, then he lifted his head, pulled himself out of his car, and staggered his way toward the front door. She could see the white bandage on his hand, noticed that he carried it gingerly away from his body.

He made it about halfway up the cobblestone walkway when a series of floodlights suddenly kicked on and Amisha found herself—and her car—illuminated in light. The blasted motion detector had activated the floodlights, and they now brightened the entire perimeter of the property. Including her hiding spot.

She ducked, prayed that Rajiv wouldn't turn to his right and notice her car parked only a score or so meters away. What would he do if he saw her? Would he jump in his car and chase her through the streets of Mashpee, like one of those foolish Hollywood movies? She would rather not find out; she had had quite enough excitement for one night.

She slowly slid her car into gear, dimmed the dashboard lights, edged her way back onto the road. She kept her headlights off, hoping to slide by Rajiv without him noticing. She accelerated past him, turned slightly in her seat to make sure he hadn't noticed her.

Don't touch the brakes, she reminded herself, *or he'll see the brake lights*. He seemed to sense the movement of her car, turned and looked toward the road. But his eyes had been affected by the bright floodlights, and she guessed it would take a few seconds for his pupils to dilate and focus. Amisha tried to stay calm, but her foot stepped down on the gas pedal despite her protestations, and she shot ahead into the dark night.

She kept her eyes fixed to the rearview mirror, willed Rajiv to remain frozen on the cobblestone walkway. *This is your castle*, she implored him, *do not flee it again*. She kept her eyes focused on his form, as if they alone kept him from sprinting to his car and pursuing her.

Suddenly a loud thump bounced her up out of her seat. A second thump followed just as she came down and banged her chin against the steering wheel. *A speed bump*, was her first thought, but she knew the subdivision had none. So what had she hit? A deer? A dog? A kid's bike?

She braked, spun in her seat, looked out the rear window. Whatever it was, it wasn't moving. Or at least she couldn't see anything moving in the darkened road. She opened the windows, listened for a moan or whimper, stuck her head out and scanned what she could see of the road behind her. Nothing. She didn't dare open the door because the dome light would go on....

The brakes. She had hit the brakes. Had Rajiv seen?

She knew she couldn't wait around to find out. She touched her hand to the bruise on her chin, remembered how it had felt when her entire face had been pummeled. And stomped on the gas pedal.

*   *   *

Officer Andrew Cleary steered his police cruiser slowly onto the tree-lined private drive and snaked his way down a slight decline. He knew that this land used to be called Smithson Bogs—he and his friends used to follow the raised paths through the bogs and down to the lake to swim and fish. That the subdivision was known today as Smithson Farm, rather than Smithson Bogs, always made him smile. Apparently a farm had more appeal as an address than a bog, especially to people paying more than a half million dollars to call it home.

To his right, Officer Cleary could see the side of the old Smithson farmhouse, a rambling red structure that from a distance looked like it belonged on the cover of a Vermont vacation guide rather than on Cape Cod. He shook his head as his angle improved and he got a better look at the old farmhouse—the home was even more dilapidated than it had been the last time that he'd seen it, almost a year earlier, when he'd done crowd control while the homeowner had been arrested on bomb-making charges. If the farmhouse was going to be part of any vacation guide, it would first need a coat of paint and a team of landscapers. And the blue tarp that covered the roof would definitely have to go. The whispers around town were that Rex Griffin was broke.

The road curved again, and he was surprised to see a group of people huddled together near where the road ended and split into a handful of private driveways that led down to the dozen over-sized homes lining the peninsula that jutted into the lake. He knew that somebody had called to report a man lying in a ditch; apparently word had spread through the neighborhood quickly on this sticky August morning.

He tapped on the brake—was there something moving in the woods, just beyond the crowd? But when he looked again there was nothing but trees and brush. Must have been a deer. Or maybe just the shadows playing tricks.

He pulled his cruiser off to the side and walked down toward the group. "I'm Officer Cleary. I received a call about a man in a ditch."

*   *   *

Amisha edged away from the sweating policeman, watched as his eyes rested on the body of Rex Griffin. The dead body lay in the culvert, flies buzzing around the open wound on his head. Had she killed him? Or had she merely knocked his already dead—or perhaps just injured?—body into the ditch? She honestly didn't know. It was just as likely that Rajiv had killed him, had finally mustered the courage to run down the demon that had haunted their lives.

It would be consistent with Rajiv's personality. He would never confront another man, one-on-one. But he would bravely attack a woman barely half his size. Or propel a couple of thousand pounds of steel at a defenseless pedestrian.

Whatever the truth, she knew now that the *thump, thump* of last night had become a vital part of her future. She may not have killed him, but she had definitely run him over. And she hadn't reported it to the authorities.

The policemen eyed the group, seemed to focus on Amisha more than the others.

"Has anybody called for an ambulance?"

Amisha looked down, trying to avoid eye contact. Was it really possible that she had actually killed a man, run him down with her car and left him to die in a bloody ditch? She pulled her windbreaker tight against her, even as the sweat ran down the small of her back.

"Well, has anyone checked to see how bad he's hurt?" Nobody responded, so the officer trudged back to his cruiser. He spoke into his radio for a few seconds, then returned. "Doesn't anybody know what happened?"

Amisha could feel her neighbors' eyes on her. She shrugged. "I found him here when I came out for my morning walk. I screamed, and everyone came running. I think it's Rex Griffin. He lives in the old farmhouse right as you come into the subdivision."

She had returned to the subdivision from her motel room early that morning, after a brief telephone conversation with Rajiv that seemed to pacify him a bit. She had parked her car, freshened up, and set out to see what she had bumped in the night. And found a corpse.

Of course, in the universe of corpses one could stumble upon, this wasn't too bad a landing spot. It wasn't Rajiv, but Rex Griffin wasn't a bad consolation prize.

Officer Cleary nodded, slid awkwardly down into the culvert on his hip, stepped around a pair of wire-rimmed glasses that must have been knocked off of Griffin's face. He examined the corpse, looked up at the group. "He's dead."

He reached into Griffin's hip pocket, pulled out a wallet. He examined it, climbed out of the ditch, studied the group for a few seconds. "Please stay away from the body. I'm going to get some tape to mark the scene." He began to walk away, then abruptly stopped and turned. "And nobody leave."

*   *   *

Officer Cleary walked back to his cruiser and backed the car up the slope until he found a soft shoulder to pull onto, then opened the trunk. But instead of police tape, he grabbed a pair of binoculars. It felt good to be doing some actual police work after a summer of traffic details and drunk college students and fender benders. He removed his hat, peered around the corner of the trunk, observed the crowd.

Cleary removed the binoculars for a moment and rubbed his eyes. The group had gathered in a circle, the neighbors shaking hands and patting one another on the back. It wasn't exactly the Munchkins singing and dancing around the dead body of the Wicked Witch of the East, but it was still a strange scene. Everyone was smiling, even as their eyes rested on the cold, broken, bowtied body lying dead in the ditch.

*   *   *

Dominique unfolded herself from the curve of the tree, slowly eased her way deeper into the woods. She wished she could have arrived earlier, before the crowd had gathered. She would have liked to have examined the body herself. As it was, it was fortunate that Vernon happened to have been listening to the police radio and heard the report of a body in a ditch in the Smithson Farms subdivision. Remarkably fortunate, in fact....

In any event, here, in the shadow of Metacomet's grave, the war had claimed its first casualty. No, that was not accurate. The war over this land had claimed thousands of souls over the centuries. The body in the ditch was merely the first casualty of the latest battle.

She was hopeful it would be the last. The world was now back in some sort of rough balance—Griffin had created a life in furtherance of his scheme, and now his had been forfeited in return. But she also understood that sometimes things don't work out quite so neatly.

*   *   *

Justin McBride shook his head. He was already regretting his decision to serve as the executor of Griffin's will. Not that he mourned the man; not in the least. And it didn't hurt to be privy to the secrets and financial details of the scoundrel's life. But it sure did create a lot of work for Justin.

They had found Griffin's body just this morning, and already Justin had been forced to devote the better part of the afternoon dealing with Denise. She had cried hysterically at the news, so much so that Justin finally brought her to the hospital emergency room. The doctor had been hesitant to give her medication because of the baby, but in the end decided the drugs were less risk to the fetus than was her thrashing and wailing. Justin shook his head—it was hard to wrap his brain around the fact that the sister Griffin had pimped now so mourned his death. But she was really just a kid, and the only adult in her life was now gone.

In any event, he now had to find a qualified mental health worker to come live with the 30-week pregnant Denise. For the time being, at least, her doctor thought it would be best for her to stay in the farmhouse.

Later he would spend more time with the young woman, try to get to know her a bit. She was, after all, his legal responsibility. As was her baby. But, for now, it was time to locate Griffin's will and the trusts he had spoken of, as well as his other important papers. And then he would have to try to get up to speed on the dozens of Griffin's outstanding lawsuits. If nothing else, it would surely make fascinating reading.

He began to wander around the old farmhouse, looking for insights into his dead adversary. And also looking for some photos. But there wasn't much to see—a few pieces of simple furniture in the kitchen and living room, a playroom which Denise had decorated with mobiles and pictures of butterflies and dozens of stuffed animals. There was even a bathroom, which for some reason surprised Justin; it had never occurred to him that Griffin's body behaved like that of a human being.

Upstairs, of course, would be where the good stuff was. That was where Griffin kept his office. He headed toward the stairwell, was intercepted by a policeman. "I'm sorry, sir, I'm going to have to ask that you not go upstairs."

"I understand, Officer. But I'm the executor of the estate. I need to start going through the papers." *And I need to find some pictures of my son massacring innocent civilians.*

"That will have to wait until we've finished our investigation."

Justin nodded. Griffin would probably have hid the pictures—it was unlikely the detective would stumble across them. Justin would have to conduct a thorough search later.

For now, the police would be focused on solving the murder. It made sense that they were treating Griffin's death as a possible homicide. Denise said she was in bed already when he went out to walk the dog—not surprising given her pregnancy. But the fact that she didn't see her brother go out really didn't matter. Everyone knew he walked Barrister every night—same time, same route. And Griffin had plenty of enemies. It would have been a simple matter to wait for him, then run him down with a car and leave him in the ditch to die. "Officer, can I ask who's in charge of this case?"

"That would be Detective Foster. I can get him for you if you want."

"Please."

Justin sat in an old rocking chair, waited. Griffin's dog, Barrister, rubbed his head against Justin's leg—the dog had befriended Justin earlier in the day when Justin had dropped some hamburger meat into a bowl for him. Before the death had sunk in and the hysteria had begun, Denise had mentioned that she had awakened to find Barrister scratching at the front door; apparently he'd been waiting at the farmhouse door all night. No surprise that he was hungry.

Justin looked around. From the inside, the farmhouse seemed simple and almost quaint, though a bit tired. How many times had he driven by, pictured Griffin deep inside the bowels of the structure concocting some evil plan? In his imagination, the house had always been dark and dank and cobwebbed. But, today at least, the sun poured in and, even with all the activity, the house seemed to invite a cup of tea and a nap. Perhaps it was just his mood.

A tall, lanky man ambled into the room, introduced himself. "Mr. McBride, I'm Detective Foster. You wanted to see me?"

"Yes, Detective. I'm just curious as to your investigation. Do you think Mr. Griffin was murdered, or was it just an accident?"

"I'm really not at liberty to discuss this with you, sir, other than to say we have not eliminated any possibilities."

Justin nodded. He realized that he, like the other neighbors, would likely be on the list of possible murder suspects. Which was why he had been kept from going upstairs and why Detective Foster was being so close-mouthed. He figured he'd make their job easy for them. "Well, Detective, I'm sure that at some point you'll need to interview me. Even though I'm the executor of his will, Mr. Griffin and I were hardly on good terms."

Foster nodded, remained silent. So Justin continued. "Anyway, I'm available whenever you need me. But, being the executor, I will need

204

to start going through the documents in Mr. Griffin's office. If for no other reason than to begin making funeral arrangements."

Foster nodded again. "Very well. I'll come up with you right now. If you have a notebook, you can take some notes. But I don't want anything taken out of the room."

"That's fine. All I really need right now is the will. If there's a copy machine up there, I can just make a copy and leave the original."

The two men climbed the stairs, stepped over the series of extension cords snaking down the hallway and entered Griffin's office.

Foster had already done a rough inventory of the office. "I think I saw the will over in that file cabinet."

Justin found it quickly, glanced through it. Pretty standard stuff. The only mildly surprising thing was a request by Griffin to be cremated and have his ashes scattered, which for some reason struck Justin as odd. Not so much that it was a strange request, but it had simply never occurred to Justin that Griffin had any spiritual beliefs of any kind.

Also tucked into the envelope was a larger document, neatly organized and updated monthly. This document listed and summarized all of Griffin's active litigation, and listed his bank accounts, safe deposit boxes and other assets. In addition, the document contained a narrative of information and instructions for the will's executor—parameters for settling the various lawsuits, including the suit against Justin; a policy number for a small life insurance policy; information regarding the Griffin Family Trust; instructions on how to pay the monthly mortgage on the farmhouse; the name and address of the family friend in Maine who would serve as Donald's guardian; and a request that Justin be appointed legal guardian for Denise and the baby, along with information regarding Denise's medical condition and needs. All in all, it was as thorough a 'death package' as Justin had ever seen.

Not that Justin wouldn't have a boatload of work to do. It would take him months just to get up to speed on all the lawsuits, and maybe years to actually litigate or settle them. And trying to care for Denise and the baby would also require a huge investment of time and emotional energy. Justin shook his head—this would likely be a full-time job. And he would be doing it for free, since Griffin's estate had no money to pay him. Even in death, Griffin was screwing him.

But make no mistake—it was worth it. No more demon lurking outside his home. No more threats of blackmail. No more spying on his friends and neighbors.

*　　　*　　　*

Two days later they held a brief memorial service for Griffin.

Ronnie approached Justin. "What, no body?"

Justin smiled. His friend was making no pretense at mourning the death of their enemy. "No, he wants to be cremated."

"All right. Where are the ashes then?"

Justin laughed softly. "The body is still at the Medical Examiner's office." From what Justin could pry from the detective, the Examiner had confirmed that the cause of death was, not surprisingly, internal injuries and trauma to the head caused by a collision with an automobile. And he had found no traces of alcohol or drugs in the body. But the Examiner was still working to confirm identification of the corpse. "I guess it's standard procedure in cases where there's no spouse to identify the body. So they need to make a final ID before they release the body. Then we can cremate it."

"Can't they just look at fingerprints or something?"

"That's what I thought. The police tried to get prints from the FBI from back when Griffin was in the army, but I guess a lot of the prints from the Vietnam era were poor quality and are worthless. And nobody can seem to find any dental records—not surprising if you ever noticed the guy's teeth. So the Medical Examiner had to take a skin sample from the corpse and is comparing the DNA to stuff found on Griffin's comb and toothbrush."

"Well, the sooner you can bury the body, or burn it, or whatever, the better as far as I'm concerned."

But nobody, including Ronnie, seemed too upset that there were no actual remains to mourn over. Justin attended the service because he felt like he had to, and because he thought someone should escort Denise. She was still being medicated, though they had begun to decrease the dosages. But they couldn't very well keep her from attending.

Justin was surprised to see most of the neighbors in attendance, milling around in the back of the church, just as he had been surprised to see Ronnie. Pierre and Carla Prefontaine, speaking with a large, imperial-looking woman he assumed to be Dominique Victor. Loretta Lemaire. Amisha Raman, without her husband. A few others.

Not that he blamed them for coming, even though not a single one of them had a fond memory of Rex Griffin. They were here to find closure, to bear witness to the man's final demise. Life with Griffin had been a nightmare. Now his death marked the end of their ordeal, and the memorial service formally sealed that death.

Other than Denise and the neighbors, the church was empty except for a few church officials. Justin tried to fight back a shiver—Griffin lived for more than half a century, and not a single person came to mourn his death. It didn't surprise Justin, but, still, it was a horrible way to die. In a ditch, without friends or loved ones. Just as he had lived.

Justin looked back at the neighbors. They were socializing with one another—friendly, chatty. Almost too much so. He could sense their thoughts, understood their need to paint on happy faces. They knew that, in all probability, a murderer was in their midst. They eyed each other, studied the masked faces around them, obsessed on the question that would never be spoken but that filled the air: *Had any of them come out of a sense of guilt? Or because they feared not attending would somehow cast suspicion on them?*

*   *   *

Rajiv waddled into the kitchen. "Woman! Come here and sit down."

Amisha moved toward him slowly, her chin raised. She took a seat between Rajiv and the door, curled her hand around a screwdriver she had snatched from a drawer on her way to the table. Rajiv's blood had soaked into the butcher-block and left a rust-colored spot the size of a small dish.

He had just returned from his business trip the night before. She had been waiting for him at their house, resigned to the fact that she would have to accept his abuse for a few more weeks. She simply wasn't prepared to flee just yet. Rajiv had immediately forced himself on her, and she had complied with his sexual demands, which seemed to curb his rage a bit. But this would be the first time they had actually spoken.

"This donkey from up the street who has been tormenting us is now dead." He leaned back, folded his hands on his bulging lap, a look of satisfaction on his face. "Now I expect you to clean up the mess he has made of our lives. Understood?"

Amisha nodded.

"In the meantime, I have made some changes. First, I will now be driving your BMW. I just this morning returned the Mercedes to the dealer."

"Why? It drives fine. And the lease is not up for another few months." *And I didn't have a chance to look for any dents yet.*

Rajiv smiled. "Because you are no longer deserving of a car. And also because my company can no longer afford to lease me one, thanks to you."

Amisha resisted the impulse to argue the point. Rajiv regularly blamed her for the problems around the house. This was the first time he had blamed her for his problems at work as well. Never mind that his company, even though it was failing, could easily afford to continue lease payments on a car. He continued. "You will walk until you have proved yourself worthy of the privilege of a car. You can begin to prove yourself by putting our finances back in order. Once a week you may take a taxi to do the grocery shopping. In addition, I have taken your credit cards."

Amisha forced herself to remain impassive. Let him think he had won. "Very well."

He eyed her suspiciously, then offered an evil smile. "You may mask your face with indifference, but I am no fool, woman. I can see your anger. Now go. Go clean up the mess you have made of our lives."

*   *   *

Pierre poured the rest of the wine into Shelby's glass, then popped the cork on a fresh bottle and refilled the glass he and Carla were sharing. "I don't like it."

Carla looked up at him, smiled. "I know you're not talking about the wine. So what do you mean, you don't like it? What's not to like?"

"I don't like that he's dead." Shelby knew Pierre was a bit drunk, smiled as she watched him concentrate on proclaiming his feeling in a steady voice. She hadn't wanted to believe Pierre was capable of murder, but she also hadn't been able to shake the feeling that—in this extreme case at least—he was. But his proclamation that he didn't like the fact that Griffin was dead would be a strange statement for Griffin's killer to make. Drunk or sober.

Carla teased her husband. "You have to understand, Shelby, that Pierre was raised to believe that the devil is immortal. And Pierre was convinced Griffin was the devil himself. By dying, Griffin disproved Pierre's theory. Right, Pierre?"

Shelby wondered if Carla had asked Pierre if he had killed Griffin. Not that she would have blamed her if she hadn't. As a spouse, how do you ask that question? And, more to the point, do you really want to risk hearing the answer?

Pierre closed his eyes, ignored Carla's jab at his Catholic upbringing. It looked like he was trying to organize his thoughts, then abandoned the attempt with a chuckle. "I don't know what I'm trying to say."

Carla came to his rescue, rubbed Pierre's knee. The last time Shelby had visited, they had seemed disconnected from each other, so it was good to see that the affection between them had returned. Even if it had been sparked by someone's death.

But their intimacy, as always, made her think of Bruce. She had not seen him since the meeting at the Victors' house, and she had found herself scanning the sidewalk for him on her drive into town today. Now that Griffin was dead, she had no excuse to remain in contact with Bruce. But she wasn't sure she was ready to have him just sail out of her life again.

Shelby had the vague sense Carla had spoken. She had missed the words the first time, but the echo of them still sounded in her ear.

Carla had said: "It's hard to believe he's really gone, really out of our lives. Just like that. Poof."

Shelby tried to shake the thoughts of Bruce from her head. What was wrong with her? Why did every conversation have to trigger thoughts of Bruce? She hoped she hadn't enlisted Bruce's aid out of some misguided hope that she might re-spark their relationship. If so, not only was she setting herself up for a huge letdown, but she was putting her friends and clients at risk as well.

She ran her hands through her hair, responded to Carla. "Have they said how he died?"

Pierre interjected. "A house fell from the sky, landed on him. Then we all stood around and sang." He jumped to his feet, did a little jig. "Ding, dong, the witch is dead...."

Carla rolled her eyes. "You stole that from the cop, Pierre. The policeman who first came to investigate told the ambulance driver that we were all grinning like the Munchkins after Dorothy's house landed on the Wicked Witch."

Shelby responded. "But didn't the Wicked Witch have a sister who came back to avenge her death...?"

Carla offered a shiver in response. "That's a scary thought, Shelby. Anyway, you asked how he died. Internal injuries. They think a car hit him, then backed over his head a few times."

Shelby grimaced. "Do they have any suspects?"

"Oh, I'm sure they have plenty of suspects," Carla responded with a laugh. "But I don't know if they've narrowed it down at all."

Shelby sipped her wine, nodded. It struck her that she was being more than a bit sexist by focusing her suspicion only on Pierre. Carla could just as easily run a man down with a car. And she had just as much reason to do so as Pierre.

"Ronnie Lemaire says they should post a reward," Pierre said.

"For information on the killer?" Carla asked.

"No, a reward for whoever killed Griffin. A big check, keys to the city, maybe a parade down Main Street."

Shelby observed her friend. Carla seemed pensive, maybe a bit disturbed. Or maybe Shelby was just being overly observant, looking for signs of guilt in the crease of a brow or clench of a fist.

"I know Ronnie's just kidding around," Carla said, "but I don't think we should be so quick to embrace the killer. I mean, I'm happy to be rid of Griffin too, but...."

Pierre responded. "Well, you at least have to admit that the killer did us a big favor. And whoever did it must have had a good reason. Maybe we shouldn't embrace him, but I don't think we should condemn him either."

"Sure we should," Carla said. "I happen to think the pyramids in Egypt are wonderful, but that doesn't mean I shouldn't criticize the fact they were built with slave labor. The ends don't always justify the means."

Pierre paused, nodded. "You're right. I can't condone murder, no matter what the reason." He set his glass down. "So I won't drink to the killer." Then he smiled and lifted it again. "But I will drink to the fact that Griffin's out of our lives." He took a healthy swallow.

"I'm almost afraid to ask," Shelby interjected. "Have the police questioned you guys?"

Pierre laughed. "Yeah, they walked in just as we were spray-painting the bumper of our car."

Carla cuffed him. "Stop that, Pierre. Yeah, they questioned us, along with everyone else in the neighborhood."

"No shortage of suspects, I would guess."

"That's for sure," Carla responded. "They even questioned Justin McBride, and Griffin named him the executor of his will."

"Really? What's that all about? They weren't friendly, were they?"

Carla answered. "No, but apparently Griffin approached Justin a few months ago and asked if he'd do it. Said he needed someone he could trust to take care of Denise."

Pierre had been gazing out into the night, but returned to the conversation. "That's another thing that doesn't make sense to me. Why would Griffin ask him? And why would Justin agree to do it?"

Shelby answered. "Good question. It seems like a conflict of interest to me. As a lawyer, it's sort of awkward to represent someone when they're suing you."

"I'm not sure it matters," Carla said. "Griffin's dead now."

"But doesn't the whole thing smell funny to you?" Pierre's eyes went from Carla to Shelby and back to Carla again.

"I suppose," Shelby offered, "we could ask Bruce to keep sniffing around a bit. If you're really concerned." Shelby hoped she had made the suggestion to help her friends, but feared she might have had an ulterior motive. Her next comment, however, she recognized as purely self-serving. "I can go see him tomorrow and talk to him about it. I mean, if you want me to."

"That's a good idea, Shelby." Carla's eyes twinkled as she smiled at her friend. "Are you sure you don't mind?"

*   *   *

Billy ran his hand along the bumper of the family's Ford Taurus. It felt smooth, but what did he know? He stretched out on the driveway, shined a flashlight on the bumper's underside, examined the grill area. No discoloration, no indentations, but, again, what did he know? Would a collision with a man—as opposed to with another car or even a bicycle—leave any evidence? Unfortunately, forensic evidence was not one of the things they taught in metal shop.

The police hadn't come to the house yet, hadn't questioned him. Or his dad. Or his mom. But they would. It was simply too much to expect that an asshole like Griffin would die in a tragic accident, the victim of some random streak of bad luck. Common sense would tell you that luck that bad—or, in this case, luck that good—was rarely random. Somebody had made their own luck.

Maybe he should do the same.

He grabbed his car keys, yelled to his mother that he was going to run a quick errand. He drove slowly, winding his way toward the main street, looking for the right opportunity. There. A delivery van, double-parked in the right lane, the driver carrying a box into a storefront. Billy buckled his seat belt, took his foot off the accelerator, lowered his head as if fiddling with the radio. He closed to what he guessed was about 10 yards, looked up, slammed on the brakes, fought to keep the wheel straight. He skidded, braced for impact. Then smashed into the back of the van.

*   *   *

Justin had spent the past few days making sure Denise's needs were taken care of. At some point she might need to move to a supervised facility, but Justin—after consulting with both her doctor and the social worker assigned by the state—thought it best that she remain in the farmhouse until the baby was born. So he finalized arrangements for a full-time aide, then brought her to her doctor for a full exam. He also made a point of sharing a meal with her once a day. She was timid and meek and intimidated by him, but slowly she was beginning to relax. Was she capable of raising a child? Not on her own, Justin guessed, but with supervision it should be possible. She at least deserved the chance to try.

It had also struck Justin that he hadn't checked on Donald since that first day when he had called the group house and asked them to inform Donald of his brother's death. Perhaps he should have made arrangements to bring Donald to the funeral. He shrugged; it was too late now. And from what Griffin had said about his brother, it was probably best to leave him undisturbed in his supervised home. But he should at least take a drive up to Medford and meet with the man, give him some of the details of his brother's death. Justin picked up the phone.

A staff member answered, and Justin re-introduced himself. "I'm the one who called last week with the news that Donald's brother, Rex, died."

"Yes, Donald took that very hard. He wouldn't leave his room for almost a week—didn't bathe, didn't eat, didn't shave, nothing. His brother was the only one who ever came to visit Donald."

Justin smiled to himself. Maybe Rex did have a streak of decency in him after all. "Anyway, since I'm the executor of the estate, I thought I should come up and meet him."

"Are you also his legal guardian?"

"No. Some family friend up in Maine is the new guardian." Justin looked at his notes, gave her the man's name and telephone number. The man had left a message on Justin's answering machine, apologizing for not making the funeral. But they had never actually spoken.

"Well, Donald finally came out of his room yesterday, so come on up anytime."

"Are there specific visiting hours?"

"No, nothing like that. This is a group home, not an institution. We try to make it as informal as we can—we give the residents as much freedom as they can handle."

"You mean Donald just comes and goes as he pleases?"

The staff member laughed. "It's not exactly like that. Autistic people live very structured lives. Our challenge is not in keeping them from running off on their own; our challenge is getting them to venture out into the world once in a while. So if Donald wanted to take a walk down to the corner store and buy a candy bar, we'd be all for it. But it's never happened—it's simply not part of his routine. Now, running out to the ice cream truck, that's part of his routine. That truck doesn't come, he's out of sorts all day."

"All right. Then I'll probably come up next Wednesday."

"That's fine. We'll let him know you're coming, so he has some time to get used to the idea. Like I said, we try to keep their routine as steady as possible."

"I understand. And thanks for your help."

*   *   *

Bruce didn't have a phone, and Shelby didn't want to bother the Victors to track him down for her, so she drove over to look for him. She got an early start, hopeful of catching him before he went out for the day.

She pulled into the driveway, noticed a tall, tanned figure bent over a small boat along the shoreline. She recognized the movements, knew the lines of his jaw and of his back and of his legs. She began to walk toward him, a bit surprised to notice that her stomach had tightened as she closed on him.

This was the man who had lied to her, betrayed her, sacrificed their love at the altar of greed and avarice. She had never loved another man since. Whether it was because Bruce had permanently scarred her, or rather because he still filled every crevice of her heart, she did not know.

She moved noiselessly, but he somehow sensed her approach, turned toward her. Maybe when you live alone in a sailboat for seven years you develop a heightened ability to feel things, to perceive

214

things that normal people can't. Or maybe he had heard her car pull in and was just playing it cool.

"Hi, Bruce. I thought I might catch you here."

He wiped his hands on his shorts, smiled carefully. "Hi. I was just about to go out for a canoe ride. Want to come? It's a beautiful morning...."

She shrugged. "All right. Sure." She could sense he was uncomfortable, knew that she was. This was the first time they had been alone together since his return. "Are you sure you know how to work those things? There's no sail, you know."

He smiled, this time not as carefully. There was no denying that he was still extraordinarily handsome. Which was, she knew, part of the problem. But only part—add in the fact that he was incredibly intelligent, and the fact that he refused to bend in any way to the norms of society, and the fact that he seemed to have a limitless capacity to find adventure in life, and the result was that Shelby was still smitten. After all these years. And despite all his betrayal. She shook her head to clear it, listened to his response. "I think I can manage. But there's two paddles, so don't think you're not going to have to pull your weight."

"I can handle it."

They climbed into the canoe and Bruce pushed them out into the small lake. It was a calm morning, and the sun was over Bruce's shoulder, so Shelby could see his profile shadowed in the water next to her. She paddled on the other side so as not to obscure its features.

Once in a while she spun her head around—to follow the flight of a bird, or take note of a feature on the shore—in an effort to steal a glance at Bruce's entire face. She realized that it had changed little over the years. Still dark and rugged, still the dimple on his chin, still the sad—even sadder than she remembered—brown puppy dog eyes. And still the dazzling smile, a display of joy that he rationed carefully, saving it for only the most intimate of moments and only for the most special of people. Or, at least, that's what she felt like when he bathed her in it.

She shook her head, dipped her paddle in the water. Enough of that. "Aren't you going to ask why I'm here?"

"Actually, no. I was afraid if I ask it might make you re-think it and leave."

Shelby could tell by the tone of his voice that he had flashed that smile at her. She stole a glimpse of it in his reflection, but resisted turning around to face him fully. He continued, a bit more tentative now. "I've gotten used to not talking. So I probably would have just kept on paddling until you said something.... It's not like I have anyplace I need to be."

She decided to focus on their business. "Well, then, maybe you wouldn't mind helping us out a bit more. Pierre still feels like things don't add up."

Bruce smiled. "I agree—things don't add up. What's bothering him?"

She sighed. She wished Pierre had been more specific. "For one thing, he's bothered by Justin McBride agreeing to be the executor of Griffin's will."

Bruce nodded. "It seems to me that a lot of questions will be answered when they figure out who killed him."

Bruce's response struck Shelby as pretty non-responsive. She wondered if Bruce was hiding something from her. "You're assuming he was murdered?"

"Definitely."

"Yeah, me too." Shelby paused for a moment, gazed across the water. Carla had, over a few too many glasses of wine, commented that she thought Bruce would do anything to win Shelby back. Did that include murder? Shelby shook her head—not only was she flattering herself, but it made no sense. How could Bruce think she'd be impressed by him killing Griffin? Then again, with Bruce things were never that simple. She sighed. "You once said that the way to find the killer was to follow the money."

Bruce nodded. "And I still believe that. So how about insurance—anybody have a policy covering Griffin's death?"

"He had a term policy, but he let it expire."

"So we probably can eliminate insurance fraud. What about all the litigation?"

"I spoke to Justin the other day—that's how I knew about the insurance. There's dozens of cases, as you know. He says he'll probably just dismiss most of the ones that Griffin initiated, says they're all bogus. So all those people stand to benefit."

"Including Justin. He was one of the people Griffin was suing."

"Right. Including Justin. But also including almost half of Mashpee."

Bruce nodded. "How about Billy Victor and his family?"

"I'm sure the police have them near the top of their list. They definitely hated Griffin, but what do they really gain by his death? Griffin had already agreed they could help raise the baby. But you tell me, you know them better than I do."

Bruce was silent for a few seconds. "Any of them could have done it, even Dominique. Billy's a pretty confused and angry kid right now. And this whole thing must be killing Vernon, knowing he can't do anything to help. And let's face it—he's got nothing to lose. He's probably not going to live more than a month or two."

"Is he still driving?"

"Yeah, I think he is. And Billy just got his license."

"All right. So they're all possibilities."

Bruce sat up, stopped paddling. "And don't forget the Mashpee tribe. I'd be curious to see if those tribal documents Griffin found turn up in Ace Awry's hands. They're worth a fortune to the tribe. And therefore to Ace. Maybe I should keep an eye on him for a while."

They're worth a fortune. The thought popped into Shelby's head a second time: Could Bruce have murdered Griffin? Had he found some angle to play, some way to scam his way to that fortune he had lost almost a decade ago? She lowered her hand into the water, tried to wash the thought away.

Bruce was still talking. "And, of course, we can't forget all the neighbors."

Shelby nodded. "Right. They definitely were the ones most under attack by Griffin. I know Amisha and her husband were having some financial troubles, and Ronnie Lemaire was dying to get his hands on Griffin."

"How about Pierre and Carla?"

Shelby lowered her voice, shook her head. "Yup. Them too. So

217

once again, Pierre is a suspect in a murder." Shelby smiled wanly at the unfortunate irony.

"Do you think he could have done it?"

Shelby started to answer, then shrugged her shoulders in defeat. She turned, looked deep into Bruce's eyes. She saw nothing but affection and warmth. And, of course, strength. But those eyes had duped her before. "I don't think so. But we all know that I'm not the best judge of character, right Bruce?"

*   *   *

Justin's first meeting with Donald Griffin wasn't exactly going as he had planned. Donald had refused to give up his chair in front of the television, refused to respond to Justin's questions, refused even to turn and face him. Justin wasn't sure whether his charge hadn't heard him or was just ignoring him.

He excused himself. He was getting too old for this stuff. How did he end up becoming the executor for the penniless estate of a man he abhorred? The answer, he knew, was because he wanted to protect his son from having his blood-lusted face splashed across the front page of the *Boston Globe*. Not that he had necessarily succeeded even in that—he still hadn't found those damn pictures.

Justin wandered around, located a staff member, described the situation with Donald. The man smiled at him. "First visit, huh?" Justin nodded. "You just gotta be patient with Donald. If he doesn't know you, it's gonna take a while before he'll even respond to you. And if he senses that you're gonna tell him something he doesn't want to hear, he'll just shut you right out."

Justin nodded. "Actually, I think he already associates me with bad news. I'm the executor of his brother's estate. He won't even listen to me when I try to talk to him about his brother's death."

"Oh, he's listening to you all right. But you won't get a reaction out of him—he'll just shut down if he doesn't want to hear what you have to say. If I was you, I'd wait a while and try again. But this time talk about something else, stay away from the death stuff, you know? Maybe ask if he wants an ice cream or something."

"Thanks."

Justin went back into the television room, sat next to Donald. They watched *Gilligan's Island* for a few minutes in silence, Donald rocking back and forth in his chair, thick glasses tight against his eyes, his face darkened by a scraggly growth of facial hair. Justin spoke. "I was thinking of going out to get myself an ice cream. Would you like me to get you one?"

Donald didn't turn to him completely, and the rocking continued, but Justin could sense his words had reached the man. Justin studied his face—the glasses were thicker and more bulky, and his hair was cut short against his head, but there was definitely a resemblance to Rex. Except for the eyes. Rex's constantly mocked and ridiculed, while Donald's one functioning eye moved slowly, empty and expressionless. The other just sat there, looking sideways.

Finally Donald spoke, in a loud monotone. "Mint chocolate chip."

Justin clapped his hands on his thighs. "Great. I'll be back in a few minutes."

The two men shared their snack in silence, Justin resisting the urge to wipe the ice cream off of Donald's whiskered chin. Then Justin tried again to reach Donald. "Listen, my boy...." He caught himself—Donald was no boy, he was over 50 years old. But it was hard to think of him as a man. "Donald, I have something to tell you about your brother, Rex. Do you remember Rex?"

Donald stared straight at the television, or at least his one eye did, but he responded. "Rex is my brother."

"Yes, that's right. Well, Rex had an accident. A car hit him, and now he is dead." This was the second time he had delivered the news, and the staff had delivered it once prior to his visit, but Justin wanted to make sure that Donald understood, that he accepted the death. "Do you understand me?"

"Rex is my brother."

"Yes. But Rex is not going to be able to visit you anymore. But he asked me to come see you, to bring you ice cream and anything else you want."

"Are you Rex's friend?"

Justin sighed. First question, and he had to lie already. "Yes, I was. But do you understand me when I say that Rex is dead? A car ran him over."

"Blue Volvo Cross-Country, SJX212; Black Acura Legend, CI3481; Red Ford Explorer, CI1715...."

Justin interrupted. "What are you talking about, Donald?"

"Rex is my brother. I made a list of cars for him. All the cars that drive into Smithson Farm Estates."

"When did you make this list, Donald?"

Donald rocked back and forth, then answered. "August 16, August 17, August 18."

"Wait. Rex died on the night of August 18. Were you there, in Mashpee?"

For a few seconds Justin feared he had lost Donald to *Gilligan's Island* again, but Donald finally responded. "Rex is my brother. He invited me to visit. We had ice cream."

Justin forced himself to slow down, to try to make his questions more precise. "Donald, were you at Rex's house the night he died?"

"Rex went out to walk the dog. At ten o'clock I went to bed. Ten o'clock is my bedtime."

Justin tried a different tack. "You said you made a list. Do you have it still?"

Donald rocked, hummed to himself, then shook his head. "Rex told me to give it only to him. Not to anybody else."

Justin reached over, put his hand on Donald's shoulder. Donald pulled away. "Yes, I understand. But I am Rex's friend. He asked me to help him—and you—if anything happened to him. I think he would want me to have the list now that he's ... now that he's gone."

Donald squeezed his eyes closed, then bolted from his seat. "I will get the list for you."

Justin watched him march out of the room, then up some stairs. Did he really have a list of every car that entered the subdivision the weekend of Griffin's death? If so, it would be key to the investigation. But why would Rex have asked Donald to make such a list?

Donald returned, handed Justin a stack of index cards. "Rex is my brother."

"Thank you, Donald." Justin took the stack, examined it. Just as Donald said, the cards logged every car that had entered the subdivision beginning on the evening of August 16 and continuing through August 17 and 18. Each card listed three entries, and each entry listed—in simple block letters—the time, the make, model and color of the car, the license plate, and whether the car was entering or exiting the subdivision. Justin's eyes went to the evening of August 18, the night Griffin was killed. Donald had noted seven cars entering or exiting the subdivision that night. Including Justin's Lexus.

He looked up from the papers. "Donald, why did Rex ask you to make this list?"

"He said bad people were trying to hurt him." Donald paused, closed his eyes. "Rex is my brother."

Justin nodded. Perhaps Griffin had been expecting another attack and had enlisted Donald to help catch the culprit. Or perhaps instead Griffin had planned to use Donald's log in furtherance of one of his schemes. Whatever the case, Justin would have to turn the log over to the police.

Or would he?

"Donald, does anyone else know about this log, this list?"

Donald shook his head from side to side. "It is a secret."

"Do you have another copy of it?"

"No. The list is for Rex." He offered Justin a proud smile.

"Donald, I'm going to take this list with me, okay?"

Donald had turned his attention back to the television, was now humming and rocking again in his chair as the *Gilligan's Island* theme song played. "Donald? Donald?" Nothing. Justin sighed, then smiled. Gilligan was never going to get off of that island. But he may have just provided Justin with the lifeline that he needed.

*   *   *

Justin spread the index cards out across his kitchen table, examined them. He recognized a number of the cars as those his neighbors drove. Based on the movements Donald had logged, there were a number of neighbors who had driven in and out of the subdivision that evening in a manner consistent with running down Rex Griffin—Justin himself, the Prefontaines, Ronnie Lemaire, Amisha, Rajiv, even the Victors. In short, the log did little to eliminate suspects.

Justin located the two index cards that logged his activity for the night and pulled them off the table. By removing them, he eliminated any evidence against himself. However, the cards he removed also logged certain activity by Ronnie, Rajiv and the Victors. For example, the activity of Ronnie entering the subdivision was duly logged, but his exit was not. Similarly, the removal of the cards made the movements of the Victors appear innocent. And it took away any evidence of Rajiv driving into the subdivision that night. But otherwise, the removal of the two cards did not create any inconsistencies in the log as far as Justin could see.

Unfortunately for the Prefontaines and Amisha, however, the now-abridged log left them alone atop the list of suspects. Which, Justin admitted to himself, was a shame. He enjoyed Pierre and Carla's company, thought they were good, decent people. And, of course, they had two young children. If he had the chance later to help them, to somehow exonerate them, he would do so. And the same was true of Amisha.

But, right now, Justin simply couldn't afford to have the police sniffing around, thinking he was a suspect in a murder. As it was, he hadn't been able to find the pictures of Justin, Jr. that Griffin had been blackmailing him with. But at least at this point the police had no reason to focus specifically on him, no reason to start digging into his relationship with Griffin. The last thing he needed was for the police to start looking for a motive as to why he might want to kill Griffin. Even if they couldn't prove a case against him, Justin knew how the game was played: the police find the pictures; rumors start to circulate about incriminating photos; the pictures get leaked to the press; his son's political career goes down in flames.

Well, not if Justin could help it.

He took the two incriminating index cards out to the deck and lit his gas grill. "Sorry Pierre, sorry Carla, sorry Amisha," he murmured as he dropped the cards between the jail-like bars of the grill rack and into the fire. He watched as the cards slid through the gaps, melting more than burning as they curled into themselves in a last desperate attempt to escape the hot blue flame.

*   *   *

222

Shelby hated it when friends and colleagues imposed upon their relationship with her at the expense of her professional integrity. So she was especially aware of how unwelcome her phone call would be. But at least her friend was on the Cape, just a short walk in any direction to a beach. Shelby was stuck in her office, her plans to take an August vacation thwarted by the demands of her profession. And the air conditioning was on the fritz, so her office felt like a steam bath.

"Hi, Pam, this is Shelby."

"Shelby, hi! What's up?"

Pam had worked for Shelby in the District Attorney's office in Boston. She had moved to the Cape, now worked for the DA's office in Barnstable. They had been close—Shelby had mentored Pam right out of law school—and still got together every couple of months for lunch.

"Sorry to do this, but I'm trying to find out some information on that hit-and-run death over in Mashpee. Rex Griffin. Can I ask you some questions?"

Pam's normally bubbly voice lost some of its enthusiasm. "One second. Let me close my door." She would talk, but she wasn't thrilled about it.

"Before you say anything, Pam, you should know that I'm friends with Carla and Pierre Prefontaine. They might be on your list of suspects, so I'll understand if you don't want to talk to me about this."

Pam sighed. "Let's do this. I'll tell you what I know about evidence we've collected—if your friends were ever to be charged, you'd be entitled to that anyway. But I can't comment on who the investigation is focusing on or stuff like that."

"Fair enough. Thanks."

"Don't thank me yet—there's not much to tell. The Medical Examiner just got the DNA tests back. No surprise, they confirm the body was Rex Griffin."

"You're treating it like it was intentional?"

"Yeah. It's hard to believe it was just an accident. The guy's got so many enemies, plus he was beat up a few months ago. And the car drove over him a few times...."

"I assume you're checking car bumpers, stuff like that."

"As much as we can. Without a definite suspect, we can't get a search warrant because we don't have probable cause. And by now anyone with anything to hide has been through the car wash a few dozen times, so we're not going to find any clothing fibers or skin or hair residue."

"Do you have any witnesses?"

"No. None of the neighbors saw or heard anything. Griffin's sister was living with him, but she says she went to bed early that night so she didn't even notice he was missing until the next morning. His brother was up visiting for a few days, but he didn't see anything either."

"I didn't know he had a brother."

"I actually just interviewed him—he's autistic, so he didn't have much to offer. Name's Donald. He lives in a group home up near Boston. Just confirmed what we already knew: Griffin went out to walk his dog, didn't come back. That's all he knows. Not surprising—from what I know about autistic people, they're in their own little world."

Shelby sensed there was something her old friend wasn't telling her. "What was he doing there?"

"Just visiting, I guess."

"That doesn't sound like Griffin. He hardly seems like the doting brother."

After a slight pause, Pam sighed and responded. "Actually, his brother came to visit occasionally. But, Griffin did give Donald a job while he was there. He was keeping a log of the license plates and car models of every car that went in and out of the subdivision."

Shelby nodded. "That sounds more like it. No doubt Griffin had something planned, some scheme. He was always plotting something against the neighbors. Maybe he even suspected someone was going to come after him and wanted to help you guys catch the killer."

"I thought about that, but then why have his brother keep the log for the whole day? Why not just keep it for the time he was out walking the dog? I think your first guess is probably right—Griffin was probably up to something."

"Did you get the log?"

"Yeah, Donald had given it to Justin McBride, who passed it on to us. Basically, we were looking for anyone who came into or out of the subdivision between eight and nine o'clock that night. Best we can tell, that's what time Griffin was killed." Pam paused here, then continued. "I'm sorry, Shelby, but the only car that fits that description is one owned by the Prefontaines."

Shelby felt her face flush. "Well, that really doesn't prove anything. They could have been taking the kids out for an ice cream or something."

"You're right."

Shelby sensed her friend was just placating her. "And don't forget, the log wouldn't necessarily include anyone who lives in the subdivision—a neighbor could have run down Griffin, then quietly rolled back into their driveway without ever passing the farmhouse."

"Good point. We've been working from the assumption that the driver just took off, drove away. But, you're right, it's possible they might have just stayed in the subdivision."

"Do you think the list is accurate?"

"It seems to be. We've crosschecked a lot of it already, and so far it matches up with what we know—people doing errands, friends visiting, stuff like that. We're assuming that since the mundane stuff from early in the weekend is accurate, the entries made at the time of death probably are also."

"That makes sense." Not that she wouldn't challenge the assumption in court if she had to. "But, even so, what if Donald just went to the bathroom and missed someone? Or what if he fell asleep for a few minutes? There seems to be a lot of holes here."

"You're right, Shelby. But you asked what we have so far, so I told you." Pam paused, lowered her voice. "Look, if you want, why don't you come down and take a look at the log yourself. Maybe you'll see something that we missed."

"Thanks, Pam, I'd really appreciate that. And sorry if I've been a bit defensive about this...."

"No problem. You'd do the same for me."

Shelby wasn't quite sure how to respond. In fact, she probably wouldn't have bent the rules, even for a close friend. Maybe she needed to think about being a bit more open-minded, a bit less orthodox in the way she viewed the world. She looked back at the notes she had made. "So if Donald was up visiting that weekend, how did he get home if Griffin was dead?"

"Limousine service, same way as he came down. The limo came and picked him up the next morning, just as scheduled. He was very earnest when he told me about it—Rex told him to be packed and ready at eight o'clock in the morning, so he was packed and ready at eight o'clock in the morning."

"He didn't see or hear anything himself?"

"Nope. Kept his log until ten o'clock, then went to bed."

"Well, the log may help narrow the suspects, but there's no way a jury is going to convict someone for murder just based on driving in and out of their own subdivision. It seems to me that you're going to need some forensic stuff...."

"Yup. That's where we're at. And so far, we've got nothing from forensics. Car hits man—that's really all we know right now for sure."

*   *   *

Ace Awry closed the donut shop at 2:30. The town was packed with tourists, but it was too hot for donuts and coffee. Plus, he wanted to go home, change his clothes and jump into the ocean.

He pulled off the main road and onto a bumpy dirt lane. It was a part of the Cape the tourists never saw—four-room homes with peeling paint, laundry hanging on a line, cars up on cement blocks. It was borderline poverty, and it was how many of the Mashpee tribe members lived. At one point Ace had dreamed that he could lead his people out of this life, return to them the rich lands that were rightfully theirs. But he had been young then, and idealistic enough to believe that the White Man's courts would do justice and return tribal lands to the tribe.

His own house, near the end of the lane, was solid and neat and comfortable. He could have afforded to move to a bigger home in a wealthier area of town, but it had never really occurred to him to do so. He lived where he had lived his whole life, surrounded by the people he had grown up with. Why should he move and live among strangers?

He pulled up to his mailbox, thumbed through the stack. He paused at a hand-written envelope, froze when he saw the return address: "Rex Griffin." He had never received mail from a dead man before.

He tore open the letter, the thought of a refreshing swim now pushed to the back of his mind.

Dear Ace:

> *If you are reading this letter, it means that I am dead. Not to be melodramatic, but I have long suspected that someone is trying to kill me. I am therefore writing this letter and giving it to a trusted confidante with instructions to mail it to you in the event of my death.*

> *Regrettably, I find myself in the middle of a high-stakes legal battle, a mere pawn in a real-life game of Monopoly. As you know, there are many people in Mashpee—and some, no doubt, who reside outside of our community—who do not wish to live through another legal battle between the tribe and the townspeople. These individuals, I fear, will stop at nothing to prevent the tribe from re-filing its lawsuit against the town. I have recently been contacted by these individuals, threatened by them, even assaulted by them to the point of requiring a week of hospitalization to treat my injuries. Their demand: that I destroy the tribal history documents and not deliver them to the tribe. You may have wondered why I have been hesitant to turn the documents over to you. Now you have your answer. But fear not; I have not destroyed the tribal records.*

> *The purpose of my letter is to inform you that my trusted confidante, who must remain nameless, will contact you soon after my sister's baby is born. He knows where the documents are hidden, and can access them. It is my desire, even in my death, that the agreement you and I discussed in general terms be brought to fruition. Such a result would ensure the long-term well-being of both my nephew and the Mashpee tribe. My confidante is aware of the details of this agreement and will negotiate the particulars of the matter with you.*

> *For his own safety, the executor of my will, Attorney Justin McBride, knows nothing of these documents. For your safety, as well, I believe it best that you keep this matter a secret for the time being—by that, I mean do not go to the police with this information, and do not*

speak of it to anyone except the other tribal council members, and only then after you have sworn them to secrecy. Our enemies, having killed me before I could deliver the documents to you, may believe they have succeeded in keeping the documents from the tribe. There is nothing to be gained by allowing them to learn otherwise. And it may be that the element of surprise will work to the tribe's advantage.

Good luck, be careful, and Godspeed.

Your friend in this world and the next,

Rex Griffin

Ace pounded his thigh, contemplated the message from beyond. *Damn.* The tribe's future depended on getting those tribal history documents. And soon. But now Griffin had entrusted them to some confidante. Another hurdle.

Griffin had been stringing him along, teasing him, promising to hand over the documents. Ace had been content to play the jolly buffoon, to allow Griffin to believe he was harmless. But Ace knew all about Griffin. Griffin would never give up the documents for anything less than a king's ransom. At least not while he was alive.

Since Griffin's death, Ace had been biding his time. His plan was simply to approach the executor of Griffin's estate and cut a quick deal to buy the documents. The executor would be ignorant of the true value of the documents to the tribe, so a few thousand bucks would probably have done the trick.

But this letter changed everything. Even in death, Griffin had a claw-grip on the documents. And there were apparently others who wanted the documents as badly as he did.

But that would not dissuade Ace. In his younger years he had charged wildly into the fray, an Indian brave in seventies clothing. He was older now, and not as headstrong or impulsive, but the fires of righteous indignation still burned hot within him. The Mashpee tribe—and Native Americans everywhere—had been treated shabbily by both the European settlers and the United States government, and those injustices had yet to be avenged. He would not pass on a second opportunity for reprisal, even in light of the apparent dangers of doing so.

It was rare, after all, to get a second chance.

And the tribe would have to do better this time. In their first suit they had swung for the fences, tried to hit a home run rather than take what the pitcher was giving them. And they had struck out.

Looking back, a better strategy would have been to ask for less, to not push for the return of all the land in the town of Mashpee. The Penobscott tribe in Maine, for example, had settled a similar claim for $30 million. And other tribes—such as the Pequots and the Mohegans in Connecticut—had extracted gambling rights concessions in settlement of their land claims. Rather than insist on the entire town, the tribe should have sought a more palatable result. There had been support among the townspeople to work with the tribe, and the title insurance companies and the state surely would have kicked in some money, but any spirit of cooperation had been poisoned by the tribe's extreme position. The tribe's position was heartfelt—the tribe's attorneys had convinced the tribe members that the land had been stolen from them. But the tribe's quest to recover all land within the town's borders had hit the townspeople where they lived, literally, and after that there was nothing to do but litigate.

This time, they would choke up on the bat and be satisfied with a clean double. The town had grown wealthy over the years—you couldn't find a decent-sized house in the New Seabury section for less than a half-million dollars. So there was plenty to go around. And speaking of New Seabury, the developers there were planning a whole new building spree; the last thing they needed was a lawsuit to cloud their title. Even more reason for them to throw some money on the table.

Which was not to say that a new claim by the tribe wouldn't be met with opposition, some of it even fierce. No matter how many years passed, and no matter how much the socio-economic mix changed over the years as empty-nesters and second-homers settled in Mashpee, the tension and animosity of the 1970s case still lived just beneath the surface of everyday life.

He would have to be careful. It wouldn't take much to spark the old grudges and hatreds. Just ask Rex Griffin.

*   *   *

The ring of the phone seemed harsher, more angry than usual. Pierre picked it up, a strange sense of foreboding passing over him as he did so. "Hello."

"Pierre, this is Shelby. I need to talk to you. But I think Carla should be on the line also. Is she home?"

"Sure. I'll get her."

Carla picked up. "What's up, Shelby?"

"I've got some bad news. I was just talking to a friend of mine who works in the District Attorney's office in Barnstable. She's part of the team investigating Griffin's death. Well, it turns that Griffin has an autistic brother, Donald, who was visiting him the weekend he got killed. Nobody's sure why, but Donald was keeping a log of all the cars that went in and out of the subdivision for that whole weekend. Since the police have a pretty good idea of what time Griffin was killed, they're using the log to narrow down the list of suspects."

Pierre interjected. "Let me guess. Our car is on that log."

"Worse than that. Your Highlander is the only car that went in and out of the subdivision during the window of time the police are looking at."

Carla gasped. "That can't be right. I don't even think we left the house that night. And there must have been more than one car going in and out...."

"You're right. There were some coming in and some others going out. But only yours went in, then out, which is what the police theorized would have been what the killer did."

Pierre grabbed the back of the couch to steady himself. This was like a repeat of his worst nightmare. "You mean the police think we killed Griffin?"

"No, they're not there yet. They agree that there could be a perfectly reasonable explanation for your car going in and then out."

"But, Shelby, I just told you that there is no perfectly reasonable explanation. That was a Saturday and we didn't drive anywhere that night. I was up in my studio finishing up a painting which I needed to deliver on Monday, and Pierre was watching a movie with the girls." Carla paused here, then addressed Pierre. "You didn't go out after the girls went to bed, did you Pierre?"

"No. I put them to bed at eight and then watched the ball game. You came up a little before ten and we watched the news together."

Nobody said anything for a few seconds, then Shelby spoke. Pierre thought he sensed some doubt, or maybe just confusion, in her voice. "Well, it's possible the log isn't accurate. But the police are pretty sure it's authentic–all the other info on it checks out with what they know to be true. Anyway, my friend is going to let me take a look at it, probably in the next week or two. Maybe I'll be able to make some sense of all this. But, anyway, I thought you guys should know about it."

Pierre forced the words out of his mouth. "Shelby, are they going to charge us with the murder?"

"I don't know, Pierre. I really don't know."

*   *   *

Shelby, as usual, was in her office. At least the air conditioning was working. But was her brain?

She put down the phone, stared at it for a few seconds. How could Pierre and Carla claim not to have left the house when the log clearly showed their car doing so? Were her clients lying to her? Or even to each other?

Shelby pictured the layout of their house–Carla's painting studio was in a room above the garage, away from the area where Pierre would have been watching TV. Carla could easily have slipped into the garage and driven away without Pierre knowing. And Pierre could have done the same without Carla noticing, though she would have probably heard the garage door opening when he left. But he could have purposely left it open. Either could then have waited for Griffin, run him down, fled from the subdivision for a half hour and re-turned by ten o'clock. And never have been missed.

Chapter 17

[September]

Justin opened the door, was surprised to see Amisha Raman standing on his front porch. *Absolutely beautiful. Dark, exotic, stately. If I was 40 years younger.* He interrupted himself, laughed quietly. *She still wouldn't have anything to do with me!*

He covered his mouth to hide his smile, escorted Amisha into the foyer. "Hello, Amisha, to what do I owe the pleasure of this visit?" He hoped he didn't sound too sappy. But she was probably used to men making fools of themselves around her.

She flashed him a perfect smile, but couldn't hide from him the sadness in her eyes. "If it's not too much trouble, I would appreciate a few minutes of your time."

"No trouble at all. Come on in." He escorted her to the kitchen table. She even smelled good—just the right combination of floral and musk. "I'll make us some tea. Now, what can I do for you?"

"I've come to petition you for a favor, Justin. We are trying to obtain a bank loan on our home, but the lawsuit by Griffin is preventing us from doing so. I believe the correct term is that there exists a 'cloud on the title.'"

Justin nodded. "Yes. No bank would want a mortgage on a property that already had an attachment on it."

"My problem is that we need the money from the mortgage to pay the IRS. Since Mr. Griffin is now dead, is there any reason his attachment cannot be removed?"

Good question. "Well, you've come to the right place. As executor of his estate, I'm the one who can make that decision. Unfortunately, my hands are tied right now because things are still being processed in the Probate Court. I can't do anything now, but in a few months I'd be happy to help you. We both know, after all, that his claim against you is bogus."

Amisha looked down at her hands, turned her face away from Justin. "A few months will be too late." Her voice was soft, almost a whisper. She turned toward him with large, wet eyes. "Justin, please, is there any way you can help me? This is more than a simple matter of money. Please?"

He had known women who had used their beauty to manipulate men, who had played the damsel in distress to their advantage. But this was different. There was no melodrama, no artfulness in her plea. She was scared. Of something.

He sighed. He was 73 years old—the worst that could happen to him was that he would be sanctioned by the court, maybe even disbarred. But so what? He was planning on retiring anyway. And, let's face it, he had recently done things far worse than releasing a property from a bogus lawsuit. These people had been victimized by Griffin long enough. Maybe it was time for a little justice in a world full of laws. "Very well, my dear. I will prepare the necessary paperwork."

She offered him a half smile, then a full hug. "Thank you. Thank you so much."

"Well, don't mention it." It was a long time since he had blushed.

She smiled at him again. "Oh, one more thing. Do you remember you offered to speak to the authorities about that e-mail Griffin sent from my husband's computer?"

Justin stammered a response. He had totally forgotten. "Well, with everything going on, I just haven't had a chance...."

She interrupted him with a touch of her hand on his arm. "Don't worry about it, Justin. In fact, I think now it would be best if you just let the investigation take its own course."

*   *   *

Billy fought to concentrate, forced his eyes away from the window and back to the mathematics equation his teacher was scrawling on the blackboard.

Mr. Peters was his name. He had been friendly with his father, had taught with him at the high school for almost 20 years. He had come to the funeral last week, had comforted his mother, had put a protective arm around Billy.

Mr. Peters would, Billy knew, cut him some slack for the first few weeks of school. As would the other teachers. But at some point Billy would have to get his shit together. Or else his son's father would not be going to college.

In some ways, it seemed like only a few days since Rex Griffin had told him about Denise being pregnant. Yet so much had changed over the past six months. His father was dead. Rex Griffin was dead. And his baby would be born soon.

Denise had called a couple of nights ago. He could tell she was nervous, even scared a bit—she had never called him before. In fact, they hadn't really spoken since his two Friday night winter pizza dates. Looking back, he knew he should have at least tried to call her, tried to be supportive. She hadn't done anything wrong. It wasn't her fault that her brother got his rocks off from pimping his sister— Griffin was probably watching the whole time through a crack in the door. Maybe even videotaped it, the sick bastard. Anyway, as tough as it was for Billy, Denise was the one who had to carry the baby.

But it seemed to Billy that the upcoming birth of her baby had somehow made her more self-assured. She may be retarded, or learning-impaired, or whatever they called it, but Denise was taking this whole pregnancy thing very seriously. And based on their conversation, she knew a lot more about this childbirth stuff than he did. Even with his mother trying to explain things.

Denise had called to tell him about her latest visit to the doctor. He didn't really understand the details, but the bottom line was that the baby might come a few weeks early. But the doctor said things looked fine. Billy had thanked her for the news and hung up.

Then he had called back. "Denise, this is Billy again. Um, I forgot to ask you something. Would you like it ... would it be okay, if I came to the hospital with you?"

He had heard a nervous giggle, then a tentative response. "Okay, Billy."

A knock at the classroom door interrupted his thoughts. He saw his mother's head lean in, make eye contact with Mr. Peters, nod toward Billy. "Billy," he said kindly, "please take your things and go with your mother."

Dominique let Billy drive to the hospital, hoping it might keep his mind occupied. She had been a young woman when Billy was born, but not this young. She saw it all the time as a school nurse at the high school—kids having kids, babies having babies. But she never thought she'd be one of the young grandmothers. Not that Billy was at all to blame.

She sighed. As if blame really had anything to do with it. A life had been created, and now must be nourished and cherished. The rights and the wrongs of it all were irrelevant.

They arrived at the hospital, took a seat in the waiting room. She saw Justin McBride seated in the corner, reading a book. She greeted him, introduced him to Billy.

"Nice to meet you, Billy. I'm Denise's legal guardian, which means I'll probably be the baby's guardian as well."

Billy shook hands. Dominique noticed that her son's eyes had originally focused on the lawyer's over-sized eyebrows, but then shifted quickly downward to look directly into the man's eyes. She was glad that he had caught himself, pleased that he hadn't stared rudely. He spoke in a strong, clear voice. "Were you friends with Mr. Griffin?"

Dominique watched Justin as he responded. She was glad Billy had asked the question—it gave her the chance to study the lawyer's response without him noticing her scrutiny. She, too, had wondered about the relationship between Griffin and Justin.

Justin laughed lightly, then spoke. Dominique studied his eyes, watched his hands, tracked his breathing. "Not exactly. We were associates, but not friends. In fact, even associates is probably too strong a word. Suffice it to say that our relationship was one of grudging respect, not mutual affection."

Billy nodded. Dominique, too, was satisfied by the reply—she sensed no artifice in it. But, then again, he could just be a good liar. She hadn't been around him enough to become fluent in his body language. Not yet, at least.

Billy continued the conversation. "Mr. McBride, do you know if Denise has decided on a name for the baby?"

"I don't know, son. Why do you ask?"

"It's just that, well, I don't really want her to name him Rex."

The attorney smiled kindly, nodded to Billy. "I understand." He started to move back to his seat, then turned again to address Billy and his mother. "You know, this is really none of my business, but I do know that your father just passed away. Would you like me to suggest to Denise that perhaps the baby should be named Vernon?"

Dominique, again, studied the man. It was a kind, sensitive offer. But was it more than that? Was it also an attempt to ingratiate himself with them—scripted and premeditated? Or had the thought really just popped into his head this moment? Again, she sensed no avarice. Yet the man was an admitted associate of Rex Griffin....

Billy looked to his mother for guidance before responding. She nodded to him, but allowed him to speak. "We would like that, Mr. McBride. Thank you."

A few hours later, a nurse appeared, conferred with Justin for a minute, then escorted him away. He turned to address them as he left. "They need to do a C-section because the baby is turned wrong. But don't worry, they say it's not a problem. I need to go and sign the consent forms. Then I'll go talk to Denise about the name."

Billy looked at his mother, concern on his young face. She took his hand, squeezed it tightly. "Don't worry, son. It's not uncommon. You, too, had to be delivered that way. And look how you turned out."

"That's not exactly encouraging, Mom." She could see him try to smile, appreciated his attempt to lighten the mood.

Another hour and a half passed, then the nurse returned to the waiting room. She was smiling this time. "If anyone would like to come meet young Vernon Griffin Victor, you can follow me."

*   *   *

Ace wiped down the countertop with a damp cloth for what must have been the three millionth time, slapped at what must have been the 30 millionth fly.

Five weeks had passed since he had received Griffin's letter from

236

the beyond. Ace was growing impatient—the tribe's lobbyist had worked his magic, and the Bureau of Indian Affairs had begun the process of making a final decision on the tribe's petition.   Unfortunately, Ace still didn't have the tribal history documents that would clinch the case, and the BIA might rule on the tribe's petition for federal recognition any day. It was crucial to get the tribal history documents down to Washington before the BIA made its ruling.

Without the documents, the tribe's chances of succeeding were less than 50-50, perhaps far less in light of the new Republican administration's track record on Native American issues. But with the Griffin documents, even a biased Bureau would have to concede the tribe's claim was valid. Then the tribe could re-file its land claim suit. Or at least threaten to do so.

But until Griffin's so-called "trusted confidante" contacted Ace, there was nothing to do but wait. And Griffin had said no contact would be made until after Denise's baby had been born.

Now, finally, the baby had arrived. A healthy boy, thank God. Who knows what would have happened if the boy had not survived childbirth.

Not that the kid had too much to look forward to. A retarded mother, a teen-aged father. And conceived by a sick uncle, now dead, as a pawn in some elaborate game.

Ace thought about it for a minute. Maybe pawn was the wrong word. Maybe the baby was the young prince. Just as ancient rulers had arranged marriages between their offspring to cement peace, perhaps the baby would somehow keep the peace between the town and the tribe.

No, that was probably wrong. This baby would not bring peace, this baby would bring war between the tribe and the town.

This was the baby's destiny. For this, the baby had been conceived.

Two days later, Ace's phone rang. Finally. He was sitting in his living room, his feet up on his recliner, enjoying a beer and the Red Sox game.

"Is this Ace Awry?"

"Yes."

"I believe you've been waiting for my call."

Ace kicked his feet down, leaned over and looked at the Caller

I.D. screen: "Unknown." Not surprising—the confidante sounded like he knew what he was doing. In fact, it sounded like he was using some voice-altering technology as well. "Yes, yes I have been."

"Good. I'm prepared to turn over the documents to you. But first I need you to sign the agreement."

"I understand. Send it right on over, Fed Ex if you don't mind. We're in a bit of a rush here. I assume the terms are as I discussed with Mr. Griffin."

"I believe so. Mr. Griffin prepared the contract before his death. But please understand—I am only an intermediary, I have no authority in this matter. In fact, I have not even read the contract. So the contract must be executed without any changes. Only then am I authorized to release the documents to you. My instructions are very specific on this matter—there can be no revisions."

Ace sighed. He knew a bit about business, had seen a few "take-it-or-leave-it" and "not negotiable" deals in the past. They were all bullshit. Everything was negotiable. But this one seemed pretty fail-safe—how do you negotiate with a dead man?

The Fed Ex package arrived the next day, as promised.

Ace grabbed a beer, sat down at his kitchen table, opened the thick envelope. The agreement itself was thick—18 pages. He'd grind his way through it later. And at some point he'd probably need a lawyer to look at it. But for now he concentrated on the cover letter, twisting his ponytail in his fingers as he read:

Dear Ace:

I believe you will find that this agreement accurately reflects the general deal you and I discussed this past summer. I realize it is long and complex—perhaps more so than it need be. But the fact that you are reading this letter means that my caution is well-founded.

As you read through the contract, you will see that I have drafted many provisions intended to make it impossible for the tribe to renege on its obligations. It may be that the tribe—at a later date, after achieving federal recognition as a sovereign entity—could renounce and repudiate any contract it might sign with a non-tribe member. But, according to the tribe's by-laws, it cannot refuse to honor a contract made with one of its own members. And since Denise's baby is both a member of the tribe and a 51% beneficiary of the Griffin Family Trust, any agreement with the trust is in fact an agreement with the baby and therefore cannot be renounced.

In addition, I have set forth in particular detail the business agreement between the trust and the tribe. In summary:

1. The tribe will receive the 19th-century historical documents.

2. On or before February 1st of next year, the tribe will pay to the Griffin Family Trust the sum of $50 million as payment for these documents.

3. In the alternative, the tribe may enter into a settlement with the town and the Smithson Farm Estates subdivision owners. The settlement with the subdivision owners shall result in the residents being ejected and all the property of the Smithson Farm Estates subdivision being deeded to the tribe, free and clear. The tribe shall then immediately enter into a 20-year lease (a copy of which is attached to the agreement) with the Griffin Family Trust whereby the trust, for a cost of $1 per year, shall have the right to use and sublease all the property in the entire subdivision, excepting the land containing Metacomet's grave (which the tribe may use as a museum and/or tourist attraction). The trust will have the right to lease these properties either on a seasonal or year-round basis and retain the income from these leases.

4. In the event the settlement in paragraph 3 is concluded prior to February 1st of next year, the $50 million payment will be waived.

Of course, as you and I discussed, this $50 million sum will never be paid. I have no doubt that the tribe will soon have assets far in excess of this figure, but it would be foolish of the tribe to pay $50 million to the trust when it can instead acquire and then lease to the trust the subdivision property, which has a value of perhaps $7-8 million. But this $50 million payment due on February 1st will be like a ticking time bomb for all parties involved. It will be in nobody's interest—not the town, not the tribe, not the title insurance companies, not even the subdivision owners *(who, no doubt, will receive quite a premium from the title insurance companies for their properties)—to allow this date to pass and this sum of money to 'leave the table.' All parties will benefit if a settlement is reached before February 1ˢᵗ. Which is why I have structured the deal this way—there is no benefit to another decades-long battle between the town and the tribe. Such a battle would enrich only the lawyers. And my family needs the money to live on now, not 10 or 20 years from now.*

Ace made a quick trip to the bathroom, grabbed another Michelob from the refrigerator on his way back to the table. That friggin' Griffin was a ball buster. Ace started to take a sip from the bottle, than thought he'd better finish the letter first.

I must, unfortunately, insist that the terms of this agreement be non-negotiable. I have instructed my confidante accordingly: He is prohibited from delivering the tribal history documents to you unless this agreement is signed in its present form, without any amendments or modifications. The tribe has two options: pay the $50 million, or acquire the Smithson Farm Estates property and lease it to the trust by February 1. There is no third choice.

I have confidence that you will be able to shepherd this settlement around the many minefields and pitfalls that await it, Ace. In the end, I think everyone will realize it is a good deal for all involved. The tribe—finally—will be fairly compensated for its loss by extracting a fair settlement from the town and the title insurance companies, a sum it can use to endow its future. The subdivision neighbors will see an end to all the litigation. The title insurance companies will scream and holler, but in the end they will see the wisdom of not litigating a case that could cost them hundreds of millions of dollars (and that's a conservative estimate—did you know that the assessed value of the town land is in excess of $1.5 billion?). And the town can avoid another civil war.

So it's up to you, Ace. Good luck and Godspeed.

Yours from the beyond,
Rex Griffin

Somehow, even in death, Griffin was holding all the cards. Then again, he was also dead, good hand or not. What was the dead man's hand in poker, the hand Wild Bill Hickok was holding when he got shot? Two pair—black aces and black eights. Ace knew he would have to be careful not to play the same hand. Of course, in the Wild West, they'd shoot the Indian before he even made it to the poker table.

Not that Griffin had given him much leeway in how to play this out. It would be Ace's decision on *how* to close the deal and *when* to close the deal, but, make no mistake, the deal itself was Griffin's. The tribe had no wiggle room—if they wanted the documents, they had to accept Griffin's terms.

But in a way, maybe it was a good thing. With those terms came limitations, constraints that would prevent the tribe from overplaying its hand as it did last time. As always, there would be members who would advocate fighting the town to the bitter end, insisting that nothing less than a return of all tribal lands would be unacceptable. Ace knew the type—it had been the face in his mirror 20 years ago. But these extremists had been effectively neutralized by Griffin's $50 million time bomb.

Ace thought about it more. No, it wouldn't be the extremists that blocked this deal—Griffin had de-clawed them. Ace's problem would come from the moderate members of the tribe, those who had been opposed to filing the original suit against their neighbors. He had little respect for most of them. They had been self-righteous in their opposition to the original suit, but their motives had been less than selfless. *It's wrong to sue our neighbors*, they had preached. Well, yes, if you happen to own a popular restaurant in town and don't want to be boycotted. *We shouldn't be trying to take people's homes*, they had scolded. Especially true if you happen to live in a mini-mansion yourself that could be forfeited to the tribe. *Our actions are choking off the local economy.* Good point, but a bit self-serving when you happen to be an electrician whose business is suffering due to the construction slowdown.

Ace had never admitted it to anyone, but in some ways the selfish-ness of the tribe members had served to prove the very point that the lawyers for the town were trying to make to the jury: that the tribe had ceased to function as a tribe, that its members had assimi-lated into mainstream society. Ace didn't really believe it to be true—he had seen too many occasions where the tribe members had made sacrifices for the greater good. But the stakes were high this time, and he knew he needed to find a way to manage the more moderate members of the tribe.

And that's where Metacomet's grave came in so handy. The tribe members could differ on the economic benefits of suing the town, but all members would agree on the spiritual value of a settlement that enabled the tribe to re-claim the great Metacomet's gravesite. Ace shook his head—had Griffin been ahead of Ace on this issue as well? Is that why he had drafted the agreement to specifically provide for the use of a chunk of the property as a home base for the Metacomet tourist attraction? Griffin could just as easily have kept control over the entire subdivision for his family, but he instead carved out a parcel for the tribe to use along with the gravesite. Intentional or not, it would be effective leverage in enlisting the support of moderates like Ronnie Lemaire.

Yes, Ronnie Lemaire. He was well-respected in the tribe—his opposition to the suit last time had almost derailed it. But he was also wearing a second hat now. He was one of the Smithson Farm Estates subdivision owners. And if this deal was going to come together, the subdivision owners were going to have to sign off on it. They would, after all, be losing their homes. So if Ronnie wanted to avoid a suit this time, he'd better be able to convince—or, if necessary, coerce—his neighbors into packing up and moving out. Ace smiled at the irony. There was plenty of open land out in the western part of the country, Ronnie could tell them.

*   *   *

Shelby was almost afraid to examine the log. The more she thought about it the more she was forced to conclude that her clients—no, make that her friends—were lying to her. That didn't necessarily make them murderers, but it sure did strike her as odd behavior.

And if they were going to lie to her, why not make up some simple story about driving out to pick up milk or something? The answer, she had concluded, was that such a story required that it be vouched for by both spouses—if one had left the house for an errand, after all, he or she would have told the other. But if one had left the house to commit a murder, he or she would have kept their movements a secret and the other spouse could not now vouch for the errand story. So, as much as her brain fought to find a reasonable explanation, the only conclusion she could reach was that there was only one lying spouse. And that spouse was also a murdering one.

Pam brought her into a small meeting room. They were in Barnstable, in a non-descript office building just down the street from the county courthouse. It took Shelby less than a second to size up the room—4 government-issue chairs around a square government-issue table. Nothing on the walls.

"You know I'm going to have to stay with you while you look through this, right?"

"Of course. And, like I said, I really appreciate it."

"No problem. Maybe you can help us solve this case. But, I have to tell you, right now your friends are on our short list of suspects."

Shelby shrugged. It wasn't exactly the news she wanted to hear, but it wasn't that surprising either.

Pam reached into a plastic storage container, pulled out a Ziploc bag. "This is the log. There are about 40 index cards, covering the three days before Griffin was killed. The last three cards are the ones that correspond to the time window when Griffin was killed. And the 12 before that are for earlier in the day."

"Thanks." Shelby pulled the three cards off the bottom of the stack, examined them. Each card contained two or three entries, each entry written in dark, block letters. Sure enough, the log showed Pierre and Carla's Toyota Highlander leaving the subdivision at 8:33, then returning later that night at 9:16. These times would support a murder theory whereby the Highlander waited for Griffin, ran him down sometime around 8:30, exited the subdivision at 8:33, then returned almost 45 minutes later.

She looked up at Pam. "How about these other entries? Whose cars are they?"

"Well, for most part, they're friends and other visitors. We're checking them out, but none of them seem to have any connection to Griffin. Otherwise, we do have an entry for Amisha Raman's car leaving the subdivision at a little before nine o'clock. And there's an entry for Ronnie Lemaire–the log has him returning at about 8:45. But nothing for him leaving, which is a bit strange."

"Have you talked to them?"

"Just basic stuff. Amisha says she had a fight with her husband and went to stay in a hotel. Interesting, but not necessarily of any relevance. Ronnie says he went out with Lorraine for dinner at about 6:30. We'll probably follow up more later, but there's a lot of things we're trying to look at here and we're a bit understaffed. It's funny—people watch these TV shows and expect us to have a team of forensic experts swarming over the crime scene. I saw one episode the other night where they found a piece of evidence by picking through the trash bags in the county dump. Like that's really going to happen."

Shelby laughed, and Pam continued. "Someone asked me if the forensic guys could tell who killed Griffin by looking at the tire marks on the body. I suppose if it had been a muddy day and the car had gone right over his face or his hand we could try to get a match. But it's not like there were any tracks on his windbreaker."

Shelby nodded. She remembered how frustrating it had been to try to investigate crimes on a shoestring budget. She picked up one of the index cards, rubbed her fingers across it as she thought about the case. Pam laughed lightly. "Hey, careful with that, don't rub the ink off!"

Shelby smiled, looked down at the dark block letters on the card. "Not likely. Donald looks like he wrote this with a dentist's drill...." She stopped mid-sentence, held the card up to the light. "Wait a second. Look at the back of this. You can see where he pushed so hard that the paper is imprinted on the back." She turned it over. "And look at the front. You can see where the card that was on top of it left an imprint also."

"So?"

"Well, have you looked to see if the imprints from one card in the log match up with the next card in the sequence?"

"I'm not following you."

"All right. Picture this. Donald has a stack of cards. He writes on the top one, but he pushes so hard that you can see the faint imprint of his letters on the card below it, right?"

"Okay."

"Here, give me the card that follows this one in the sequence."

Pam handed Shelby the card, then reached into a drawer and produced a magnifying glass. Shelby studied the cards, then sat back and grinned. "Here, check this out. This is the last card. You can see the two entries written in pen, but can you also see the imprint of an entry below those two?"

"Um, yes. I can't see what it says, but there's definitely an imprint there."

"Right. Now take a look at the card that supposedly preceded it in the sequence. How many entries?"

Pam dropped the magnifying glass onto the table. "Holy shit. You're right. There are only two. Based on the imprint, there should be three entries. There must be some cards missing."

"Didn't you tell me that you got these from Justin McBride?"

"Yeah...."

"Well, isn't it possible that McBride, when he gave you the cards, might have removed one or two cards from the stack?"

"Sure, but why?"

"You tell me. But so much for my clients being the prime suspects in this murder."

✻   ✻   ✻

Shelby got back in her Saab, lowered the convertible top. She decided to drive straight to Mashpee to tell Pierre and Carla what she had discovered. Not that it necessarily exonerated them. There was still the small matter that they were insisting that they hadn't left the house at all that night. She would, of course, represent them if they wanted. But only if they played it straight with her. She didn't need to be lied to by clients, especially ones that were supposed to be friends.

A half hour later she was sitting on the deck with Pierre and Carla. They only had an hour before the girls came home from school, so Shelby got right to the point and summarized her discovery of the lost log cards.

Pierre nodded. "Justin must have pulled some out."

245

"Which, it seems to me, he would only do it he had something to hide," Carla added.

"That seems to be the most obvious explanation. But it's also possible that Donald simply lost a card or two. In any event, it definitely helps you guys because it makes it possible there are other suspects. But it still doesn't explain what your Highlander is doing out driving around at night with you guys sitting at home."

Pierre and Carla looked back at her blankly. Finally Pierre shrugged, then spoke. "I suppose it's possible that somebody stole our car and then returned it later that night...."

Shelby pursed her lips. "Look, guys, you have to be straight with me. Are you absolutely certain you didn't drive anywhere that night? Think about it over night, talk about it, then give me your answer tomorrow, okay? And remember a couple of things: anything you tell me is confidential and can't be used in court against you." She paused here, took a deep breath. "And the same goes for anything you tell each other. Nobody can make you testify against your spouse. But the bottom line is, if I'm going to help you I really need to know the truth."

Carla answered without even looking at Pierre. "Look, Shelby, I understand why you're skeptical, but we don't need to talk about anything over night. We already told you: we didn't leave the house that night. I can't put it any more clearly than that."

Shelby nodded, smiled. "All right then. There must be another explanation that we haven't thought of." She stood up, hugged Carla, then turned and did the same to Pierre. "I'll talk to you guys tomorrow. Good night."

*   *   *

Pierre walked Shelby out to her car. He needed a few minutes to be alone, to think. What was that old expression? When you've eliminated all the other possibilities, the truth, no matter how improbable it seems, reveals itself. Was it possible that Carla had killed Rex Griffin? What other explanation could there be for the Highlander being on the log? It would have been easy for Carla to slip out without him noticing. And the whole idea that someone had stolen–

or, more accurately, borrowed–the Highlander was ridiculous. The car had been locked in the garage and alarmed, and there was no evidence of any tampering or break-in.

But was his Carla capable of murder? The same Carla that scooped up house spiders and dropped them out a window rather than squashing them? And, yet, she did support the death penalty in certain cases....

He began to make his way back to the house. Carla met him at the door, a coy smile on her face. "So, you think I might be a murderer, huh?"

He stammered a response. "Well, no, of course not...."

She took his hand, led him to the couch. "Look, Pierre. I've been through this already once before, remember? You were accused of murder, and all the evidence pointed to you. And I had a decision to make: Should I ask you if you did it? But in the end I decided just to trust you–I knew, in my heart, that you were incapable of it. So why insult you by even asking? Well, it's the same thing all over again. I'm not going to drive myself crazy wondering if you slipped out and murdered Rex Griffin. I'm just not going to do that."

He smiled. But she still hadn't come right out and said she didn't do it. "I guess that's good advice. But I know I didn't do it, and yet our car is on the log...."

"Look. Would you have ever thought Bruce was framing you for murder?"

"No."

"That's my point. Sometimes there's a perfectly reasonable explanation that nobody has thought of yet."

"Well, I'd feel better if we had one here...."

"All right, so let's brainstorm a bit. Why was Donald keeping the log in the first place?"

"Shelby mentioned two possibilities. It could be that Griffin was worried he was going to get attacked again and wanted to be able to give the police some evidence...."

Carla cut in. "That seems far-fetched to me. He was attacked last time by a guy coming from the woods, not by a car. And Donald was only up visiting for three days. Why would Griffin be so sure that he would be attacked that particular weekend? It just doesn't add up to me."

"Okay, I agree. The other possibility is that he was planning some other scam and wanted to keep track of all of our movements."

"That makes more sense to me."

"Yeah, but it still doesn't explain how the Highlander ended up on the log."

"Well, how about this? Griffin, in general, is worried he might get attacked. So he tells Donald that, if he doesn't come back, Donald should add the Highlander to the log. Maybe Griffin even wrote out the make and model and color for him before he left."

"But why?"

"Just for revenge. One last chance to screw us. Or maybe he thought he'd survive the next attack and wanted to be able to point the finger at us."

Pierre nodded. It was a reach. But, then again, so was the thought of Carla running down a man in cold blood, then returning to calmly watch the nightly news with him before bed.

Carla put her hand on his knee. "Or how about this one: We know Justin had custody of the log, and we also know he may have tampered with it. Maybe he added the Highlander to it himself."

Pierre nodded again. But why? "That one seems possible...."

"Look, I don't know if any of my theories are right, but my point is that there are lots of possibilities here. I'm not ready to jump to the conclusion that I'm sharing a bed with a murderer. I'm just not going to. And I won't have any trouble sleeping tonight."

Pierre wished he could say the same.

*　　*　　*

Ronnie had been surprised to get the call from Ace Awry—the two men rarely spoke, even though they were first cousins. But that meant it was probably important, so Ronnie agreed to swing by Ace's donut shop later that afternoon.

He had no doubt that the conversation would involve Metacomet's grave. For some reason, the tribal council had been secretive about the discovery; Ronnie had heard about it from Pierre

Prefontaine, not from the tribe. Probably not a bad strategy in this case—if word got out, excitement would build, and that would just give Griffin more leverage over the tribe. But now that Griffin was dead, why the need for continued secrecy?

Ronnie shrugged. An hour with Ace and he'd probably know more than he cared to.

He sat down at the counter, took Ace's outstretched hand. "How ya' doin', Ace?" It struck Ronnie that Ace had not aged well. As a young man, Ace had been handsome and athletic. And more—the girls not only flocked to him, they stayed with him, captivated by his charisma and idealism. He was going to change the world. It had worked when he was younger, but the whole thing was a bit comical now, an overweight, pony-tailed donut shop owner plotting a Don Quixote-like quest to win back America from the White Man.

"Can't complain. How's business?"

"Like you said, can't complain." He swatted at a fly that had landed on his arm. "Lots of construction, so we're putting in lots of systems. Plus the regular stuff." Actually, that was a lie. Business was okay, but he was barely keeping his head above water. Loretta had gotten into the habit of taking monthly shopping trips to the Boston boutiques, and Ronnie had been spending so much time trying to land the big contracts to justify his purchase of some fancy new equipment that many of his steady customers had left him. Any kind of slowdown in the local economy, and he was in trouble.

"Glad to hear it. Can I get you some coffee or something?"

"No thanks, I'm good." The cheap bastard would probably have charged him for anything he ordered. "So what's up, Ace?" He knew Ace didn't want to talk about the septic business. Unless he wanted some work done for free.

Ace dropped his voice. "The shit is gonna hit the fan in the next few weeks. I'm talking big stuff."

"I heard something about Metacomet's grave, over in my neighborhood...."

Ace nodded. "That's part of it. But it's bigger than that. We're getting ready to re-file the lawsuit. And this time we're pretty sure we can win."

Ronnie rolled his eyes, turned his head away in disgust. "Damn it,

Ace, let it go already." Ronnie wasn't surprised. He had done some digging after he had first heard from Pierre and Carla that Ace was working with Griffin. So he knew that Griffin had found some historical documents that validated the tribe's claim of continuous existence. Or, at least, Griffin had claimed they were historical. It wouldn't have surprised Ronnie if they turned out to be fake. In any event, he had hoped that Griffin had taken the documents with him to his grave, away from Ace and his plans for civil war. A battle like that would likely drive Ronnie and his business straight into bank- ruptcy.

Ace held up his hand, cut him off. "Let me finish. It's not gonna be like last time." He described the documents Griffin had found, then outlined the agreement Griffin had dictated from the grave. "So that's it—if we want Metacomet's gravesite, we have to do this his way."

"Why not just go buy the land from Pierre Prefontaine? Then just forget about all this lawsuit bullshit."

"Because the grave is partially on Griffin's land also. And the only way to get Griffin's land is to do his deal."

Ronnie nodded. Griffin dead wasn't much better than Griffin alive—he was still making trouble, still screwing things up. "Shit, Ace. This is exactly what happened last time. Everyone said we were filing the suit just to put pressure on the town to settle. But that's bullshit. You know what happens once you sue—the press gets involved, then you got yourself a circus. A bunch of yahoos from around the country fly in waving their Indian Nation flags, the townspeople get pissed, shit like that." *Businesses fail.*

"But that's the beauty of Griffin's deal. If we don't settle, it'll cost us $50 million. So we'll *have* to settle. I've thought about this a lot, Ronnie. It's the only way to get Metacomet's grave."

Ronnie sniffed. "Yeah, like that's what you really care about. You've always just wanted this fight, Ace. Wounded Knee without the bullets."

Ace surprised Ronnie with his answer. "You know what, Ronnie? You're right. I was more interested in proving a point last time, more interested in revenge. And I was wrong. But it's not like that this time. We have a chance to get a huge chunk of cash for the tribe, plus get

Metacomet's grave. And we won't have to tear the town apart to do it. I really believe that."

Ronnie stared out the window. He was surprised to realize he actually believed his cousin was being sincere. "Even if I believed you, Ace, I still don't see how you can do this without screwing up this town again. It's like last time—in order to get the title insurance companies to pay attention, you have to file the lawsuit. And once you file it, people get pissed. You guys forget that other tribes, when they sue, they sue the states or the feds. But we gotta sue the town— our own neighbors. I mean, the suit basically says, 'Get the fuck out of your homes, this is our town.' It's hard to make that sound too friendly."

Ace nodded. "I know it's hard. But I think we can do it. We just have to explain to people that the lawsuit is just a formality, some- thing we have to do to get the title insurance companies involved. That's why we need people like you to help out. Everyone knows you were against the last lawsuit. So they trust you. If you tell them it's no big deal, they'll believe you."

"I don't know about that, Ace. Most of the people who live here now weren't even around during the last suit."

"Yeah, but the new people aren't the ones we care about—I mean, they're just here on weekends anyway. But the ones we do care about, the old-timers, they're the ones that matter. And they'll listen to you, Ronnie."

Ronnie sighed. "I don't know, Ace...."

"Look, I gotta tell you, the council has pretty much decided. We're gonna do this. But it sure would make me feel better if you were with us."

Ronnie felt his face redden. "You can't just ram something like this through without consulting the tribe!"

"We're not ramming anything through, Ronnie. If you had been at the meeting last night, you would have heard all about it. We took a vote...."

Ronnie sat back on his stool. It had been his choice to skip the meeting to go see the Red Sox play. What was that about Nero fiddling? He sighed. "All right. I'll help you. But do me one favor."

"What's that?"

251

"Keep it quiet until next week. I'm going to the dentist tomorrow, and, I'm not kidding you, he was so pissed off last time we sued that he tried to kill me with that drill. I can still smell my friggin' teeth burning...."

*   *   *

Bruce knew, from Dominique, that Ace and the other tribal council members had signed the agreement Griffin had drafted, then mailed it to a post office box in Boston. And, as promised, Griffin's trusted confidante had delivered the documents to Ace a few days later. But they didn't come by UPS. Instead, a Federal Express envelope arrived one day at Ace's house. Inside the envelope Ace had found a safe deposit box key taped to an index card with the name and address of a local bank. No note.

Ace, of course, had headed right to the bank. He had been surprised, Dominique reported, to see that his name—alongside a decent forgery of his signature—was listed as a co-owner of the box. He had opened the box, examined the documents, and left them there. That was three days ago.

Since then, Bruce had been watching him, trying to get inside his head. Not that it took too much insight: The man was scared. The question was, why?

It was possible Ace had murdered Griffin, in which case he would, understandably, be nervous and skittish about getting caught. But, if Ace was the murderer, it was doubtful he was also responsible for the beating Griffin took over the summer because, from what Bruce had learned, Griffin and Ace hadn't even met until after Griffin's recovery. So, even as a murderer, Ace might fear that the same person who attacked Griffin might also attack him, since he now had the documents. After all, anybody who had been tracking Griffin—as Bruce had been—would have seen Griffin meeting with Ace, and probably would have also seen Griffin stash the documents at the bank in the safe deposit box. And now Ace had gone right into that same bank.

But if Ace was not the murderer, he would have even more reason to be frightened. Someone had killed Griffin, presumably to block the delivery of the documents to Ace. Now that Ace was planning to deliver those documents to Washington, the same motive for murder applied.

So, either way, Ace had reason to be a bit jumpy.

And lack of sleep apparently wasn't helping.

The first night after Ace had visited the bank, Bruce had sat outside Ace's house, watching him pace and fidget the night away. On the second day, Ace had closed up the donut shop early and driven to Sandwich, just north of Mashpee, where he spent a half-hour inside an antique shop that, according to a sign in the window, specialized in historical documents. Bruce's guess was that Ace wanted to authenticate the documents before he submitted them to the BIA, but first wanted to interview the antique shop owner to make sure he was trustworthy before actually presenting the documents. At least that's the way Bruce would have handled it.

After visiting the antique shop, Ace had checked himself into a small motel in Falmouth—his light had been on all night again. And this morning, the third day, Ace skipped the donut shop entirely. Instead he drove straight to Mashpee Commons, to the bank in the building that looked like an old Wild West saloon. He waited in the parking lot for it to open. Bruce parked down the street, watched from behind an adjacent building. Bruce's guess was that Ace would grab the documents, bring them to the antique shop for authentication, then head right to Logan Airport for a flight to Washington to make his delivery. Then come home and sleep.

Another car pulled into the parking lot, slid into a spot between Ace and the bank. American car, black, older model, full-sized. Two men in the front seat. Bruce focused his binoculars on Ace, watched as an anxiety-ridden and sleep-deprived Ace studied the back of the men's heads. Bruce imagined the picture Ace's mind was drawing— thick-necked, brown-toothed, unshaven. Maybe even a lazy eye. Definitely big.

At nine-thirty, the bank lights flicked on. Ace grabbed a briefcase off the passenger seat, opened the car door, made no effort to hide the fact he was watching the other car as he walked briskly toward the front door. Bruce saw a man get out of the car, heard the distant thud of a car door being slammed. Ace, too, heard the slam, scurried into the bank lobby.

Bruce tucked his binoculars behind a bush, followed the men into the bank. He doubted the men in the car had any interest in Ace—in fact, nobody beside Bruce had taken any interest in him at all over the past three days. But Bruce couldn't be sure.

The man from the car was standing at a teller window, his back to Ace. Bruce watched Ace study the man. Broad-shouldered, average height, probably about 30 years old. Blue jeans, work jacket and boots.

Apparently satisfied that the man was no threat to him, Ace signed in, then walked with a bank employee into the vault. A few minutes later, he emerged, briefcase in hand. He walked past the man from the car, who had moved over to the ATM machines. The man turned as Ace approached, offered Ace a tight smile. Ace nodded, headed toward his car. Nothing—no pursuit, no confrontation. Just a guy in the bank, his buddy waiting in the car. Or perhaps a guy trying to look like he was just some guy at the bank....

Bruce followed Ace into the parking lot. Ace was leaning against his car, breathing deeply. He took one more deep breath, then headed back to the bank. Bruce smiled—Ace had been testing them, had tried to bluff them. He had left the documents in the bank, would have gladly handed them the empty briefcase had they confronted him. Not a bad move. But Bruce could imagine Ace's next thought: *Had the men known, somehow, that the briefcase was empty?* Poor Ace. Lack of sleep, paranoia, fear—his world had become a video game, full of shadowy villains with x-ray vision.

More likely, if they were thugs—which Bruce now doubted—they had simply concluded it was too risky to make a scene in the Mashpee Common parking lot. They would take Ace later—force his car off the road, maybe just run him down and leave him to die in a ditch like Griffin.

Ace exited from the bank a second time a few minutes later, closed his eyes in some silent thanks as he noticed the car had left. Then he tensed again, and Bruce again sensed his thoughts: *Maybe the car isn't gone. Maybe it's tucked behind the building, waiting.* Ace stood in the shadow of the building, his eyes alert to any movement, the briefcase clenched tightly against his sweat-stained shirt. Bruce watched him pull a pocket knife from his back pocket, open the largest blade, hold it tentatively in his shaking hand. It wasn't much of a weapon. But it might make him feel better. Bruce was actually beginning to feel sorry for the guy—he looked like he was on the verge of having a heart attack.

Ace crossed the parking lot again. His leather soles clapped on the pavement, then were muffled by the roar of a car engine turning over. His eyes darted—which car had roared, where was the predator? A slow jog now, no reason to play it cool. Ten feet from his car.

Then he froze. Bruce watched as he circled the car warily, trying to peer through the windows. Bruce smiled. Of course—Ace had left the doors unlocked, and was now imagining that one of the thugs was lying on the floor in the back seat, waiting to stick a gun in his ear or press a knife to his throat.

Ace ducked behind a pickup truck, dropped to his knees. Pushing the briefcase ahead of him, he crawled between the rows of cars toward his vehicle. He was panting now, and his hair was matted with sweat. But Bruce nodded in approval—there was no way anybody hiding on the floor of the back seat could have seen his approach. Ace may be paranoid, but at least he was making rational decisions in response to his delusions.

Ace pushed himself to his knees, raised the briefcase up to his chest and, using both hands, slammed the face of it down onto the pavement. Thwack! The sound echoed in the morning air, interrupted by the fluttering wings of a flock of birds fleeing in fear. Ace touched his hand to the car, felt for any movement. Another slick move—a well-trained assassin might resist the urge to bolt up in the seat, but few people could have remained completely immobile in response to the mini-thunder bolt that Ace had just unleashed.

Still, Bruce couldn't help but laugh. The men had driven away ten minutes ago, probably on their way to some construction job. Bruce would follow just to make sure, but Ace should have no trouble delivering the documents to Washington.

*   *   *

Ace sat in his old Buick, tried to keep his heart from pounding. He pulled a T-shirt from his overnight bag, wiped his face. This was silly. It was one thing to be cautious, another altogether to be paranoid. He looked at the grease stains on his hands, the holes in the knees of his pants, the sweat stains on his shirt—he had crossed the line. Sure, there may be people who wanted to stop him from delivering the documents to Washington. And it was even possible that they would be willing to kill him if necessary. But he needed to put things into perspective—they weren't the friggin' Mossad. They were, if anything, amateurs like him.

He started the car, resisted the urge to brace for an explosion, headed north toward Sandwich. A quick stop to authenticate the documents, then up to Boston for a flight to Washington.

Fifteen minutes later he was at the antique shop, a couple of cluttered rooms in an old yellow Victorian home that had been chopped up into small offices and retail shops. The proprietor greeted him, complied with Ace's request that he lock the door to the store, then returned and spread the documents out on an old green farmer's table. He examined them with a magnifying glass, rubbed them between his fingers, smelled them. Ace shifted back and forth, forced himself to breathe as the man fussed over his task.

Finally the expert spoke, rendered his decision. "These are real. No doubt."

Ace smiled, sighed. "How can you be sure?"

"They don't make this kind of paper anymore. Same thing with the ink. Even the handwriting is conclusive—see how the 's' looks like an 'f' right here? Whoever wrote this was taught their penmanship around 1800, I would guess."

Ace nodded. He had never stopped to wonder who, indeed, had authored these documents. First tentatively, a child just learning to write, probably one of the few in the whole tribe who was literate. Then continuing, dutifully, decade after decade, as an adult. And, finally, scribing the last of the 61 entries with the shaking hand of an old man or woman. But always anonymously, the scribe's identity lost forever to time and history.

But the documents remained. The documents, which had been

written to chronicle the tribe's history, would now be used to transform the tribe's future.

*   *   *

Justin, bless his kind old heart, had dropped off the paperwork to Amisha a few days after her plea for assistance. She had stashed the documents, which released her house from the Griffin litigation, in the freezer wrapped in a waterproof bag with some chicken breasts. And waited.

Rajiv was leaving today for another business trip. Four, maybe five days. He had not reported the knife incident to the police, as she knew he wouldn't. What could he say? His wife held up a knife to block his punch? No, he had been handling this his own way. Like a man.

Which, in his mind, was to treat her like some disposable kitchen wench. By day, brusque orders—no conversation, no greeting, no kindness. And no freedom—in addition to taking her car and canceling her credit cards, he had closed her bank account and locked her jewels in the safe with her passport. Every day he tried to tried to come up with new ways to punish her, to humiliate her, to demean her. Nights, of course, were the worst. He forced himself on her with renewed vigor and frequency, venting his anger at her through his perversity, his depravity. Biting her nipples. Tearing her insides with his violent thrusts. Ejaculating in her face. Trying to break her, to make her cry, to beg for mercy. Cruel, stupid man.

She knew she could not live like this. Griffin's death had freed her of one demon, but the one who shared her bed continued to torment her. Too bad Rajiv couldn't be eliminated as neatly as Griffin had been.

She phoned the bank. The one asset that was still in her name was the house; it had been frozen by the Griffin litigation, so Rajiv hadn't bothered to switch it into his name. "Yes, this is Amisha Raman. I'd like to schedule that closing for tomorrow, if possible. The title problem has been eliminated." She smiled, appreciated the way the words sounded. *The title problem has been eliminated.*

Tomorrow, then. She would hand over the documents Justin

257

prepared, show the bank some picture identification, sign a couple of pieces of paper. And they would give her a check for $300,000. Then, in a few months, the bank would foreclose on the house, probably evict Rajiv. Hopefully into the winter cold.

In the meantime, she needed to pack. She boxed her family heirlooms and silver, sent them by UPS back to India with a short note: *We are in the process of relocating—no room for these treasures. Please hold for me. All is well. Amisha.* Then she pulled out two suitcases. The smaller one she filled with essentials—personal papers, health and beauty supplies, pictures of her family. The other she began to load with clothes and shoes.

She had scores of outfits to choose from. She looked at them—would it be tough to give them up, along with the catered dinner parties, the marbled bathrooms, the Oriental tapestries? She would miss them, no doubt, but the choice was an easy one. They were things. This was life.

But packing clothes begged the question—where was she going? Rajiv kept her passport locked away, so leaving the country was impossible. And she didn't want to fly because that left a paper trail. She would take a bus to Boston, then grab the train, then ... where?

Well, maybe it would be easier to decide where not. Not another small town—she would never be able to blend in with her accent and exotic looks. Not Los Angeles, where they had lived for a few months—that would be the first place Rajiv would look. And he definitely will look. It simply wouldn't do for a man of Rajiv's stature to lose his wife.

She sighed. Not that he would be the only one looking. He wasn't smart enough to find her, but the police were. They had already questioned her twice about Rex Griffin's death. If she disappeared—with a few hundred thousand dollars in cash, no less—she could hardly hope they wouldn't be suspicious.

But that was irrelevant. If they thought she murdered Griffin, they would hunt her down and arrest her, whether in Mashpee or someplace else. If they didn't, they would leave her alone. Either way, it was out of her hands. And how much worse could jail be than living with Rajiv?

But she could escape Rajiv. He simply wasn't clever enough to find her. New York made some sense. She could disappear there, maybe even find—or buy—a new identity. Lay low for a while, stay away from the Indian community. It would be tough, alone in a strange city. But anything was better than living as a wench in her own house. And at least she'd have some money.

She would have a check for $300,000, but how would she cash it? She pictured herself walking into a bank in Manhattan. *Yes, I'd like to cash this check. I'll take that in fifties, if you please. And could I have a wheelbarrow with that as well?* Not good.

She picked up the phone again and hit the re-dial button. "Yes, Amisha Raman calling again. I was wondering, for the closing tomorrow, would it be possible to get thirty separate bank cashier's checks, each in the amount of $10,000? We are doing some estate planning, and that would be quite helpful." She offered a light laugh. "We have a rather large family, you know."

Amisha could almost hear the unspoken words from the other end of the phone line: *Who can figure what those crazy foreigners will do with their money?* The actual words were much more mundane. "Hold on please, Ms. Raman. I'll have to check on that."

Cashing a check for more than $10,000, Amisha knew, required a stack of paperwork. This way she could cash the checks periodically, as she needed them. And since they were bank cashier's checks, they were almost as good as cash. Still, maybe she'd travel to Philadelphia to cash them, so they couldn't track her to New York. Or maybe go to Atlantic City and turn some of them into casino chips.

"Ms. Raman, there's a $15 fee for a bank check. So we can do it for you, but we will have to charge you $450."

Of course. For a price, anything was possible. "That's fine. Please have them made out to 'Cash.'"

"All of them, Ms. Raman? That's not very safe."

"Yes, all of them. Thank you." The banker was right—it wouldn't be safe to travel with all that money. But it would be a lot safer than staying here in Mashpee.

Chapter 18

[October]

The tribe filed its lawsuit against the town just as many of the vacation-home residents had packed-up and left for the winter. The litigator in Shelby appreciated the strategic value of the timing—it would be far more difficult to mount an effective defense to the tribe's action when more than half of the defendants were scattered around New England.

But, to Shelby, an even more impressive maneuver was the tribe's decision to delay actually serving the lawsuit on any of the defendants. It had been filed with the court, but not yet delivered to the town's residents. It was a subtle distinction—the suit was no less "real" because it hadn't been served. But, psychologically, it kept the matter less personal, less intimate. Reading about something in the newspaper was far less traumatic than having a sheriff appear at your door with court papers.

Which was not to say that the townspeople were unconcerned. The suit was specific in what it was requesting from the court: the ejectment, or eviction, of every property owner from all property in Mashpee. The tribe would settle for less, Shelby knew, but the headline writers were having a field day.

Carla had phoned her at 7:30 in the morning, catching her in her Back Bay condo right in the middle of her morning workout. She had climbed off the elliptical machine, dried her face with a towel, and listened as Carla read her excerpts from the legal papers.

Shelby could imagine the buzz of activity in the law firms around

Boston that represented the title insurance companies. For some reason that Shelby still didn't understand, the title insurance companies had reached the conclusion that the Supreme Court decision had decided this matter once and for all. As a result, they had continued to issue title insurance policies for Mashpee properties as if there were no potential title problems. She recalled a conversation she had had a few weeks ago with an attorney who worked for one of the title insurance companies:

"I have a client interested in buying some property in Mashpee," Shelby had fibbed. "But I remember something about an Indian land claim down there...."

"Yeah, that got resolved back in the '80s. Went all the way to the Supreme Court. Had us a bit nervous for a while," he had responded with a laugh. Shelby guessed he would not be in such a jovial a mood this morning.

"So there's no problem now?" Shelby had asked.

"Nope. We're issuing policies in Mashpee the same as anywhere else."

"Is there any chance the Indians could re-file the case?"

"Actually, I think they tried that once, after they lost the first time. Case got thrown out on *res judicata* grounds."

Shelby had nodded and hung up. She had read the second case, and he was right. The court had dismissed it as well, ruling that the issue as to whether the Mashpee Indians constituted a federal tribe had already been litigated once and that the doctrine of *res judicata*—which stated that the same case could not be litigated twice—precluded the identical case from being argued a second time. But what the title insurance lawyer had not known—or if he knew, had not understood the importance of—was that the Bureau of Indian Affairs had been, even then, in the process of reviewing the tribe's petition for recognition as a federal tribe.

And, now, the title insurance companies' ignorance of the tribe's BIA application had come back to haunt them. Armed with the historical documents Ace Awry had somehow obtained from Rex Griffin and delivered to Washington, the BIA had just last week made a preliminary ruling in favor of the tribe's petition for formal tribal status. Absent startling new evidence, or some showing of fraud on the part of the tribe, the ruling would become final in a matter of months.

The BIA's decision opened the door for the tribe to re-file its case, despite the *res judicata* doctrine. The title insurance companies would surely argue that *res judicata* continued to apply and that the matter should not be re-litigated. But Shelby thought the tribe had the stronger legal position. In fact, she had found a footnote buried in a 1993 federal court case in which the judge expressly questioned the decision in the first Mashpee case, a highly unusual signal from the court that it would be open to revisiting the Mashpee claim.

The issue in dispute in any new case would no longer be whether the Mashpee group constituted a federal tribe—the BIA had effectively settled that question once and for all. Rather, the question would now be a different one entirely: Who owned the Mashpee property? And no court had yet heard a word of evidence on that matter.

Hopefully, no court would hear the case this time, either. Dominique Victor had warned Pierre and Carla that the suit was coming, but had assured them that the tribe hoped to settle the case quickly. Still, Shelby knew that settling a case was often more difficult than winning one. It took only one person to fight, whereas everyone had to agree to a settlement.

Which, naturally, made her think of Pierre. Who knew how things might have gone if he had agreed to the settlement with Griffin? Griffin might still be alive, for one thing. Or maybe not. And if Griffin were still alive, this lawsuit might never have been filed—somehow Ace Awry had obtained the historical documents from Griffin after Griffin's death. Was it possible Ace had killed Griffin to somehow speed up their delivery? Or, on the other hand, had someone killed Griffin in a futile attempt to prevent the documents from being delivered to Ace? As always, all roads seemed to lead back to Rex Griffin. She just hoped that one of them led to a killer not named Prefontaine.

Her friend Pam in the D.A.'s office was still working on deciphering the imprints on the log, so Shelby had no new information to work from. The police seemed to still consider Pierre and Carla suspects, but at least they were no longer focusing on her friends exclusively. And Carla's theory that perhaps Justin had added the Highlander to the log was at least a possibility. Unfortunately, the log was written in simple block letters, so any handwriting analysis would likely be inconclusive.

Shelby wondered if Bruce had learned anything new. She checked her calendar—nothing pressing for the rest of the week. Maybe it was time to spend a couple of days on the Cape.

*   *   *

They were back in Pierre and Carla's living room. But not as large a group this time, probably only ten neighbors instead of fifteen or twenty. "So," Carla began. "Here we are again. Anybody having fun yet?"

Her comment elicited nothing more than some nervous laughter. She had hoped to ease the tension a bit—in addition to the pressures of the latest lawsuit, the neighborhood was burdened by the reality that, in all likelihood, one of them was a murderer. The fact that whoever it was had done them all a huge favor was really beside the point. A murderer was, after all, hardly the neighbor of choice. At least when Griffin was alive everyone knew who the enemy was. Now, any one of them could be the killer. Including Pierre and her.

She shrugged, continued. It would just have to be that way until they found the killer. "Anyway, we thought that it might be a good chance for everyone to get together and talk about the Mashpee tribe's lawsuit. Justin and Shelby both said they'll try to answer some questions."

Justin cleared his throat. "Before we begin, has anybody seen Amisha Raman in the past few days?" He scanned the room. Carla noticed he seemed anxious, even a bit concerned. Or it could just be that she looked at him differently now in light of the possibility he might be a murderer. "No?" He sighed, shuffled a few papers. "All right then. I guess the first thing we should discuss is whether we're all comfortable with Ronnie Lemaire being here. For those of you who don't know, Ronnie's a member of the Mashpee tribe."

Ronnie stood up before anybody had a chance to respond to Justin. "Look, I came over here tonight because you're my neighbors.

263

Many of you are also my friends. We've been through a lot together already. I just wanted to say that I wanted nothing to do with this lawsuit. I thought it was wrong 25 years ago and I think it's wrong today."

A voice interrupted. The preppy golf pro. "Yeah, well, that's not really much good to us, is it? I mean, can you get the case dismissed?"

"No, I can't get it dismissed. But I can fight to make sure it settles quickly. Last time things got out of hand—everyone took it too personally."

"I don't know, Ronnie. To me, it's pretty personal when somebody tries to take my home, you know?"

"I know, I know. But that's not gonna happen here, no one's gonna take your house without you agreeing to sell it to them. That's not what this is about. The only reason the tribe filed this suit was to get the title insurance companies' attention. That's why I came tonight, to tell you guys not to worry. This is gonna settle."

The debate continued. "You know what? Even if it does settle, it's still a major pain in the butt. And you know what else? We can all forget about refinancing our mortgages or selling our houses. This is going to mess up our title just like Griffin's lawsuits did."

A few eyes turned to Shelby, waited for a legal response to the comment. "I think that's accurate. But that's more your area of expertise, Justin."

Justin nodded. "You're probably right. Last time, during the first lawsuit, the title insurance companies basically redlined all of Mashpee until the litigation ended—you couldn't get title insurance at any price. It'll probably be the same this time. And without title insurance, nobody'll be able to sell their property or get a mortgage."

Carla made a point. "But most of us have title insurance already."

Justin nodded again. "Most of you probably do. The problem with title insurance is that you're only covered for the policy amount, which is usually your purchase price. So if you bought your house a couple of years ago for $400,000, and now it's worth $500,000, you stand to lose $100,000. For some of you, the gap in coverage may be even larger if you've made improvements to your property, or if you've owned your property for a number of years and it's appreciated in value."

An angry voice belonging to one of neighbors challenged Justin. He was a single doctor from Connecticut; Carla saw him on weekends—always, it seemed, with a different date. "It's not like it matters anyway. We still have that Griffin lawsuit hanging over our heads. The title insurance companies aren't gonna pay us a penny until that gets settled. You're the executor of the will, Justin, why don't you just dismiss that case already? I was all set to sell my house and get the hell out of here—had a guy ready to pay cash just last month. Now I'm stuck here until this Indian thing gets settled."

Justin sighed. "I'm sorry about that. But these things take time, the Probate Court is backed-up...."

"Jeez," the doctor continued, "with friends like you guys.... I mean, think about it a second. Pierre says he's gonna help us out, then he deep-sixes the settlement with Griffin at the last minute. Ronnie says he's our friend, hopes we understand when him and his cousins file this friendly little lawsuit. No big deal, they're just trying to take our houses. But don't take it personal. And Uncle Justin over here, all of a sudden he's executor of Griffin's estate! How did that happen? And does he make this bullshit Griffin lawsuit go away? Of course not. What a bunch of idiots we are, listening to you guys. I'm outta here."

The man left, and a few other neighbors followed. A handful of people remained in the room, but the angry words hung in the air like a cold mist, and the group soon broke up for the night.

*   *   *

Shelby sat on the floor, Valerie and Rachel side-by-side on the floor in front of her. For some reason her mind turned to Bruce....

She shook the thought away, finished twisting each of the girls' hair into a French braid. "There we go. One blond, one brunette. But both beautiful."

Shelby held a mirror up for them to see. They smiled, then Shelby presented them each with a key chain she had bought in the Copley Place mall. Attached to the chain was a miniature device that played single-song CDs through a small earphone. The Back Street Boys,

Britney Spears, Christine Aguillera. Perfect for a couple of little girls riding on the school bus.

They gave her a tight hug, then Pierre walked them—earphones firmly in ears—up toward the bus stop at the end of the subdivision drive.

She watched them go out the door, sighed. She had finally decided to take some time off and had come down to the Cape on Thursday night for a long weekend. But she had a feeling this would be a working vacation.

Pierre returned, joined Shelby and Carla for a cup of coffee on the deck overlooking the lake. Shelby wasn't 100 percent certain that her friends hadn't killed Rex Griffin. But she had come to the conclusion that she would try not to judge them for it if they had. Not that she was sure she could just let it go. But Griffin had terrorized them, threatened their children. Murder was obviously an extreme solution to the problem, and she didn't think she herself would ever be capable of it, but she wasn't prepared to totally condemn them if their fear and desperation had pushed them over the edge.

She looked at her friends. Carla seemed her usual carefree and upbeat self. But Pierre looked haggard, distracted. It reminded her of the way he looked when he had been first accused of murder. Was he worried about himself, she wondered, or about his wife? Well, whatever the truth was, Carla had made it clear that they had told Shelby everything they were going to tell her. So no sense in pushing it further.

Shelby sighed, sat back. The leaves were changing colors on the trees, and the effect was doubled because the trees were reflecting off the glass-like lake. A fish jumped, mixing the colors on the water surface into a collage of reds and yellows and oranges. No wonder Carla liked to paint down here. "What a peaceful spot."

Carla nodded. "It seems we don't really get to enjoy it that much. I thought once Griffin was gone, things would return to normal."

Shelby smiled at her friend. "I'm not sure you guys have a 'normal.' First Bruce, then Griffin, now the Mashpee tribe's lawsuit. Not to mention being suspects in a murder. You should seriously think about sending the girls to law school, just to save on legal fees."

Pierre responded. "Nothing against you, Shelby, but I'm not sure that's what I want my little girls to spend their lives doing."

"No," Shelby laughed, "I can't blame you for that. It's usually not fun. And it's never pretty."

"How ugly do you think this Mashpee case will get?" Pierre turned to face her while she answered. She noticed that his eyes were puffy and bloodshot.

"I really don't know; a lot of it will depend on what the tribe's looking for. But I will say this: It always gets *really* ugly right before things settle. It's just human nature—go right to the edge before pulling back. It's like a game of chicken."

Pierre nodded. "I remember feeling that way myself. I knew I was innocent, and I wanted to keep fighting, but it just seemed like the stakes kept getting higher and higher."

Shelby reached over, squeezed her friend's hand. "That was partially my fault. Bruce had all of us in the DA's office convinced you were guilty. We felt we had to go after you. It never occurred to us that you were being framed by your own attorney."

"Yeah, well, it never occurred to me either." Pierre paused, then spoke again. "Speaking of which, do you think we can trust Bruce now? I mean, there's hundreds of millions of dollars at stake in this whole land claim mess—I have a little trouble believing Bruce could just swim past all that chum and not stop for a nibble or two."

Carla nodded. "Good point. What do you think, Shelby?"

It struck Shelby that Pierre and Carla had probably planned this conversation, had probably discussed it between themselves last night. Perhaps they even sensed that she was beginning to fall for Bruce again. "I really don't know. I do know that people are capable of changing. I have a cousin who's a few years younger than me. He was a real womanizer—he would say anything to get a woman into bed, then move on to his next conquest. He used to tell me all about it, sort of use me as a sounding board. Everyone thought he would make the worst husband, including me. Then he got married, and it turns out he's Mr. Monogamous. He's the best husband. So I asked him about it, and he looked at me kind of funny, like he was insulted. I still remember what he said: 'It's not like I *couldn't* be a good boy-friend, it's just that I didn't feel it was that important. But once I decided to get married, I knew I'd have to change. So I did.' So maybe it's like that with Bruce. Maybe he just needs to decide it's important to him, then he'll change."

Carla glanced at Pierre, then focused directly on Shelby. "You know what? I think he really has changed. I think he would do anything to win you back. Anything. And I think you want him back in your life, too. So just go for it, Shelby. Just do it."

Pierre rolled his eyes. "Come on, Carla. Don't forget who you're dealing with here. It's one thing to use him to track Griffin. But don't start kidding yourself that you can actually trust him...."

Shelby turned away from her friends. She knew that Pierre was probably right, but she had been allowing herself recently to hope that Bruce might actually have reformed himself, and it was nice to hear that Carla thought it could—and should—happen. After all, it had been Bruce's obsession with money that had motivated him to cheat and steal and betray those around him. But he had deprived himself of all material comforts the past seven years, so how money-hungry could he really be?

Still, she knew that Pierre would never agree, and she didn't feel like arguing the point right now.

Carla seemed to sense Shelby's discomfort, quickly changed the subject. "Well, we'll have plenty of time to talk about Bruce later. But I heard some people talking at the grocery store. They think the tribe's just trying to get the state to let them open a casino. Like Foxwoods down in Connecticut."

Pierre responded. "Really? Here on the Cape? The traffic would be a nightmare."

Shelby pondered that possibility for a minute. "No, that doesn't make sense to me. The situation in Connecticut is different than in Massachusetts—the tribes get to have gambling down there because the state had already legalized it for other groups, like churches."

"Churches?" Pierre asked. "You mean like bingo nights?"

"Yeah, believe it or not. That's how Foxwoods started—high-stakes bingo. But, legally, the reason they were able to open in the first place is because the state had already legalized some sort of gambling. That's not the case in Massachusetts."

"But isn't there some tribe on Martha's Vineyard trying to open a casino?" Carla asked.

"Yes. They're also part of the Wampanoag tribe, just like the Mashpees. But they need permission from the state, and they haven't been able to get it. That's why I don't think the Mashpees are interested in gambling—it's seems like pretty much a dead end in Massachusetts."

Pierre nodded. "So what do you think they really want?"

"You tell me, Pierre. You're friends with the Victors. And Dominique is on the tribal council. What do you think they're doing this for?"

"They've never discussed the lawsuit with me, but Billy and I talk sometimes about his feelings, about being a Native American. I think a lot of it goes back to their feeling that they got ... you know, shafted. They see the Holocaust survivors getting reparations from the Germans, and African-American leaders are talking about reparations for slavery, and they just feel like they deserve something too. I don't remember how it came up, but Dominique was telling me the story of how some state official in the early 1800s basically embezzled all the tribe's money and nobody did anything about it. They just feel like they're owed something."

Shelby nodded. "Makes sense."

"Plus," Pierre added, "they see all the other tribes raking it in from gambling. You can't help but feel like you want a better life for your family."

Carla asked, "What about Ronnie's comment last night, that they just want to settle this quickly?"

Pierre responded. "I believe him. From what I've heard about the first case, he was one of the few members of the tribe who didn't want to sue. So it makes sense that he'd be looking for a quick settlement."

"He may be, but the rest of the tribe might have a different agenda." Shelby looked at her friends. "My concern is that you guys seem to be right in the cross-hairs again because Metacomet is buried right in your backyard. So, no matter what happens, they're going to want your property."

Carla laughed. "Tell them to get in line."

*   *   *

Shelby and Bruce met late in the afternoon at a beach in Falmouth, one town west of Mashpee. She had invited Carla and Pierre to join her to see what Bruce had learned, but they had declined.

Warm sun, cool wind, miles of empty beach. No wonder the locals say that the fall is their favorite time of year on the Cape.

Bruce was waiting for her, seated cross-legged in the sand, a shy smile on his face.

She sat down next to him, careful to leave some space between them. "So, counselor, what do you think of the latest lawsuit?"

"I think I'm glad I'm not representing the title insurance companies."

"Aside from the fact that you're disbarred, you mean?" As she spoke, she realized this was the first time she had been able to speak of their past in a light-hearted manner.

Bruce flashed her a smile—he must have sensed the breakthrough as well. "Well, there is that small detail.... But I'm still glad."

"Yeah, me too. I'm not sure how they dropped the ball on this, but it's going to cost them."

Bruce looked out over the ocean. "In some ways the title companies are like banks—all conservative and risk-averse and buttoned-down. That's their culture. But that's also their weakness. They're not really very clever. So they don't see things coming at them from different angles, like this one did."

"So you think the tribe has a strong claim?"

"Morally or legally?"

Shelby smiled, teased her ex-lover again. "Since when do you judge things on their morality?" She tried to keep any bitterness out of her voice. But her message was clear.

Bruce bowed his head, pursed his lips together. "Fair enough. I'll stick to the legalities. Legally, I think it's a pretty strong case, especially if they get a judge willing to look past all the politics of throwing people out of their homes. That's what happened last time—I read through the cases and the commentary afterward and the judge

270

seemed to be looking for a way to make the case go away. He just couldn't get past the fact that all these people were going to lose their homes. But the law is pretty clear: Massachusetts had no right to sign a treaty with the tribe to alienate the tribal lands back in the 1860s. Only Congress could do that."

"But when you say 'alienate,' you make it sound like they took the land from them. That's not what happened—the land was just parceled out and given to the individual tribe members."

Bruce smiled. "That's where the morality comes into play. You're right, this wasn't like some of the other cases where the state coerced the tribes into selling the land for a handful of beads and baubles. This was actually done at the request of the tribe, as a way of trying to give the tribe members the same rights as other citizens had."

"It's hard to argue with that."

"True. But maybe we need to go further back, look at how the Mashpee tribe ended up in Mashpee to begin with."

"Okay."

"Basically, the Wampanoag Indians—those that weren't killed, that is—were rounded up from all over the Cape and southeastern Massachusetts and settled in Mashpee. It was like a reservation. They called it a 'praying town' because the missionaries came in and Christianized them all."

"Let me guess. All their other lands—just taken, right?"

"Yup."

"So what you're saying is that maybe the moralities swing both ways here."

"I guess what I'm saying is that it's hard to argue the whole morality thing in light of the way the Native Americans were treated. We take their land, then justify it by waving a bunch of laws and treaties in their face. 'A deal's a deal, the law's the law,' we tell them, even if the whole thing wasn't even close to being fair. So now they're waving the law back in our face. Doesn't seem right when we say now that the law doesn't matter, that we have to look at what's fair."

"But where's the morality of people like Carla and Pierre losing their houses for something that happened over 100 years ago, something they had nothing to do with? They didn't take the land from the Mashpees."

"No, they didn't. And it's not fair to them. But you and I both know it's not going to come to that. The title insurance companies will have to kick in a pile of money, and there's no way the state is gonna let 10,000 people lose their homes. There's been a bunch of these cases around the country, and nobody's ever lost their property. They all eventually settle."

"Sure, in the end they do, Bruce. But in the meantime people go through hell. That case up in the Finger Lakes region of New York, those people are stuck. They can't sell their houses, they can't get mortgages, nobody's putting money into their property.... That's what happened here during the last lawsuit. Everyone in Mashpee was on, like, a ten-year holding pattern."

Bruce nodded. "That's a good point. I was looking only at the end game. But you're right—I heard this morning that they stopped construction over at New Seabury. They don't want to put any more money in until the lawsuit is resolved."

"And that might take years. In the meantime, all these people are out of jobs."

"And lots of those people are Mashpee Indians."

"That's Ronnie Lemaire's point," Shelby said. "In many ways, the tribe is suing itself. Don't forget, the tribe members still own a lot of the property in town. It's all part of the lawsuit."

"That's why we both agree that this thing should settle."

"Yeah, but you know how this works. Everyone wants to settle, but it becomes this giant game of chicken. So we go right up to the brink of trial, then hope somebody blinks."

Bruce laughed. "And in the meantime, the lawyers make a bundle."

"Not this lawyer. I've written off most of my time on this case."

Bruce nodded, then Shelby could see his mind wander off. She waited a few seconds, then he spoke. "I'm not sure if I should be telling you this. Not yet, at least...."

She smiled. "But you're going to anyway."

He grinned back at her. "Of course. But I need you to keep it to yourself." She nodded. "I can't give you all the details, but Griffin set this up so that it almost has to settle by February 1. If it doesn't, the tribe has to pay a $50 million penalty. So that's pretty good incentive for it all to get resolved."

Shelby nodded. The information, sparse as it was, did explain some things. "That explains why they brought the suit so soon—I thought maybe they should have waited until the preliminary BIA ruling became final, just to be safe. But I hadn't counted on Rex Griffin. Still controlling things, from the grave. Unbelievable.... Speaking of which, did you know Amisha Raman disappeared?"

Bruce seemed surprised. "What do you mean, 'disappeared?' Was she kidnapped or something?"

"No, she waited until her husband was out of town, got a $300,000 mortgage on their house, cashed the check and took off. Nobody's heard from her since. I just got the story from my friend Pam in the DA's office—I haven't even had a chance to tell Pierre and Carla."

"She could be dead...."

"Maybe. But it looks like she took off. She packed a couple of bags, sent some stuff back to her family in India. Plus the $300,000's missing."

"Interesting."

"The police think so. She was already on the short list of suspects—Griffin had almost ruined her husband's career, plus the lawsuits had made it impossible to take any money out of their property. And they owed the IRS a ton of money. Not to mention the fact that Griffin made her look like an idiot in front of her friends and family with that fake e-mail he sent."

"But how was she able to get a mortgage on the property with all the lawsuits clouding title?"

"Good question. Apparently Justin, as the executor of Griffin's estate, released her from the lawsuit Griffin had filed."

"Any idea why?"

"Could be there's something going on there. Or it could be he was just being a nice guy. Though it strikes me that Justin seems to be involved in lots of these strange relationships...."

Bruce nodded. "Interesting. So much for my sleuthing abilities. I didn't even know Amisha was gone."

"All right, so you owe me. What else have you found out?"

Bruce looked off again, almost as if the answer to Shelby's question could be found in the crash of the waves. "Nothing definite. But I've looked at everything I can find that relates to Griffin—old lawsuits, all his land dealings, the family trust he formed, his will. I even drove up to Boston to check out his brother Donald. And I have a hunch. Even with Amisha disappearing, I think it's still good."

"Care to share it with me?"

He turned, faced her straight-on for the first time today, looked deep into her eyes. "I'd like to Shelby. I really would. But I think it might be dangerous...."

"Please, Bruce, don't insult me. I'm a big girl."

"I know that, Shelby. I know. And I don't mean to insult you. But you're gonna have to trust me on this."

Shelby felt the anger rising inside her. "Hah! Trust you?"

She wished she could pull the words back, just rewind a few seconds and erase them. But they had left her mouth, had found their mark. She could see Bruce try to fight through them, try to hide the pain they had brought. "I know I don't have the right to ask you that, Shelby. But if you can't trust my motives or my honesty, at least trust my ability to unravel this whole thing. Trust my sleazeball instincts. That is, after all, why you brought me here."

"Fine. I trust your instincts to figure this all out. But what does that have to do with telling me your hunch? What does that have to do with danger?"

"Forget the danger. You're right—you're a big girl. But I need to stand back and see how things play out. And if I share my suspicions with you, it can't help but alter your behavior. I know you—you'll want to make things right, want to protect your clients, your friends. And then things will play out in a different way. It's like one of those science fiction movies where someone goes back in time and does everything possible not to change the time line, not to change the future. If I tell you, that will change the future. The only way to prove my hunch is to let things play out as they are supposed to. I don't have any other choice, Shelby, I really don't...."

Shelby studied the man sitting next to her. She had never loved anyone so much, nor hated anyone as viciously. She had agreed to meet him today with a sense of giddiness, a bit of anticipation. It had been so long since she'd found a man attractive, so long since she'd felt the stirrings in her soul. And in her body. Tonight, she had been open to anything.

And then he had asked her to trust him. She was ready to forgive, prepared perhaps even to love. But trust.... That would come last. It was backwards, she knew—normally trust came before love. But trust was a matter of the brain. The heart could be fooled into loving again, could be seduced into carelessness and indiscretion. But the brain remembered forever. Or at least hers did.

*   *   *

Bruce jogged along the edge of the beach where the waves lapped onto the shore, his bare feet sinking with every step into the cold, wet sand and his eyes squinting into the early morning sun. The wind came up from the south, a warm autumn breeze that nudged him slightly shoreward as he jogged along. If he kept going as the crow flies, east into the sun, he would end up in Europe. Or he could just follow the curve of the Cape as it elbowed to the north and jog all the way to Provincetown. Or he could just stay right here in Mashpee and see this through....

He had a theory. He just didn't have any way to test it.

Which, apparently, was more than the police had. Mashpee, despite its recent growth, was still a small town—it was tough to keep many secrets. Especially in a murder investigation. So Bruce had heard from Dominique, who heard it from one of the tribe members, who had a boyfriend on the police force, that the police still had no idea who the driver of the hit-and-run vehicle was. Amisha's disappearance made her an obvious choice, and the missing log entries made Justin's behavior highly suspicious, and Pierre and Carla's car on the log implicated them, but there was still no hard evidence tying any of them to the crime.

Everyone was working from the assumption that the death was intentional—nobody accidentally runs down a pedestrian, backs over the head, and then leaves the victim in a ditch to die. And everyone was pretty convinced that the killer was the same person who had been responsible for the attack on Griffin a few months earlier, though he had enough enemies that the attacks could have been unrelated. But there were no eyewitnesses to either incident other than Bruce and Griffin's dog Barrister, and neither was talking.

The police had finally convinced the obvious suspects that it was in their best interests to allow for their cars to be examined: Ronnie Lemaire, Pierre and Carla Prefontaine, Amisha and Rajiv Raman, the Victors, Justin McBride. Plus a few other neighbors and enemies of Griffin. None of them wanted to jump to the head of the suspects line by refusing to cooperate. But other than the Victors' car, which had needed a whole new front end after Billy's accident, none of cars or trucks showed evidence of a recent collision. Which, of course, didn't eliminate anyone from possible guilt—any of them could have hired someone to run down Griffin, or rented a car, or used a company car, or somehow masked or repaired the damage to their vehicle. And, in Rajiv Raman's case, he had returned his lease car to the dealer, who in turn had sold it at auction. It was now somewhere in Pennsylvania, any dents having long since been repaired.

Bruce looked at his watch—he'd been running for 30 minutes. Time to turn around, get a fresh perspective.

Griffin's murder may have been born of anger or hatred or revenge, but there was more to it than that. The whole thing, especially when coupled with the earlier attack, had been too methodical. This wasn't a situation where a neighbor was driving home through the rain one night and couldn't resist the impulse to ram his car into the hated Griffin. This had been planned.
Planned by somebody who knew Griffin's routine, planned by somebody who not only *wanted* Griffin dead, but *needed* him dead. And Bruce thought he knew who that somebody was.

But it was still just a hunch. He needed a way to test it.

Somehow Griffin's death had solved somebody's problem, fixed something that, but for murder, could not be fixed. If Bruce could somehow un-solve things, or un-fix things, the killer would have to react.

And then Bruce would have him or her. Would it win him Shelby? By itself, probably not. But he had to make things right with her—and with Pierre and Carla as well—before she would even consider taking him back. He had told them he would help; he didn't relish the idea of telling them he had failed. It was bad enough that he would have to explain why he hadn't told them about Justin being a spy–he knew they would have confronted him, which would have neutralized the one edge Bruce had over Griffin.

But before he could tell them anything, he had to find a way to test his theory. Just as he couldn't voice his suspicions to Shelby, he couldn't take his theory to the police. They might take him seriously enough to investigate, but they were bound by all sorts of due process and legal constraints that Bruce was free to ignore. Anything the police did would be heavy-handed, would likely spook the killer. Bruce, on the other hand, could be subtle, clever, even duplicitous– the very reasons Shelby and Pierre and Carla had enlisted his aid originally.

So he would have to do this alone. It might even get a bit danger-ous. One man was already dead and, in the killer's eyes, there wouldn't be much difference between one lifetime in jail and a second. Not that Bruce was afraid to die; in fact, he had contem-plated ending his own life a handful of times over the past seven years. And he really didn't have that much to live for. But the decision to live or die was one he preferred to make by himself, thank you very much.

And one more thing. It was one thing to be helping Shelby and Pierre and Carla–he owed them that much. And he was happy to help out the tribe if he could. But this had gone beyond a simple chess match. If he was going to be risking his life, he expected to be well-rewarded for it. The grand prize, of course, was Shelby. But short of winning her back, there was pile of money just sitting there on the table which would make a decent consolation prize.

Chapter 19

[November]

As Ronnie had feared, things were starting to get ugly.

Unlike during the first lawsuit, Ronnie was pleased to see that the tribe was doing its best to calm and placate the townspeople. As the political operatives would have said, they were doing a good job 'staying on message.' "Don't worry," Ronnie and the other tribe members had preached at countless meetings and forums and coffee shops, "the title insurance companies will be the ones who have to pay us, not you."

And, for a while, that approach worked. Then the title insurance companies got smart. Ronnie left his house, turned toward the lake in the direction of Justin's home. He kicked the leaves along as he walked, smiled as he glanced over his shoulder at the old farmhouse. The lawsuit between the town and the tribe might get ugly, but at least Griffin was out of their hair.

He lifted the brass knocker on the old lawyer's red door, let it drop against the strike plate. Justin's eyebrows, followed by the rest of his face, appeared in the doorway a few seconds later.

"Hey, Justin. You got a minute?"

"Sure Ronnie. Let me get my coat, I'll come for a walk with you." Justin disappeared and returned with a bright red windbreaker. He and Ronnie continued walking along the subdivision peninsula, toward the lake. "I was just reading this nice letter I got from my title insurance company." Justin held it up for Ronnie to see. "Any chance that's what you want to talk about?"

Ronnie glanced sideways, studied his friend's face. At least, he thought Justin was still his friend. He had come right out once and asked Justin to explain why he had agreed to serve as Griffin's executor, but Justin had refused to go into any details. "It's confidential," Justin had shrugged. "I'm sorry, Ronnie, but I can't talk about it." It was a bullshit response—where Ronnie came from, friendship and loyalty were more important than niceties like attorney-client privilege. But Ronnie also recognized that, for someone like Justin, it might be harder to dismiss the professional rules of conduct he had observed for almost 50 years.

Whatever the case, Ronnie was no longer 100 percent sure he could trust the old lawyer. But, for today at least, he needed some counsel. "Sure is. I got the same letter. What do you think?"

Justin studied the document for a few seconds. "It's funny. Title insurance companies are notorious for denying coverage. It's a big joke with lawyers—you can't get them to admit that the policy covers anything. You know, your house burns down, your insurance company comes right out. They might screw you for a few bucks when it comes to rebuilding, but they don't tell you that a fire is for some reason not covered in the policy. But these title companies, they start off by denying coverage for anything. You gotta hire a lawyer to fight them before they even take your phone calls."

"But not this time."

"Right. This time they send a nice letter, come right out here and say, in no uncertain terms, that they will defend this action and pay under the policy if necessary."

"So, why?"

"I think, for once, that somebody's giving them some pretty good advice. Look at the bold type in the middle of the letter. I'll read it: 'We will defend this action and, if necessary, pay to you an amount up to and including your policy limit of $325,000.' Now, in my case, I've owned my house for almost five years. It's worth almost twice that amount now. But they're only going to pay $325,000. So what am I thinking as I read this?"

Ronnie was used to his friend's Socratic methods when discussing legal matters. "So you're pissed off because you may be out a few hundred grand." He looked around the subdivision, wondered how many of his neighbors would be out six figures.

Justin beamed. "Exactly. And whom am I angry with?"

Ronnie smiled at Justin's refusal to adopt his crude terminology. "Not the title insurance company. They just sent you this nice letter, telling you they're going to go to war for you. So now you're pissed at the Indians who are trying to take your house."

Justin nodded again. "Right. I think what the title companies are doing is trying to drive a wedge between the tribe and the towns-people. You guys have been doing a good job so far making this seem like nobody was going to lose anything here because the title companies would come in and pay. But nobody took the time to look at their policies to see what 'paying' actually meant. Lots of these people have been here twenty, thirty years. What do you think they have for policy coverage—$20,000, $30,000? They're not going to be real happy when they realize they're only getting ten cents on the dollar."

"So we're the enemy again."

"Looks that way to me. Looks like you're going to have some pretty angry neighbors around here."

"Story of my life. Angry neighbors." And, unlike Griffin, it wasn't likely they would all just go stand in front of a speeding car and make this problem go away.

*   *   *

Dominique tiptoed into the living room, smiled down at her son. Billy was splayed out on the couch, snoring. Baby Vernon was asleep on Billy's chest, breathing softly.

She thought about waking them, moving them off the couch. But why bother? Neither of them had been sleeping much lately—Billy because he was trying to be father, student, athlete and teenager all at the same time, and the baby because, well, because he was being a baby. Dominique turned off the television, tucked a blanket around them, made sure Vernon could breathe freely, and kissed them each softly on the cheek. "Good night, my darlings," she whispered.

But instead of leaving the room, she sat down in a chair opposite the couch. Billy had amazed her over the past couple of months. He had always been a good kid—a bit quiet, and sometimes even morose, but kind and thoughtful. Yet still a kid, interested in sports and music and girls and cars. Now, all of a sudden, he had become a man. He still played hockey, and he still glued himself to his music videos whenever possible, but these interests had become secondary in his life. He was working hard in school, taking extra shifts at the restaurant when possible to help with the family finances. He had even gotten his hair cut short.

Most of all he had become a father. It would have been easy to allow his bitterness and resentment at the way Griffin had mistreated him to poison his feelings toward Denise and, even, the baby. Nobody could have blamed him if he simply ignored Baby Vernon. Sure, he was the child's biological father, but in many ways his relationship with the mother was little more than that of a sperm donor—he had been drugged and tricked into contributing his sperm to some fiendish scheme devised by a sick man.

But Billy seemed to have succeeded in walling-off his hatred of Griffin from his relationship with Vernon and Denise. No doubt it helped that Griffin was dead. But, beyond that, she had never sensed from Billy a single moment of regret at the way his life's path had veered. No brooding. This was his life, and he would live it as best he could.

And, so, every morning he dragged his teen-aged body out of bed at 5:00 so that he could be at the farmhouse in time to feed the baby his morning bottle. He stayed with Vernon until school began at 7:30, then swung by after work or hockey practice to help put the baby down for the night. And on Fridays he packed up Vernon and brought him home for the weekend. Sure, Dominique and Billy's sisters helped out, but for the most part Billy willingly took on the mundane tasks of diaper changing and bottle feeding and bathing.

The real surprise for Dominique was in the way Billy interacted with Denise. Somehow, he intuited the need to support her without in any way questioning her competence. Denise was intent on nurturing her baby, even as the state sent child-care specialists over on a daily basis to instruct and monitor her care giving. Like any mother, Denise was fiercely protective of her right to care for her child, even as her competency for the job was being questioned. So Billy totally deferred to her—and, Dominique recalled with a smile, insisted that Dominique do so as well. Denise, growing more confident by the day, was the primary caregiver, and Billy merely her supportive assistant. It served them both well. And Baby Vernon seemed to be doing fine....

Dominique heard the angry voice even before she heard the crash of glass. "That's the house. The brown one!"

A fist-sized rock bounced once and rolled to a stop up against her slipper. She kicked it away, stood, turned to find Billy thrusting Baby Vernon into her arms. "Take Vernon and get down!"

Dominique watched Billy gallop through the living room, toward the front door. She tried to control the fury in her voice. "No, Billy, wait. Let me call the police." A second rock thumped against the front door, then a third crashed through a kitchen window.

"No way, Mom. We can't wait for them. Those mother-fuckers could have hit Vernon with those rocks."

Another shout from outside. "Let's torch the place!"

Dominique felt the heat rise within her, saw the fire in her son's eyes. "All right, then. But go out the back way, sneak around behind them. And grab the baseball bat. I think there's a bunch of them. But be careful!"

Dominique shielded the baby with her body, intercepted Billy's sisters before they came into the front of the house. "Take the baby. Go into the basement and stay there." She quickly dialed 911.

Through the broken windows Dominique could hear the angry voices from outside. "Goddamn Indians! Go back to your reservation!" Another barrage of rocks thumped against the house; she could feel the old structure vibrate as the heavier stones hit. "Yeah, or we'll scalp you!" Young voices, young laughter, lubricated by a few beers. Great—another generation learning how to hate.

She edged along the wall, peeked out from behind a curtain. Four boys, a couple of whom she recognized. The big kid was from Billy's hockey team—a bully that Billy had had some trouble with before. She saw a beer bottle sail through the air, crash against the roof. But she didn't see Billy.

There. Across the street. Edging his way toward the boys' car. Now sprinting at the group. Bat raised high to strike.

Dominique had a moment of panic, then nodded in pride. Billy was too smart—even in his fury—to crush someone's skull with a bat. He swung the bat low, cracked it across the closest boy's knee, buckling his leg like a folding chair. Dominique felt a pang of sympathy for the boy—he would likely spend the next few months in a cast. And he was somebody's son.

The group turned as the fallen boy bellowed in agony, descended like a pack of wolves on Billy. He backed himself against the car, swung the bat menacingly to keep the three boys at bay. It should have ended there, but the beer had made them more brave and less smart, and the bully from Billy's hockey team, even sober, had more brains in his fist than in his head.

The bully shoved one of his buddies in the back, propelling him into the path of one of Billy's swings. The boy crumpled to the ground, holding his ribs, moaning. He would be no further threat to Billy either. But the bully's path to Billy was now clear. He charged, drove his shoulder into Billy's midsection, pinning him against the car. The fourth boy charged as well, grabbing Billy's arm, pinning it behind his back as the bully stepped back and swung his fists wildly at his outnumbered teammate.

Dominique watched as the boys' fists pummeled her son. She rushed to the front door, out into the yard, toward the melee. She was no fighter, but she could use her bulk to shield one of the boys, give her Billy a chance. He was fighting valiantly, but already his face was bloodied and one arm hung limply by his side. She lumbered toward them, her heart pounding in her ears.

Then, suddenly, a body flashed in front of her, jumped into the swarm of fists and kicks and elbows. She panicked—had one of the two fallen boys recovered, returned to the fight? She could shield Billy from one boy, but not two.

But the new figure was taller, sturdier than the boys. A man's figure. His back was to her, but she saw his foot fly up, catch the bully under the chin and send him reeling backward. Then his fist swung around, buried itself into the other boy's midsection, folding the boy in half on the ground. The bully stood up again, rushed at the man like a bull.

She saw the man's face as he turned. Bruce. Dark and handsome and calm.

He smiled confidently, waited until the bully had closed to within a foot, then simply stepped aside and spun away, allowing the bully to crash shoulder-first into the side of the car. He roared in pain and anger, dropped to his knees. He tried to stand again, but Billy walked over, pushed him gently with his foot. The bully toppled over onto his side. He spit out some blood and a couple of teeth, hissed at Billy and Bruce. "Fuckin' Indians."

Bruce smiled at Billy, tilted his head toward the crumpled body of the bully. "Looks like General Custer over there's gonna need a doctor."

*   *   *

Pierre sat at the edge of the lake on a large rock, his feet dangling in the cool water. He had just spoken to Billy, learned of last night's brawl. Billy and his family were shaken but okay. The four boys had been arrested.

He and Carla had lived in Mashpee for barely a year—they carried with them none of the decades-long bitterness that seemed to have resurfaced just as it had almost forever faded away. The history buff in Pierre knew that it took at least a generation to heal the wounds of conflict, to replace the hatred with the sweet memories of peace. Mashpee had almost made it. Now this.

In many ways, Pierre felt like he and Carla were ground zero in the conflict. On the one hand, Metacomet was buried in their back yard, so their property was a prime target of the tribe. Now that Griffin was dead, they had finally settled in, finally felt comfortable walking the neighborhood or letting the girls play in the yard or going fishing on the lake. Even with the threat of a murder charge hanging over their head, their house had finally become their home, and they had no desire to be ejected by the tribe.

On the other hand, they had grown increasingly friendly with Billy and Dominique, and were sympathetic to the tribe's cause. Pierre still remembered Dominique's words when she drove over to personally tell them the tribe was going to file the lawsuit: "Personally, I want nothing to do with this. The risks to this community are too great. But I'm charged with doing what's best for the tribe, not for myself or my family. There's simply too much to be gained—we have to file the suit. I just pray it settles quickly, before things go too far." Yet Pierre couldn't help but think of that assassination scene in *The Godfather* movie. *It's not personal, it's just business.* Then bang.

And that, most of all, was the problem with the tribe's lawsuit. It was personal, no matter how much the tribe tried to portray it as just some procedural formality to get the title insurance companies to pay. The suit prevented people from moving, from getting second mortgages to pay for college, from sleeping at night. Pierre understood perfectly: The suit had turned people's homes into houses.

He also understood this: The quicker the townspeople could have their homes back, the better it would be for all. From talking to Dominique and Ronnie, the tribe understood this as well. But did the title insurance companies? The longer they waited to settle the case, the more difficult it would be to reach that settlement. Because once things turned personal, even the most well-reasoned settlement agreement was subject to the personal caprices of any single participant. Pierre knew from experience.

But more than that, when things turned personal, people tended to get hurt. Just ask Billy Victor.

Or Rex Griffin.

*   *   *

Amisha balanced herself on the edge of the bed, careful not to fall into the black hole that had been her mattress for the past three nights. It was mattress-with-bedbugs number eight, covered by bedspread-with-cigarette-holes-and-semen-stains number eight, next to side-table-with-a-bible-and-nothing-else number eight. In her entire life she had never spent even a single night in places like this. Now she was trapped in them, needing the anonymity they offered, musty little hellholes catering to drug dealers and prostitutes and people on the run. Like herself.

And the seediness wasn't even the worst of it. Sure, she missed her custom furnishings and her plush carpets and her designer appliances. But mostly what she missed was some structure in her life. She was hiding, not living. She had no purpose in her day other than to not be found. But how long could this continue? At some point she had to begin to make a life again.

She had been hoping, then planning, to escape from Rajiv for years. Now that she had done so, what next?

She had been on the run for over a month. A bus to Boston, a train to New York, a subway to a series of cheap hotels. Moving, blending in, fading into the anonymity of the city. Days in front of the TV, dinners from a hot dog vendor or pizza stand, on to the next hotel, cash paid up front.

If the police were looking for her, they could probably find her. But she had likely succeeded in eluding Rajiv and any lackey he had hired to track her. For the first week or so, she hadn't slept, startled by every footstep in the hall or voice outside her door, fearful that at any minute her snorting husband would come bursting through the door. But she had moved so many times now that the trail was cold. Now the noises in the night didn't scare her, they just disgusted her.

It was time now to stop hiding, to peek out from under her rock. Slowly, at first. But eventually it would be nice to actually have a conversation with another human being again. Oprah was interesting, but she did a lot more talking than listening.

She would start by trying to find a guy to make her a fake passport. And then get out of the blasted country before the world came crashing down on her head.

*　　　*　　　*

Justin poured coffee for his three guests, offered some cookies he had scrounged from a tin in the back of his pantry. He sat down, his back to the window, allowing his guests to enjoy the view of the lake through the large picture window.

So much for keeping his personal and professional lives separate—since he had semi-retired and moved to Mashpee, it seemed like he was always holding business meetings around his kitchen table. Not that it was a bad place to sit around and talk; the eating area off the kitchen was bright and airy, and the birdfeeders in the back yard provided just enough activity to offer a diversion if the conversation lagged. And, of course, the lake gave a pair of tired eyes a place to rest for a few seconds.

Even so, his wife would have been mortified at his skills as a host. Unannounced guests or not, she would have been prepared to entertain. Especially now that she was the mother of a United States Congressman. Justin, Jr.–his secret still unexposed, though the pictures were still floating around somewhere–had won the election and would be on his way to Washington when Congress reconvened in January.

Justin sighed. He was plenty busy, that was for sure. But he missed May, missed being able to discuss things with her, missed her insights into human behavior. She would have urged him to stay far away from Rex Griffin, no doubt. Not that even she could have prevented his blackmailing. But at least she died never learning of the atrocities their son had committed. And if there was a heaven, Justin trusted that its guardians would continue to shield May from that information.

And May would have offered counsel on the whole mess he had created with Donald's log. That was just bad luck–how was he supposed to know that Donald bore down so hard when he wrote? Even so, he had patiently explained to the police that he had turned over every card that Donald had given him, had suggested that perhaps Donald had lost some of the cards himself. And it wasn't like they could ever charge Justin with tampering with evidence–the only one who could possibly testify against him was Donald, and he would hardly make a credible witness. Even so, the whole episode had definitely blown up in his face. He had altered the log to remove himself from suspicion. Now, if anything, their suspicion of him was heightened.

He turned to his guests. Ronnie Lemaire, of course, he knew. And, in his role as Baby Vernon's guardian, he had spent a considerable amount of time lately with Dominique Victor as well. But this was his first personal contact with Ace Awry, though he had met him a few times around town. "So. What can I do for you?" Justin assumed, since his guests were all prominent members of the Mashpee tribe, that this visit somehow involved the lawsuit.

Ronnie responded. "Thanks for meeting with us, short notice and all. And congratulations on your boy's election—he'll be a helluva Congressman, no doubt."

"Thanks, Ronnie. I hope you're right."

"Anyway, I'll get right to it. We were wondering if you'd be willing to help us out."

"Do you mean as an attorney?"

"Sort of...."

Justin tried to keep the surprise off his face. As a property owner, he was one of the defendants in the case. He couldn't help the tribe.

Dominique interrupted Ronnie. Gently, Justin noticed, so Ronnie wouldn't be offended. "Perhaps Ronnie wasn't clear. When he said 'us,' he was referring to all of Mashpee, not just the tribe. Mashpee needs your help, Mr. McBride."

Justin smiled at the woman, impressed by her ability to read his thoughts. She was right—Justin had misinterpreted his friend's words. "I'll do what I can. But can you be more specific?" He realized he had unconsciously directed his question at Dominique.

"Our problem is that we desperately want to settle this lawsuit. And we are prepared to be generous in our terms. But we need to do this quickly—every day that passes causes divisions in this town that may never heal."

"I agree with that assessment. And if the tribe is prepared to be generous, I see no reason why the case can't settle. But what can I do to help?"

Ace Awry jumped in. It was Justin's sense that he just couldn't stand to be silent for so long, especially when such an important conversation was taking place around him. "Our problem is we can't get the title insurance companies to come to the settlement table. We can't very well call them up and beg them to settle with us—they'd just take that as an invitation to screw us. And none of our lawyers have any relationships with the title insurance guys, so they can't send out any signals either."

Justin nodded. "That makes sense. The firm you're using has some very good litigators, but they don't do any real estate work. And it's the real estate guys who work regularly with the title insurance companies."

"Right," Ace said. "That's what we're looking for. Somebody who has a relationship with the title insurance companies, somebody who can just call them up–unofficially–and suggest that the tribe would be interested in a quick settlement."

"And you think I might be that person?"

Ronnie responded. "It was my idea, actually. I know you used to do a lot of real estate. I figured you know a bunch of the guys at the title insurance companies."

Justin nodded. When he had first met Ronnie, he had allowed himself to judge the man by his line of work, his coarse manner of speech, his taste in clothes and cars and wives. But over time he had learned to appreciate his friend's street smarts and common sense. Ronnie may not be able to discuss French existentialism, but he knew how the world worked. "You figured right, Ronnie. I do have some old friends at the title companies. And I'd be happy to make a few calls. Whisper in a few ears, as it were."

*   *   *

A still November mist shrouded the lake. Bruce heard the splash of a fish jumping, waited for the ripples to radiate toward shore and lap gently onto the sand.

A voice intruded on his early morning solitude–he hadn't heard the footsteps approaching, even though they must have passed over the gravel drive only a few yards behind him.

"Good morning, Bruce." He smiled to himself. Of course he hadn't heard them. Dominique hadn't wanted him to. Or maybe she had simply floated through the mist.

"Good morning, Dominique."

"I hope I didn't startle you." She said it teasingly, a knowing smile softening her face.

There was no sense trying to lie to her. "You did, a bit. I'm not used to anyone else being up so early."

"The baby woke me. Plus, I wanted to speak with you; I figured I could find you down here. I wanted to thank you for coming to our rescue the other night."

Bruce shrugged. "No problem. Billy was outnumbered, so I thought I'd make it a fairer fight."

"You've fought before, I could see."

It was a statement, not a question. "Yeah. A few times."

"And, Bruce, I think you like it. You seemed ... I guess the word is untroubled. Most people become very agitated when fighting. You were at ease, calm. Perhaps even happy."

He turned away from Dominique. What kind of response could he possibly make to such a comment? She was right—he knew it, and she knew it. There was no sense denying it. "Do you think that makes me a bad person?"

"No, not at all. If anything, it makes you a good person because you're able to control the impulse. But it does add to your complexity. I knew you were smart—you have the intelligence and curiosity of a scholar. And now I see you have the soul of a warrior. And your heart, well, I have some theories on that as well."

Bruce laughed softly, almost gaily. So what if she knew his secrets? It was like being shy in front of Mother Earth. "I'm sure you do."

"By the way, my sense is that, in time, love will wash away the problems of the past. It doesn't usually work that way, but in your case I am hopeful."

He nodded. "Thank you."

"You know, Bruce, we have a saying: 'Even the wild mountain stream must someday join the river.'"

Bruce smiled. "Am I the stream?"

Dominique shrugged. "You tell me." She turned to leave, then called back over her shoulder. "By the way, we've set up a meeting with the title insurance companies for next week. Hopefully we can settle this whole lawsuit before things get even uglier around here."

"Great. Good luck."

She stopped abruptly, turned her head slowly as if in response to a distant voice. She stared at a point across the lake, her body rigid and regal. Her words came slowly, in a low voice, her eyes fixed on the trees as if she were reading a message printed on their leaves and branches. "In the meantime, Bruce, be careful."

*	*	*

The high school auditorium was packed, and it was still a half hour before the meeting was set to begin.

Dominique sighed. In light of the recent violence, she had hoped that the police would search everyone before entering the building. The chief had seen it differently. "This is a community meeting, set up to allow the townspeople to ask questions of the tribe. We're trying to heal some wounds here. Let's give people the benefit of the doubt. But we'll keep our eyes open." Maybe he was right.

Ace, of course, was sweating as if he were wearing a wool suit at a mid-summer picnic. His shirt was already drenched, and his hands were trembling. It was Dominique's house that had been stoned, but Ace was convinced he was being followed, stalked, targeted. She smiled at her old friend—he was paranoid, and he was so frightened that he barely slept, but he refused to take a less visible position in the tribe. This was his life's work—it was almost as if he was intent on martyring himself. Dominique was more worried he was going to have a nervous breakdown.

She scanned the crowd. Many of the faces she knew—at one point or another, most of them had wandered into her office during their high school years in search of aspirin or first-aid or even abortion advice. Many of the faces had aged a decade or two, but Dominique couldn't help but remember them as they had looked at sixteen.

Of course, there were scores of faces she had never seen before. Mashpee's new residents—mostly wealthy urbanites who had purchased luxury homes in the New Seabury resort section of town. For them, this was the first town-tribe battle; few of them had been around for the original bout. Dominique guessed that their approach to the conflict would be more businesslike, more measured. High-priced lawyers, not rock-wielding teenagers. Dominique wasn't sure which was worse.

The crowd had basically divided itself into three sections. On one side, the Mashpee tribe members gathered, their backs to the wall,

291

their eyes focused warily on the crowd entering the auditorium. Dominique had suggested they arrive an hour early to avoid any conflicts in the parking lot on the way in to the meeting. In the middle of the auditorium, the golf-shirted New Seabury crowd had assembled. They had likely never been in the high school before; in fact, they probably had never even voted in Mashpee, or bothered to learn anything about the town history. But their trophy homes were in jeopardy, so they were here en masse.

The townspeople—that is, the residents who voted and sent their kids to school and worked and actually lived year-round in Mashpee—milled about together on the side near the entrance. Many of them were trying to stare down the tribe members on the far side of the auditorium. A few of them took it a step farther, baiting the tribe with mock rain dances and war cries. Dominique made eye contact with the police chief; he nodded quickly, sent a couple of uniformed men over to try to calm things a bit.

Dominique signaled to the other tribal council members—might as well get started, before things got out of hand. The seven council members took their seats at a table in the front of the room; they had decided not to bring their lawyers to the meeting. But they had invited Ronnie Lemaire to sit at the table with them as well. Dominique had developed a close relationship with many of the townspeople over the years, but her position as a tribal council member made her too much of a lightning rod to be seen as the voice of compromise and reason. So they needed Ronnie to champion some kind of middle ground.

Dominique tapped on the microphone, stood, raised her chin and addressed the crowd in a slow, deep voice. "Thank you all for coming out here tonight. We do not kid ourselves—we know that our lawsuit has made many of you angry, has made many of you bitter, has even made many of you vengeful. Our job tonight is to convince you that we value and treasure you all as part of the community of Mashpee. Yes, we have filed a lawsuit. Yes, we understand that seems like an attack on you and your homes. But no, we do not want to tear this town apart like it was torn apart 20 years ago. It will never, I promise you, come to that again."

She paused here, trying to judge her audience. The newcomers, who viewed Mashpee as a vacation destination rather than as a community anyway, seemed unmoved by her words. Which was fine. The issues with them would be settled by the lawyers. But the long-time residents seemed to have focused on her message, seemed at least to be listening. Not that they were convinced—a voice called out the ripe question: "Why should we believe you?"

Dominique waited for the cheers and applause to begin to die down, then silenced the audience with her response. "You should not. I would not."

She nodded her head, scanned the crowd. "That's right. Don't trust my words. Words are cheap. I can stand up here all night and promise you that we want this lawsuit to be over. Soon. That we're not going to drag this out, that we're not going to take anyone's homes. But I'm not stupid—we just sued you; we've done nothing to earn your trust. So I won't ask you to trust me." They were listening, she was sure of that.

"But I will ask you to trust your own common sense. I'll give you an example: The lawsuit the tribe filed asks for *all* the land in Mashpee to be returned to the tribe. But what you all may not have realized is that *all* the land includes my house. It includes Ronnie Lemaire's house. It includes Ace Awry's donut shop. I've got a boy going to college next year, and I was planning on taking out a second mortgage on my house to pay for it. But, just like all of you, I can't because of the lawsuit.

"I'll give you another example. Ronnie Lemaire had the contract to put in the septic systems for those new homes over in New Seabury. That's a big contract for him. He went out, bought new equipment, hired and trained a bunch of new guys, many of them tribe members. And guess what? Construction's stopped because of the lawsuit. You think Ronnie's happy about that? You think the guys he laid off are happy?

"And Ace, do you think he hasn't felt the boycott down at his shop? Many of you used to make a stop at Ace's part of your morning routine, but not any more. Do you think Ace likes seeing a third of his business disappear?"

Dominique stopped, let her words sink in for a few seconds. "Look, you can think that we're a bunch of greedy back-stabbers for filing this lawsuit. You can even think we're immoral, that somehow this lawsuit is just plain wrong. But don't make the mistake of thinking we're stupid. We understand that this lawsuit is bad for you. We also know full well that it's bad for us. If it takes us a decade or two, and in the end we've won a boatload of money but in the meantime we've lost our homes and our businesses and our livelihoods, then we've won nothing.

"So trust your common sense. It should be telling you that we have nothing to gain by letting this go on much longer."

Another voice, but this one with less venom in it. "Then why'd you file the lawsuit to begin with?"

Ronnie stood, looked to Dominique for permission to respond. "Personally, I was against it. Dominique mentioned some of the reasons, but also because I just thought it was wrong to go around suing your neighbors. But they convinced me we had no choice. To get those title insurance companies to take us seriously, we had to file the damn lawsuit. And so far it's worked—we've got a meeting set up with them next week. Hopefully we can just settle this and go back to our lives."

One of the newcomers stood, cleared this throat. "It's all well and fine that you've set up a meeting with the title insurance companies. But I've had quite a bit of experience in these matters," he proclaimed as he cleared his throat a second time. "What makes you think these title insurance companies will settle with you? It's not that simple, you know."

Dominique could see that Ronnie's face was reddening at the man's elitist attitude, so she responded before he could. "Yes, we're fully aware of the difficulties in negotiating with the title companies. We know we're not going to get as much now as we would if we pushed on to trial."

"So why are you doing it?"

"Because we think it's worth it. We want this to end quickly, and we're willing to take less now to save the community from ripping itself apart."

Bruce stood, waited for Dominique to notice him. She hadn't even seen him come in. His eyes met hers for the briefest moment; she thought she noticed the hint of a wink. Then he opened his mouth to speak. "I'd just like to clarify one thing. There are a group of us in the tribe who are not so willing to settle this lawsuit."

Dominique felt her knees begin to buckle. She had always sensed a benevolence in Bruce, a generosity of spirit. And she did still. Yet his words were assaulting her, undermining that which she had worked so hard for. What was he doing? He was technically a member of the tribe, because his grandfather had been. But he had never expressed even the slightest interest in the tribe's affairs. Or, at least, he never had to her. He continued his verbal assault. "I, for one, don't think we should settle for less than $500 million, maybe more. After all, the property in town is worth almost two billion dollars. That's *billion*, with a *b*. And this case is airtight. So why should we sell ourselves short?" Dominique noticed that a few of the tribe members, mostly the younger ones, nodded in agreement. Were they crazy? Five hundred million dollars? The title companies would never pay that much. The tribal council would be thrilled with one-third of that amount.

Bruce continued. "I don't mind waiting around for five or ten years for the courts to decide. I'd rather not, but there's no reason to settle this for a bag of peanuts and $22 worth of beads just because we don't want to hurt anyone's feelings."

Dominique sank back in her chair, only half-aware of the angry shouts and hisses that buzzed through the air. All of their efforts to diffuse things, all of their attempts to maintain peace in the community—gone. What was Bruce doing?

*   *   *

Bruce sat alone in his one-room cottage. It was late, and the book he was reading had hit a slow spot, but he kept his light on—he knew he would soon have company.

Female company, actually. But not Shelby.

It was well past midnight when a firm knock rattled his door. He opened it, ushered Dominique into the room, offered her a chair. She lowered herself slowly into it—somehow she managed to look regal doing so, even though the throne was a rickety folding chair and the castle a rustic shack. And even though, as Bruce knew, he had put her through hell tonight.

Her voice was steady, powerful. "So, Mr. Arrujo, that was quite a little speech you made tonight. Would it be too much to ask for an explanation?"

He smiled to himself. They both knew he had been waiting up for her, just as they both knew she would visit and expect an explanation. But he would have to be careful—he was about to lie to Dominique. It would be a good lie, a well-reasoned and perfectly believable lie, wrapped neatly inside a bunch of truths. But a lie nonetheless.

"I'm sorry to blind-side you like that, Dominique. That wasn't what I planned on doing. But I noticed a guy in the back, a partner from my old firm. He was trying to just fit in, but I recognized him. He was there to spy. He represents one of the title insurance companies."

She was silent for a moment. "That's interesting, but not surprising."

"I agree. But the more I thought about it, the more I pictured him running back to the office and dictating some long memo to the effect that the tribe is desperate to settle. Well, so much for having any leverage in your negotiations."

"Continue."

"So I figured I could neutralize that a bit by making it sound like not everyone in the tribe was so anxious to see this case resolved. And, believe me, the guys at my old firm will have no trouble believing I'm leading an insurrection."

Bruce could feel her studying him as he spoke, could sense her mistrust. But she was tired, drained from the day's events. And there was simply too much she didn't know to be able to ferret out the particulars of Bruce's deceit. "I see your logic, Bruce, but that's a pretty high price to pay for some negotiation leverage, don't you think? I mean, the townspeople left there tonight convinced there's some radical band of young tribe members ready to take to the streets and do battle. Tomahawks and all." Bruce heard no humor in the comment, only bitter irony.

"Is that really such a bad thing? Why do you think the Israelis sometimes negotiate with Arafat? Because, as much as they hate him, they like him a lot more than the Hamas and the other radicals."

"Please, Bruce. I'm not Arafat, and you're not a suicide bomber. Let's not get melodramatic here."

"But you see my point, right? In their minds, they can make a deal with you or take their chances with a bunch of young punks like me. What would you do?"

Dominique dropped her hands onto her knees, focused on a point just behind Bruce's eyes. Her mouth curved into a smile as she spoke, but the words cut through the air like a cold wind. "Unlike them, I don't have a choice. I have to take my chances with the young punk."

＊　　＊　　＊

Justin and his son were seated at a booth in the original Cheers bar in Boston. Justin had wanted to meet someplace close to Beacon Hill so as not to inconvenience his busy son, but he also didn't want their conversation to be overheard. Since no self-respecting Bostonian had set foot in the bar since it had officially changed its name from the Bull and Finch Pub to Cheers in order to draw tourists, he knew it would be safe to talk.

"You know," Justin began tentatively, "in all your years as a legislator, I've never once tried to influence you, never once asked for a favor of any kind."

"No, you haven't, Dad."

"Well, I'm afraid that's about to change." Justin sipped his scotch, took a deep breath. "Over the past few months I've done some things I'm not very proud of...."

"Such as?"

"I'd rather not give you any specifics, but suffice it to say that my actions were in response to the threats of a blackmailer."

"Come on, Dad, what could anyone possibly blackmail you for? You're clean as a whistle."

Justin lowered his voice. Even tourists sometimes heard things they shouldn't hear. "Unfortunately, my son did some things in

Vietnam, things that were captured on film by someone in his battalion."

Justin saw the shock, then the panic, then the humiliation in his son's face. So, it was true. His son had led a massacre. Justin felt an ache in his heart—he had always held out hope that the pictures had been fake, that his son hadn't really committed the atrocities Griffin had captured on film. Justin waited a few seconds for both him and his son to adjust to the changing realities of their lives, then continued. "Well, as I said, in response to this blackmailer, I've done some things that keep me up at night, wondering what kind of man I really am."

"This blackmailer, who is he?"

"It doesn't matter now. He's dead."

His son nodded, looked at his father quizzically. Justin could hear the unspoken words: *Dad, did you kill him?* Justin had anticipated this moment, cut him off before the question could be asked. "That's all I'm going to say on the matter." The ambiguity would serve his son well—he could lessen the burden of his own guilt by believing his father had also killed, or, alternatively, could continue to hold his father in high esteem by imagining him innocent of such a crime. Justin watched a couple of co-eds purchase some Cheers t-shirts. Probably gifts to bring home for Thanksgiving. Maybe even for their parents....

"Dad, I want to try to explain what happened in Vietnam, what it was like there...."

Justin put up his hand, interrupted his son, spoke in a gentle voice. "Please, Son, don't. Make peace with yourself, or with your God if you believe in one. But it's not necessary to explain yourself to me. You've devoted your life to public service, and I'll always be proud of you for that. Perhaps you've done it as some type of penance, I don't know. Whatever the reason, you're a good man. As I said, I'm proud of the man you've become."

"Thanks, Dad."

Justin took another long sip from his drink. "And now I need your help so that I can also try to repent for my sins, as it were."

"Whatever I can do."

"Thank you. You know about the lawsuit the Mashpee tribe filed against the town, right?"

"Sure."

"Well, this case could really foul things up down there. Already, people are losing jobs, fights are breaking out, businesses going under. It could get really ugly, all the old prejudices coming out into the open again. This is a case that needs to settle. Soon."

"Okay. What can I do?"

"The state needs to kick in some money. I'm trying to get the title insurance companies and the town to reach a settlement, but they need a push. If the state put up, say, $30 million, and made it clear it was only available for a short time, that might get the parties to agree."

"Wow, that's a lot of money. I can do fifteen, maybe twenty...."

"Son, I think we really need thirty."

He sighed. "All right. I can probably pull it off. Ever since I got elected, everyone in the State House has been fawning all over me, trying to get on my good side before I go to Washington."

"Good. Thanks. What do they say—make lemonade out of lemons? Well, maybe we can make something good happen out of this whole mess." Justin lowered his voice. "I know I won't sleep well at night, but maybe some other people will."

*   *   *

Bruce wandered through the cemetery in front of the Old Indian Meeting House. It had become a favorite spot to walk and think—a flat, open area ringed by majestic old maple and oak trees, the tombstones scattered haphazardly about like oversized leaves that had fallen in the autumn wind.

He stood among his ancestors, wondered if they had somehow intervened and influenced the younger members of the tribe to follow his lead. At a hastily called meeting two nights after the town forum, dozens of tribe members—fire in their eyes—gathered to fight under the twin banners of ethnic pride and socio-economic justice. They were no different than the youth who marched for civil rights or protested the Vietnam War or rioted against world trade in

Seattle and Quebec and Genoa. The causes were different, but the burning passion to fix the world that their parents had screwed up was the same for every generation.

Bruce's message was simple: *Why should we accept the same type of deal that the previous generation derided as insulting?* He quoted from letters to the editor Ace had written 25 years earlier: "This is not about money. This is about respect. This is about righting the wrongs of the past." Why, Bruce asked, should it be about money now? Was it because the tribal leaders had grown old, soft, comfortable? If so, perhaps it was time for a new generation of leaders.

And Bruce appeared to be the perfect candidate to be that leader—handsome, charismatic, a graduate of Harvard Law School. So what if his bloodlines had been diluted? None of the Mashpee could claim 100 percent Native American blood, and Bruce was no interloper—his grandfather had participated in tribal events a full half-century earlier.

But the reality was that Bruce had no interest in becoming the leader of the tribe. He would lead them on for a while. And perhaps, in the end, even lead them astray. But he had no interest in leading them anywhere they would want to go.

They, on the other hand, would lead him straight to the killer.

*   *   *

Somehow it had been decided that the meeting between the tribal council and the title insurance companies would be held in Boston, at one of the lawyers' offices. Maybe the council had feared that Bruce and his merry gang would disrupt things if the meeting was held on the Cape. Or maybe it was just easier to get all the title companies and their teams of lawyers together in a central location.

Whatever the reason, the decision played right into Bruce's hand. Thanksgiving was only a week away, and media outlets were preparing their yearly pieces on the Pilgrims' landing at Plymouth Rock. And also the counterbalancing piece on the Native American protest of the Thanksgiving holiday. Bruce would give them a little spice to add to their stories. He and his group took to the sidewalk just as the council and all the lawyers were arriving.

It was the kind of story the media ate up. A high-stakes battle over ownership of an entire town, couched in the historical conflict between native and colonist, with a couple of dozen protesters, dressed in traditional Wampanoag clothing, marching in front of a downtown office tower. And the signs didn't hurt: *We want OUR land, not YOUR beads!* seemed to be the favorite, though the politically incorrect *Now Who's the Indian Giver?* was also popular.

Bruce counted five television stations, did four interviews. He had scripted his comments: "The bottom line is that we want our land back. The title insurance companies think they can buy us off, but this isn't about the money. It's about our heritage, about the legacy we want to leave for our children. Our land was wrongly taken from us, and we want it back. And if the tribal council won't do as we ask, we'll have no choice but to remove them from office. We're staying right across the street in the Parker House hotel, and we're not leaving until the tribal council abandons these settlement negotiations."

*   *   *

Inside the law firm conference room, Dominique peered down from the 31st floor window, barely able to make out the line of protesters below. She had her doubts about Bruce's motives, but she had to give him some credit: the title insurance companies seemed anxious to cut a deal with the current council. It was either that, or take their chances with Bruce and his band of renegades.

She appreciated the irony of the situation. A generation earlier, the title insurance companies had adopted a strategy of stall and stonewall. Like all insurance companies, they had been in no rush to settle. They knew they might have to pay in the end, but if they could hold onto their cash for an extra few years while the parties did battle, well, the cost of the fight would be worth it to them. And they also knew that the time and energy and expense of a long legal battle would wear down their adversary.

But, this time, a long delay could hurt the insurance companies. The threat of Bruce's insurrection was an obvious incentive. But the insurance companies would also see the wisdom of settling before the tribe was on the hook for the $50 million penalty to the Griffin Family Trust—by February 2, the tribe would need $50 million just to get even, never mind meet its expectations of a windfall.

For the umpteenth time, she did the rough math in her head. The value of all the land in town was approximately $2 billion. The tribe had 2,200 tribe members. A successful lawsuit would, therefore, under a best-case scenario, yield $900,000 for every man, woman and child in the tribe. Enough for them all to retire on. Enough to get fat and lazy. Enough to addict them to a life of luxury. Enough, in short, to ruin the spiritual wealth of the tribe. She had seen it happen in other tribes, tribes that had been both blessed and cursed by the riches of casino gambling. She would not allow it to happen to the Mashpees.

On the other hand, she wasn't stupid. The tribe was poor—its members needed money for health care, education, housing, basic living expenses. And they needed it now, not ten or twenty years down the road. It was her job to find the balance, to find the level of wealth that would enrich them but not corrupt them. And then convince the title insurance companies to pay it.

But what was the proper balance? She had adopted an informal test, had polled the tribe members: *How much money would it take for you to quit your job?* In her mind, any number that caused the tribe members to quit their jobs would be too much. Enough for a comfortable retirement. Enough to pay for college for the kids. Even enough to pay off the mortgage. But not enough to retire. Not enough to buy a mansion. Not enough to change who they were.

The number she had settled on was $300,000 per family. That was $70,000 per tribe member. In round figures, a total of $150 million, or less than 10 percent of what the lawsuit sought. In the end, she knew, it would be a bargain for the title insurance companies.

Even so, that didn't mean a settlement would be easy. Getting someone to write a check for $150 million was never easy. Plus, there were a number of factors weighing against a quick settlement. Dominique took out a legal pad, scrawled a list. First, the state had yet to offer to kick in any money. Both the tribe and the title insurance companies expected some public funds to be thrown onto the table at some point; it would be difficult to reach a settlement knowing that the state had yet to be squeezed. The good news was that Justin McBride's son, newly elected to Congress, was pushing for some state funds in his last days in the state legislature. Maybe he'd have some success before he left office by dangling the promise of future favors from Washington.

Second, the title insurance company executives still hadn't cleaned the egg off their faces. Unlike the first suit, which came completely out of left field, the companies should have seen this one coming. As long as the title insurance companies insisted that the claim was bogus, jobs would likely be safe. But once they admitted the claim was legitimate, Dominique knew that heads would roll. Dominique looked around—some of those heads were likely in the room with her right now. The mouths attached to them would fight hard against any settlement. She shrugged—they were not the final decision-makers anyway. And they were expendable. They would thrash about, but in the end the top executives would simply sacrifice them and approve the settlement over their objections.

The third problem was egos. She was sitting in a room full of lawyers, hundreds of millions of dollars at stake. They would all want their say, all want to earn their fees, all want to be the straw that stirred the drink. So she would need to keep Ace and his righteous indignation in check, allow the egos to believe they were controlling the agenda.

Finally, there was the issue of the subdivision neighbors. In the end, they would have to agree to sell their homes and move. This would be the last hurdle, after the deal had been agreed to. It would be tough to get all the neighbors on board—nobody liked to be evicted, and at least one or two would try to hold out for a few extra bucks. But there should be enough money on the table to buy them out. And it wasn't like their subdivision had been a breeding ground for suburban bliss the past couple of years. In fact, she had just learned from her contact at the police department that they had finished deciphering the log imprints from the night of the murder. Not only did the missing entries implicate Justin McBride, but they also recorded that Amisha Raman's car had entered and exited the subdivision at incriminating times. Bottom line: Whatever the terms of the settlement, it was likely that at least a few of the neighbors would be far more focused on clearing their name than on protesting a settlement with the tribe.

But all that really was beside the point right now—she needed to focus on the settlement. Dominique looked back at her notes. All of the obstacles she listed were formidable, but none of them should be insurmountable. So the case should settle. Unless Bruce carried his little insurrection too far.

*   *   *

Amisha was sitting at the window, peering through the crusted window at some rats scurrying back and forth in the alley below her hotel room. She shuddered—snakes and bugs and spiders had never bothered her, but rats seemed to trigger some primitive terror. Perhaps she had been attacked by them in a previous life. And now it seemed like every hotel she stayed in overlooked a rat-infested alley. She raised a cup of instant coffee to her lips; along with a granola bar, that would be her breakfast. If the rats hadn't taken away her appetite.

A knock on the door jolted her. Coffee bounced down her chin and onto her blouse. A second knock—firm and insistent.

Nobody had ever knocked on her door before. She didn't know anyone in New York, and even if she did, they had no way to find her. And it wasn't likely to be a chambermaid offering to fluff her pillows.

She tiptoed across the thin carpet to the door, peered through the eyehole, saw the blue uniform and badge. Her heart jumped—cops wouldn't come just to bring her back to her husband. Did their visit somehow relate to the fake passport? Or to the SEC investigation? Or even to Griffin's death? She took a deep breath. "Yes?"

"Mrs. Raman, New York City police here."

Mrs. Raman. How did he know her name? She had been using an alias since she arrived. "Be right there." She straightened her skirt, ran her fingers through her hair, dabbed at the coffee stain on her blouse with the bedspread. At this point, the only thing she had going for her was her looks. Not that her charms were likely to hold much sway with the police. But being attractive and guilty was probably better than being uncomely and guilty; the cops were, after all, only men. She opened the door, smiled innocently. "Yes, what can I do for you?"

There were two of them. She caught the younger, Hispanic-looking officer peeking down her blouse. But the older man was gruff and disinterested. "Are you Amisha Raman, formerly of Mashpee, Massachusetts?"

She nodded. No sense denying what they already knew.

The younger cop smiled at her. Or maybe it was a leer. "The cops in Massachusetts want you. Said you ran some guy down in a car. Your husband dropped a dime on you."

Blasted Rajiv. Speaking of rats—he probably figured he could get his revenge on her and clear himself all at once. Bastard.

She couldn't help asking. "But how did you find me?"

The younger cop flashed a photograph of her. "Not too hard. Your picture's been passed all over the city." In the hallway, Amisha noticed a man peering into the room at her, his eyes darting between her face and a photo in his hand. The guy she had tried to buy the passport from. "Your husband's offering ten grand to whoever turns you in to the cops...."

The older man cut him off. "Shut up, kid." He turned back to Amisha, slipped a pair of handcuffs over her wrists. "You're under arrest for the murder of Rex Griffin." She felt her knees buckle beneath her. "You have the right to remain silent...."

*   *   *

Bruce watched himself on the evening news that night from his classically-furnished hotel room, listened to the words he had spoken only hours earlier. *We're staying right across the street in the Parker House hotel....* Good. His message to the killer hadn't been edited out. The killer would be watching, would not miss Bruce's words. The expressed words—*in the Parker House hotel*. And also the implied—*Come and get me.*

In the killer's mind, this would be a game of cat and mouse, with Bruce as the mouse. The killer would stalk Bruce, surprise him, pounce. Bruce smiled, remembering the old cartoon shows where the

305

mouse led the pursuing cat straight into the jaws of the waiting bulldog.

He grabbed a newspaper, took the elevator down to the lobby. Bruce's guess was that the killer would come tonight. He would be ready.

*   *   *

Shelby looked at her watch—9:15. Another night in the office, another day like all the others. Time to pack up her things, take a taxi to her condo in the Back Bay, pop some popcorn in the microwave, click on the ten o'clock news. It was her normal weekday routine—she had no family to rush home to, and by working 13-hour days she was able to keep her weekends free for travel or an occasional date. If she wanted to see her friends, she met them for lunch. It wasn't much of a life, she knew. And it looked worse in the light of her fast-approaching 35th birthday.

The phone rang just as she was turning off the light. She glanced at the display, noted that the call was coming in on her direct line, a number she gave out only to friends. "Hello."

"Shelby, hi, this is Carla. Have you spoken to Bruce at all lately?"

Shelby noted the alarm in her friend's voice, put down her briefcase. "Not for a couple of weeks. Why?"

"I just saw him on the news. I only caught the end of it, but it looks like he's leading some protest against the tribe settling the lawsuit. I guess they had a settlement meeting today, up in Boston."

"Are you sure it was Bruce?"

"Oh yeah. They interviewed him. He was all bent out of shape about the tribe selling out, selling its legacy. And he had a bunch of other tribe members demonstrating with him. They were all dressed up in Native American clothes, even Bruce. It was a big story."

Shelby stared out the window, stammered a response. "I, I don't know what to say, Carla. I don't know anything about this."

"I hope I'm wrong, but it sounds to me like he's up to something. I mean, why should he care if the tribe settles or not?"

Shelby tried to focus. "I have no idea...."

"Well, they were demonstrating outside of one of the law firms' offices. Someplace downtown. It was on the cable news. They'll replay it again at 9:30."

"All right. I'll try to figure out what's going on. Thanks, Carla. I'll call you when I learn something."

Shelby set the phone down, stared out her office window at the Boston skyline. Somewhere out there Bruce was plotting, planning, scheming. But to what ends? Was he still trying to catch the killer? Or had he, instead, sniffed the leafy scent of the mountain of money at stake in the tribe's land claim?

The question flashed into her mind: Could a bloodhound ever truly ignore the scent of its prey?

She replayed her last conversation with Bruce in her head. He thought he knew who the killer was, he had told her. And he had a plan for catching him or her. But he couldn't tell Shelby anything about it, couldn't share his suspicions or his plan. *Trust me*, he had implored. *Trust me.*

And now this. She shook her head. Dressing up in Native American clothing and demonstrating in front of an office tower seemed like a strange way to catch Griffin's killer. She was willing to cut Bruce a lot of slack—he was brilliant, and he was tenacious, and he was capable of crafting elaborate schemes. But what possible connection could his behavior have to catching the killer?

He had asked her to trust him. She had, in effect, laughed in his face. Had she driven him away? She tried to look at it through his eyes. She had exiled him for seven years, then beckoned him back with an opportunity at redemption. Painfully, he had asked for forgiveness. Dutifully, he had performed his tasks. Patiently, he had awaited a sign from her that their love might again be free to flourish. In return, she had laughed in his face.

If she had, indeed, driven him away, she would have to pay for that mistake for the rest of her life. It had been seven years, and she hadn't found a single man for a single moment to be the least bit desirable. She knew she would never love again. She would either reconcile with Bruce, or live her life alone. That was just the way it was.

But she would not make others pay for her mistakes. She had unleashed Bruce on the Mashpee community, had introduced him as some sort of bad bacteria that would eradicate an even worse bacteria and then somehow be purged from the body once its work was done. But, if her suspicions were correct, the experiment had gone bad. The bacteria was intent on devouring the body it was supposed to save. And only she could stop it.

She left her office, walked down the darkened hallway toward the conference room. She tried, unsuccessfully, to suppress a shudder—she was frequently alone in the office at night, but tonight she felt a lurking evil, a sense that danger loomed in the darkness. For some reason she could not articulate, nor even understand, she heard Dominique's deep voice as she walked: *Be careful tonight.*

Shelby moved slowly, further into the darkness, finally reaching the conference room at the end of the hallway. She exhaled, pushed open the conference room door, groped for the light switch with one hand as she clutched a pair of scissors tightly in the other.

Light flooded the room. Shelby's eyes darted back and forth, scanning the room for a danger that—somehow—her gut had already concluded did not exist. She cursed herself: *Stop acting like a melodramatic teenager.* The self-admonition sobered her, calmed her. Danger may, indeed, be lurking tonight. But it wouldn't be found in the sterile confines of a downtown law firm. It would be out on the street, prowling in the shadows, shrouded in the darkness.

She turned on the TV, found the news channel, glanced at her watch. Eight minutes until the news recycled, eight minutes until she had the privilege of watching the face of the man she loved betray her, betray her clients, betray her friends.

Finally, the headlines began again. A Eurasian woman, whom Shelby had actually met at a cocktail party the week before and found incredibly beautiful and equally empty-headed, spoke to Shelby from the anchor desk. "Our lead story tonight involves the land claim filed by the Mashpee band of the Wampanoag Indian tribe. Earlier today a splinter group of tribe members protested outside a downtown office tower, threatening to derail settlement discussions between the tribe and the title insurance companies that reportedly had begun to make significant progress...."

Shelby gasped as Bruce's face—steely, resolute—filled the screen. Carla had warned her, but the three-dimensional image of his betrayal knocked her deep into her chair like a knee to the gut. She forced herself to breathe, listened to his words as the camera followed him and his fellow protesters as they marched in front of the One Beacon Street office tower:

"...Our land was wrongly taken from us, and we want it back. And if the tribal council won't do as we ask, we'll have no choice but to remove them from office. We're staying right across the street in the Parker House hotel, and we're not leaving until the tribal council abandons these settlement negotiations."

Our land? Our children? Who was he kidding? Bruce had no stake in this battle, no true ties to the community, no burning identity with the tribe's heritage and culture. He was pursuing some hidden agenda, the most generous interpretation of which was that Bruce was using the tribe as a playing piece in his chess match with the killer. But even that interpretation was a stretch, was based on the belief that Bruce was behaving in a totally selfless manner. Anyone with an ounce of cynicism in them would conclude that Bruce was maneuvering himself into a position to grab a share of the tribe's soon-to-be-acquired wealth.

Whichever it was, Shelby wanted some answers. She would likely find them just a few blocks away, at the Parker House hotel.

*   *   *

Bruce sat in the lobby of the Parker House. The lobby was long and wide, easily large enough for Bruce to lose himself in a leather chair in the corner. A team of flight attendants had just arrived and was checking in, but it was almost ten at night and otherwise the room was empty.

He peeked out from behind his newspaper, recognized the face of the man entering through the revolving doors. Rex Griffin moved slowly, cautiously, his right hand deep in the pocket of his trench coat. Probably gripping a weapon. But probably also not expecting to need it until he had surprised Bruce in his hotel room.

Bruce stood, circled around behind Griffin, watched as he conferred with the front desk staff. Griffin would have learned Bruce's name from the news broadcase; he would now attempt to get Bruce's room number, would likely be rebuffed by the well-trained staff, would then settle for a phone number. Bruce made his way to the house phones, tucked away in a shadowy corner of the lobby. He slipped on the busboy hat and apron he had stolen from the laundry room, picked up a tray of empty drinks he had stashed—it wasn't a great disguise, but it should be enough, along with the element of surprise, to give Bruce the edge he needed.

Griffin argued for a few seconds with the desk clerk, then resigned himself to accepting the phone number. Bruce turned his back to the man, dropped to one knee, busied himself cleaning up an imaginary spill on the carpet.

Griffin reached for the phone, dialed, waited for Bruce to answer. "Damn it," he hissed. Bruce imagined the words escaping through the small, brown teeth he had observed at the Burger King. "Answer the phone."

Bruce maneuvered his way behind him, scanned the room to make sure nobody was watching. The angle was such that they were out of view of the main desk, and the lobby was otherwise empty. He stood slowly, confident that he had surprised his prey, then lunged. Bruce locked his arm around Griffin's exposed neck, forced his jaw back with a turn of his forearm. Griffin gurgled, fought against Bruce's grip for a few second, then bent his smaller body to Bruce's strength.

Bruce whispered into his ear. "Hello. This is Bruce. I can't take your call right now."

Griffin's hand darted into his pocket, pulled out a small revolver. But Bruce had anticipated the move. He spun Griffin around, locked Griffin's arm behind his back, twisted the gun away from him. "Nice try. Now we go into the bathroom to make sure you don't have any other weapons. Then we go for a walk."

*   *   *

It was 10:00 p.m., a cold, windy Tuesday in November in a city that was known for going to bed early. Shelby noticed a few people in Bruins jerseys making their way to their cars after the game ended, and a few other lawyers like herself dragging briefcases toward the subway stops, but for the most part the streets were empty.

She breathed in the cold air, felt her adrenaline pump, wondered at her heightened sense of awareness. Tonight, for some reason, she saw everything, noticed the smallest details, perceived things at a magnified level.

Friends who had experimented with drugs had described a similar sensation—the world, which had previously existed as an Impressionist painting, had suddenly become perceptible on an almost microscopic level. For Shelby, it was like putting on eyeglasses for the first time, like shaking the water out of her ear, like tasting food after the throat lozenge had worn off, like smelling the bread baking in the oven after a long cold. It was all of those things, together.

She tasted the pizza, flavored by a gritty mix of salty ocean air and dust from a construction project, as it wafted over the cobblestones of Quincy Market. She watched the wind currents blow across City Hall Plaza, squeeze between two buildings, then churn over an overflowing dumpster. She saw the joyful bounce in the step of a young Bruins fan as his sticky fingers clutched his father's hand, and she knew that the home team had won tonight. Even the homeless woman huddled in the shadows near the entrance to the Parker House hotel looked strangely familiar, the large brown eyes dancing in the moonlight from above the scarf shielding her face.

Shelby pushed through the revolving doors of the Parker House, the pizza and the dumpster and the Bruins and the homeless woman quickly forgotten. She spotted Bruce immediately, his back to her, huddled together with another man near the house phones in a corner at the far end of the lobby. She could not see their faces, but she could feel the tightness in their backs, could sense the tension between them, even imagined she had caught the faint scent of Bruce's after-shave.

Bruce and the man ducked into the men's room. Shelby crouched behind a couch, waited until they emerged a few minutes later. Bruce's hand rested on the other man's back, and it seemed to Shelby as if he was pushing him ahead. The men were still at the far end of the lobby, and Bruce's companion had pulled a hat low over his face and walked with his head bowed, so Shelby couldn't see his face. But she saw their overcoats, smelled their hostility, sensed that Bruce, at least, preferred that their conversation—and whatever else might transpire between them—be continued on the darkened streets rather than in the warm glow of the lobby's crystal chandeliers. She quickly darted back through the revolving door, out onto the sidewalk. She ducked behind a luggage cart, peered between the bags bound for Chicago, waited for Bruce and his companion to appear.

They pushed through the revolving door, squeezing together into a single compartment, Bruce's hand still on the man's back. They spun out onto the sidewalk, turned away from Shelby, walked up School Street half a block to the corner, then turned left onto Tremont. Shelby waited a few seconds, followed at a safe distance. They walked a block—past a mid-sized office building, a small cemetery, a church.

Shelby still hadn't seen the man's face, but there was something eerily familiar about his posture, his bearing, his carriage. She toyed with the idea of running ahead on the opposite sidewalk to get a better view, but rejected the idea because she didn't want Bruce to see her.

They had now reached the Boston Common park area. Like the rest of the city, the Common was mostly deserted—the vendors and business people and shoppers and tourists had abandoned the cold park to the homeless for the night. The men passed by the subway entrance, then circled around a stone fountain. Bruce shoved the man down onto a bench, then warily sat next to him, his right hand still glued to the small of the man's back.

Shelby waited until they were settled, then kicked off her shoes and ducked, noiselessly, into the shadows of the park. She approached the bench from the rear, forcing herself to move slowly, carefully. Finally, a few feet from the bench, she slipped behind a tree. She could hear Bruce's words clearly in the night air, saw his breath rising above his head.

"Look, it doesn't matter how I figured it out. But I knew you'd come out of your little hole when you saw me on TV."

"That's right. I can't have you interfering with the settlement." Shelby gasped. She knew that voice. But her brain refused to believe what her ears were telling her. She fought to stifle her panting, held her hand over her heart to quiet the drumbeat in her chest. Had they heard her? And did it matter? A ghost could see her even behind the thickest tree.

She took a deep breath, peeked out cautiously. As she stared in disbelief, Rex Griffin turned, spotted her, offered her a wry smile.

She gasped again, spun away, slumped to the ground in the shelter of the tree. *He was alive.*

She heard Griffin's words in the distance. "That sounds like a fair deal. I accept. I'll give you a million dollars if you keep your mouth shut."

Bruce started to react. "What are you talking ab-...?!"

The echo of Griffin's words hit her, enraged her. *A million dollars.* How could she have allowed Bruce to do this to her again? She stormed out from behind the tree before Bruce could finish his sentence, hissed at the man she once loved and thought she might someday love again. "You son-of-a-bitch! You lied to me again! How could you, Bruce?"

Bruce spun toward her voice, stood. She could see the confusion, then the panic, on his face. "Shelby, what are you doing here?"

"Me?! What about you?"

The question hung in the air. Bruce opened his mouth to answer, but the only response in the night air was a sharp pop. Shelby was vaguely aware of having seen Griffin wrench something from Bruce's hand, of noticing the fear in Bruce's eyes, of seeing Griffin's out-stretched arm pointing at Bruce's waist. But only when the echo of the gunshot pounded its way into her consciousness did Shelby understand what had happened.

Shelby's eyes followed Bruce's, settled on the gun. Bruce's voice cut through the night as he toppled onto the bench. "Run, Shelby!"

She watched him list to one side like a torpedoed ship, then noticed Griffin turn her way, the gun sweeping steadily toward her like the second hand on a clock. She dove for the same tree that had sheltered her, heard the crack of a bullet bounce off the trunk as she tumbled to the ground. *Unbelievable. He's shooting at me.*

She scrambled to her feet, ran for the shadows deeper in the park, trying to keep the tree between herself and Griffin for as long as she could. She crouched as she ran, zigzagging like she had seen in the movies. She was a fast runner. She was in good shape. And she was scared to death. Even barefoot, she knew he wouldn't be able to catch her. But a bullet was another story. She would need to put a few hundred feet between her and the gun to feel safe.

And she wasn't there yet. She heard the clap-clap-clap of a pair of shoes pursuing her along the pavement, then a second shot pierced the night air. She tensed for a moment, waited for the impact of a bullet. Nothing. She kept running, searching for a path that would keep her in the shadows.

Out of the corner of her eye she saw a movement, a figure lurking in the darkness. Then a voice shouted, deep and robust. "Police! Police! Some idiot's out here shooting! Someone call the police!" Shelby spotted the body attached to the voice—the same burly bag lady she had seen earlier by the hotel.

Shelby cringed. The old crone was going to get herself killed.

But instead of more gunshots, Shelby heard Griffin's footsteps veer away, retreat down a path heading out of the park. Apparently the presence of another person—or, more accurately, another witness—had been enough to cause him to end his pursuit.

She waited for a moment, listened to the fading clap of his footsteps. He was gone. Shelby turned, looked for the bag lady. She, too, had disappeared.

But Bruce was still on the bench, maybe already dead. Shelby ran back toward him, her rage at his betrayal replaced by an almost enfeebling feeling of dread. She reached a tentative hand out to him. "Bruce...."

He held his hand over his side, his fingers already red with blood. "Shelby, listen. This is not what you think...." He coughed, cringed in pain.

For some reason she thought of her parents' and brother's death, their bodies mangled in a collision with a drunk driver. Asshole or not, Bruce didn't deserve to die here on a park bench at the hands of Rex Griffin. Or Rex Griffin's ghost. "Be still. I have a cell phone. Let me call 911." Her tone, she knew, could have been more compassionate.

"Wait. I need to talk to you first. I can explain everything, I promise...."

"Later. Let me call first." She took out her phone, dialed the emergency number. "They're on the way."

"Shelby, listen to me. Don't tell them Griffin is alive. Please."

Shelby felt her anger rising. "What, so you can collect your hush money from him? Sorry, Bruce, I'm not going to let you screw us all again."

"That's not it, Shelby." He took her hand, squeezed it in his even as she recoiled from his bloody touch. "I really can explain. But please, please, don't tell the police Griffin is alive. If you do, the whole settlement will fall apart." He almost sobbed the words. "I want so much to make this right. Please, Shelby...."

She looked into Bruce's eyes. How could she trust him again? She had heard Griffin's words, had heard him accept Bruce's million-dollar offer. But Bruce's eyes bore into her, feverish, imploring her to keep his secret even as the life seeped out of his body. She heard sirens approaching, knew she had only a few seconds to make her decision. Here was a dying man, a man she had once loved and thought she still might, a man who had betrayed her, begging her not to tell the police who had shot him. Had anyone, anywhere ever had to make this decision before?

She sighed, nodded her assent. Her experience in the District Attorney's office had taught her that dying men rarely lied. So she would trust him for now. If he died, she would figure out what to do then. If he lived, she would demand a full explanation, then make a final decision. "All right, Bruce. I won't say anything. For now."

He leaned back, smiled through his pain. "Thank you. I promise I'll tell you everything. Just tell the police we were sitting on the bench and some guy came up from behind, asked for my wallet. I refused, then he shot me and ran." The words seemed to drain him, but his eyes stayed focused on her, waiting for a response.

She nodded, turned away, retrieved her shoes. The police car pulled to a stop a few yards away. After everything he had done, she was going to lie for him. Probably get herself disbarred.

Suddenly Bruce jolted up, grabbed her arm, whispered in her ear. "Shelby, Griffin saw you. And he knows you saw him. He might come after you. Especially if I die. Be careful, please be careful...."

*   *   *

The bag lady slowly rotated her body around the large oak tree as Rex Griffin jogged past, the gun still in his hand. She, like Shelby, had been following Bruce, though she had disguised herself so she would not be seen by Griffin. But, unlike Shelby, Dominique had not been so surprised at what she had found. She watched Griffin trot away, pulled the scarf back up over her face, and shuffled back toward her hotel as the sounds of sirens filled the night air.

*   *   *

Rex Griffin heard the police sirens, slowed his pace. Running now would only draw attention to himself.

He pulled the handgun from his pocket, wiped it clean with a handkerchief, began to drop it into one of the trashcans scattered around the Common. Then he stopped. Why bother? If the police arrested him now it would be because Bruce and Shelby had identi-fied him—it wouldn't matter whether he had the gun or not. So why not keep the weapon? He might need it later.

He breathed in the cool night air, savored the solitude of the park at night. He had been shut up in that group house for what seemed like a decade. But it would end soon, one way or another. He knew one of two things would happen. If Shelby identified him to the police, they would be sweeping the city within a few minutes looking for him. He didn't like his odds if he had to evade an entire police force. He was unprepared and ill-equipped to play the part of prey tonight—he had expected to be the hunter.

On the other hand, it was possible that Bruce—if he was still alive—had convinced Shelby to keep her mouth shut, in which case the police would attribute the whole episode to some random act of urban violence and were looking for some 20-something urban thug.

Griffin hoped it was the latter, but he knew he couldn't bank on Shelby's silence. He hailed a cab, directed him toward the airport. He would camp out there for a while, catch the news, try to get a sense of how the police were treating the incident. Then he would have to

316

make a decision. Return to the group home in Medford before he was missed, or flee.

Of course, it never should have come to this. If Bruce hadn't somehow figured everything out, the tribe and the title insurance companies would be on the verge of agreeing to a settlement that would allow him—finally—to escape the nut house he had imprisoned himself in the past few months. Donald's room wasn't a jail cell, but it was almost as bad.

And wearing Donald's goddamn glasses were giving him a constant headache. As a kid he used to fool around sometimes and wear Donald's glasses, and he knew they would make it appear as if he, too, had a wandering eye. Apparently a prism was inserted in the lens in order to allow Donald's bad eye to see straight ahead. However, the prism worked in both directions, so that anyone looking through the lens at his eye would also see a distorted image. In Donald's case, it make the wandering eye appear worse than it actually was. Not that he cared, or even noticed. When Rex wore the lens, it made it look like he, too, had a wandering eye. Not as extreme a case as Donald's, but who really would notice that Griffin's right eye was directed at two o'clock on the watch face rather than three? It was a great disguise, which was why he had been so careful not to crush them when he ran over Donald, but the headaches were a killer.

All in all, life in the supervised setting, surrounded by a bunch of retards and their fawning zookeepers, his head constantly pounding, was hardly the idyllic retirement on a beach in Thailand he had planned for himself. For that, he needed the settlement to go through. The deal he had structured would give the Griffin Family Trust control of a cluster of homes that would provide him a generous income for the rest of his life. More importantly, the settlement would permanently whitewash the fraud he had committed on his mortgage lender because the title insurance companies would pay the lender in full. And the tribe would be unable to repudiate the deal even after they discovered Griffin had manipulated them—Baby Vernon was the majority beneficiary of the Griffin Family Trust, and the tribe would be legally, as well as morally and politically, bound to honor a contract entered into with a tribe member.

Not that the tribe should even care that they had been duped: His little manipulation would enable them to extract a pile of money from the title insurance companies, as well as a parcel of land for a shrine to their fallen Chief Metacomet. Manipulated, yes. But not cheated.

The only one who really had a right to feel cheated was poor Donald, who lay buried beneath a headstone that bore his twin brother's name. Good old Donald. Griffin had spent a lifetime trying to distance himself from his twin—it was bad enough to have a retard for a brother, but a retard who was an identical twin was like being overcharged for a root canal. So Griffin had long ago simply reinvented Donald as a younger brother, confident that differences in hairstyle and weight and carriage and eyewear would suffice to shroud the truth, especially as they got older. But in the end it was Donald's identical DNA that had enabled Griffin to succeed in deceiving the police. So, yes, Donald had every right to feel cheated.

As, Griffin admitted, did Pierre Prefontaine. If he ever learned the truth, that is. Pierre, alone among the neighbors, had refused to do a deal with the devil. But he would likely be more than willing to sell his property to the Mashpee tribe for a fair price, especially because the income from the property would then be channeled to Billy's son, Baby Vernon. Little would Pierre know that the devil himself—back from the dead—would also be sharing in that income stream. So, yes, if Pierre ever learned the truth, he, too, would definitely feel cheated.

And the deal wasn't dead yet, so Pierre still might be duped. Bruce had, somehow, figured out that Griffin had killed Donald and adopted his identity. But, for some reason, Bruce had not yet gone to the police. So Bruce must have some other agenda. Unfortunately, their little meeting had been cut short by Shelby's interruption and the unfortunate gun incident, so Griffin had never learned what Bruce had in mind. Whatever it was, if Bruce could somehow keep Shelby from running to the police, things still might be salvaged. Griffin had thrown out the million-dollar offer in the heat of the battle merely to distract Bruce. But why not throw some money at Bruce to buy his silence? Bruce seemed like a man who could be bought; in fact, that was probably why he had not yet gone to the police. And Shelby—based on the emotional exchange between her and Bruce that Griffin had viewed tonight—apparently had some romantic interest in Bruce, which gave Bruce some influence over her as well. So, if Bruce survived, maybe this whole thing could be saved. But Shelby would surely go to the police if Bruce died.

Griffin smiled. Maybe he should have shot Bruce in the knee instead of the gut. Life was funny. An hour ago, he had wanted Bruce dead. Bruce was impeding the settlement, was scuttling a finely crafted and elaborately planned scheme. A dead Bruce had meant a live settlement. Now a live Bruce was probably his best chance.

He didn't even know who this Bruce guy was, though he certainly appeared to be a formidable adversary. Bruce had been lying in wait for him, had foiled the assassination attempt even before it began. If it weren't for Shelby's surprise arrival from behind a tree, Bruce would still have the upper hand.

The reality of the situation was that, even lying in a hospital bed somewhere, Bruce still did have the upper hand—unless he died, of course. Bruce could blackmail Griffin. Or turn him over to the police. Or just string him along for a while. Shelby's arrival had delayed Bruce, but it had not derailed him.

In fact, Shelby's surprise appearance, which Griffin had so welcomed only an hour earlier, may not have been so fortuitous after all. It had allowed him to escape from Bruce tonight, but he was still in Bruce's trap. Worse, there were now two people who knew he was alive. That was two more than Griffin had expected when he sneaked out of Donald's room earlier tonight. Maybe he should have shot Shelby first, then turned on Bruce. At least he could try to buy Bruce. Shelby, on the other hand, seemed to be fiercely loyal to her clients.

Perhaps, in the end, Bruce would be Shelby's downfall, much as he had been Griffin's.

*   *   *

Shelby sipped a Diet Coke, alone in the middle of a large cafeteria at Massachusetts General Hospital. The doctors had stabilized Bruce. He would, at least, survive. Her heart was relieved at the news. Her brain wasn't so sure.

And the police had taken her statement. She gave them a general description of the assailant, enough so she could later not contradict herself if she ID'd Griffin, but not so detailed that she would be breaking her promise to Bruce. Their story—a middle-aged white man mugging them in the park—seemed a bit bizarre, but her status as a former Assistant District Attorney cloaked her in credibility.

So here she was—lying to the police, abetting a con artist, betraying her clients and friends. Not to mention shielding a murderer. All in a day's work.

She looked around her. How had she ended up here, in the middle of the night, the sound of a gunshot blast still ringing in her ears?

She remembered the feeling of frustration, of helplessness, when her parents and brother had been killed by the drunk driver. It had been so random—if her mother had only taken a few extra seconds in the woman's room, or if her father had chosen another lane in the tollbooth, or if.... It was paralyzing, she knew, to think this way. If every trivial decision in life had such ramifications, how could anyone ever decide to do anything? She had finally just thrown up her hands and concluded that it was just the way life was—roads diverged, paths taken, history made. Some people called it fate.

But this, tonight, was different. This was not some random series of events. She had purposely initiated many of the events that had brought her to this point. She had written to Bruce and enlisted his help in Mashpee. She had settled on the litigation strategy against Griffin. She had followed Bruce tonight, surprised him so that Griffin could turn the gun on him. And she had lied to the police.

And she would live with the consequences, good or bad. But the scary thing was that her decisions could potentially have a dramatic impact on others. A murderer was still on the loose because of her. The homes of thousands of people were still at risk because of her. The financial fate of an entire tribe was in flux because of her. Tonight, she was the drunk driver plowing into the tollbooth, she was the random event that would change thousands of lives.

She buried her face in her hands. Bruce better have a good story.

*   *   *

They finally let Shelby into Bruce's room late in the morning the next day. It was no different than all the other hospital rooms she had been in—white walls, white sheets, bright lights, a single chair under a single window next to a single bed. But no flowers, no cards. She had thought about bringing something but rejected it.

Bruce was out of danger—they had removed the bullet, and it had not damaged any critical organs. He was drugged to mask the pain, but clear-headed and coherent. And, Shelby guessed, happy to be alive. She wasn't so sure how she felt about it.

"Look, I did what you said. I lied to the police. Now I want to hear the whole story."

He was propped up in a hospital bed, an I.V. running into his arm. "I'll tell you everything, I promise. But first you have to believe me—I never asked Griffin for any million dollars. He just made that up after he saw you, said it just to distract me."

"Whatever, Bruce." She hadn't slept at all. And somehow coffee didn't seem to be giving her the same high as the morphine was giving Bruce.

He sighed. "All right. Here goes, from the beginning." He told her of his visit to the group house in Medford, about meeting Donald. "I didn't figure it out until later, after I had researched their birth records, but it turns out that Donald is Rex's identical twin."

Shelby could feel her eyes widening. "So that's who got killed! It was Donald's body in the ditch."

And then the revelation hit her. "Oh my god, Griffin did it. He killed his own brother."

"Right. He sent his brother out to walk the dog, then ran him down. Made Donald put on a bow tie and carry his wallet. Probably even got out of the car and switched eye-glasses with him before driving over his head."

"And then switched identities."

Bruce nodded. "I still haven't figured out a few things, like how come nobody noticed that Donald suddenly didn't have a wandering eye anymore. But Griffin's pretty clever, so he probably figured out something. Anyway, that's why he asked to be cremated in his will—so they couldn't reexamine the body if anyone ever got suspicious."

"And because they're identical twins, the DNA matched."

They sat in silence for a few seconds as an older, overweight nurse waddled in to take Bruce's temperature and check on his medication. She was competent, but gruff. Shelby noticed she had no wedding ring. Was she widowed? Or perhaps a bitter old spinster?

Shelby tried to wrap her brain around Griffin's crime, tried to imagine what could have driven him to murder his own brother. But she failed. She would give anything to have even one of her family members back, alive. And here was Griffin, sacrificing his only brother like a pawn in a chess match. She shivered, slipped her jacket over her shoulders.

Shelby watched the nurse work on Bruce, caught a glimpse of his upper thigh as the older woman checked his wound. Her mind began to remember how that thigh had felt wrapped around her own.... She shook the thought away, stared out the window at the Charles River below.

The nurse left, and Bruce continued. "But all that was later. When I first saw Donald up in Medford I still had no idea what Griffin was up to. So I just filed it in the back of my mind....

"Anyway, then I started looking more closely at the records at the Registry of Deeds. I noticed that Griffin had a $2 million mortgage on the farmhouse that was coming due this February. But then I saw it had been discharged last fall, which seemed weird to me. I mean, where did Griffin come up with a stack of money to pay off his mortgage? So I called the bank, made believe I was Griffin. You know the routine, give them the right social security number and mother's maiden name, and they'll tell you anything. They told me the loan was still outstanding and the payoff amount was $2 million."

Shelby tried to focus on the details of Bruce's narrative, fought to put the murder of Donald Griffin in the back of her mind for a few more minutes. What kind of demon would send his own brother to his grave in that way? The answer, she now knew, was the same kind of demon that would drug his retarded sister and breed her like a farm animal.

"All right then. Griffin had to come up with $2 million before February. So he's desperate. And he's got a twin brother who's autistic."

"Yeah, but it's more than just that his loan was due. Turns out he forged the bank's signature on all the closing documents, so he was facing some serious jail time if he got caught. And the only way he wouldn't get caught was if he paid back the $2 million before February."

Shelby nodded, impressed that Bruce had been able to unravel Griffin's plan. "So that's why he was willing to pledge the farmhouse in the settlement with the neighbors. We thought he owned the property free and clear. Stupid us for believing the public records. We didn't know the bank was still owed $2 million."

"I think he was just trying to buy some time."

"For what?"

"For gestation."

"Gestation?" For some reason she felt her face flush.

"Right. He planned all along to get the $2 million, and more, from the tribe." Bruce explained about the tribal history documents and how the very documents that Griffin hoped to sell to the tribe would give them the authority to renege on their promise to pay him.

Shelby knew she wasn't at her sharpest. The lack of sleep, the stress from the night before, the revelation about Donald Griffin—all of them had drained her. She stood up, looked out the hospital room window at the river below. The paths of the Esplanade ran along it's banks. On her first date with Bruce they had walked those paths for hours in the rain....

She turned back toward Bruce. "I'm not sure I followed that. Why wouldn't Griffin be able to enforce a contract with the tribe?"

"The documents he found proved that the Mashpees had existed continuously as a tribe since the 1800s. And that's the litmus test for tribes trying to win recognition from the federal government. Once tribes are recognized, they're treated like sovereign nations. They can't ignore U.S. criminal laws, but the civil laws don't apply to them like they do to the rest of us. It's called sovereign immunity. So, as a sovereign nation, the Mashpee tribe—or, more accurately, the Mashpee Nation—could just turn around and repudiate the contract it signed with Griffin."

"I get it now. So Griffin needed some way to enforce the contract with the tribe. Since the baby would be a member of the tribe, the baby could enforce the contract. The tribe wouldn't repudiate a contract with one of its own members."

Bruce coughed. Shelby could see him cringe as he did so, even as he tried to hide it from her. She pulled her chair closer to his bed so he wouldn't have to talk so loud, sat down, rested her foot on one of the wheels of the bed. He continued. "Right. Especially since the baby's grandmother was on the tribal council. So Griffin set up this family trust and made the baby the 51 percent beneficiary of the trust. And it was the trust that owned the documents, the trust that had the contract to sell the documents to the tribe."

"Okay, so that explains why Griffin drugged Billy and ... violated ... his poor sister. But why did he have to kill Donald?"

"That wasn't part of the original plan, I don't think. But, at a certain point, Pierre made it clear that he wouldn't sign off on any deal with Griffin. Especially one that let Griffin walk away with a pile of money. And Griffin needed Pierre because Metacomet was buried partially on Pierre's and Carla's property. Griffin knew that the tribe had to have Metacomet's grave as part of the settlement—it was going to be the centerpiece of a big historical attraction they were planning, plus the grave had all that spiritual value for the tribe members. So the bottom line was that the whole settlement between the title insurance companies and the tribe that Griffin envisioned couldn't go through unless Pierre and Carla also agreed to sell their property. And nobody—not even Griffin—could make them."

Shelby could see that the long explanation had tired Bruce. She offered a tired smile. "You mean because they had the best lawyer in town?"

"That, of course." Bruce winked at her. Again, she felt her face flush. "But also because Griffin knew how stubborn Pierre is."

"You're right. There was no way Pierre would agree to any deal with Griffin."

"And, like I said, Griffin knew that. So he had himself killed."

"And we all bought it."

Bruce shifted himself onto his back, took a deep breath. "Well, he set it up pretty well. My guess is that before the murder he arranged to have himself beaten up, hired someone just to make it look like he had violent enemies. To make the murder look more believable."

"You mean the assault was fake?"

"Not fake. Griffin was really attacked and beaten. I was there, I saw it. But I think Griffin set it all up himself. He probably figured it was a good trade—a few broken bones in exchange for a few million dollars."

Shelby admitted to herself that she took some satisfaction in knowing the assault had been real. And if Griffin were capable of that, maybe he really did make up the million dollar offer to Bruce just to distract him. Which meant Bruce hadn't been deceiving her....

"Once you know the ending, the beginning and middle fall right into place. But how did you figure it all out?"

Bruce smiled. "His dog."

Shelby shook her head. "I don't get it." She noticed she was smiling too.

"When he got beaten up, the dog stood next to him the whole time, barking until help came. The newspaper made a big deal about that—you know, loyal dog saves man. But when he got hit by the car, the dog took off, went home. Some neighbors found the body in the ditch the next morning, dead. So that made me wonder—why no dog?"

"Because the body in the ditch was Donald, not Rex." She looked at Bruce's strong, chiseled features. "I can't believe you figured this all out, Bruce." She reached out, squeezed his shoulder.

He laughed, cringed a bit in pain from the effort. "Yeah, that makes me almost as smart as Griffin's dog...."

A tall, thin blond woman entered the room. Bruce looked up, smiled. "Hey, Doc."

She smiled back at him—a bit flirtatiously, Shelby thought. Shelby sat up, straightened her hair.

The doctor turned to Shelby. All professional and serious now. "I'm sorry, but I need to examine him. Then he needs his rest. You'll have to come back in a few hours."

Shelby nodded. It would likely be a thorough examination. She would go home, take a shower, freshen up. She smiled at Bruce. "I'll be back. And don't go anywhere. You've still got some 'splaining to do."

*   *   *

Shelby returned two hours later, waited another hour for Bruce to wake from his nap. This time she had some flowers and chocolate. And she was wearing a bright red blouse that Bruce had given her as a gift.

He smiled at her. "Nice shirt."

She smiled in return. She knew he would recognize it. "Just some old thing I found in the back of my closet."

That sat staring at each other for a few seconds, then she spoke. "All right. So you figured out that the body wasn't Griffin."

"Well, that was my theory. I figured Rex had simply taken Donald's identity, moved into the group home in Medford for a few months until everything blew over. He did the lazy eye thing, switched glasses, probably cut his hair to match Donald's, maybe did a few other things to fool the staff—remember, they really were twins so it wouldn't have been that much of a stretch. After that, he sent a few letters to Ace—anonymously, of course—but basically all he had to do was sit around and wait."

Bruce coughed, caught his breath, continued. "The whole thing was pretty much on automatic pilot—he'd drafted all the agreements before he died. Then, once the deal closed, he was going to take off, use Donald's share of the family trust income to live on. His share was only 49 percent, but that's 49 percent of a pretty big number, so Griffin could live pretty comfortably once he got out of the group home."

Shelby nodded. "But how was he going to get out? Isn't it supervised?"

"It's supervised, but it's not like they have guards or anything. I mean, Griffin had no trouble sneaking out last night—probably down a fire escape or something. And he's allowed to go walk around town by himself if he wants. They actually encourage the residents to do stuff on their own. That's probably what happened the weekend he killed Donald—a limo picked Donald up for a weekend visit with his brother, then Griffin just showed up a couple days later and walked in the front door dressed as Donald. Nobody would have given it a second thought. Limo picks up Donald, then drops him off at the end of the weekend...."

Shelby interrupted. "Wait, it's even more clever than that. Someone might have wondered why Donald was visiting Mashpee in the first place—it's not like Griffin made it a habit of entertaining his brother for the weekend. But Griffin made us all believe Donald was down there logging license plates, just part of another Griffin scam. And then Griffin gave Justin the log, which had practically everyone's name on it. Just to make sure all the neighbors would be suspects in the murder."

Bruce nodded. "That was always part of his strategy, to make sure there were plenty of suspects for the police to focus on."

"Including Justin. His name was on the log until he altered it." Shelby got up, poured a couple of cups of water from a plastic pitcher, returned to her chair. She slid up tight against the bed, held the cup out to Bruce.

He took a sip, then continued. "Right. Anyway, the last few months, everything Griffin did was done to just add to his list of enemies. And don't forget, Donald was out walking the dog and getting run over on the night of the 18th. So Griffin was the one who kept the log for that night, probably even added a few extra entries just to keep the focus as broad as possible. It would have been easy enough for him to copy Donald's block handwriting."

Shelby stood up again. "That's it! That's how Carla and Pierre's Highlander ended up being on the log. Griffin added it in later, to implicate them." She paused for a moment, dropped her head. "I really thought they were lying to me."

"Hey, come on, it seems like you stuck by them pretty good."

Shelby offered a sad smile. "Yeah, I guess so. But I wasn't totally convinced they were innocent. But you know what? The really amazing thing is that, with such a long list of suspects, it turned out that *nobody* was the killer."

Bruce laughed. "Good point."

She allowed her eyes to rest on his for a few seconds. And she didn't feel funny about it.

He held her gaze for a few more seconds, then sighed and responded to her earlier question. "Anyway, as far as Griffin escaping the group home for good, it'd be pretty easy just to forge some letter from a lawyer saying he was the new family guardian and was moving Griffin to another home or something."

Shelby closed her eyes, tried to process everything Bruce had told her. "One thing doesn't quite add up. If Griffin was planning on killing himself off, why did the February 1 date matter anymore? I mean, so what if the bank noticed the forgeries? It mattered when Griffin was alive—he didn't want to get caught and go to jail. But now that he's, quote-unquote dead, why would he care if the bank figured out he had scammed them?"

Bruce took a deep breath. "A couple of reasons. First, he was worried that, if the police learned he had been scamming the bank, they might sniff around a little more carefully. Maybe they'd even start checking dental records or something—he had somehow gotten rid of his own, but they could have checked Donald's if they became suspicious. So he was just being careful; I would've done the same thing. But also, he didn't want to sit up there and rot away in that group home; he wanted this all settled quickly so he could get on with his life. Without the February 1 deadline, the tribe and the town might have fought this out for years."

Shelby nodded. "All right. Enough about Griffin. But what about you? Why didn't you just drive up to Medford and confront him?"

"I thought about that. But I still didn't have any proof, you know? I kept trying to find stuff, but Griffin covered his tracks pretty well. I looked at his pickup truck for evidence of a collision, but I'm not a forensics expert and the thing's so old it's got dings and dents all over it. And I found the limo driver who brought him back to Medford, but by then Griffin had already morphed himself into Donald, so all the driver remembered was picking up some autistic guy and driving him home."

Bruce took a sip of his water, continued. "So all I really had was a gut feeling. If I drove up there and confronted him, and he just babbled back at me like Donald would, what would that prove? I mean, if he could fool the staff at the group home, he could fool me. And by confronting him, I would be forfeiting the one advantage I had over him—he didn't know who I was, or even that I had figured out his plan. Which is the same reason I couldn't tell you guys about

Justin spying; you would have confronted him and blown my advantage. So, anyway, what I needed was a way to lure Griffin out of his lair. I needed to test my theory."

Shelby nodded. "I get it. That's why you started your little tribal insurrection. You figured if it looked like the settlement was on the rocks, Griffin would come out and try to put things back on course."

"Right. I knew he wouldn't just sit there and watch as I ruined all his plans. He'd come after me, try to shut me up. He figured that without me the insurrection would fizzle out. You know, to kill the monster, cut off its head. And I am the head. My guess is he was planning to kill me."

The words stunned Shelby. She had witnessed the attempt last night, and was sitting at the injured man's hospital bed this afternoon, but the victim of that attack had—in her mind—been the Bruce who had betrayed her. Suddenly, as Bruce had explained everything to her, things had changed. The target of Griffin's bullet was not some rogue, but was the man she might still love. She turned away, wiped a tear from her eye. She tried to hide the gesture from Bruce, then shrugged and smiled at him as a second water drop dripped down her cheek.

He reached up, wiped the tear away with the back of his hand. "Please don't cry. At least not for me."

She leaned her cheek against his palm, closed her eyes for a few seconds. "Why not?"

"I don't deserve it. Not yet, at least. I'm trying, I'm really trying. I want more than anything to win you back. That's all I've thought about for the last eight years...."

"Is that why you're doing all this?"

"Yes. But I'm not sure that's the right reason. All I'm doing now is paying the price: *Capture Griffin's killer and win back the beautiful Shelby.* Well, does that make me a good person? Or am I just still being selfish, doing the right things because I want the reward?"

Shelby wondered how much the drugs and the trauma of the injury were causing Bruce to be more candid and open the usual. She didn't doubt his sincerity, but Bruce was usually more reticent. "I don't know, Bruce. Sometimes it's hard to separate one motivation from another. But, it seems to me, the fact that you're thinking about this at all is a pretty big step in the right direction."

Bruce sighed. "Maybe."

Shelby studied Bruce, then shrugged the issue away and gently removed his hand from her cheek. There would be time to discuss Bruce's morality—and their future together—later. "So if you knew Griffin was going to come after you, why didn't you just go to the police? Or were you just trying to impress me by taking a bullet?" She reached out, covered his hand with hers.

He smiled, then she noticed a flash of concern harden his features. "The reason I didn't tell the police is the same reason I didn't want to tell you."

She abandoned her light tone, squeezed his hand. "Which is...?"

Bruce took a deep breath, sat up straighter in his bed. His mouth opened, but no words came out.

"Come on, Bruce. Why didn't you want to tell me?"

He whispered a response. "I don't want Griffin to get caught."

Shelby leaned forward in her chair. "What did you say?"

Bruce took a deep breath. "I said that I don't want Griffin to get caught."

Shelby started to respond, was cut off by the return of the old nurse. The spinster checked on Bruce, looked sternly at Shelby. "Only a few more minutes, okay? He needs his rest." Had the blond doctor sent her in?

Shelby waited for the nurse to leave, tried to stay calm. "I don't understand what you're saying, Bruce. Griffin killed his brother, almost killed you. And you want him not to get caught?"

"Look, I'm not saying that the ends justify the means here, but the final result of everything he did is a pretty good deal for everyone. The tribe is going to end up with a huge amount of money—maybe even a hundred million dollars. They can use that for education, health care, job training, all sorts of worthwhile things. Plus they get Metacomet's gravesite—I only have a few drops of Indian blood in me, but even I think it's a fabulous discovery. I mean, other than Geronimo and Pocahontus, can you name another Native American hero?"

"No. And I agree it'd be great for the tribe. But what does that have to do with Griffin?"

"Let me finish." He adjusted his tubes, pulled himself into a sitting position. "Because this deal's not just great for the tribe. The town ends up way ahead also—they get to settle this whole land claim thing once and for all, without having to pay a dime, without having a town-wide battle. And let's not forget Denise and Baby Vernon; they each get enough money from the deal to live well for the rest of their lives."

"All right. So I agree it's a good deal for everyone. But you haven't told me why Griffin can't rot in jail for the rest of his life. Assuming he hasn't skipped town already."

"I was worried about that too, so I called the group home this morning—he's still up in Medford, probably waiting for my call. But to answer your question, he can't rot in jail because the whole deal is predicated on Griffin being dead. If it turns out he's alive, everything changes. You know how hard it is to get everyone on the same page in a deal this big. As soon as the news hits that he's alive, all the dynamics change. The whole $50 million penalty thing will be in question, which will give the Native American activists from around the country the leverage they need to push the tribe to take this to trial."

Shelby nodded, continued Bruce's line of reasoning. "And all those lawsuits between the neighbors will be resurrected, which will mess up the title to the subdivision properties. Plus the state will get cold feet about throwing money into a deal that benefits a killer's family...."

"Not to mention that I can't fool the title insurance companies forever; eventually they'll figure out that my little insurrection is a paper tiger. This deal gets done this week, or it dies forever. And if it dies we're looking at a decade of litigation, town versus tribe."

Shelby began to argue the point, then relented. She knew that Bruce was probably right—she had been involved in enough multi-party settlements to understand the unique dynamics of the process. It was next to impossible to get all the parties to agree even on where to meet; once you actually got them around the conference room table with a general consensus on a deal, you either sat there until the deal was done or retreated to your bunker to re-arm for a long battle. There was never a second round of settlement discussions if the first round failed. The planets aligned only once.

"Look, Bruce, I don't want the settlement to fall part either. But that doesn't mean I'm willing to let Griffin get away—literally—with murder. He has to be punished."

Bruce nodded. "I know. I agree. I wish we could have it both ways, but I don't see how. Either he walks, or this settlement dies."

Shelby didn't have to voice her ambivalence—Bruce could see it in her face. He continued. "Look, if it makes you feel any better, my bet is he's had a pretty miserable last few months. Not to be insensitive, but I could see where all the babbling and jabbering and *I Love Lucy* re-runs would start to drive anyone crazy."

"That's small consolation—he can still come and go as he pleases. And soon he'll be on some beach somewhere, working on his tan. I want him in jail."

"That's the one thing that'll never happen. He'll run first, even kill himself. From what I've been able to find out about the guy, his one phobia is being locked up. I guess he was a POW in Vietnam, and he is scared to death of being put into a cage or a cell again. I was talking to one of the cops that arrested him after that bomb scare...; oh, by the way, my guess is that he called the police himself that day, he was the anonymous tipster. He wanted the neighbors to see him arrested on bomb-making charges, figured it would terrorize them."

Shelby nodded. "Why am I not surprised?"

"Anyway, the cop said Griffin was freaking out about the thought of having to spend the night in jail. Claimed he had some phobia about being locked up, ever since Vietnam. I believe it, too. I've been watching him—he sleeps on the roof of his house, he won't get into elevators, he always drives with the windows of his pickup open, even in the rain."

She smiled, raised an eyebrow. "Even more reason to tell the police."

Bruce laughed quietly. "The thought of him in a jail cell is tempting, I admit. But it all comes back to the same choice: If we expose Griffin, the settlement dies. I'm sorry, but there really is no choice at all."

Shelby thought about what Bruce was saying for a few seconds. "This is wrong, Bruce. Who are we to decide what Griffin's punishment should be or not be?"

"Well, if it helps, I'm not asking you to make the decision with me. I'm telling you about it only because I promised I would. But you shouldn't feel any responsibility for this decision. It's mine. I'm comfortable with it. I'll take full responsibility." Bruce dropped back into his bed, his eyes now closed.

Shelby let him rest for a few minutes while she weighed their options, then smiled as she heard a light snoring. She leaned over, kissed him on the cheek, whispered into his ear. "Don't think you've won this argument yet."

*   *   *

Bruce had been sleeping for an hour when the nurse came in. She woke him to change his bandage and check his vital signs. It had always struck Shelby as ridiculous the way nurses and doctors constantly woke sleeping patients just to check on them. Sleep was what their bodies needed, not blood pressure cuffs and thermometers. But Shelby knew the hospitals were worried about malpractice suits, so they poked and prodded and fussed on a regular schedule.

When the nurse left, Shelby continued their discussion. It wasn't really an argument, because her heart told that Bruce was right. Or maybe her heart had lost its objectivity. "If you let Griffin walk, I could still go to the police."

Bruce sat up. He sensed she was bluffing. "Yes, you could. But I don't think you will. At least I hope you won't."

"You still haven't answered my question. Who are we—or 'you,' if you prefer to think of it that way—to play judge and jury, to just decide that Donald Griffin's murder should go unpunished? We're lawyers, not gods."

"First of all, forget the lawyer stuff. That has nothing to do with it. My answer to you is that I am a human being. A living, thinking human being." At the word 'living,' Shelby noticed that both hers and Bruce's eyes dropped to his bullet wound. The conversation about Griffin seemed to lose some of its import.

He continued. "Eight years ago you told me I wasn't fit to be a member of society, that I should go away alone and try to find some type of moral compass by which to live my life. Well, I did that. And I'm comfortable with who I've become, comfortable that I'm capable of weighing the pros and cons of this. This whole 'follow the law' thing is an interesting debate to have sitting around a dinner table late one night with a bottle of wine and a bunch of friends. But here, today, in the real world, the best I can come up with is to let Griffin walk in order to save the settlement. Sure we could follow the law, take our pound of flesh. But that would ruin hundreds of lives—homes foreclosed on, jobs lost, families splintered. And for what? Just so we could watch Griffin rot in jail? There's nothing just about that. That's just petty revenge."

"Whatever your reasons, you have no right to take the law into your own hands. That's no better than being a vigilante."

He smiled at her, attempted to lighten the tone. "A vigilante. That's fine. I've been called worse." He smiled again, a smile, she knew, designed to remind her of how far he had come in the past eight years.

Only yesterday she had been convinced that he had betrayed her and betrayed the tribe in some elaborate scheme to secure the millions he had always craved. Instead, it turns out he had been working like a dog—without pay or recognition or even gratitude—to track Griffin. But that still didn't make it right. "Bruce, right or wrong, you can't just ignore the law."

Bruce's eyes looked deep into hers. He took both her hands in his. "No, Shelby, that's not right. The law is *not* always just. You know that. We both know plenty of lawyers who practice law their whole lives and wouldn't recognize justice if it walked in and paid them a six-figure retainer. It's not justice when O.J. Simpson gets acquitted." He lowered his voice. "It's not justice when the drunk driver who killed your family walks away."

Shelby turned away, whispered a response. "That's not fair, Bruce."

"Yes it is, Shelby. You know it is. Justice is something that lives in our hearts, in our souls. Not on some piece of paper in a law library. Don't hide behind your law degree, don't use your training as an excuse not to think and feel. You're elevating form over substance. You're better than that."

She sighed, closed her eyes. She could feel herself being swept away by the passion—and, she had to admit, the logic—of Bruce's words. The professional in her had fought against this exact argument for years. As an Assistant District Attorney, she had fought against the policeman who swore out a false affidavit to secure an arrest warrant for a known drug dealer, fought against the colleague who withheld evidence to ensure a criminal didn't go free on a technicality. It didn't matter that their motives had been pure, didn't matter that her rigidity might unleash evil back onto the streets. What mattered, she had argued, was that the law be respected. Whatever the consequences. It was hard to admit that she might have been wrong this whole time.

"I don't know, Bruce. I need to think about all this." She paused, then continued. "And I at least need to tell Carla and Pierre. They're my clients. They have a right to know."

Bruce mulled over her comment for a few seconds, shook his head. "Do you think that's a good idea? There's no way Pierre would go along with this. If we're going to tell Pierre, we might as well just hand Griffin over to the police."

Shelby weighed Bruce's point. "I guess you're right about Pierre...."

"Look, take some time. This is a big decision for you; I know it goes against everything you believe...."

Shelby interrupted. "Or thought I believe. You know, I've been doing a lot of re-thinking of things today...."

Bruce smiled. "Well, that's encouraging to hear. But it's still a big decision. I'm asking you to break all the rules."

"And will you understand if I say no?"

Bruce was quiet for a second, then locked his eyes onto Shelby's. For the first time since he had returned from his exile, he was looking at her with the self-assuredness that had so beguiled her a decade ago. He had found himself, was speaking to her now as an equal rather than as some kind of supplicant kneeling at her feet begging for her forgiveness. His voice was steady, deep. "I'll understand if you say no, but I'll be surprised, and I'll be disappointed. You used to tell me that you became a lawyer because you wanted to fight for justice. Well, here's your chance."

*   *   *

Dominique rocked the baby, allowed him to wrap his fingers around her pinkie. "Do you have any idea how much trouble you've caused?" she cooed at the infant. "Such big, big trouble...."

"Hi Mom." Billy walked in, plopped onto the couch next to his mother and son, lifted the baby from her arms. "You said you wanted to talk."

"Yes, Billy. I want to do something, but I need to ask your permission first."

"Sure. What?"

"You know they arrested Amisha Raman, right?"

Billy nodded.

"Do you think she murdered Rex Griffin?"

Billy shrugged. "I don't know. I don't even know her."

Dominique smiled. He had grown, matured so much in the past year. Yet in many ways he was still a teenager, quick with an 'I don't know' or a 'Whatever' or a 'Guess so.' "Seriously, Billy, have you given it any thought?"

"A little."

"So who do you think did it?"

Billy looked away from his mother, took a deep breath. Dominique sat up, watched her son. She hadn't expected this conversation—or at least not this part of it—to distress her son. But the boy clearly had something on his mind, something he had been carrying around with him for quite a while. She should have sensed it earlier.

Finally, he spoke in a tight whisper. "I think Dad did it, Mom. I think Dad killed him."

Dominique reached out, took her son's hand, resisted the urge to wrap her arms around him and rock him like a baby. "Oh, Billy. Poor boy—is that what you think? No wonder you look so miserable."

He looked back at her, his eyes questioning her, hopeful that she might relieve him of the burden of his suspicions. "He didn't...?"

"No. I can promise you that. I think he may have wanted to, but

336

I'm not sure your father was capable of that kind of thing. Anyway, why didn't you talk to me about this before?"

"I don't know."

"Come on, you can do better than that."

"Well, it was almost better not knowing for sure. If I asked you and you told me he did it, then.... I don't know. I guess I was just afraid."

"I understand. But I can assure you he didn't do it."

Billy nodded, then Dominique saw his brows furrow a bit and his eyes focus on her. He looked into her eyes for a few seconds, then spoke. Dominique knew the question even before it came out of his mouth. "Did you do it, Mom?"

"No, Billy. I did not."

Dominique fought to suppress a smile as she realized that her son was not nearly as relieved to hear this news as he had been to hear that his father had been innocent. Probably because he had, over the past couple of months, convinced himself that his father had murdered a man before he died and was now paying for it in some hell of an afterlife.

"So," he sighed, "who did kill Griffin?"

"Well, that's what I wanted to talk to you about. First of all, the police are wrong. It wasn't Amisha Raman."

"If you know that, then you must know who it was."

"Good point. You're right, I do."

"So why don't you tell the police?"

"It's not that simple."

"Look, Mom, you're talking in riddles. If you want to talk, then talk."

Dominique nodded. "Fair enough. The truth is that Rex Griffin is still alive. I saw him with my own eyes."

"I don't get it. Then whose body was in the ditch?"

"His twin brother, Donald. Griffin was driving the car that night. He ran down his own brother and left him to die in that ditch. Then he stole his identity. I don't know all the details, and I can't sniff around too much because I don't want anybody to know I've figured it out, but somehow Griffin set this all up so that he could walk away with a pile of money from the settlement."

337

"Wow. So Griffin's still alive—that sucks."

"Yeah, but I doubt he'll ever be back here again. He'll probably take his pile of money and disappear forever."

"So why can't you tell the police?"

"Because if I do, the entire settlement we just negotiated will probably go down the drain. Then we'll be stuck with a decade of civil war in this town."

"I don't understand why the settlement would go down the drain."

"Because the settlement is all very tenuous. For one thing, Bruce can only fool them for so long with his threat to take over the tribe. And, for another, who knows if the state'll still be willing to kick in some money next year? If this deal doesn't happen now, it won't happen."

Billy nodded. "All right. But you can't just let Amisha Raman sit there in jail."

"You're right. I have a plan. But I won't do it unless you agree...."

* * *

Shelby returned to Bruce's hospital room the next day. She noticed his face light up when she entered, felt a flush of excitement rush through her body.

He squeezed her hand, smiled into her eyes. She resisted the urge to bend over him and kiss his face; there would be time for all that later, if things were meant to go in that direction. First, they had to deal with some pretty big issues. She removed her hand from his.

Bruce continued to smile up at her, then spoke. "Well, have you made a decision?"

She sighed. "I thought I had, but I'm not sure it matters anymore. The police arrested Amisha Raman two nights ago. For the murder of Rex Griffin."

Bruce jolted up. "You're kidding. Based on what?"

"I spoke to an old friend who works in the District Attorney's office down on the Cape, and she said they think they have a decent case. No hard evidence, but her husband pointed the finger at her. Said he got suspicious when she went out in the car the night of the

338

murder and didn't come back until the next morning. He asked her about it the next day, and she told him she knew he'd be out walking his dog. She waited for him and ran him down. Now that she's skipped town and left him, he figures there's no reason to keep quiet about it anymore."

"That's bullshit—the guy's just pissed because Amisha left him. Is that all they've got on her?"

Shelby felt the need to defend her friend Pam a bit. "Well, Amisha had a motive to kill him. She couldn't get the money out of her house as long as Griffin was alive, and she needed the money to get away from her husband. Plus, the log records Amisha's car going out of the subdivision during the murder window. When the police got the call from Rajiv, they decided they had enough...."

He interrupted. "That's it, just the log? We know that log is fake. And half the people in Mashpee had a motive to kill Griffin."

"True. But nobody else cashed out $300,000 and disappeared like she did. And nobody else had their spouse tip off the cops. And don't forget, the detectives don't know that Griffin altered the log— they still think it's accurate. She was hiding out in New York; the police found out she was trying to buy a fake passport. They were worried she was getting ready to leave the country, so they felt like they had no choice."

"Still, none of that means she killed Griffin."

"You and I know she didn't, but, unfortunately, nobody else does. At least not yet."

"So you're going to tell them?"

"Come on, Bruce, even you can't justify letting Amisha take the rap for this, no matter how much it may screw the settlement up. She's innocent. We have to tell them."

Bruce looked off into the distance, absorbing Shelby's news. She interrupted his thoughts. "Before that brain of yours gets too wrapped up in this, you should also know that the tribe and the title insurance company reached a tentative agreement last night."

"Well, that's good news. How much?"

"The tribe gets $150 million, plus Metacomet's gravesite."

"Really? That's great, more than Dominique had hoped for."

"Yeah. From what I heard, some of the lawyers from your old

firm pushed for the high number. They convinced the title insurance companies they really didn't want to have to deal with you. At any price."

Bruce smiled. "Well, at least I'm good for something."

"So, anyway, it's not a done deal yet. It all depends on the state kicking in some money, plus all the subdivision owners have to agree to sell their properties. But it looks like the heavy lifting is done."

"Which brings us back to Rex Griffin. Any way I can talk you into waiting to see if Amisha can beat this on her own? I mean, it's not like they have a strong case against her. We know there's no evidence."

"That's not fair, Bruce. She may beat it, but she'll have to go through hell in the meantime. She's a flight risk, so there'll be no bail. Not to mention what it must be like to be accused of a murder you didn't commit. I saw what it did to Pierre...."

"Yeah, you're right, you're right." He pounded his thigh. "It's just that we're so close. Another month or two and this whole deal would be wrapped up. Then we could go to the cops and tell them the truth, clear Amisha."

"No. You're wrong about that, Bruce. We either go to them now or we never do. If we wait, Griffin will be long gone. They'll charge us with obstruction of justice, maybe even accessory to murder. We know Griffin did it, we know where he's hiding. We can't wait to say anything until after he disappears. No, it's now or never."

*　　*　　*

Rex Griffin sat in Donald's room in the group home. He picked up the glasses. Four minutes until breakfast—Donald would have been on time, so he would have to be as well.

But it was driving him crazy. The encounter with that Bruce Arrujo guy on the Common was the only intelligent conversation he had had in months. Even with a gun pressed into his ribcage, it had been a pleasure to actually speak in a normal voice and full sentences.

He hid the travel brochures he had been studying, checked his watch a final time, painted a dazed look on his face and marched down the stairs and into the cafeteria.

Griffin sat in the blue chair, ate his Fruit Loops with milk and a banana, greeted the other residents and staff members in a loud cheerful voice. "Good morning, Russell! Good morning, Christopher!" He now knew Russell was the Asian one and Christopher the white one. His head pounded. At least Denise let him read his newspaper while he ate.

Clark shuffled into the room, took the seat next to him. He brought his dark-skinned face close to Griffin's, bathed him in a stale, ketchup-like breath. "Good morning, Donald. Did you sleep well?"

His face a mask of indifference, Griffin wiped Clark's spit from his cheek, then recited his response in a loud voice. "Good morning Clark. I slept good." Eyes closed, as always, when he spoke. At least his head didn't hurt so much when his eyes were closed.

They ate in silence for a few minutes, each of them bouncing rhythmically in their chair as they chewed. Griffin wondered if he'd ever be able to eat sitting still again.

Hopefully, he'd find out soon. It had been two days now, and the police had not come for him. He had returned to the Medford home that night after the encounter in the Common, confident that somehow Bruce—if he lived—would succeed in keeping Shelby from exposing him. Of course, if Bruce had died, Griffin was prepared to flee immediately. But hourly phone calls to the hospital the first day had satisfied Griffin that his victim would survive.

Not that the news was all good. He knew Bruce's silence would cost him a million or so in hush money. But it was worth it. He'd still have plenty to live on. And if he didn't buy Bruce's silence, the alternative would be a lifetime in jail. Half a fortune on the beach in Thailand shouldn't be too tough to take.

*   *   *

So. He would have to lie to Shelby yet again.

Bruce glanced over at her, smiled sadly as she scribbled notes on a legal pad. The doctor—an older Asian man with a perpetual smile on his face—was instructing her on how to care for him. She had spent the night in his room, curled into a reclining chair with a blanket and a small pillow, her hand resting in his while she slept. Tubes protruded from his arm, bandages surrounded his abdomen, nurses poked and prodded him every couple of hours. But, as he watched her sleep, he couldn't remember feeling more content.

The doctor had wanted to keep him in the hospital for another couple of days, but Shelby, at Bruce's urging, had charmed him into releasing Bruce to her care. Bruce was anxious to get back to Mashpee and set things straight.

At least that's what he had told Shelby. In reality, he was planning on further confusing things.

Yes, he would explain to the police that Amisha was innocent, just as he and Shelby had discussed. And, yes, he would explain to them how Griffin had been plotting and scheming to profit from the tribe's lawsuit against the town. But, no, he would not tell them that Griffin was still alive.

That would not be necessary. Bruce was going to confess to the murder himself.

He wouldn't actually call it a murder. He'd describe it as an accident, a tragic accident that became a hit-and-run when he panicked and fled, inadvertently backing over the already-dead body as he did so. He had been tracking Griffin—the night was dark, the roads were slick, the stars misaligned. Bruce had felt the impact, had checked Griffin's pulse, had found him dead. The story wasn't airtight, but how critically would the police look at it in light of the fact that Bruce—not even a suspect in the case—was admitting to a felony?

He'd likely have to serve some jail time. But probably only a few years—this was an accident, not a murder. Involuntary manslaughter. First offense. Bruce, unlike half of Mashpee, had no motive to kill Griffin. And he would be walking in and confessing to the crime himself.

It was a fair price to pay—he had sentenced Pierre to a similar fate for a lesser cause. Amisha would walk. The settlement would settle. And he would, finally, be able to look at himself in the mirror and know he was worthy of Shelby.

Shelby helped him into her Subaru Forrester, buckled his seatbelt, fluffed a pillow. Then she smiled and brushed her lips over his, lingered for a few seconds. He could get used to this. Even if he would have to wait a couple of years.

She pulled out of the parking garage, exited the medical area onto

Storrow Drive. She merged into traffic, came to a stop at the traffic lights at Leverett Circle. Bruce looked out his window, read the billboard: *If You Lived Here, You'd be Home Now.*

Home. Maybe someday.

Shelby climbed the on-ramp to Route 93 South, fought her way through a bottleneck caused by the Big Dig construction project. Bruce scanned the raised highway around them. "Doesn't look much different than it did eight years ago."

"Except that there's a 10-lane underground tunnel running the length of the city right beneath us. There going to take this whole structure down in a couple of years, build some parks or something here."

Bruce pointed to a giant red-ribbon wrapped around a medium-sized office building butting up against the highway. "I remember that. Must be getting close to Christmas."

Shelby nodded. "Yup. They wrap it every year. The old Grain Exchange building, I think."

"Yeah." He paused for a few seconds. "It's good to be back in Boston. Even with the traffic."

They eventually emerged from a tunnel on the south side of the city. Shelby headed south toward the Cape, one hand resting gently on Bruce's thigh.

Bruce tried to sound casual. "When we get there, I think it would be best if I went in alone. You're right about the whole obstruction of justice thing—they might be pissed we didn't say anything earlier. No reason for you to get dragged into the muck with me."

"Come on, Bruce. Like you said, I'm a big girl."

"No, seriously. It's one thing for me to get disbarred—I never really wanted to be a lawyer anyway. But you're devoted, you're talented. And you actually do some good. Don't risk your career for this, Shelby. It's not worth it. There's no reason for you to get involved."

He watched her consider his words. "All right, I guess you're right." She smiled at him. "But it would be a good story if we were both disbarred...."

"You mean like Bonnie and Clyde?"

Shelby laughed, squeezed Bruce's hand. "No, I was thinking more like Nixon and Agnew. Our neighbors would love us."

Our neighbors. There was so much implicit in those words. Not the least of which was that Shelby felt him worthy of her now. Today. This minute. Without him having to prove himself by confessing to a crime he didn't commit.

But this wasn't just about her. It was about him. He hadn't really proved anything yet. Sure, he had resisted the temptation to swoop in and swipe a juicy slice of the settlement pie—it would have been simple enough to grab a few million for himself, either by blackmailing Griffin or by actually following through on his phantom campaign to take over the tribe. But he had long since learned that money no longer interested him, so his decision to forego the millions was no more laudable than that of an ex-smoker passing on a cigarette. The true test for Bruce was whether he could act selflessly, whether he could sacrifice his own happiness for the benefit of others.

He had read once that the true way to judge a man's character was to observe him under times of duress. Most people were decent and fair-minded when the stakes were low. But how would they react when things got tough? His generation never had the opportunity to observe one another in a foxhole, never had to muster the courage to walk into the Deep South and register Blacks to vote. That was the type of trial he was referring to.

What he was about to do today would be more than a fair test. In Shelby's eyes, he had already redeemed himself, was now worthy of a second chance. He could, if he chose, simply tell the police the truth, leave the police station, and begin a new chapter in his life with Shelby by his side. It would be a perfectly justifiable choice. After all, it was not his fault that the settlement agreement was so tenuous—he had done his best to preserve it, done his best by the tribe and by the townspeople and even by Shelby.

But, he knew, he had not done his best by Bruce Arrujo. He could do better. He *had* to do better, he *had* to prove to himself that the Bruce that had schemed and lied and betrayed and abused was gone forever, replaced by a man who was worthy of his own self-respect. A man who could look in the mirror each day without cringing in shame, without recoiling in disgust. A man deserving of Shelby.

He and Shelby made small talk the rest of the drive, Bruce sneaking a look at her whenever he could, knowing that it would be a while before he would have the luxury of doing so again. She, on the other hand, was animated and carefree, oblivious to the fact that—once again—their lives' paths would soon diverge. He wondered how she'd handle the news. He, at least, had a say in the matter. She was about to be dropped on her head. Again.

She turned to him as they crossed over the bridge onto the Cape. "Should I go straight to the police station?"

"Might as well. Amisha's probably scared to death."

Twenty-five minutes later she pulled into the long circular drive in front of the brick station house and turned to face him. "You sure you don't want me to come in with you?"

"Thanks, but no. But why don't you give me your cell phone number so I can call you if I need you...."

"You mean if they start torturing you or something?"

He forced a smile. "No. I just don't want you sitting out here in the parking lot waiting for me. It might take a while. Go grab some lunch, and I'll call you when I'm done."

She leaned over, kissed him gently on the lips. She lingered again, then rested her head on his shoulder. When she looked up, there were tears in her blue-green eyes. She made no attempt to hide them from him, even as they spilled onto her cheeks.

"Why are you crying?" he whispered.

"I don't know." She stroked his cheek, looked deep into his eyes. "I've missed you, Bruce."

Bruce sighed. So much for fair tests. It would be so easy—blissfully so—to simply walk into the police station and tell them the truth about Griffin. And then walk out and back into Shelby's arms. Forever. "I love you, Shelby. No matter what happens, don't forget that."

He saw the alarm in her eyes. "What do you mean by that?"

Bruce smiled, tried to disarm her suspicions. "Just that. Don't ever forget that I love you."

He held her gaze, repelling her efforts to peer within him. He knew he was only partially successful, knew that if he stayed in her car any longer, it would be too late. "All right. I'm going in. Talk to you soon."

He closed his eyes to her gaze, kissed her again. Then he opened the door, pulled himself to his feet and, resisting the urge to look back, began the long walk across the hard pavement.

*   *   *

Dominique watched Bruce struggle to push open the door. She shrunk deeper into her black vinyl chair in the white-walled waiting room, pulled a newspaper in front of her face. She studied his back as he spoke across the counter to the officer on duty. "I'd like to speak to the detective in charge of the Rex Griffin murder investigation. My name is Bruce Arrujo."

She wasn't surprised to see him. She had called the hospital, had learned he had checked himself out. She had expected he would come straight here.

She just wasn't sure for what reason. The fact that he was here indicated he had rejected the selfish course, had resisted the temptation to grab the money and run. But would he go one step further? Would he choose the selfless path rather than merely reject the selfish one? Would he sacrifice his own freedom for some greater cause?

Not that it mattered, she knew. But he didn't know that. To him, this was a life-defining moment. She knew it was all merely academic.

One look at his slumped shoulders and sad eyes told her the answer. She smiled, proud to see that her instincts had been right. She had taken her chances with the young punk. And not been disappointed.

She beckoned him with her eyes, smiled kindly as he turned slowly around to face her. "Hello, Bruce."

He stammered a response. "Dominique. Hi. I was just...."

She silenced him with her hand. "I know, Bruce. I know what you're doing. And I also know you would have gone through with it. As hard as it would have been."

"What do you mean, 'would have gone through with it'?"

She walked over, took his hand. "Go back to Shelby. I've already told the police everything."

346

"About Griffin? You mean...."

"That's right. I've told them how my Vernon killed him, ran him down and left him to die in the ditch. They're letting Amisha go right now."

He looked back at her, speechless. But she saw that he had processed her words, knew that he understood the simple brilliance of her deed. Vernon was dead; he could not be punished. And from his death, the settlement would live.

She kept his hand in hers, guided him toward the door, toward Shelby, toward the rest of his life. "Thank you, Bruce. Your grandfather would have been very proud of you."

Chapter 20

[December]

Griffin endured yet another spittled greeting from Clark, finished yet another breakfast of Fruit Loops with milk and a banana, watched yet another rerun of *The Beverly Hillbillies*, spent yet another hour practicing the fine art of shoe-tying. It had been more than a week now since his encounter with Bruce and Shelby in the Common. He should have heard from Bruce by now.

He knew he couldn't wait much longer. He felt trapped, confined, enclosed—he had been sleeping on the fire escape all fall, but it was getting too cold even to keep that up much longer. As it was, he wasn't really sleeping much anyway. Which made it even more difficult to constantly stay in role—to bounce when he ate, to stammer and shout when he spoke, to follow his daily routine down to the minute. He had a newfound respect for Donald—it took a lot of work to act like a retard all day long. He wondered if he'd ever be able to break some of the habits he had acquired, ever be able to walk without a stiff back or handle a set of keys without fondling and counting them. More to the point, he wondered if any day now he'd snap and go completely insane from the drudgery and sheer monotony of his existence.

One thing was certain: February 1 was just around the corner. And one way or another, things would be resolved by then. He had left Justin with enough money in his estate to pay the mortgage every month. But not the $2 million balloon payment. By February 1 he needed to be long gone. And he would need a few weeks before then

348

to make the necessary arrangements—a fake passport, some airline tickets, a disguise.

There was, of course, no family friend in Maine serving as Donald's legal guardian, so Griffin's disappearance would alarm nobody. Griffin had invented the man; he was nothing more than a post office box, an answering machine and a bank account. The bank account and answering machine Griffin accessed and controlled by telephone; the mail he had arranged to be forwarded to another post office box in Medford. When necessary, Griffin responded on behalf of the guardian to messages and mail from Justin or the group home administrators or the social services agencies. Likewise, it would be a simple matter for him to prepare a letter transferring himself to another facility, then send the necessary vehicle to pick himself up and transport himself to the new home. And an equally simple matter to funnel the money deposited by Justin into the Maine bank account to another account in Thailand. But, again, he needed a few weeks to pull everything together.

He returned to his room, rubbing the doorframe as he entered, and immediately noticed the small piece of paper wedged between the window frame and sill. He bounded over to the window, looked out onto the fire escape, scanned the yard below. Whoever had left the note was long gone. Not that it mattered—he knew the note was from Bruce.

He closed his door, took off the damn glasses, unfolded the handwritten note: *I'm out of hospital. Sit tight. I'll contact you soon.*

Excellent. He was beginning to wonder if Bruce was going to contact him. The newspapers had been reporting that a settlement between the tribe and the title companies had been reached, and that the state had agreed to kick in the money it had promised, but Griffin knew that, with one phone call to the police, Bruce could turn Griffin's cushy retirement into a maximum security prison sentence. The sooner he and Bruce met and agreed on a mutually satisfactory arrangement, the quicker he could get the hell out of this nut house and begin to live his life again.

Griffin pulled out the travel brochures again. Bruce said to sit tight. He could do that, at least for another couple of days, torturous though it may be.

*   *   *

Justin arose from the wooden bench, approached the front of the courtroom. He rested his briefcase on a heavy wooden table, pulled out a manila folder. He took a deep breath, looked up and addressed a clean-cut young man in the black robe. The judges seemed to get younger every year. "May it please the Court, Justin McBride here for the plaintiff. Your Honor, thank you for hearing this matter on such short notice."

"I must say, Counselor, your pleadings caught my eye. Are you sure your facts are correct?"

"Yes, Your Honor. There's simply no evidence of the man. I've even hired a private investigator. Nothing."

"You mean to tell me that this guardian is a figment of someone's imagination? How could that be?"

"I'm not sure how to answer that, Your Honor. I just don't know. But I do know that there is a young man with autism living in a group home in Medford who needs someone to look after his needs. And this gentleman in Maine—whether he's real or imagined—obviously isn't doing it."

"Okay, then. I agree that an emergency situation exists. And I find your proposal to be an acceptable solution. Your motion is granted. So ordered." He banged his wooden gavel. "Next case."

*   *   *

Bruce watched from the back of the courthouse as the old barrister ambled away from the judge's bench. Justin may have been willing to undertake the task without the threat of blackmail, but Bruce couldn't afford to take that chance. He had approached Justin, told him he knew that Justin had been serving as Griffin's mole. And then had given him his marching orders.

Justin had begun to put up a fight, then had sighed and relented. "I suppose if I'm going to let myself be blackmailed by Griffin, I can let myself be blackmailed by you as well." Bruce had nodded—both men understood that Justin was getting off easy for his duplicity with

350

Griffin. In some cultures, they would have poked out Justin's eyes for spying. Bruce had just demanded the use of his mouth for a few minutes in front of the judge.

Bruce looked at his watch, slipped out of the courthouse. Everything was in place now. Unless there was a screw-up, he might actually be able to pull this off.

*   *   *

Shelby and Carla had just returned from a morning of Christmas shopping at the outlet malls with Valerie and Rachel. Not only did it prevent the adults from buying gifts for the girls, it also prevented Shelby and Carla from discussing the Griffin case.

Now they were sitting around the kitchen table with a cup of coffee. Shelby had no choice but to act surprised when Carla told her the news. After all, there was no way Shelby could have known about Dominique's confession, since nothing had appeared in the newspapers yet. She listened to her friend's account. "Billy told Pierre that it was his father who killed Griffin. And Dominique went to the police and confessed. Otherwise they would have put Amisha on trial."

Shelby painted a surprised look on her face and asked the expected questions. "Wow. I didn't even know Vernon was well enough to get out of bed."

"Well, apparently he still drove once in a while."

"Did Dominique know he was going to do it?"

"If she did, I'm sure she didn't admit to it. She said Vernon just took the car one night after dinner, said he had some business to attend to, came back an hour later. Then, on his death bed, he told her that he'd run down Griffin, then rolled him into a ditch."

"I didn't see anything in the papers...."

"There hasn't been anything yet. I guess the Victors have some friends on the police force. They're trying to keep it all quiet. I mean, Vernon's already dead, so what does it really matter? And it's not like anyone's really bugging the police to solve the crime."

Shelby turned away from her friend to hide her smile. In reality, the reason the newspapers hadn't yet carried the story was because the police—at the request of Shelby's friend at the District Attorney's

351

office—had agreed to keep it quiet for a few days. Shelby didn't like calling in so many favors, but in this case it was worth it. They needed a few days before the news officially broke.

"I see what you mean. Griffin doesn't have—I mean, didn't have—a lot of friends around here." Shelby cursed herself. She just wasn't very good at this lying stuff. Especially lying to close friends. Time to move to safer ground. "So they let Amisha go?"

"Yeah. Turns out she was just trying to get away from her husband. She had nothing to do with the murder. She did what she should have done in the first place--got a restraining order against him and moved out to California with her sister."

Shelby turned to Pierre. "I didn't think Amisha did it. But I didn't think it was Vernon either. What about you, Pierre?"

Pierre was silent for a minute, then responded. "I guess, in retrospect, it's not surprising. Vernon probably figured Griffin had messed with his family so he deserved it. And it's not like he would ever have to pay for his crime; he knew he was dying. But I thought all along it was Bruce."

Shelby laughed lightly. "That's just because you didn't trust him."

"I still don't. Never will. But at least he didn't screw us over this time. Not yet, I mean."

"What do you mean, 'Not yet?'"

"Hey, there's still time. There's $150 million sitting there on the table. Would you leave Bruce alone with it? I saw him on TV, saw him protesting the settlement. Sure, he says he did it to help the tribe get their settlement, but that seems like an awfully convenient excuse to me...."

Shelby wanted to defend Bruce, wanted to tell Pierre and Carla how hard he had toiled on their behalf. Hours and days and weeks, tailing Griffin, following him, spying on him, finally exposing him. Organizing the protest to help the tribe, not hurt it. Taking a bullet in the gut. Resisting the million dollars Griffin had offered. Bruce deserved Pierre's gratitude, not his disdain. But she knew she could voice none of that. Not without revealing Griffin's secret. So she changed the subject again. "Speaking of the $150 million, has anyone contacted you about the settlement?"

Carla nodded. "Yeah, we got a call yesterday from one of the lawyers. Basically, they're offering us ten percent over fair market value for our house, plus moving expenses and closing costs to buy a new place."

"That seems fair."

"Yeah," Pierre responded. "They need everyone to agree, so they know they need to make us decent offers."

"Are you going to accept?"

Carla laughed. "Are you kidding? Of course. This is a great deal for the tribe, great for the town, great for Baby Vernon. Plus, this house—no matter how much money we put into it—is still a piece of garbage. It'll be nice to put this all behind us."

"How about the other neighbors?"

"I think everyone will do it. We're all ready to move on with our lives. I mean, we've been sued, we've been harassed, we've been bomb-scared, we've been suspects in a murder case. Nobody will miss this place."

"Where do you think you'll go?"

"We like it here in Mashpee. Pierre likes coaching, plus we've made some good friends. So we're going to stay." She paused, smiled at her husband. "But this time, I get to choose the house."

*   *   *

"Is it safe to talk here?"

Griffin eyed the man standing across the room from him. He was a formidable opponent, both physically and intellectually. In fact, Griffin had to admit, Bruce had him by the balls. Now it was just a question of how hard he was going to squeeze. "Yes, it's safe. They'll leave us alone here." Griffin sat on his bed, motioned for Bruce to take the chair.

"All right. First of all, I need to know everything—how you're planning to escape, where you're going, how you're going to access the money...."

"Why?"

"I'm a professional. You're not. I figured out your little scheme; others might also. I'm taking a big chance just meeting you here today. I don't like taking chances."

"Fair enough. But, first, please stand up and take off your shirt and pants. I want to make sure you're not wearing a wire."

Bruce did as requested, then sat back down after Griffin had searched him. "Okay. Talk."

"Not so fast. First, who else knows you're here?"

"Nobody."

"What about Shelby? You didn't tell her?"

"No."

"How do I know she won't hold me up also?"

"Don't worry about Shelby. I can control her. Now tell me what you've got planned."

Griffin nodded. Bruce had kept Shelby from going to the police, so he obviously had some hold over her. "All right. I've got a few bucks stashed away, just enough to get out of the country."

"Where you going?"

"Asia. That's all I'm going to tell you." Bruce nodded, so Griffin continued. "The way I've set up the trust, Donald has a 49 percent share. Under the settlement, the trust gets to keep the rental income from ten houses in the Smithson Farm subdivision. I figure we'll start seeing money in May, when the houses get rented for the summer. Figure ten grand per house per month for the summer, plus two grand per house for the other months. Comes to $400,000 per year after expenses, rough figures. Donald's take is about $200,000 per year. For twenty years."

"That's it? Hardly a fortune."

"You're right. But—and I'm sure you figured this out already— they also paid off my $2 million mortgage, so I'm happy with it. And my needs are simple."

"All right. I'll take half."

Griffin offered a wry smile. "That's a bit steep, don't you think? I've spent over a year on this. You're asking for $2 million."

Bruce shrugged. "Sorry. It's not my fault you didn't cut a richer deal."

"I'll give you a quarter share—$50,000 per year. That's a million in total."

Bruce stood, hovered over the smaller man. "I said half. Or you're going to jail."

Griffin sighed. It was worth it just to get out of this nut house. And he could cheat Bruce later, after he was safely hidden away. "All right, sit down. But if Shelby shows up looking for a cut, it comes out of your share."

"Fine." Bruce sat back down. "Now I want to know more details. How are you planning on getting the money?"

"I've set up a phantom guardian up in Maine."

"I know about that. Pretty sloppy, if you ask me."

Griffin tried to hide his surprise. This Bruce Arrujo had completely checkmated him. Of course, Bruce had the advantage of knowing his opponent. Griffin never even had any idea a match was on, much less any knowledge of who Bruce was or what his stake was in this whole affair. It might have been a closer match if they had been on even footing. Not that it mattered now—Griffin was just fighting for a draw. "Sloppy or not, it's worked so far. I've set up a bank account in the guardian's name that only I can access. Justin McBride will send the money up to that account every month."

"How will I get my share?"

"You'll have to trust me for it. I'll wire it every month to your account."

"Fat chance."

"Sorry, but that's the only way. Look at it this way: If I screw you, you just go to the cops, and they tell Justin to stop sending checks. Then I get nothing. So don't worry—you'll get your money."

Bruce nodded. "All right. One question. What have you got on Justin McBride?"

Griffin arched an eyebrow. "Why do you think I have something on him?"

"I don't think, I know."

"How?"

"Because you were careless. You flipped your french fries onto the floor, then kept right on talking while I swept them up. Idiot."

Griffin remembered the Burger King incident, recalled the sloppy worker with the 'Bruce' nametag. Bruce was right—he had been careless. "I'm impressed. All right then. I have some pictures of Justin's son. He was in Vietnam. He massacred some civilians."

"Good. Give me the pictures."

355

"Why?"

"Because eventually Justin might get suspicious. Let's face it, your little phantom guardian ploy up in Maine may be cute, but it's hardly foolproof. I figured it out without even going up there. If Justin starts asking questions, I need some way to keep him in line."

"I don't know...."

Bruce raised his voice, clenched his fist. "Look, this is bullshit. I thought you had made a real score here, but this is fucking amateur hour. A hundred grand a year—shit, that's chump change. So if you want me to go ahead with this, I need it to be airtight. I need those pictures."

Griffin nodded. He couldn't very well argue with Bruce's judgment on these matters. Not after Bruce had so deftly played his hand. "All right." He reached under his mattress, dug out an envelope, handed the pictures to Bruce. "Here. Be careful with them. There's no other copies."

"Good. Anything else?"

Griffin shook his head. "Nope."

Bruce scribbled out the name of a bank and account number, handed it to Griffin. "Don't lose it, and don't fuck with me." He offered a cold smile. "And have a good trip."

*   *   *

Justin sat in the car, waited. He had made small talk with the two deputy sheriffs sitting in the front seat for most of the ride up from the Cape, but now he was content to sit quietly as they listened to sports talk on the radio. Something about the Bruins management being too cheap.

There. Bruce came out the door of the group home, bounded down the steps, began walking toward Justin and his two law enforcement companions. Justin hadn't appreciated being blackmailed by the young man, and he didn't totally trust him. But Bruce now held all the cards in this particular hand of poker, just as Griffin had held the winning hand in the previous game. It would be nice, Justin thought, to have a winning hand himself. And, in a few minutes, he expected to draw the ace he needed.

He leaned forward in his seat. "That's him, leather jacket, coming down the street right now."

"What do you want us to do?"

"Sit tight. It depends on what he does."

Justin slumped down in the back seat, waited until Bruce was abreast of the car, then opened his window. He called out in a firm voice. "Bruce."

Bruce stopped, noticed Justin's companions, smiled knowingly. The plan had been for Bruce to meet Justin at a diner a couple of blocks away. "Didn't trust me, huh Justin?"

Justin shrugged. "Just being careful."

Bruce smiled again, this time with what appeared to be genuine warmth. "No need to be." He reached into his pocket, withdrew a wrinkled envelope. "Here are the pictures. Don't worry, I didn't even look at them. I don't think there are any other copies." He handed them through the window.

Justin reached slowly for the envelope, tried to keep his hand from shaking, forced himself to open the envelope. He had no desire to view the photos, but he needed to make sure Bruce hadn't tricked him and given him a stack of random pictures.

He removed them one by one, bore witness to the blackness that somehow possessed men's souls. Bodies—actually, in many cases, merely body parts—strewn across a field, wet with blood, organs exposed, hands clawed in a final grasp for life. Piles of them, mostly children and women, faces turned away from the camera, apparently mowed down while running for the woods in the distance. And his son, his boy, his baby, standing among them, gun raised, firing bullets into what Justin's mind told him must have been writhing humans and twitching corpses. Justin's stomach churned, his eyes watered. He pushed open the door, vomited onto the sidewalk.

Of all the things Griffin had done, of all the terror he had inflicted, the worst had been forcing Justin to view these pictures. Justin would never be able to love his son again. And, for that, he would hate Griffin forever.

Justin tucked the envelope into his jacket pocket, walked up and down the street in hopes that the cold winter wind would blow away the horror from his mind's eye. He focused on trees and birds and clouds. After ten minutes, the red had begun to fade from his vision—the clouds were becoming white, the trees green, the birds black. Or at least partially so. The birds, especially, seemed to be streaked with red as they flew, seemed to cry out in pain as they cawed. Perhaps it would always be so.

He rubbed some snow on his face, returned to the car. He had work to do.

Bruce was waiting, addressed him in a soft voice. "I have a favor to ask."

Justin found his voice. "What?"

"Can I come with you guys?"

Justin nodded. "I don't see why not. Get in."

Justin slid over, instructed the driver to pull up in front of Griffin's group house. "Okay, gentlemen, let's go in."

*   *   *

The four men climbed the stairs to the old Victorian, Bruce in the lead. Justin had called ahead, had spoken to the staff. They were waiting for him. But Bruce knew that Justin would defer to him if things turned ugly.

A heavy-set woman with sad eyes addressed Justin. "Are you Mr. McBride?"

"Yes, I am. Here's a certified copy of the court order appointing me as Donald Griffin's legal guardian. Where is he?"

"In his room. Second floor, first door on the left. He doesn't know you're coming, as you requested."

"Good. We'll be taking him with us, right now. I'll send someone over later to pack up his stuff and settle his accounts."

The woman began to argue. "Now? So soon? I'm not sure the sudden change will be good for Donald...."

Justin lifted his hand. "I appreciate your concern. But this is best, I assure you."

The four men climbed the stairs, Bruce motioning them to remain silent. When they reached Griffin's door, Bruce pushed it open without knocking. No reason to give Griffin any chance to flee.

The door swung open. Griffin bolted from his chair, locked eyes with Justin, began to stammer out a comment in Donald's voice. Then he saw Bruce.

Bruce closed the door, motioned to one of the officers to block the window. The other deputy began to search the room. Under the mattress he found the gun.

Justin turned to the deputies. "Thank you, gentlemen. You've both witnessed the fact that we just found a gun hidden under Donald Griffin's mattress—I'll ask you to sign an affidavit to that effect later." The men nodded. "Now, would you please escort Mr. Griffin out to the car?"

The men moved in, grabbed Griffin by the elbows. Justin threw a jacket over his shoulders, smiled at him. "Come on, Donald. Time to go."

Bruce could see Griffin struggle, watched him fight to stay in character. Griffin took a deep breath, began yelling as they dragged him down the stairs. "NO, NO, NO! I do not want to leave! Mrs. Kennedy, please make them stop! Make them stop!"

The concerned worker moved her wide body to intercept them. She blocked the doorway, reached for Griffin's elbow, turned to address Justin. "Now wait just one minute here. You can't just drag him away like this." She turned to Griffin, spoke in a soothing voice. "It's okay, Donald. Hush, now."

Justin smiled kindly at the woman. "Were you aware, Mrs. Kennedy, that Donald kept a loaded gun under his mattress in his room?"

As she stared back at him in horror, Justin nodded toward one of the deputies. He pulled the handgun, now sealed in a plastic evidence bag, out of his pocket. Justin continued. "As you can see, we are doing this for both Donald's safety and the safety of the other residents here. Now please step aside."

Mrs. Kennedy stared at the gun, released Griffin's elbow, edged away from him. He called to her, pleaded for her to help, but she merely shook her head. "Goodbye, Donald."

Griffin continued to scream and protest, but the deputies dragged him down the front stairs, pushed him into the back seat of the car. Justin and Bruce slid into the seats on either side. Justin spoke to the deputies in front. "Could you close the dividing window please? I would like some privacy."

Justin waited until the window was tightly closed, then turned to Griffin. "Well, Rex, you almost pulled it off."

Griffin sneered at Justin, sniffed in disdain. "Please, Justin, don't act so smug. You're like the water boy running around celebrating after his team won the game. Like you had anything to do with catching me. You had no clue. You're just here at the end, carrying Bruce's jock strap for him."

Even in defeat, Griffin's words hit their mark. It would make Justin that much more anxious to taunt Griffin with his plans for him. Justin responded. "Interesting analysis. After all, your fate is now in my hands."

Griffin shrugged. "Whatever, Justin. If you were going to turn me over to the cops, you would have done it already, but that would mean killing the whole settlement, which I know you don't want to do. So what are you going to do, rough me up? You're feeling pretty brave, I bet, now that you got your pictures back. And you've got your boys here to protect you."

"No, Rex, we've got a better idea than that."

"Oh, I suppose you could steal my money. Or, at least, the half Bruce hasn't already taken. But, hey, easy come, easy go. I'll survive."

Bruce saw Justin actually rub his hands together, like a bad actor in a cheap film. The old barrister was relishing the fact that Griffin thought they had no choice but to let him walk. Penniless, yes, but still free. "Actually, Rex, you won't be needing money where you're going...."

Griffin looked at Bruce for some hint at what Justin was getting at, but Bruce offered only a slight shrug. He would allow Justin to enjoy his moment.

Griffin turned back to Justin, responded to his comment about not needing money. "Nice try, Justin. Like I said, I know you're not sending me to jail."

"No, not jail. But I happen to know about this wonderful old mental hospital up in upstate New York. It's a beautiful granite building—if you like the gothic period, that is. You know, lots of towers and turrets and iron bars on the windows. Small rooms, a couple of roommates to keep you company. Right out of the 19th century in many ways. I don't think they still do lobotomies, but it really is a perfect place for a dangerous patient like yourself."

For the first time, Bruce could see some concern in Griffin's eyes. Still, their prisoner tried to remain flippant. "Scary thought, Justin, I must admit. But you can't just stick me up there. Even the retards have legal rights."

Justin nodded. "Yes, they do. And those rights are protected by their legal guardians." He paused here, pulled out a piece of paper from his pocket. Bruce could see Griffin's eyes boring into the paper, trying to read the words even before Justin had unfolded it.

Justin smiled at Griffin, held the document up for him to see.

Bruce had let Justin deliver the news, but in reality this was Bruce's plan, Bruce's victory. He turned to Griffin. He really didn't like the man. "Meet your new legal guardian, Justin McBride. That's the court order. Once the judge learned that this guardian of yours up in Maine didn't really exist, he agreed that Justin was the natural choice to be Donald's guardian. After all, Rex himself had entrusted Justin with the care of his sister and his entire estate. So who better to watch over his brother Donald?"

Rex shifted, his eyes moving toward the door latch. Bruce anticipated the thought. "Don't bother. They're locked from the front seat."

Justin smiled, spoke. "Don't worry, Rex. You'll like it there. Donald has a lot of money now, as you know. And I'm not going to scrimp on making sure you have the best care available. Every day we'll bring in therapists and aides and specialists. I've done a lot of research on this—they'll teach you how to answer the phone, how to order from a restaurant menu, how to make change. Just think, seven or eight hours a day of this type of specialized instruction."

Bruce pictured Griffin being passed from one fawning, cheerful therapist to the next, day after day. Good morning, Donald. How are you today? Today I want to work some more on the correct way to shake hands when you meet someone. Now, give me your hand.... Justin, a grin spreading across his face, apparently was having similar visions.

Griffin glared at Bruce. "What if I won't go?"

"Well, it's a little late for that. But, once you get there, I suppose you could tell them who you are, what you did. They might even believe you...."

Justin interrupted Bruce. "Or they might give you electric shock treatments...."

Bruce cut him off. "Whatever. But my bet is you'll keep your mouth shut. You're facing a lifetime sentence in jail for murder. Probably maximum security, locked up with other murderers and rapists, maybe an hour out of your cell every day. As bad as this mental hospital is, I still think you'd prefer it to a lifetime in jail. But, hey, it's your choice."

Bruce stopped here, waited for a response from Griffin. Bruce knew that the one thing that could derail their little plan for Griffin was if somehow he had learned that Dominique had implicated Vernon in the murder. Armed with this knowledge, Griffin would be immune to the threat of jail time—he would know that he wouldn't be pursued for a murder that had already been solved. Which is why it had been so crucial that Shelby convince her friend at the District Attorney's office to keep the news quiet for a few days.

But even without the knowledge that Vernon had been implicated, Griffin could still ruin things. It wouldn't surprise Bruce if Griffin chose jail instead of the mental institution, just to deny them their little victory. And that, of course, would derail the settlement. So there was some risk. But they were counting on Griffin's fear of being locked up in a jail cell. For Griffin, anything was preferable to that. And, knowing Griffin, he was probably planning on some future escape attempt, which would be far easier from the hospital than from a jail. Griffin did not yet know that Justin had arranged for a permanent electronic monitoring bracelet for his ward.

Bruce could see that Justin was holding his breath, waiting for Griffin's decision. Somehow, after all their strategizing and scheming and cunning, Griffin still controlled the game.

But, at least for now, Griffin simply glared at Bruce, his choice implicit in his silence.

Bruce continued. "All right then. The mental hospital it is. And who knows, Rex? After 10 or 15 years of constant treatment, they may even cure you."

Epilogue

[Six Months Later]

Bruce stood at the edge of Metacomet's grave, the May sun warming his neck and a light breeze cooling his face. He stared deep into the moist soil. Somewhere inside his veins a small amount of Metacomet's blood flowed. It was a good day to be alive.

The construction of the tribe's Wampanoag Historical Center building was almost complete. In two weeks, the site would open to the public, and thousands of people would visit Mashpee to attend the festivities. Bruce would be one of those people, but he also wanted to spend some time at the gravesite now, before all the commotion. He reached down, gently rubbed the earth.

Dominique's voice startled him. As always, he hadn't heard her approach, wasn't even aware she was at the construction site. "Hello, Bruce. I'm glad to see you." She surprised him, kissed him softly on the cheek. "Is Shelby here with you?"

He smiled. She wouldn't have asked the question if she thought the answer might have been no, wouldn't have put him in the position of having to explain that their steadily-rekindling romance had been snuffed out. "Yes, she's here. But you knew that, right?"

Dominique chuckled. "I haven't seen her, if that's what you mean. But I doubt the two of you are spending too much time apart these days."

He smiled again. "We're getting there. There's still a couple of things we need to work through."

Dominique stared off into the distance for a moment, then responded. "Shelby is not the type of person who can keep secrets from her friends, Bruce. The dishonesty eats at her, undermines her, interferes with her understanding of her self. She will never be able to move ahead with her life until she unburdens herself and tells Pierre and Carla the truth."

Only after a few seconds did Bruce realize that Dominique's comment had been in direct response to his. He nodded his understanding. "But do you think it's safe to tell them? So far, only you and Justin and Shelby and I know. But we all have a reason to keep it quiet. Pierre might feel cheated, might insist on his pound of flesh."

Dominique shrugged. "The settlement has gone through, this building is almost complete—it's too late for him to do much damage. And let's be honest, Bruce. It's not Griffin's flesh he wants. It's yours. Always has been. You're the one who sent him to jail, who cheated and scammed him."

Bruce thought about her words. As usual, she was right. "Makes sense."

"So, give him his flesh."

"I don't get it."

"I'm no lawyer, but it seems to me that they could make a pretty good case against you for obstruction of justice. Not to mention whatever crime it is when you lock a man away in a mental hospital when he's perfectly sane."

"You're right. I'd be in trouble if the truth came out."

"Well, my bet is that if you give Pierre the scalpel, and if you lie down on the table and take off your shirt, he's not going to have the guts to actually slice into you. But he'll feel pretty good about everything afterwards."

Bruce nodded. "You're right. I think a big thing for Pierre is that he never had a chance to even the score with me."

Shelby approached, greeted Dominique, reached for Bruce's hand.

Bruce smiled at Dominique, turned and spoke to Shelby. "Hey, do you think there's any chance you can talk Pierre and Carla into going for a drive up to upstate New York next weekend? I know they still hate me, but I think it's time we shared our little secret with them."

*   *   *

Pierre was sullen, irritated at having to spend a beautiful June day stuck in the car with a man he despised. But Shelby had insisted they make the trip, promised them it would be worth the effort.

Bruce quietly suggested that Pierre drive. It hardly made Pierre the Alpha male, but it was better than making him sit in the back seat. And it gave him something to do other than glare at Bruce.

Bruce sat silently, watching the heat rise off the tarmac, listening as Carla updated Shelby on the latest Mashpee gossip. Carla and Pierre had bought a new house in Mashpee—cute neighborhood, lots of kids and dogs and swing sets, no terrorists. Denise and Baby Vernon were still living in the farmhouse; Justin had used some of her money from the settlement to renovate the structure and create a separate apartment to house the full-time aide that helped care for Denise and the baby. Billy had been offered a bunch of hockey scholarships around New England, but had settled on nearby Providence College in Rhode Island so that he could be near his son. Justin, like all the neighbors, had sold his house to the tribe as part of the settlement, but had stayed in Mashpee and had opened a small office where he provided free legal aid to the needy. Amisha was still in Los Angeles—her divorce had gone through, and she was doing some modeling. Ronnie seemed to be doing fine, though there were rumors around town that his business would have been in some trouble had construction not begun on the new development that had been halted by the tribe's lawsuit.

And Ace continued to hold court at his donut shop. Bruce smiled to himself as he pictured Ace breathlessly recounting his harrowing journey to Washington. Outrunning and outmaneuvering those enemies of the tribe who would have denied the Mashpees that which was due them. Little did Ace know that he had been nothing more than the hand puppet of a man whose arm reached out from behind the black curtain of an illusory death.

Finally, after two hours of driving toward a still-secret destination, Pierre's frustration boiled over. He pulled off the highway into a rest area. "All right, everyone get out of the car. We're not going any further until someone tells me where we're going."

He got out, slammed his door. Carla turned and shrugged at Shelby and Bruce, and the three of them got out as well.

As Bruce stepped from the car, Pierre hit him with a quick punch to his midsection. The blow doubled Bruce over. He gagged, began to defend himself, then resisted the impulse. An odd thought passed through his head. *Finally he hit me. Now maybe we can get beyond this.*

He allowed Pierre to spin him around and pin him against the side of the car, much as a cop would do when making an arrest.

Carla ran over, grabbed at Pierre's arm from the side. Bruce stopped her. "It's okay, Carla." Bruce knew he could overpower Pierre, but that wouldn't really solve anything. He'd let it play itself out for a bit.

Pierre spoke through clenched teeth, his breathing loud and quick. "Now. Where. Are. We. Going?" With every word he shoved his palm into the small of Bruce's back.

Bruce looked over at Shelby, smiled in a way he hoped would be comforting. "I guess we have to tell them."

Shelby nodded. "All right, but not like this. Pierre, calm down. Then let's go sit over at one of those tables."

Pierre nodded, slowly released his grip on Bruce's jersey. "Fine." He trudged off toward the picnic area.

Shelby and Carla started to walk with Bruce, but he motioned them ahead. He didn't want Pierre to think they had taken sides against him. Bruce took a quick detour to the vending machines, came back with a stack of cold drinks.

He sat down opposite Carla, nodded to Shelby sitting next to him. She spoke. "Okay. Here's the story."

Bruce listened as Shelby slowly recounted the entire saga, explained that Rex Griffin was still alive, attempted to justify their decision to invoke their own brand of justice in order to save the settlement agreement. Bruce studied her—it was almost cathartic for her, he guessed. Finally telling the truth to the friends she cared so much about. He knew she was nervous about their reaction, but her sense of relief dwarfed even that.

Pierre was silent for a few seconds, his hands clenched in front of him on the light blue plastic picnic table. The revelation seemed to pacify him in the same way it had unburdened Shelby. "I knew something was up. I knew it. It made no sense that Justin would be helping out Griffin. And I knew there was stuff going on that Bruce wasn't telling us." He still hadn't looked at Bruce, but at least he had used his name without an expletive in front of it. "Of course, I thought it was because Bruce was trying to scam the tribe out of some of the settlement money. But the whole thing never added up for me."

Bruce nodded a commendation. "Good instincts, Pierre." He hoped it didn't sound patronizing. Then he offered up his flesh, handed Pierre the scalpel. "I know we have no right to ask you guys to keep this quiet, and I'll understand if you think Griffin should be in jail. At this point, the settlement has gone through, so it really wouldn't matter if you went to the police."

Bruce focused on Pierre's face, studied him as Pierre put the pieces of the puzzle together.

A sardonic laugh escaped from Pierre's throat. "Wouldn't matter, my ass. It would matter to you." He now looked straight at Bruce. "What do they call it, accessory to murder? Or obstruction of justice?"

Bruce nodded. "Probably both." He continued to eye Pierre, watched as the man he had cheated and scammed and framed realized he finally had him right where he wanted him—open and vulnerable and defenseless.

Pierre left the table, walked a few feet off and stared into the woods. He returned after a minute or two, took Carla's hand. She nodded to him, somehow understanding his unspoken question, and he sighed. He looked back and forth at Shelby and Bruce, spoke in a soft voice. "Well, it seems to me that you guys were able to get the best of both worlds. If this asylum or hospital or whatever it is is really as scary as you said, then it's as bad as being in jail...."

Pierre hadn't come right out and said so, but implicit in his statement was that he wouldn't go to the police. Generous in victory, just as Dominique had predicted. Bruce reached over, squeezed Shelby's hand.

They returned to the car, continued north on their trip.

An hour later they pulled off the highway, followed a country road for a few miles, and exited down a long private drive. They stopped outside a massive iron gate, waited as the security guard checked them against a list and allowed them to enter.

Bruce had visited the building before. He had driven up the day after Dominique had implicated Vernon in the murder, after they had hatched their plan but before they had grabbed Griffin from the group home. He and Justin had been fairly certain that the news that Vernon had killed Griffin would not spread all the way to upstate New York—it was a minor case, and the police were purposely downplaying it. But the one thing that could have ruined their plans would have been if Griffin somehow learned that the murder had been solved. Griffin could then have simply discarded his autistic mannerisms and walked away, miraculously "cured," confident that he would never be arrested for a murder that had already been solved. So Bruce had spent a day just hanging around the facility, satisfying himself that no stray Massachusetts newspapers or radio waves or cable television broadcasts had somehow penetrated the thick granite walls.

Even though this was Bruce's third visit, he was still awed by the sheer heft of the structure. Everything seemed to be cold and heavy and dark—granite slabs, iron bars, blackened hinges, stone buttresses. It was the type of place where you expected to see the townspeople storming the front door by full moon, armed only with giant crosses and garlic necklaces.

They went to the front door, waited to be buzzed in. The door creaked as they pushed it open, and an unsmiling white-smocked woman creaked at them from behind a reception desk as they entered. "Can I help you?"

Bruce stepped forward. "Yes, we're here to see Donald Griffin. I called yesterday—my name's Bruce Arrujo."

The woman pushed a button, spoke into an intercom. The high-tech buzzers and intercoms and television monitors stood in stark contrast to the dank, heavy feel of the dungeon-like fortress. "Bring Donald Griffin to the meeting room." She turned back toward a computer screen on her desk.

Shelby whispered, her eyes wide as she studied the cold surroundings. She shivered. "Bruce, this place is horrible. What have we done?"

Carla reached out, rested her hand on her friend's shoulder. "Hey, whatever happened to Griffin he did to himself. He's the one who spent a lifetime trying to scam people. He's the one who terrorized the neighborhood. He's the one who drugged Billy and Denise and bred them together like rats in a science experiment. And he's the one who ran down his own brother and left him to die in a ditch. You guys just did what you had to do. It's not pretty. But I think it's called justice."

A short, fat security guard with greasy hair and pimpled skin escorted them down the hall, the sound of his hard-soled shoes echoing off the stone walls.

The guard spoke in a high-pitched voice. Bruce thought he saw him try to peek down Carla's shirt. "The patient will be here shortly."

They entered a small, dimly lit room with a couple of old chairs and a dusty couch. Carla turned to Pierre, took his hand. Then she reached over and touched Shelby on the shoulder. She took a deep breath. "You know what, guys, I don't need to see this. Griffin's here, locked away where he can't hurt anyone. That's enough for me."

Shelby nodded. "I agree. I've been to these places before. It's not going to be pretty. It almost seems sadistic for us to have him paraded out so we can gloat over him."

Pierre shrugged. "Fine with me. As long as I know he's here. I don't need to see him drool and babble."

Bruce stood up. He tried to hide his disappointment–he knew it was a bit perverse, but he was sort of looking forward to showing off his handiwork. "Then what are we waiting for? Let's get out of here and go have some fun. I saw a marina a few miles back—maybe we could rent a sailboat for the afternoon. What do you think, Pierre? I hear you and Carla are pretty good sailors...."

Pierre looked at Carla, turned to Bruce. He teased his old enemy, a slight edge to his voice. "Well, we're not the clipper ship that you are, Bruce. What was it, the perfect combination of the ocean and the land...."

Bruce laughed. "That's what I thought. But I thought you guys decided I was the muck instead."

Pierre pushed him gently in the back, propelling him toward the door. "We did. But it turns out you're just a guy, Bruce. Sometimes you screw up; sometimes you do good. This time you did good." He paused, waited for the women to follow. "Now let's get out of here and go for a sail."

*   *   *

Dominique scanned the crowd crammed into the bright new building. She felt the tingling in her chest. So many people. Many of them were Native Americans from around the country, here to celebrate the opening of the new historical center, here to pay their respects at the grave of the great Metacomet. No, not a grave. A shrine.

Toward the back of the large exhibition hall she saw Pierre and Carla and Shelby and Bruce chatting and smiling. Carla and Shelby stood shoulder-to-shoulder, with the men to the outside. Every time she had seen them, they had arranged themselves in that configuration. Wounds didn't heal that quickly. But they did heal.

Valerie and Rachel were in the back of the room in an open area, one on either side of Baby Vernon as he toddled along over the blue carpet. Occasionally he would plop onto his rear end and the girls would rush to lift him. Denise, of course, was nearby, as was Billy. But they were content to let the girls entertain him.

A glint of light caught her eye as Shelby gestured with her hand. *A diamond ring.* Good for them.

She caught Bruce's eye as he moved his way toward the back of the hall. She smiled at him, offered a small wave, held up her ring finger and rubbed it. He laughed, shrugged his shoulders.

There were many strangers in the hall as well, many townspeople and tourists and dignitaries—smiling, mingling, taking interest and perhaps even some pride in the shrine to a man who was part of the history of all Americans. Best of all, their interest was sincere and dignified. No war dances from the children, no questions about taking scalps.

The tribe had been intent on avoiding the stereotypes and kitschiness that defined Native American culture for so many Americans, intent on creating a historical site rather than a tourist trap. There would be no peace pipes or teepees or tomahawks at

Metacomet's grave. Visitors were here to view the grave of a great warrior, a great leader, a great figure in American history. And, from what Dominique had seen so far, visitors had approached the shrine with solemnity and gravity, with respect and dignity.

She smiled. In life, Metacomet had taken up arms, organized the northeastern tribes, fought for the rights of Native Americans to be treated with dignity and fairness and respect by the European settlers. It was only fitting that his gravesite was now a shrine to the fact that the battle, at least partially, had been won.

The shrieking of children caught her ear. Bruce and Shelby had sneaked up on the girls from either side. They were crouched down, their hands pawing the air like lions, slowly moving toward their prey. Over the buzz of the crowd Dominique could hear Bruce roaring. The girls scampered away, dragging Baby Vernon with them, a happy grin on his face.

Dominique turned, focused her eyes on Pierre as he watched his former enemy play with his daughters. There was no concern in his face, no hatred. She touched the stone that marked Metacomet's grave, said a silent prayer. Maybe the wounds would heal quicker than she thought.

The End